HOLD FAST

HOLD FAST

SARAH LE MARCHAND

The Book Guild

First published in Great Britain in 2025 by
The Book Guild Ltd
Unit E2 Airfield Business Park,
Harrison Road, Market Harborough,
Leicestershire. LE16 7UL
Tel: 0116 2792299
www.bookguild.co.uk
Email: info@bookguild.co.uk
X: @bookguild

Typeset in 12pt Adobe Jenson Pro

Printed and bound in Great Britain by 4edge Limited

ISBN 978 1835741 504

British Library Cataloguing in Publication Data.
A catalogue record for this book is available from the British Library.

For my family: past, present and to come.

St Peter's Valley, Jersey

DECEMBER 1942

Is this his chance? The fat guard's distracted. Chasing young Kirill who stumbles away from the work detail into the onion field. So he's got a chance. Heart pounding, eyes darting, he stands still; the others plod on. Mustn't think what they'll do to Kirill; he has to concentrate on his own survival. The guard's boots clog and sink into the mud at the gate; his back is turned. His head is down. The green uniform strains at the shoulders.

Here's his chance.

Ahead of the slow-moving, ragged procession of workers, the younger guard hasn't stopped; the red glow of his cigarette swings in his hand. Rifle rests on his back. Its muzzle, a black spike, pokes up over his shoulder, stabs the gloom of the evening. He's probably thinking about his supper.

The world spins and the air is sucked from his lungs. He turns and lurches back up the road, expects a shot in the back. Shoulders rounded and eyes down, he staggers around the bend. Through an open gate. Into a ploughed field. Oily mud grabs at his feet. He stumbles. Blood pumps loudly in his ears. A smell of soil and decay rises. He clings to the slimy gatepost, looks back up the road. There's a yell in the distance. And another. The shriek of a whistle.

Gavno! Shit!

No. He's not going back. Energy courses through him. He can do this.

He runs on.

He needs cover, a hiding place. There's a copse of skeletal trees, branches sharp against the marbled sky, on the other side of the field; he heads for it, avoids the soft earth where ridges of soil glisten in the light rain. Keeping his head low, he runs close to the hedge, his knees aching. Brambles scratch at his legs. Wet grass and nettles drag on his feet. He pitches forwards over an invisible tree root. Lands hard on his hands; his elbows fold and stinking leaf mould smears his face. He scrabbles on hands and knees for a few moments, his feet sliding in the mud; he can't propel himself forward. He crawls; it's darker close to the ground, and wetter. He must run. A tree stump, soft with yellow lichen, helps him to his feet and he runs again, lopes and limps like a wounded animal until he falls into the blackness of the copse.

He crouches low against a tree, listens. He can hear the wheeze of his breath in the silence. The dull thump of his heart. Nothing else. He looks back. In the distance, the gate of the field. The road is empty. He picks up a stout stick and wields it against the dripping weeds, clears a path through the undergrowth deeper into the murk of the trees. He's thinking of making a nest, burrowing into a bush when his route brings him out onto the far side of the copse. He stops, listens again, the rasping of his breath hisses in his ears. Behind him, the thickets and shadows block his view; in front, a leafy crop greens the field and in the far corner there's a crumbling wall, the remains of a building. Shelter. A refuge.

He forces his legs towards it. His feet sink into earth, trample spinach leaves. Until his hands meet a rough wall and he collapses behind it. He fights the heaviness, listens, taut for pursuers. He should run on, but he's so tired, so tired... he blinks hard. Imagines the beating he'll get when they find him. Pulls himself to his feet. One leg starts to shake, out of control. Dizziness swirls in his head. Vision blurs. Sinks to his knees. Blackness descends and bubbles around him; sleep suffocates and soothes and a cloudy wall of nothingness covers him. He sleeps, curled like a rat in the straw, until the breeze grows into wind.

Confused, he twitches awake. Gusts of icy, salty air snap at his face and he snatches great mouthfuls of it until his pulse slows. Darkness has thickened. On his hands and knees, shaking with cold, he feels along the tumbled stones and hauls himself to his feet. His hand finds a damp sack caught on a hawthorn and he pulls it over his shaven head, leans back again the wall. He must run on. He'll take his chances. He's not going back. The wall prods his back, as he rocks back and forward. Above, in the void of night, a sickly moon moves behind a mass of black clouds. It hangs low, pinning glitter in his eyes.

One man in his work group collapsed shovelling rocks for ten hours, didn't get up. He was tipped into the liquid concrete of the wall as if he was rubbish; his stick legs and feet, wrapped in sacking, poked up and gradually sank until they were consumed by the grey slop. It's an image he can't shake from his head. He won't die like that; better a bullet in the back.

He's never going back.

The old man who sleeps on the shelf below his, had an arm broken by a rifle butt for working too slowly. It hangs useless now and he works by wedging the spade into his armpit. He never speaks, the old man, never has in the months they've worked together. Since his beating, he doesn't even look up. The top of his head is bald and scabby; lice run in his ears.

The old man is dead already. But he's not. He's young. He's going to live. He draws his legs to his chest, hugs his shins, feels his breath warm on the damp knees of his trousers; his buttocks prick with pins and needles.

What they are building he doesn't know, only that he must hew stone walls with a pickaxe in a dark cave, shovel granite into trucks and wheel them back into the light. The trucks return filled with bags of cement and sand. The tunnel is always wet; the workers know only pain and hunger and cold. He thinks hell must be like this.

But he's escaped the grave and is going to live.

He listens for a search party; the only sound is that of wind in the trees, like an angry tide, whispering unceasingly. Why haven't the guards come? They'll come in the morning. He could be miles away by then. He can rest for a few hours. He allows his knees to sag and sits against the wall, pulls the sack over his trembling legs. Waves of sleep force his eyes to shut and he's back in the echoing tunnel. It's closing in on him, choking him. He can't move. Fragments of dreams leap: the face of his father, scowling and shouting at him; a bloody wound on a disembodied leg; the limp corpse of a naked child. He wakes to relieve himself, eases his heavy legs out of the sack and stands up, fingers clutch the wall behind him. The sharp stink of iron-yellow rises from the steam. His stomach churns, cramps and rolls with nausea; sour saliva fills his mouth and he retches and twitches.

But he's still free. Free. The word bounces in his brain and hisses in his ears. He's never going back. He must eat and he must run again. They'll be looking when it gets light. It's hard to move. The wall is solid behind him.

Grouville, Jersey

JUNE 1ST 1940

OVER TWO YEARS PREVIOUSLY

From the wireless on the dresser, the newsreader's clipped vowels were stiff with optimism: '*The heroic feat by the fishermen and boat owners who had sailed across the channel to rescue the men from the beaches of Northern France was hailed by one war correspondent, who saw boats return to British shores, packed with exhausted and injured men, as a miracle. The reporter spoke of the selfless courage of the British, helped by French and Dutch sailors, who brought their loads back across the hostile channel, then went back undaunted into the inferno to rescue more of the thousands waiting...*'

None of it seemed real. Not in the balmy warmth of the June evening with the kitchen door open to the smell of the farmyard. A bird tweeted and was answered by another. The crackle of static. Michael felt light-headed. He took a shallow breath and looked at his family seated around the scrubbed pine table. In his usual place, at the head of the table, his father was bolt upright, the weathered lines on his forehead drawn together, his eyes down. His mother had put down her knitting and was rubbing her fingers over her knuckles. His parents looked old, he thought. Why had he never noticed that before? His stomach lurched.

Michael's older brothers sat opposite him, side by side: dark-haired, frowning Jacques, his elbows on the table, rested his chin in his hands; Yves, two years younger, sat back in his chair, biting his lip, pushing his hands through his thick, fair hair. The touch of Amy's elbow against his own made him turn to his twin sister and raise the corners of his mouth in a thin smile. She had pulled her fuzzy plait over her shoulder and was twisting the end between her fingers. He saw himself in her open, freckled face and returned the gentle pressure, happy to feel the warmth and solidity of her arm.

They had listened to the news of Germany's advance in France and the retreat of the British army every evening this week. Michael found it unsettling.

Easing his back with his hand, his father got up and switched off the wireless, shaking his head as he retook his seat. Yves folded his arms and sighed, and kept his eyes on the table in front of him.

'They're heroes, real heroes,' muttered his mother, nodding and glancing around the table. She took up her knitting again but it remained still under her curled fingers.

With a scrape of his chair on the flagged floor, Jacques leapt to his feet, his eyes flashing. 'Heroes? What is the damn government doing? What happened? Why's it left to old men and boys to rescue the army? It's a disaster, a bloody disaster.'

His mother's horror at his language showed in her face. 'Jacques, please! Don't talk like that.'

His brother's use of expletives was nothing new to Michael. Recently, the swear words had been worse than 'bloody', though rarely in front of his parents. Jacques was angry and he let everyone know.

Amy was frowning and nodding in response to Jacques' outburst. Michael caught her eye and raised his eyebrows. Did she agree? What did *she* know about it? She shrugged almost imperceptibly. She understood as little as he did but covered her ignorance in a way that he couldn't. A hollow, sick feeling turned his stomach.

He knew that the German army was to be feared and Adolf Hitler was threatening to take over the whole of Europe, but details of the politics and history were hazy. France was a foreign country to him, despite its close proximity to the Channel Islands, and they relied on Mr Churchill's Britain for protection. History lessons at school were on medieval England, castles and kings – an age that seemed almost as remote as the evacuation stories which were coming across the airwaves to the wooden wireless crouched on a shelf on the dresser.

Many of his school friends were thrilled to think of British soldiers fighting for King and Country and proud of the owners of the little boats who risked so much to help those stranded on the beaches. Yesterday he'd overhead a group talking about the rescue of soldiers from the French beaches as he left when the school day was over.

'Bloody Jerries. Jesus Christ!' one of the lads had said. Michael had never heard him so animated. 'They're no match for our lads. We'll be back.'

Michael walked away without saying anything, head down and blood racing; he couldn't help thinking that the situation was more complex than that.

Other friends had already left Jersey with their families because of the threat, the proximity to France. Some businesses had been abandoned; the hardware shop in St

Helier, where Michael's father bought tools and containers for the farm, was boarded up.

Yves cleared his throat after the heavy silence that followed Jacques' outburst. His gentle voice was cautious: 'So many people are… evacuating. Dad, I know you've said that you don't want to leave, but have you thought…'

His father's head snapped up and Michael could see the fire in his eyes. He was normally a man of few words and rarely expressed strong emotion. 'You don't abandon your home,' he said. 'This farm has been in our family for generations, and anyway, what about the animals?'

His mother nodded, her face serious. 'We've made that decision and we will stay.' She put one hand over Amy's on the table and caught Michael's eye, her face creasing into a smile. 'We'll be all right.'

'Jacques, Yves. You are both old enough to make up your own minds, but I hope you'll stay too,' said his father. 'We need you here. We'd struggle with the milking yard, if you went, Jacques. And the island needs milk. Yves, you've made such a good start with the plumbing business…'

Yves nodded and blinked rapidly, folded his arms in front of him. Jacques held his head between clenched fists, his shoulders raised. Michael felt the prick of tears. Why would the Germans want to invade the tiny Channel Islands? And anyway, the British government would defend them, wouldn't they?

15TH JUNE 1940

The tide was far out and the pebbles and pools of Le Hocq lay exposed to the heavy heat of the June afternoon. Michael surveyed the barren landscape of rocky outcrops and glimpses of bisque-blond sand stretching from the distant mirage of Seymour Tower to the outline of Green Island, beyond the headland. Behind the smudged, still horizon was the coast of France and horrors he could not imagine.

He was digging for razor fish in a favourite spot, Stone Beach, a sandy patch in the centre of the bay about half a mile from the shore. Called Red Rock by some locals when it glowed in the evening sun, the rocky pile of volcanic stone stood above shining wet sand littered with rounded boulders and smaller pebbles worn smooth. Now, at low tide, it looked like a small, wild beach backed by a craggy headland; at high tide, everything except the rough, bulk of the rock, smelling strongly of guano, was invisible, drowned by the chilling water of the English Channel.

Alone on the newly-washed seabed below the rocks, the sun glinting on his wire-framed spectacles, he felt the heat of the sun through his bleached shirt. At his feet were a jam jar of salt stolen from his mother's kitchen and a tin box squirming with shellfish. Michael hoped razor fishing might make him feel better. But the feeling of heaviness wouldn't lift.

He sighed and wriggled his sore foot carefully. He would normally have gone barefoot, his feet hardened by beach pebbles. The clammy cling of seawater and the sting of the wound in his plimsolls were Jacques' fault. Why was he driving so fast this morning? The farm truck sped past him in the lane and forced him to jump back into the hedgerow. Thorns had pierced his foot as he'd fallen. Jacques should have stopped. He had never been a protective sort of brother, but recently he'd become distant and aggressive, angry, frustrated by the situation on the island. He needed to join up, he'd told Michael impatiently, as if it were obvious why he was bad-tempered, and the authorities were not moving fast enough.

Michael bent to his task again, tipping a teaspoon-sized heap of salt on a small hole in the wet sand and a few drops of seawater scooped from a puddle. Seconds later, a translucent floppy shape, like the fat finger of a jellyfish, emerged from the hole, followed by the tip of a hard tube. Gripping the shell, he pulled gently, feeling the satisfying give as the razor fish, after initially sucking back, let go and the ugly creature popped out, the striped pipe followed by the distinctive soft, yellow body with the rounded 'foot' on the end.

He dropped the razor fish into the open tin and turned towards the common, his shadow pointing back up the rocky beach, unnaturally thin and spiky. On his right King's and Queen's rocks rose from the beach. Never covered by the high tides, they were topped by grey-green patches and fringed with sparse grass and hares' tails, which wilted and swayed in the thin breeze. The stone was oyster-pink in the sun, rising above shadowed black indicating the height of the tides. In the main channels, small fishing boats leant at angles on their hulls, attached by rusting chains to buoys. Water puddled blue-grey in uneven ridges left by the retreating water, like miniature fields ploughed by a drunken horse. Scattered rocks were dark and slippery with vraic, the broad, brown ribbons disguising the jagged stones beneath. Seabirds ruled here; gulls and oystercatchers, calling and settling on rocks in groups and rising smoothly, lifted on unseen currents of air. A lone, white egret delicately dipped his long legs into a pool.

He couldn't define or articulate the unsettling feelings of change that crowded his life. They'd been told that school might end the summer term early because so many teachers had chosen to leave with the threat of German invasion hanging over the island. It isn't fair, he felt like shouting, aware of how childish the thought was. He wanted that fluttery, airy sense of anticipation that comes when the weather looks set fair and examinations are over. He should be looking forward to surfing on the board he had been renovating since March, an old wooden one which belonged to his father. Battered and discarded in the barn for years, he had sanded it down and applied a coat of varnish.

Cool water circled and his feet sank into the wet sand. Time to go; he couldn't avoid the tide any longer. He stuffed his tin of shellfish and jar of salt into his bag and started the long walk up the beach, stepping carefully around sandy pools and avoiding the sharp stones. The sun was hot, as it had been for the last few weeks. Great weather for the potatoes, as his father had said only last night; the Jersey Royals, which they began to harvest at the end of March, continued to be lifted from the sandy ground in large numbers. Only another couple of weeks before potatoes were over and the workers turned their attention to tomatoes. The glasshouse crops were already being picked and the outside ones, plumping up, were just beginning to lose their intense greenness. A hint of red was rising.

Splashing in the channel where the boats were moored, he walked towards the Round Tower. A weathered pink and grey granite fortification, circled by deep-set, shadowy windows, it stood high above the beach. Below was a groyne of tumbled boulders protecting the sandy beach where the family often swam at high tide. Most people called it a Martello Tower, but his history teacher said that only eight of Jersey's coastal towers were true 'Martellos'. The towers circled the coast of Jersey, like a group of pawns, lost from a giant chess set. Le Hocq's tower was used by local fisherman to store nets. Last summer he'd been allowed to climb the steep ladder in the dark circular chamber to the roof and had walked around the low wall, enjoying the new view of Le Hocq's vast expanse of rocks and channels on one side and La Rocque, with its hooked harbour wall, a mile or so away, on the other. To the east, the coast of France, its bright beaches gleaming, had been clear and peaceful. Only a year ago. When things had been so different.

Ahead of him, on the stone slip, was a small group of men, talking and gesticulating in a way which seemed to him unlike the usual slow, sociable chat between fishermen or the older men who played pétanque on the common. He quickened his pace as he recognised the dark head and stocky figure of Jacques, who would normally be supervising the late afternoon milking, and the suited figure of Mr Le Marquand, from the Post Office at La Rocque. Something must have happened. He half-raised his hand to attract his brother's attention, but the men moved before he was within calling distance. Two men walked away at speed east along the coast road. Four others, including Jacques, got into the

Le Breton farm truck, and sped off towards town, leaving a puff of grey smoke behind.

His bicycle was propped up against the tower. He slung his bag over his back and was on the bike and peddling up Le Hocq Lane within seconds of getting off the beach, using the heel of his right foot to avoid the shooting pains. Most of the way back to the farm was uphill and it took him about twenty minutes of tough peddling before the farmhouse appeared, its granite face glowing in the sun, red geraniums fiery under every window.

Michael turned off the rough road straight into the garden, panting with the exertion of the climb and skidding on the white rose petals which had fallen from the trellis over the door. Dropping the bike on the flagstones, he hurried through the front door and kicked off his damp plimsolls. The tiled floor was cool and soothing on his sore foot as he padded down the hallway into the kitchen at the back of the house.

Eight men, all familiar to Michael as neighbours and family friends, were gathered around the table, talking in urgent, low tones with his father. His mother was filling teacups and flitting between the range and the table. His questions were silenced before he could vocalise them by her raised eyebrows and his eyes darted from face-to-face to catch fragments:

'…have been asked to help. They've reached St Malo… we have to try…'

'…potato boats in the harbour, small yachts, fishing boats… there are hundreds of men.'

'I'm not in favour, me…'

'No one is really sure of the situation. British soldiers are setting fire to oil tanks.'

'They need to get away and we…'

'...do our bit...'

'It's only forty miles away, Reg. We can get there...'

'...look what happened at Dunkirk...'

'...Germans advancing quickly, eh'

'Will they be brought to Jersey, Paul?'

The words overlapped and repeated as the deep voices filled the room. Michael swallowed and pulled a stool out from the corner of the room, sitting just behind his father, hoping to understand. He cleaned his blurry glasses on his shorts as his father stood up, clearing his throat. The talking subsided.

'This is what I know: there's a meeting at the Yacht Club soon... at six. The bailiff has called it. I was told he's had a telegram from London. The potato boats are to be used to rescue men from St Malo. Four large ones are leaving now and smaller boats will be organised to ferry men out to the larger ones. That's where we come in. The men are to be brought to the island, we think. We have to leave tomorrow.'

His father's voice was calm, but the lines on his forehead were twisted with anxiety and his hands were tucked beneath his folded arms. Michael glanced at his mother. She was biting her lip. His breath caught in his throat and a weight settled in his stomach.

Chairs scraped on the stone floor and the men rose together. Murmuring, and setting down cups noisily, one muttering thanks to Michael's mother, they squeezed through the back door leaving silence, heavy in the warm room. His father returned within a minute, collecting his jacket and hat from the hook on the back of the door.

'I'm going now, Hélène. Jacques is meeting me there. Yves is still at work. I want to talk to a couple of people before the meeting.' His father laid a hand briefly on her shoulder. Michael willed him to turn and look at him. He opened his mouth and stood up, but his father intervened. 'No, son, not now. We'll talk later. Go and tell your sister what's happening. She's picking tomatoes.'

The door opened and closed with a rattle, a dog lead on the back swinging. He was left in the kitchen with his mother who sat down on the edge of a chair and folded her arms on the table. A moment of stillness was accompanied by a deep breath in, a heave of her shoulders and a sigh out before she lifted her chin and held his eyes with hers. The unknown and the unspoken hovered between them.

*

Two days later St Helier's harbour was teeming with crowds and vehicles when Michael and Yves joined the queue as directed on Albert Pier. Last night's *Evening Post* had appealed for volunteers to transport weapons for the defence of the island and supplies from British navy frigates to temporary stores. Reluctantly his mother had given him permission to help, as long as Yves kept a close eye on him. Eager to do something useful, to be involved, Michael felt full of energy. His stomach fluttered as he leapt out of the truck and looked around, while Yves went to find out what they needed to do.

He jumped when he felt a hand on his shoulder and turned to see a red-faced, bulky man in a tweed jacket, smiling at him. 'Hello, you're Yves' little brother, aren't you?'

'Oh. Yes. I'm Michael.' He held out his hand, regretting the formality when the man laughed loudly, bowing with a mocking raise of his eyebrows and taking Michael's hand in his own large sweaty mitt.

'I'm Bob. Yves and I work together at Huelin's. Told me to come along and see if I can help too. No vehicle, I'm afraid, but I thought I might help you. Ah, there he is. He'll know what we're doing, eh lad?' He slapped Yves on the shoulder and rubbed his hands together. 'Where do we start?'

'Hello, Bob. Mr Huelin managing without us?'

'He's certainly not doing any of the jobs on the list. Fiddling around with paperwork. Wouldn't be surprised if he was thinking of evacuating.'

'Oh, Lord! No! What about the business?'

'Who knows? Cross that bridge when we get there, 'spose. What's the deal here?'

'Well, we just get on with it, I think. Let's leave jackets in the truck.'

From the neat piles against the harbour wall, which were being off-loaded by uniformed soldiers from two metal-grey transport ships towering above the quay, the men were directed to collect boxes to drive them to the town hospital grounds. They stacked wooden crates into the farm truck, still dusty from its usual cargo of potatoes, sweating in the heat of the midday sun. When Bob and Yves had passed the last of their load to Michael in the back of the vehicle, a heavy box stamped with the words 'NAAFI ENFIELD RIFLES', they stepped back and moved into the shade under the wall. Michael jumped down, slammed the tailgate and joined the others.

'Wouldn't it be easy… to cream off some of this stuff?' Bob said as he leaned his head back, panting, his eyes closed.

Michael looked at him, surprised.

'No checks or lists… rifles… medical supplies. And whiskey. Did you notice, Yves?'

Yves snorted, sweeping the back of a dirty hand across his damp forehead.

Bob did not look at him. His eyes were on the cigarette he was rolling. 'It's about time we got our hands on some weapons.'

'What do you mean?' Yves' brow was furrowed.

'The Defence Force. We aren't being trained. We're being lectured at.'

'I thought… as part of the Jersey militia… aren't you supposed to… what are you doing at those meetings?'

Michael knew that Yves had hesitated to join the Volunteer Defence Force, despite being encouraged by Jacques to sign up. He had been evasive when Michael, who would have jumped at the chance if he had been old enough, asked him why he was reluctant to get involved. Yves was less outspoken, perhaps less sure of his opinions, than Jacques. Michael couldn't remember a time when he had shown anger or frustration. His mother recently had said something about how Yves was 'just growing into his own person' and he thought he understood what she meant; Yves took his time to make decisions, to do what he thought was right. He admired that.

Bob's cigarette flared and crackled. He blew out a long stream of smoke.

'We're buggering about, listening to fat, arrogant officers and looking at pictures of anti-aircraft guns. Oh, and it gets really exciting when the Colonel rambles on about the history of Jersey's coastal defences!'

A flock of seagulls was flapping over a bucket. It rose in a whirl of white screams.

'It wouldn't be difficult to lift a crate or two, would it?'

Yves looked at Bob with his mouth open, blinking. Michael swallowed and felt a stab of fear in his chest.

'What? Don't talk like that, Bob. What are you thinking? Who could… could betray their country like that? It would make you a… traitor, wouldn't it, not just a criminal…'

Michael felt a rush of pride in his brother's response.

Bob stood up and grinned. 'Forget it, Yves. I'm talking to the wrong brother, aren't I? I think Jacques would have been up for it. Pity he's gone off to St Malo… doing his bit for the war effort, as they say. Just wanted to do mine.' He grabbed his jacket. 'See you later, boys. I'll go and see if anyone else needs help.'

Michael could see Yves' unease in his pursed lips. Bob walked quickly down the quay hesitating beside other vehicles, nodding at the men and boys loading crates, before moving on.

Yves pushed himself away from the wall and looked at Michael. 'Let's go, shall we? I think we just follow the others to the hospital.'

As they drove slowly down the quay, they passed Bob in conversation with two men standing next to a baker's van, back doors open, wooden crates stacked to the roof.

'Do you think Bob would do that? Steal rifles?'

Yves shrugged and steered left joining the stream of vehicles heading towards Gloucester Street, as directed by a policeman. 'I don't know. I hope not. But he's quite… hot-headed. I've heard him ranting about how useless the Defence Force is a number of times.'

'What about Jacques? Bob said he thought that Jacques would be up for it. Would he do it… do you think?'

'It wouldn't surprise me. He's frustrated about not being able to join up. Did he tell you about the interview at the States office?'

Michael shook his head. Jacques rarely told him anything important.

'He managed to see someone, last week I think, to ask why his application hadn't been processed. He was told that Jersey is in an 'unusual position' because of British laws in the Channel Islands. Apparently, discussions were taking place and he must be patient.'

Michael knew the thinness of Jacques' patience. 'I don't suppose that went down very well.'

Yves laughed. 'You can imagine, can't you? I had to listen to him for hours. We'd gone for a drink at the Le Hocq. There was quite an atmosphere. Most of the chaps agreed with him – that it was badly organised. A few defended the government, saying that it was… complicated. I don't know what to think. Fighting's not for me… unless I have to.'

Yves drove through the open gates of the hospital and was beckoned by a policeman into a gap between two large khaki tents.

'So yes, he's angry. And I worry about what he'll do.' Yves sighed and brought the truck to a halt. They sat still for a moment as the engine ticked quietly. 'Well, here we are. Ready to unload, Michael?'

*

When Michael came down to the kitchen early next morning, following the smell of breakfast, his father and Jacques were sitting, looking tired, dirty and unshaven, at the table. His mother topped up their tea mugs and loaded bacon and fried eggs onto plates. Neither of them picked up their knives and forks. They looked stunned. His mother was leaning back against the range, her eyes fixed on his father.

Pulling his chair up to the table, he waited for a minute, desperate to know about the rescue mission, reluctant to ask, struggling to find the right words.

He could wait no longer. 'Dad… Jacques… how did it go?'

Jacques pushed back his dark hair and exhaled loudly.

His father raised his eyes to Michael's and smiled at him. 'Well… we are glad to be back. Ah, here she is.'

Amy went straight to their father, bending down and folding both arms around his neck. 'Are you all right?' she murmured, sitting down next to him and leaning her head on his shoulder. She always knew what to say, what to do. He wished he had given his father a hug.

'What was it like?' Michael pressed, leaning forward.

'St Malo was… chaotic. The smoke and noise… I've never seen anything like it.'

'And did you bring soldiers out of the city?'

'Many of the men had already been evacuated… by the advance party, but the lifeboat was a good size for getting groups out to the bigger boats – we took about thirty at a time. Most men we saw weren't injured and they were… cheerful, pleased to see us. I don't know how many trips we made. Did you count them, Jacques?'

Jacques shook his head. 'Must have been at least a dozen…'

'This is wonderful, Hélène', said his father as he drained his mug. 'A cup of tea never tasted so good.'

'Eat, both of you…' said Hélène, pushing the plates closer to them.

The scraping of cutlery was the only sound until both men had cleared their plates.

'Did you bring back the British soldiers to Jersey?' Michael asked.

'Not as many as we thought, eh, Dad? When the potato boat we were transporting men to was full, we were told that orders had changed. Most of the big boats were to take the men to England… typical… bad planning. Couldn't organise a piss-up in a brewery.' Jacques paused to light a cigarette.

'We think some injured men and some French soldiers were brought here, though it was difficult to know exactly what was going on,' continued his father. 'Our last journey was to pick up the demolition party.'

'What? Demolition party? What do you mean?' asked Michael.

'Some of the engineers had to lay explosives. Last men to leave. They didn't want to leave the Jerries any equipment… wanted to destroy the oil storage, tanks near the harbour. We saw it as we rowed them away… massive explosions… the noise was…' He puffed out his cheeks and shook his head.

'…Bloody deafening… my ears are still ringing,' said Jacques. 'Fire way up above the walls of the town. Could feel the heat too. That last journey was the worst. We all felt so tired, our arms were burning…'

Jacques got up and turned his back, looking out of the window. His father had closed his eyes.

'I'll fill up the bath, and then you can both get some sleep,' called his mother, already in the scullery. Michael could hear her pulling the tin bath off its hooks on the wall. 'Everyone else out… go and see what needs doing on the farm.'

'Not for me, Mum. I'll get back to the milking yard. Make sure they are coping without me. Quick wash then I'm going into town,' said Jacques, dropping his cigarette end in the sink where it hissed and smoked. 'There are a couple of things I need to do.' His face was set and his mouth a thin line when he turned back to the family.

'Can… can I come with you?' Michael asked.

'No, Michael… I don't think…' his mother murmured.

Jacques frowned and then nodded. 'You should know what's on,' he said. 'I'll pick you up in half an hour.'

*

Their first stop was the Royal Engineers' Yard on Mount Bingham, the home of the Royal Militia. The gravelled yard was busy. Men in uniform were packing boxes into vans and the atmosphere was one of business-like speed. A tall man with rolled-up sleeves and stripes on his shoulder was moving from one group to another with a clipboard, handing out slips of blue paper.

'Stay here,' Jacques ordered, slamming the truck door and marching towards the man. Michael watched as the officer waved him away, turning on his heel and mounting the steps of the single-story building. At the entrance, he pointed with his clipboard to a notice tacked to the door. It was printed in large bold type:

WITH IMMEDIATE EFFECT.
BY ORDER OF THE BRITISH GOVERNMENT.
ROYAL JERSEY MILITIA RECALLED TO MAINLAND.
ALL WEAPONS AND AMMUNITION TO BE SURRENDERED.
VOLUNTEER DEFENCE FORCE DISBANDED.

Jacques strode back to the truck and got in behind the wheel, his jaw clenched and colour in his face.

'What's going on? What does that mean?' Michael pointed to the sign and turned to his brother.

Jacques was shaking his head. 'We need to find out…'

Gravel flew and Michael clung to his seat as his brother reversed, causing uniformed men to curse and shout, bumped out of the drive and down the hill towards St Helier.

The bird's eye view of the harbour revealed large naval boats on the quays and crowds of soldiers. Families with suitcases and children were milling like insects around the piers. As they descended, the verges became full of stationary vehicles, abandoned in the rush to get to the evacuation ships.

Horses had hauled their empty carts into the hedgerows and were grazing on the long grass and weeds. Eventually the road was blocked and they could go no further. Jacques shook his head, pulled hard right on the steering wheel and tried to cut through South Hill. He narrowly missed a car stuffed with children, suitcases tied on the roof. Michael swallowed down a gasp. He knew better than to say anything. Sweat beaded on Jacques' red forehead. There was a squeal of brakes; he scraped a parked van before they regained the main road and drove quickly down the hill towards Havre des Pas and another route into town.

By the time they had found somewhere to leave the truck, Michael was able to unhook his hands from the seat, but he felt sick and dizzy. He waited, hoping for stability to return, not looking at Jacques. The heat buzzed in his ears; his stomach churned.

He had that helpless, panicky sensation of being at the mercy of a strong current, like being knocked off his surfboard by a wave which had risen out of nowhere. He was being tumbled in bubbles and murky water. Suffocating. Breathless. It wasn't Jacques' driving; it was forces beyond their control.

*

The queue for the bank extended around the Royal Square, unmoving. Michael and Jacques stood in the shade of a towering chestnut tree, heavy with white candles and spreading leaves. Around them a group of muttering men was forming, most looking at the States building.

'…what's going on… why aren't we being told?'

'Are we being thrown to the dogs?'

'…it's betrayal…'

'I heard that they are going to demilitarise the islands…'

'I need to get some money out,' Jacques muttered. 'Just in case. Wait here.'

In case of what? Was his brother planning to leave Jersey? What did demilitarise mean? He understood the literal meaning: remove the armed forces. But it didn't make sense. Why would they remove the professional soldiers stationed in Jersey? No. He didn't believe it.

Michael glimpsed Mr Ferrand, a neighbour of his grandfather's, close to the front of the queue and watched as his brother strolled with his head held high past the waiting families and men. He slipped into the line behind Mr Ferrand, raising his hat to him, and smiling at an elderly couple who frowned but shuffled back a few paces moving their suitcase closer to the wall of the bank.

The bank doors stayed shut when the clock on the town hall indicated nine. Behind the pulled blinds of a window there were dim lights. Jacques rapped on the glass with his knuckles and a man further back in the queue nodded at him and banged on another window. 'Come on! It's opening time!' yelled a voice and the elderly man at the front of the line raised his walking stick to tap on the door.

The manager emerged, face red, sweating in his navy wool suit, squeezing though a gap between door and frame. He stepped forward as the door closed behind him. He licked his lips and raised his chin, fumbling with his jacket button. The queue fell quiet.

'I have been ordered, by the… authorities, not to open and not to allow anyone to withdraw money from the bank. I'm sorry… I'm sorry. I am following instructions…'

There was a surge and Jacques was propelled forwards. The crowd was growing noisy: 'It's our money… whose orders… what right… if you don't… Come on. Open up!'

The manager backed away as the crowd pushed closer, shouting for his assistant; he stumbled inside and the door was slammed.

For a few minutes Michael was worried that the crowd might force the door open, or break a window. He lost sight of Jacques amongst the heaving, shouting group surrounding the bank. He had no idea what to do, who to turn to, whether he should join the group, help his brother. But the noise gradually faded and some men and family groups started to drift away, leaving fewer people who chatted in twos and threes. Now he could see Jacques again, talking with Bob, who he hadn't noticed earlier. He was wearing the same jacket as he had had on when they were helping at the harbour and a brown trilby hat. Michael felt the heat of the sun in his face as he stepped out of the shade to join the two men. Jacques glanced in his direction, shaking his head, and then turned to Bob, pulling him away with his hand on his arm and walking across the Royal Square in the direction of The Peirson pub. Michael hesitated, his body tense. His brother often treated him like a child, even though he was only five years older. After all, Jacques had said that he should know what was going on and he was fourteen years old, hardly a baby. He took a deep breath and walked slowly across the square, prepared for a rebuttal, watching the two men closely.

Bob looked up and smiled at him: 'Here he is. Mike. How are you doing? Glad to have big brother and dad back?' Before Michael could reply, Bob turned back to Jacques, nodded and touched the brim of his hat. 'That's settled then. I knew I could rely on you. See you both soon.' He stuck his hands in his trouser pockets and walked away.

Jacques' eyes were narrowed. 'We've got one more job, Mike. You up for it?'

'What is it? What was that about? He didn't... did he? You won't...'

Michael knew. Hoped he was wrong. Jacques' clenched jaw and cold eyes told him he was not wrong.

Jacques stood off in the direction of the truck. Michael, his legs shaky and his mouth dry, followed.

Nothing was said as Jacques drove out of town and onto the coast road winding towards Le Hocq. The beach was quiet with the sun glinting off the glassy pools of the retreating water. The common was empty and Jacques pulled off the road and bumped the truck over the tufted grass, slowing to a halt close to the Round Tower's door.

'I'm going in there to collect a crate.' His brother stared out of the windscreen. His voice was firm. 'Are you with me?'

Michael licked his lips and felt a bloom of sweat on his forehead. His voice came out as a murmur: 'A'right.' He cleared his throat and forced his heavy head to nod. 'Yes.' What else could he say? What would Yves have said? He had no choice.

'We have to move them.'

At the door of the tower Jacques felt around under a slab of granite, pulled out a key and let them into the dark chamber. The high windows shed light only on the upper walls, leaving the base in damp, grey gloom as Jacques closed the door behind them. Light rippled above, as if they had dived down towards the seabed; at their feet, shadowy piles of nets, tools, boxes, rusty chains, buoys, a smell of salt and fish.

His eyes adjusting to the light, Michael watched Jacques make his way towards a blackened barrel which he rocked forwards and out of the way. He reached down and pulled at a tarpaulin; the fresh wood of the NAAFI crate shone pale.

Michael's heartbeat increased and he shivered, feeling the

sweat on his face cool. He took a step forward. If they were going to take the crate, he wanted it done quickly. But his brother was rooting around in the pile of fishing gear.

'What are you doing?' He heard the panic in his own whisper.

Jacques picked up a metal rod with a hook on the end and levered open the box. Rifles nestled in straw, neatly cradling each other. Jacques picked one up, stroked it slowly, a smile on his face, before settling the curve of the stock into his collarbone.

'Here. Feel this.' He handed the gun to Michael, guiding it into a position for firing. It was surprisingly heavy, the metal cold and the wood smooth. His right index finger curled into the trigger guard. He squeezed until a metallic click vibrated along the barrel. Although his father had a shotgun for controlling vermin on the farm, Michael had never used one. Never wanted to. But now… holding the Enfield, he felt strong. Yves' face, his look of disapproval when Bob had suggested stealing the rifles, flashed into his mind. He blinked it away and swallowed hard as he handed the rifle back.

'Where are we taking them?' His voice sounded firmer. Jacques was trusting him; he must step up. He'd deal with his qualms later.

'The farm for now. Hide them in the barn at the milking yard. Probably best split up the box. I thought a few at the plumbers' yard. Bob's not so sure.'

Jacques put the rifle back as carefully as if he was putting a child to bed, tucking the straw around it. The lid was tight and it took both of them to push it into place on the corners until there was a muffled snap. Michael felt a twinge of pain in his thumb.

The common was still deserted when he emerged blinking

into the sun; he could hear crickets chirping in the dusty heat as he opened the truck's boot and pushed an old horse blanket and a couple of empty potato boxes to one side. The murmur of an engine made him look up; the bus from Gorey trundled down the hill towards the common. He froze, heat prickling in his neck, as an elderly woman got off the bus at the top of the slipway. She adjusted her headscarf and, as she started to cross the road, glanced over and smiled at him, a bag of shopping bulging and bumping at her knees. He'd turned back when a voice close to his shoulder startled him.

'It's Michael Le Breton, isn't it?'

'Oh, Mrs Le Brun.' Her faded blue eyes held his. He cleared his throat and tried to smile.

'I haven't seen you for ages. How are your parents? Paul and Jacques went with the boats to St Malo, eh? All well?'

'Yes, yes… They're back. Early his morning. Tired but fine. I'm… going fishing with a friend.' His throat tightened on the lie.

She narrowed her eyes and looked out at the beached boats, leaning at awkward angles on the wet sand. 'Tide's not in until later, eh?'

He mumbled, 'I have to help out at the farm… Jacques is helping me to bring down the gear for later. Can I help you with that bag?'

'You've cut yourself!' She nodded towards his right hand, dripping blood at his feet. Sourness filled his mouth as he crammed his thumb into it.

'Looks like you've enough on, lad.' She raised her eyebrows, hoisting the bag up. 'Give my best to Hélène and Paul, eh? I'll be up to see your granny as usual, later in the week.'

She crossed the road. Sucking the wound hard, his teeth sharp in the raw flesh drawn into his mouth, Michael pulled a handkerchief from his pocket and wrapped his thumb tightly. Red seeped through the white cotton. He moved quickly back into the tower. Jacques had the crate lifted on his shoulder, the tarp drooping down his back.

'All clear?' I heard that nosy old bag…'

'It's fine. She's gone.'

He helped Jacques manoeuvre the crate into the truck, returned the key to its place under the block of granite and swung himself up into the passenger seat, feeling the heat of the worn leather seat on the back of his thighs.

Jacques was silent, his eyes fixed on the towering rocks on the beach. Michael looked at his profile, dark curls pushed back off a tanned forehead, nose straight, mouth narrow, the sinews in his neck taut. His chest rose and fell. He turned to Michael, fixing him with cold brown eyes, and nodded. What did that mean? Approval? The sun burned through the windscreen.

They drove through Le Hocq under heavy, overhanging trees. Towards the top of the lane, Jacques changed into a lower gear as the track became steeper, set deep between banks and hedgerows, until it broke free into the expanse of flat farmland. Fields of grass, divided by hedges, were cropped by groups of toffee-coloured cows, their heads lowered and their tails sweeping away summer flies from angular haunches. Pink udders bulged.

20TH JUNE 1940

There was a buzz of conversation at Rozel Stores when Michael pushed open the door. A crowd of people gathered around the counter. One man was jabbing his finger at the large black letters of the headline of last night's *Evening Post*: *Demilitarisation: British Government to withdraw troops from island.*

'What does it mean?' A middle-aged woman in a headscarf addressed another similarly clad. Both held baskets over their arms.

No one answered the question. Michael felt anxiety rise from his stomach to his throat. He picked up a paper from the pile. No. It couldn't be true. After supplies and weapons had been brought to the island?

'That's sixpence, please. Others are waiting!'

He pushed his way out with the newspaper and sank down on a bench next to a box of apples displayed under the shop window.

The States had been in session for most of the day, the article reported, following a decision from London that all troops and military equipment are to be withdrawn immediately from the Channel Islands, in the belief that such action would protect citizens from a German bombardment. What he and Jacques had learned at the Royal Engineers' yard was confirmed: the Royal Militia was to leave Jersey, volunteer defence troops were to be disbanded and all weapons handed in to police stations. Weapons handed in? The crate stashed behind a wall of hay bales in the barn? Jacques wouldn't hand those in. How would demilitarisation protect the islands?

Michael sat still and looked at the words until they blurred into black creeping spiders. He jammed the paper into his jacket pocket, loosened his collar and grabbed his bicycle from where it was leaning in the hedge. The bailiff was going to make a statement this morning in the Royal Square.

*

He had never seen so many people walking towards St Helier; the streets were alive with people rushing, men shouting. He'd left his bike on the slipway at La Colette, propped up against their farm truck; Jacques or his parents must be in town.

As he ran down Hill Street, he heard a voice behind him. 'Oi! Mike. Mike.' He turned to see Bob, shouldering his way between two women in his old tweed jacket and tie, hat in hand. His face was red and sweating in the June heat.

'Did you…? Where's your brother? I need to see Jacques,' he puffed.

'I don't know.' Michael strode on, wanting to shake him off. Bob panted close behind him as he turned into the narrow path between The Peirson and Gallichan's the jewellers which opened into The Royal Square. The States building loomed high over on his left, its grey granite walls symmetrical with closed sash windows. The library and court house made up the shorter end of the square with shops and the bank lining the side to his right. Outside The Peirson, men in small groups huddled over barrels set out as tables, many with drinks in their hands. Michael stood still and scanned the crowd, Bob at his shoulder, uncomfortably close.

'There he is… Jacques! Jacques!' He pointed and waved his hat.

Jacques looked up at Bob's shout, nodded at a couple of men and came to join them.

Bob grabbed Jacques' arm and spoke into his face. 'Where did you…?' He glanced at Michael. 'Does he know?'

Jacques nodded. His voice was quiet and his mouth close to Bob's ear. Michael caught hissed fragments: 'Don't worry… look… need to talk… not here… we've been left in the lurch.' Jacques straightened up and pulled his shoulders back. 'I'm not going to take it… What 'bout you, Bob?'

'But… it'll be illegal to have them… and we can't leave them in the tower. Anyone could see them. I can't afford to be in trouble. My mother depends on me…'

'Keep your voice down. They're not in the tower.'

Michael could see some relief on Bob's face and his bulky body relaxed. He opened and shut his mouth, blowing out a deep breath before he replied. 'Where..?'

'Not here… tell you later,' Jacques said looking around at the growing crowd. 'Don't worry, eh, we'll sort it… I'll sort it. I don't trust anyone…'

Royal Square was filling up, men in dark clothes, creating gloomy shadows in the dappled shade of the trees, families standing around piles of suitcases. Queues for the bank were confused with groups talking animatedly, looking up at the States building. The bank was open, but a scribbled sign in the window stated that customers were limited to taking out a maximum of £25. Faces were serious; people looked nervous, angry, dressed in heavy coats despite the heat, ready for the walk to the harbour to board one of the evacuation ships. A fight broke out as one man accused another, a well-dressed gentleman in a bowler hat and black suit, of jumping the queue; they had to be appeased by a clergyman and a woman with a small child.

Michael recognised the bailiff, Mr Coutanche, when he appeared on the balcony of the senate house and the crowd fell silent, shuffling to get as close as possible. The bailiff introduced Judge Pinel who stood next to him, stepped forward and raised a megaphone, speaking slowly, his voice echoing around the square.

'The States of Jersey have been discussing the current situation and we understand that you are anxious about the demilitarisation of the islands. I hope I can allay some of your fears and want to confirm that we have every confidence that the island will be safe. Do not panic. The States Assembly members are unanimous in their decision to stay on the island and we hope that many of you will do the same thing. Think about your homes, your businesses, your farms. The cost of abandoning them will be high.' He paused, lowering the loudhailer. A dog barked and a child cried. Mr Coutanche raised the green cone to his mouth again. 'But, for those of you who want to leave, there will be plenty of ships available. Those of you who are of an age to join the armed forces may wish to consider where you will be most useful to your country and your families. Strong young men will be needed here to keep the island and its economy running.' His firm voice and clear statement suggested confidence and Michael thought of how deeply rooted in the island his family was. He was proud that they had already decided that they wouldn't leave.

The bailiff's final words brought a prick of tears to Michael's eyes. 'I will never leave and my wife will be at my side. The Union Jack and the Jersey flags are flying from Fort Regent and, if it ever becomes necessary, only I will take them down.'

There was a moment of quiet before the bailiff began to sing the national anthem. 'God Save the King' was picked up by the crowd, first in a subdued manner before it built and quickened to a stirring chorus; men pushed out their chests and women straightened restless children. Michael joined in but Jacques, arms folded, pursed his lips and kept his head down as Mr. Coutanche departed and the crowds swirled and thinned around them. The queue for the bank re-formed, snaking around the square.

Jacques was silent, his face set and his mouth a thin line, as they headed back to the farm, Michael's bike rattling in the back of the truck. His half-formed questions were ignored until they turned into the milking yard where a group of workers was herding the last of the cows into the milking shed.

'We'll talk later,' said Jacques. 'Come and help with the milking.'

Settled on a stool with a cow's rough flank on his cheek and the sharp reek of manure in his nose, Michael's shoulders fell as the familiar task took over and the milk fizzed into the pail. The only sound was of shuffling Jerseys and the metallic tinkle of liquid. His tight chest loosened and his hands worked automatically on Rose's leathery teats. Rusty marks filled the cracked skin of his right thumb.

In the quiet yard, after the cows were back in the top field and the milking team had dispersed, Michael paused in his sweeping. He leaned on his broom and watched Jacques who was standing in front of a disused shed, abandoned after the new barn was built, rolling a cigarette. He flicked open his battered Zippo lighter, inhaled deeply and closed his eyes as the smoke drifted into his face. He rolled his shoulders back and rubbed at the back of his neck. When he turned to Michael, his face was serious, his dark eyebrows drawn close together. 'This shed would be better than the barn. No one goes in there. And let's get them out of that crate. The inscription's a bit of a give-away!'

The door stuck in the warped frame as they pushed their way in. The corrugated iron roof sagged over old tools, broken boxes, piles of old sacking and discarded bottles and tins. Michael's head jerked towards a scuffling in a corner. Out of the corner of his eye, he saw movement along the wall and a flash of pink tail. He moved a rusting milk churn to one side and revealed a pile of shredded material, paper and sacking. Grey baby rats, their feet pale and snouts square, were squirming, half-obscured in the gloom. On the farm they poisoned them to protect the crops. 'Leave them,' said Jacques. 'Deterrent… in case anyone's nosy.'

Between them they carried the crate, draped in the tarpaulin, from the main barn into the shed. Jacques levered off the lid and they carried the shining rifles, six of them, into a corner, close to the rats' nest, standing them on their ends and covering them with the tarp and pieces of sacking before barricading them in behind a wall of pitchforks and brooms and boxes. From the door, they were invisible, part of the junk of a farmer's shed. Jacques stuffed a small, rattling box into his pocket. Bullets. The crate collapsed under their boots as they stamped on it and collected the shattered pieces and the packing straw in a sack before pushing the door back into its frame and piling bricks against the bottom.

Jacques nodded at Michael, smiled and swung the sack over his shoulder. 'Thanks. I wasn't sure you had it in you… you've… done well. I'll burn this. I shouldn't need to say this… but I will: keep it to yourself.' He looked hard at

Michael. 'You should get back to the house. I'll be down later for supper.'

Tired and shaky, Michael watched Jacques move towards the steel drum they used to burn rubbish. The milking yard was unusually quiet; no birds sang. Across the yard, flames flared in the incinerator. Jacques' face distorted in the heat haze.

25TH JUNE 1940

The following Tuesday, just before the end of their English lesson, there was a tap on the classroom door and one of the prefects appeared, his face serious. 'Sorry to disturb, Miss. The headmaster wants everyone to assemble in the hall, now.'

Miss Bisson struggled to make her voice heard through the buzz of excitement and slamming of desk lids. 'Right, everyone. Pack your things away and make your way to the hall.'

The noise faded to a murmur as they entered, lining up in forms in front of a row of grim-faced teachers. The absence of so many of the boys and girls, and some of the teachers was clear. Normally when the whole school gathered, the hall was full. Silence fell. Even Jeremy Cole, usually the clown of the school and often suspended by the headmaster, was quiet as Mr Wooley announced:

'School is suspended. The end of term has been brought forward.' He paused and cleared his throat. 'I know you are all worried about the future. We are all worried because we can't predict what is going to happen and life feels unsettled. Many of our friends and some of our family members have left the island; more are planning to go. Speculation about what is going to happen is unhelpful and panic is destructive. All we can do is stay calm and help our families in what might be a difficult and unusual time. I hope that all of you will stay faithful to the Christian values which are the foundation of our school. I hope that you will not forget your studies; many of you will return to them when this is all over with renewed vigour and I know that you are ambitious. Take your books home, read and study what you can. Be obedient to your parents and loyal to your friends. We will reopen in September, God willing. Now we will pray. Bow your heads, as we listen to the prayer we always use at the end of the school year. Its words are particularly relevant today.'

Miss Bisson stepped forwards, *The Book of Common Prayer* in her hands. Her voice, so familiar to Michael, was strong, warm and comforting.

'*Go forth into the world in peace;*
Be of good courage;
Hold fast that which is good;
Render to no one evil for evil;
Strengthen the faint-hearted;
Support the weak;
Help the afflicted;
Honour everyone.'

A rousing chorus of 'God Save the King' ended the school year, sung with gusto and accompanied by a few sniffling girls, one of them crying so loudly that she had to be led out of the hall by the school nurse.

The mood of the pupils changed as Michael walked out of the main door. He was buffeted by laughing teenagers. His friends were grinning, punching shoulders and making plans in the sunshine of the school playing field. He wasn't able to join in; he felt unsettled and not ready for what was happening so quickly.

Amy waved to him as she left on her bicycle with her friend Esme cycling beside her and a pile of books precariously towering over the top of her basket. He looked around for Laura, though he had been told that her family was among the first boatload of evacuees to leave Jersey. He caught the eye of one her friends, Emma, he thought she was called. She looked Michael in the face and smiled broadly, showing large white teeth. He walked over to her and asked, with his head down, if she had heard from Laura.

'Oh, hello, Michael, isn't it?' She spoke with confidence. 'Laura asked me to let you know that she was leaving, but I wasn't sure which one was you,' she said, giggling and glancing at a group of boys on the other side of the playground.

'Do you know where her family have gone?' Michael followed her gaze to see Jonny and Keith watching. She pursed her lips and pushed her thin, fair hair behind her ear, displaying a sparkling gold earring. She was so different from the quiet, thoughtful Laura and he wondered why they were friends.

'I believe she has gone to relatives in Poole. I don't know where that is exactly, but I think it's on the south coast.' She spoke with a careful formality and a practised smile on her face.

'Do you have an address?' he blurted out as she seemed to be preparing to depart, delving into her satchel.

'No, but she left this for you.' Emma handed him a small book in a worn paper cover and gave him a toothy smile. 'My family are staying. Are yours?'

Michael did not hear her. The blood was rushing in his ears and he felt the heat in his face as he looked at the book in his hand. The sun in his eyes, he turned away, aware of Emma's raised voice, but not what she said. He ignored Jonny and Keith's shouts, pushed the book into his bag and looked around for his bike, cursing when he spotted it leaning against the fence next to Keith and his scruffy Raleigh. He turned on his heel and jogged, head down, out of the playground.

When he reached the marsh at Le Hocq, he stopped in the shade of an oak tree, its leaves heavy, creating a cool green world beneath. He searched through his bag for the little volume. It was a leather-bound edition of Thomas Hardy's poetry, with a tattered dust jacket. He didn't know much of Hardy's poetry and was surprised to see a whole volume of it, thinking of the writer primarily as a novelist. He had been trying to read *Tess of the d'Urbervilles*, recommended by Laura, and wondered if there was significance in the poetry book, a message maybe. He flicked through it hoping for a note, address or dedication to him and found nothing.

'Regret Not Me', arrested his glance down the contents page and he shivered in the gloom of the shade. Leaving his bag under the tree, he took the book and walked down to the beach, crunching and rolling on the pebbles until he met the smoother surface of sand as he walked parallel to the sea towards the headland. He sat against the wall of the cottage called The Croft and read the beginning of the poem, shading his eyes from the glare of the sun:

Regret not me;
Beneath the sunny tree
I lie uncaring, slumbering peacefully.

Swift as the light
I flew my faery flight;
Ecstatically I moved, and feared no night.

I did not know
That heydays fade and go,
But deemed that what was would be always so.

His vision blurred and his eyes pricked. He allowed one tear to tickle his cheek resisting the urge to wipe it away. He removed his glasses and, blinking, gazed out to sea, seeing Laura, in a white dress, under a tree in blossom by the misty waters of Poole, which looked like Greve de Lecq in his vision. He ignored the word 'uncaring' and decided to take the title of the poem as ironic, a concept that his English teacher was keen on. They'd meet again, he knew. *What was would always be so* – yes, that's what he wished, but knew that it couldn't be. Things changed. He wished he had a picture of her. He closed his eyes, leant his head back against the rough surface seeing red behind his lids.

Barking and the cries of seagulls roused him. On the common, a pack of dogs was chasing the birds, which swooped down again after being hurried away, taunting and provoking a surge of flying fur and howling until the birds glided off the sea wall under the tower mocking the dogs by their graceful exits and settling out of reach on King's Rock. Why were the dogs running loose? Michael went to investigate, tucking the book into his trouser pocket. Among the animals he recognised Mrs Lawrence's over-fed poodle and a sheepdog which he thought belonged to Mr Bride from Green Island. As he approached, they ran away, crossing the road, and vanishing into the trees on the marsh. Michael followed but he did not see them again.

Under the oak, a small black cat was sitting on his school bag. It mewed at his approach and wound itself around his legs, crying and pawing at the fabric. A collar indicated that 'Lettie' lived in Le Hocq Lane and she followed him, calling gently, as he walked past the pub on the corner and the granite cottages on the left-hand side, their doors, which gave directly onto the lane and usually open all day, firmly shut.

Le Maret was opposite, a larger French-looking house with shutters, an elaborate white balcony and a shiny blue front door with a knocker in the shape of a fish. Michael checked Lettie's collar, opened the wooden gate to a small courtyard and lifted the brass fish door knocker, heavy and cool in his hand. The cat jumped in a fluid movement onto the wall and sat with her tail neatly furled around her haunches watching him, continuing her melancholic noises. She was hungry.

No reply from the quiet house. Michael opened one of the shutters and peered through the window to see the scattered remains of a meal on the table and clothes on the floor. With a sinking feeling, he recalled Jacques' stories of abandoned homes and pets. A loud scream and guttural muttering of 'Poor Dolly' made him jump back in alarm, knocking the shutter open further as he banged his shoulder on it. Catching the light was a swinging cage and a grey parrot, pecking at her bars, an empty dish and water tray at her feet. 'Poor Dolly! Poor Dolly!'

He tried the window, pulling at the sash, but it was locked from the inside. And still the parrot called.

Around the front door were pots of geraniums, leaves yellowed and wilting in the heat. He looked under each, hoping that they'd left a key. Nothing. But under a pile of small, rounded boulders which looked as though they'd come off Plémont Beach, he found a set of keys on a rusting ring. The boulders were warm and familiar to his hands. He'd collected a few for his mother last summer when she was building a rockery in the garden. Perfectly smooth in spheres or oval shapes and in delicate shades of pink and grey, they were piled up by the strong tides at Plémont, rolled into the caves and half-drowned in rock pools. If you could carry them up the rotting wooden ladder and onto the steep path to the headland, they were beautiful in gardens and, when it rained, they glowed with the clarity of the beach after the tide retreated.

Michael tried two keys in the front door before finding the one which turned in the lock; he looked up and down the lane before opening the door, feeling a strange sense of guilt. The mewing Lettie ran in front of him, trotting to a sticky looking enamel bowl on the black and white tiles of the hall, pushing at it with her nose. In the kitchen, towards the back of the house, he found a box of cat food, filled the bowl and looked around for water. A flowery dish sat on a dresser and he filled it from the dripping tap and put it down for Lettie who silently tucked into her meal, her little paws pushed neatly together.

Opening the door of the parrot's cage was a mistake. The bird flew out in a grey flash and raced around the room, squawking and dropping feathers and pellets over the furniture. Michael refilled her water dish and found some seeds and fruit for her in the dresser, but the bird would not return to the cage; she sat on the back of a chintz sofa, cocking her head at him. He put the food and water down on the floor and she edged towards the bowls on her scaly feet, beady eyes watching him. He couldn't leave them. What would happen when he opened the front door? Could a domestic parrot and a house cat fend for themselves in the wild? He'd only ever seen parrots in pictures and knew nothing about them. Cats were feral on the farm and they rarely fed them; this one seemed to rely on its owners.

When the parrot had finished the food, it walked, head bobbing and feet turned inwards towards Michael, who had perched on the edge of a wooden chair. He smiled as it clambered up his leg, ignoring the pricking of the sharp claws. It settled on his shoulder and pecked gently at the buttons of his shirt, crooning: 'Pretty Dolly. Pretty Dolly.' He stroked the soft grey feathers and she blinked and bent her head under his hand. 'Hello Dolly,' he said quietly.

Michael carefully shut and locked the front door, replacing the keys under the stones. Dolly stayed on his shoulder, looking backwards towards the house and Lettie followed him on the top of the wall before jumping off and shadowing him as he walked up the lane.

The school yard and playing fields were deserted; the school caretaker was sweeping the paving in front of the big doors. He stopped when he saw Michael, who pointed to his bike, askew in the hedge, and then raised a hand and went back to his brushing, seeming not to have noticed the grey parrot balancing on Michael's right shoulder and a black cat, tripping him up as he reached for the bike.

He wobbled as he tried to pedal slowly down the school path. Dolly squawked and flew off his shoulder swooping around his head as he increased his speed. He would walk up the hilly part of the route; it was hot and, though the animals were following him quietly, it would give them a breather. Dolly immediately flew to his shoulder when he dismounted, the left one this time; her claws sank into his bag's strap rather than his flesh. At the top of the hill, he turned, as he often did, to look back at the sea. The coast of France was clear and he made out houses and the thin mustard strip of a sandy beach. Smoke was still rising but was turning white and wispy. As he gazed out, a large ship rounded the headland heading away from the harbour, no doubt filled with evacuees. How many people on the ship did he know? When would they be back? Fear was not something he had experienced before and the heaviness of his breathing and tightness of his throat were new to him.

The house was deserted when he cycled into the yard and he dropped his bag in the kitchen before taking Lettie and Dolly out to the barns to find them a home. They seemed happy in each other's company and he left them sharing a dish of water.

Leaving his shoes outside the back door, he lugged his bag upstairs and climbed onto his bed, the volume of Hardy's poetry in his hand. The late morning sun was warm and the open window offered little in the way of breeze. He felt heat rise up his neck as he held the volume to his mouth, breathing in that musty book smell he associated with school. As he turned the pages, he found a poem that he recognised, one studied in an anthology at school a few months ago and chosen by Miss Bisson for its relevance to the world situation. He could see her now, sitting on the edge of her desk; she was a favourite among the pupils, blonde hair up in an untidy bun, enthusiastic and energetic, quick to praise and never talking down to them. The poem had given the pupils an opportunity to talk about the war, but they had left the classroom uplifted, despite the prospect of Chemistry next lesson. Michael read it aloud:

IN TIME OF 'THE BREAKING OF NATIONS'

I
Only a man harrowing clods
In a slow silent walk
With an old horse that stumbles and nods
Half asleep as they stalk.
II
Only thin smoke without flame

From the heaps of couch-grass;
Yet this will go onwards the same
Though Dynasties pass.
III
Yonder a maid and her wight
Come whispering by:
War's annals will cloud into night
Ere their story die.

Miss had had to explain a few of the archaic words but they had all felt the weight of the message and were able, with a bit of prompting, to see what Hardy was suggesting when he was living through war: the important things will remain and thrive despite times of conflict. The traditions and customs of the country and lovers' meetings will survive. Michael repeated under his breath 'a maid and her wight', loving the rhythm of the simple words, and imagined Laura, her hand in his, walking down through the marsh to the beach, the clouds over France lifted and a perfect summer's day ahead of them. Was he being sentimental or 'soft' as Jonny had called him? Maybe. And maybe things had to change. But why now?

'Anyone home?' Amy's voice rang up the stairs and he jolted out of his fantasy and pushed the book under the pillow. He sprang off the bed and was reminded of his sore foot for the first time in days.

He trotted down the stairs, smiling at his sister standing at the bottom. 'Just me!'

'You'll never believe what I have found in the barn?'

'A grey parrot and a little black cat? Just a guess!' He grinned at his sister's open mouth and raised eyebrows. 'I… rescued them. They'd been abandoned and sort of followed me home.'

'The parrot's cheeky. He swore at me when I opened the door.'

'I think it's a she. She says 'pretty Dolly' quite regularly, so that's what I have called her.'

'The cat was asleep.'

'I hope Mum and Dad aren't unhappy about keeping the animals. I couldn't leave them. I can't believe how people are just going. There must be hundreds of pets left. So many people seem to be leaving.'

'I've just been riding with Mum and it looks like some of the farmers have abandoned cows and pigs too. We passed a herd near Rozel which needed milking; they were making an awful racket.'

The noise of their father's motorbike distracted them, and they moved into the kitchen. It was Yves who came in the back door, ducking his fair head through the low entrance.

'Salut, twins.'

His usual greeting was given the traditional response in unison. 'Bonjour, Yves.'

'Are you both all right? School suspended?'

'Fine and yes. Not enough teachers.'

'Who wants a trip out to St Ouen's? The tide's coming up and there is a little swell, I think. My boss has left me and Bob in charge, so we decided to close up shop for the day! Play hookey.'

'I'm not sure I feel like it,' said Michael.

'What's the matter? We should make the most of it!'

'Do you really think we should?'

'Why not?' Yves' smile was infectious and Michael felt his mouth turning up, imitating his brother's. 'If we are staying, we have to carry on as usual. Jacques has the truck, so it will have to be just bodyboarding. We can go on Dad's bike. Oh, sorry, Amy. Can't take two!'

'You boys go ahead. I was going to help Mum anyway. And there is a parrot to babysit!'

*

They rounded the bend at La Pulente, high above the long Atlantic beach and the Five Mile Road which stretched along the western side of the island. Yves pulled the bike into a small gravel area and they dismounted. Corbière lighthouse rose, white and tall, on the rocks to their left. With the tide coming in, it was surrounded by the heaving blue; the causeway was covered. A favourite haunt of the family, when they could all get out for a Sunday picnic in the truck. When they were younger it was the scene of many rock pool competitions at low tide. They found red anemones, tiny crabs and shells, twisted into pale pink shapes, keeping them in buckets before releasing them as the water crept higher in the rocks. Then it was time for a swim or surf as the sun moved slowly down towards the horizon at St Ouen's. Mum would sit in the dunes, in her long sleeves and hat, and open her basket after their swim: tea, metallic in flasks, thick cheese sandwiches, tomatoes and apples. Michael had a sudden vision of his mother cutting up a rosy apple with a penknife.

The tide was nearing its height and they could see the white tops of the waves rolling silently towards the dunes. As they descended the hill, Michael closed his eyes and breathed deeply, willing the fluttering in his stomach to settle.

He kept his eyes shut, feeling the sway of the last bend before the straight run of the Five Mile Road. Yves pulled left and the motorcycle bumped into the rocky foreshore. He cut the engine and Michael opened his eyes to the whispering swish of the waves and a blue horizon. Together they ran towards the beach, the rucksack bouncing on Michael's back.

Down the stone steps the beach opened up, shining and clean. Waves were turning over and smoothly swirling into the shallows. In the distance, a faint mist obscured the headland at L'Etacq.

Yves raised his hand at a group of lads sitting under the low wall. Michael trailed behind, not knowing if he'd be welcome in this company of young men older than him and most of them working, like Yves. But the boys seemed friendly and Yves' introduction of him as 'my clever brother,' made him feel better. One of the young men was John Coutanche, who Michael knew was the bailiff's son, about the same age as Yves. They had been at school together. He was tall and confident with dark hair and pale blue eyes, skin tanned and healthy-looking. He'd stayed on at school when Yves left and was hoping to go to university.

The boys raced into the clear water, gasping at the cold, and dived through the first wave, surfacing and shaking their wet heads like dogs. Michael caught wave after wave, laughing as he collided with Yves and allowing the momentum to take him into the shallows where the sand roughened his belly. He lay still, his body sinking into the soft sand as water swirled around his legs. The war's dark clouds receded in the glitter of the moment.

When the tide began to retreat and the sun started its descent, in a blazing ball towards La Rocco Tower, the Martello just reachable on a very low tide, the boys lay on the beach and talk turned to war. A few of them, reminding Michael of Jacques, were angry and determined to get to England and join up, though they didn't seem old enough. Others were quieter and less sure of themselves. Yves, typically, said very little, but asked John about his father's situation.

'I haven't seen much of him,' John said drawing heavily on his cigarette, and swallowing a cough. 'He's at the States until all hours. Ever since he was sworn in on Friday.'

'Sworn in as what? asked Yves.

'I know, it's complicated. Mum had to explain to me. The lieutenant governor had to leave… because it's a military position.'

'So your father is…'

'He was sworn in as "civil governor".' There was pride in his voice, but a tremble too and the boys went quiet, all looking out to sea.

One of the boys, whose name Michael couldn't remember, broke the silence. 'Well, I'm glad my family is staying. Have you seen the posters around town? "Keep your heads!" and "Why go mad?" Catchy, eh? Apparently, the chap who put them up was on the next evacuee boat!' Everyone laughed and Michael felt strengthened by their optimism.

There was quiet for a few minutes before John spoke again. 'Did you see the message from the king? He says it was in our interests that the island was demilitarised. I don't know what to think… and dad won't express an opinion. At least, when I asked him last night, he wouldn't give a straight answer. And he rushed back to his study as soon as he'd eaten. I wanted to talk about it.'

Michael looked from face to face. The boys all seemed lost in their own thoughts. He wished they would discuss it; he wanted answers too but was afraid to appear naïve and childish to them.

The sun was visibly moving below the horizon, blazing a dangerous orange, throwing paths of fire on the glassy sea. They dispersed, murmuring goodbyes. Yves draped his arm around Michael's shoulders as they walked back to the motorbike and straddled the warmth of the dusty engine.

'Let's go back through St Mary's', Yves called as he revved the engine, skidding slightly on the gravel before they regained the road.

'Can't you go any faster!' Michael shouted. He wanted speed and a rush of danger.

The wind on his face, tugging at his hair, stole his breath. He tightened his hold on Yves' waist and turned his cheek to the solidity of his brother's warm back. How could any of this change?

JUNE 28TH 1940

'I'm going to visit Meg at Overdale later today…' said Michael's mother. The family had finished their breakfast and were sitting around the table, the usual time for the discussion of daily plans. 'It's a while since I've been…' She was looking pointedly at Jacques as she spoke; he'd said very little since the start of the meal, when he'd railed against the British authorities. Now his face was closed. 'She must be feeling worried… in her situation… don't you think?' There was a silence. Michael waited, though he didn't expect Jacques to respond; he looked as though he hadn't heard their mother.

'I'm sure she'll be her usual calm self,' said Michael's father. 'But she'll appreciate a friendly face and a chat.'

Meg Vibert was a friend of the family who Michael had known, like a big sister, all his life. Meg's mother and his had been close friends since school. When Mrs Vibert died five years ago, Meg had spent more time with the whole family and everyone was delighted when it had become clear that she and Jacques started 'walking out together' at Christmas.

Michael had noticed them chatting during the traditional Boxing Day party in the Caldwell Hall, not thinking anything of it until his mother had nudged his father and nodded in their direction.

'Look at that, Paul. Am I imagining it, or are they flirting?'

His father had looked across and smiled. 'Are they? You might be right. Well, that's a turn up for the books. She'd be good for him!'

'But would he be good for her?'

'What do you mean? She'd be a welcome addition to the family.'

'Well… let's not count our chickens! Of course, I'd love her and Jacques to… But… well, they are so different, aren't they? And I feel… protective towards her.'

Michael watched, fascinated by the change in Meg. Usually, she was quiet and talked with a careful, serious manner. Michael often discussed literature with her and she had started lending him books. But at the party she had seemed so animated and… 'girly'; it was the only word he could think of to describe her. She was looking up at Jacques showing a row of white teeth, shaking back her fair, frizzy curls. Her cheeks were flushed. Next to Jacques, she seemed very small and fragile, like a bird, he thought.

'Different?' questioned his father.

'I think so. I suppose I shouldn't speak ill of my eldest son, but he can be so moody sometimes, don't you agree? She's… the opposite, I'd say. I've never seen her anything but composed.'

'He has a temper at times, I'll give you that. She'll be a good influence on him,' his father said.

Since then, Meg and Jacques had become a couple and, at first, his father's predictions had been correct. Jacques had seemed more relaxed and came back smiling from their walks and cycle rides and occasional trips to the cinema. But it was short-lived; in February, as the war in Europe intensified,

Jacques joined the Volunteer Defence Force and his brother and Meg saw less of each other.

Meg's diagnosis, a few weeks ago now, had stunned the family; she had TB of the hip joint. She had seen a doctor for increasing pain when she walked. Treatment required her to keep her pelvis completely still. She would spend about twelve months in a hospital bed in Overdale Clinic, resting, in a plaster of Paris shell.

Jacques had told them one evening in March, raising his voice as he explained the medical issues, questioning the treatment and appearing to be angry with Meg. His tone was full of indignation as he called her 'passive' and said she was too happy just to do as she was told. He seemed to find her acceptance of the situation irritating and after visiting her once, Michael knew he had not been back.

'Shall I come with you, Mum?' Michael asked. 'I haven't been yet. I'd like to see her.'

It still felt very warm in the late afternoon when the bus descended to the coast road and turned west. As they trundled through Le Hocq towards St Helier, Michael narrowed his eyes against the white-hot sun hovering over the flashing ocean. A drift of cloud lined the horizon. A salty breeze from the open window ruffled his hair and he pushed it off his forehead, catching a whiff, a whisper of the earthy sourness of just-picked tomatoes on his fingers. He'd been glad of the excuse to leave the chattering girls in the greenhouse, have a cool wash and put on a clean shirt, though he'd lost the argument with his mother about wearing shorts. The feeling of freshness had not lasted; he'd felt sweaty again almost immediately, as he helped his mother pick sweet peas in the garden. Now, the leather seat of the swaying bus was hot under his cotton trousers and his feet swollen in his school shoes.

He tried to ignore, to swallow down, the shaky feeling in his chest, the cloud of the unknown, which had been building for weeks. The danger was everywhere, and increasing daily, not just in the threat of the invasion and the knowledge that it would happen. Massive change was descending, though what that change would be, he couldn't tell.

He felt it most powerfully in the evenings spent in the kitchen with the murmuring wireless. His father faced the future by working harder than ever on the farm and refusing to show any fear or answer the 'what if' questions any of them asked. He'd always been a man of few words, as his mother once described him. It was Jacques who did the talking, arguing about the way the British were handling the crisis, repeating his resentment, asking unanswerable questions and never listening. Last night's rant as his mother had served up their meal was typical:

'I don't see why men from the islands aren't called up in the same way as those on the mainland. It's ridiculous! I could have gone to England months ago, like some of the other lads, joined up there. I wish I had now. I could kick myself. Bob and I decided to go down the official channels and register at the town hall for National Service. I've heard nothing since. It's months now.'

Breathing in deeply, feeling the prickle of dust in his throat, he ran his tongue over dry lips and glanced at his mother sitting beside him, looking cool, one hand on the basket of flowers she held on her lap.

She turned and smiled at him. 'Did you see any planes today? I didn't. It felt quiet, almost normal.'

'No, I didn't see them today. Yesterday there were loads. What do you think they are looking at?'

'Jacques says they are reconnaissance flights – gathering information, I suppose.'

'They remind me of bats, with their black crosses.'

'I know what you mean. They are sinister… like vermin.'

'What information could they want? They'll see fields, beaches, cows, if they fly low enough.'

His mother laughed. 'What a view they must have! I suppose our island will look like… paradise, a secret green world, away from the battlefields of France.'

The window vibrated against his temple as he looked up into the empty sky, trying to visualise the island from the air: patchwork farmland, flashing greenhouses, clusters of granite cottages and squat-towered churches, ancient manor houses in their rolling grounds, all enclosed by cliffs, coves, beaches and the vast green sea.

The bus turned off the coast road, into the outskirts of town, and the view became crowded with terraced cottages. As the bus pulled in to allow a family to alight, he looked down over a rickety fence into one small front garden glowing with red and orange roses, climbing over a lattice arch. Next door, tall agapanthus, with their sprays of bluebell heads exploding on thick straight stems, leant over a low wall, in front of a square of well-tended lawn.

At the Weighbridge, most of the passengers disembarked, weaving into the crowds around the harbour where potatoes and tomatoes were being unloaded from trucks and carts. Tall cranes, chains dangling, were swinging crates and sacks onto rusting cargo vessels, towering over the fishing boats. Fishermen competed for space to bring in their nets and buckets. Seagulls circled and called. Normality had resumed since the initial panic.

The bus, quieter now with only an old couple seated in front of them, drove slowly behind a horse and cart along the Esplanade and Victoria Avenue, turning right to skirt the park before crawling up the steep slope of Westmount Road.

The bus dropped them at the gates of the clinic and it was with relief that Michael followed his mother out of the dusty heat of the gravelled drive into the shade of the tiled hall. Shared with three other women suffering from a variety of invisible ailments, Meg's ward had tall windows and, with its west-facing situation, a sunny outlook. In the heat of the day the blinds had been pulled down and the room had the quality of a clear pool: ripples of light moved across the walls and children darted like fish between beds. Flowers, on a central table, fading pink and yellow chrysanthemums, emitted a funereal smell and scattered dusty pollen on the polished surface.

Meg's bed, in the corner, was a bank of crisp white sheet. From the doorway, Michael could see her frowning, concentrating on her knitting, holding a pattern close to her face. She looked small, almost child-like, with her legs encased in the curved shell of plaster-of-Paris. Her pink nightgown had ruffles around its neck. She looked up as they made their way down the ward, her face transformed into a wide smile.

His mother drew up a chair and set down the basket of flowers and tomatoes. Michael was wondering if it would be all right for him to perch on the end of the bed when a series of muffled crumps and bangs made him glance up. The chatter continued. He looked at his mother, then caught the eye of a middle-aged man seated next to Meg's neighbour. A hand pouring tea was stilled. Then a loud crack, and a boom bounced in the vaulted ceiling. Fear jumped in his chest. Silence. Meg's pale face, eyes wide and staring, was frozen against her pillow. Michael turned to the window. Evening sunshine flooded yellow into the room as a nurse raised a blind. Behind the white-painted houses and conifers, a billow of smoke rose, grey at first and then blacker and denser. More bangs and smoke. He gasped and, as if the volume of a wireless had been turned up, the ward was full of noise again, this time urgent, high-pitched. A screaming child was grabbed by her father. He moved to his mother, put a hand on her shoulder. She looked bewildered, scanning the room, her mouth open. Women's voices rose and repeated in the confusion of outrage and questions.

'What's that? What is it?'

'Bombs? No! No! It can't be!'

'Jerries?'

'Where? Where?'

'Oh my God! Oh my good Lord. What's happening?'

Visitors started gathering baskets. One woman knelt down, praying loudly. 'Holy Mary, mother of God…' Pulled to her feet by her husband, and dragged from the ward, she didn't stop, her plaintive voice fading down the corridor.

Meg spoke, her voice gentle: 'You need to go, Hélène. Get back to your family. I'm fine. We're safe here.' Her calmness steadied Michael and he watched his mother taking Meg's hand and bending to kiss her cheek. 'Go Hélène. Michael, take your mother. Just go…'

Family. They must get to the family.

'I'll see you soon, I p-promise,' his mother stuttered. They left the ward as Matron entered, heels clicking, her mouth pressed into a grey slash in her flushed face, and a group of navy-clad nurses behind her, starched white headgear gleaming.

Outside, his mother grabbed at his arm and they attempted to run down the hill, but her shoes, heeled ones for the trip to town, slowed them to a brisk walk. The unimaginable had happened. They were bombing the defenceless island.

Michael's stomach dropped and he felt nauseous. Did

Dad say he was taking potatoes down to the harbour? Was it today?

'Mum! What was Dad doing this evening?'

He'd stacked the boxes in the yard, waiting for the boats to resume the regular collections for export. Or did he say it would be better to take them tomorrow? Why hadn't he listened properly?

'I'm not sure. Was he going to the harbour? I can't remember.' There was fear in her voice and Michael put his hand on her arm. 'The harbour…' She didn't seem to know how to finish the sentence.

They stopped, looking at each other before being bumped from behind by a woman pushing a pram. They were in the middle of a river of people, all hurrying down the hill; only a few laboured up, pushing against the flow. Michael pulled his arm through hers as they moved swiftly down Cheapside and into the Parade. Once they had to stop, his mother clutching her side and drawing in deep breaths. 'Just a stitch. I'm all right.'

He could see that her feet in the smart shoes were hurting her; she limped slightly and gripped his arm. In the middle of the Royal Square, she stopped, panting. All around them people were running, running away from the dusty smoke and the choking, acrid smell coming from the harbour. A woman, pulling a small child by the hand, yelled, 'Harbour, run… Bombs…' It didn't make sense; they were undefended. They had been assured that the enemy would be told. Why would they bomb the harbour?

'Come on, Mum. We must…'

She looked at him and nodded, her lips compressed. They set off again towards the smoke, down Bond Street, until the scene opened up into one he had seen in pictures of the bombings in London. They stood still in the middle of the road. His body, tight and heavy, refused to move and his eyes swivelled to take in the scene: the Pomme d'Or, and beyond it, The Yacht Club, were both damaged, windows shattered, rubble on the road knee-deep. Flames were bulging out of the windows of Norman's warehouse across the Weighbridge. Two men emerged running, one in a brown boiler suit, the other in a formal jacket, weighed down with a typewriter. He watched, hand over his open mouth, as bricks began to rain down around the men onto the flagstones and the man in the boiler suit tripped and fell. Michael's mother gasped as a window frame crumbled; glass was blown out shattering a rain of diamonds over a group of girls in overalls who were running, screaming, from the depot next door, used for packing potatoes.

His pulse racing, he pulled at his mother's arm. Only one thought… his father on the Albert Pier. As they got closer he saw, with a sharp intake of breath, that men were lying amongst potatoes and splintered wood in front of the row of farm vehicles. Others were running away, up the pier towards the Weighbridge, limping and stumbling. One man stopped suddenly, his head jerked up looking back over his shoulder. Michael followed his gaze to see three low-flying planes approaching, engines screaming. The man flung himself to the ground, behind a bollard, protecting his head with his hands, others scrambled under trucks as bullets slammed and thumped into the metal doors. Fighting for breath and with shaky legs, Michael instinctively covered his head as his mother pulled him into a crouching position. A woman in a paisley headscarf dropped her wicker basket in the road and ran into the doorway of a newsagent's shop. The planes, revving, banked, flicking their black crosses, following the line of Victoria Avenue towards St Aubin's.

He helped his mother to her feet, but she shook him off, kicked off her shoes, dropped her bag and ran, ignoring a policeman yelling at her. He ran after her, across the square and down the line of trucks. The Le Breton farm truck was not there; he'd recognise the patched paintwork anywhere. His mother was panting, breathing deeply, bending over her hands on her knees. 'Thank God. Oh, thank God he's not here,' she whispered. Then, after looking back at the line of trucks, a number dented by bullet holes, she spoke again, her voice stronger: 'So many people hurt… we should see if we can help…'

Michael took her arm, feeling a liquid emptiness in his stomach, a sense of helplessness. Fire, smoke and dust filled the air. Gulls were crying overhead, screaming and whirling. Men were shouting.

She leaned on him, her stockings torn and her feet bleeding, and they moved slowly towards the smoke rising from the Weighbridge.

Poking out from under a black van, Michael saw a pair of legs in workman's trousers and heavy boots. His mother snatched her arm from his and sank to her knees. 'Are you hurt?' she called out, touching the exposed bony ankle. She raised her voice. 'Hello. Are you hurt?' The legs moved. Michael squatted beside her as a thin, wiry man with the tanned skin of a farmer wriggled out, holding a hand to a bleeding cut on his head.

'I… no… just a scratch,' he said. 'But I think Jim here might be… I can see blood… Oh God!' On all fours, he peered under the damaged van, reaching out and calling, 'Jim! Jim!' before lowering himself onto his stomach and crawling into the shadows behind the wheels. His voice was muffled and sharp with fear. 'Jim! Are you all right?'

'I'll get help', called his mother, getting to her feet. 'Come on, son…' Michael, took her arm again, glad to move from the sharp reek of leaking petrol and the shrill voice of the man. The sound of sirens increased. On the Weighbridge, two fire engines approached, pulled by stamping horses. A motor ambulance, its red cross glowing, was stationary next to the harbourmaster's office. Men were piling stretchers on the concrete.

A policeman, red-faced, hatless, his white gloves spattered with dirt, approached as they reached him, touching his mother's arm. 'Are you hurt, miss? Your feet…'

'No. No! I'm fine,' She pulled away and frowned. 'There are injured men… on the pier. Help them.'

'Mum, we can't do anything… the police and ambulance are here and your feet…'

She nodded and allowed him to lead her over the swollen firehoses snaking across the Weighbridge. They turned back only when they reached the other side of the square. Michael could see the blue suit of the policeman bending down next to the black van.

His mother's abandoned shoes and bag, covered now in dust, lay where she had left them, outside the Pomme d'Or. Michael bent to pick them up. Clutching them to his chest with one hand, he supported her as they moved away from the sounds of screaming and shouting down Bond Street and into the almost deserted Royal Square. His mother stopped under the shade of a tree, and leaned into him, breathing out a shuddering sigh.

'I'd better get my shoes on,' she said. 'We must get home. Make sure everyone is all right.'

Michael looked down at her feet, white and blooded like skinned rats, and glanced at her. She was pale and dusty; dark curls stuck to her damp forehead, but there was a determination in the set of her face that Michael knew well.

He placed her shoes side by side in front of her and held her arm, feeling a pang of sympathy, as she forced her swollen feet into them.

She nodded at him, taking her bag from his hand, her mouth a thin line. 'Right… we need to find a bus or a taxi. Let's go home.'

Without warning, tears pricked, his eyes gritty and sore. Something lifted in his chest and he grasped his mother's outstretched hand.

Michael and his mother were lucky; as they made their way out of the Royal Square, up Hill Street, an old black saloon car had pulled over and Michael, with relief, recognised the driver who stuck his head out of the open window and called out to them, offering a ride home. Mr Bideau owned the farm adjacent to theirs; he and Michael's father helped each other out at busy times, though recently they had seen less of him. Michael had been told that he had lost his wife to cancer.

Little was said on the drive back to the farm after his mother had explained why they had been in St Helier. Mr Bideau looked grim, gripping the steering wheel tightly and tutting at the erratic driving of vehicles and carts as he negotiated the narrow lanes. Michael, glad to get out of the noise and chaos of the town, felt himself sink into the warm leather of the back seat. He closed his eyes and allowed his body to sway with the movement of the car. He desperately wanted to get back home, to his father and siblings and the solidarity and quiet of the farm house. But everything had changed. He knew that now. Nothing would be the same.

As Mr Bideau drove into the farm yard, Michael saw the whole family: his father and Jacques looking as if they were about to get into the farm truck; Yves and Amy standing by the kitchen door. His eyes pricked again as they all ran towards the car, wrenched open the doors and reached in for him and his mother, talking all at the same time.

'Thank God… we've been so worried.'

'Are you both all right?'

'What happened?'

Michael allowed himself to be pulled out of the car by his twin sister. His tongue was dry and thick in his mouth. He shook his head and tried to smile.

'Fine… Mum's feet…' He pointed. 'She…' But his father had already seen the blood. He picked her up, as she protested that she could walk, and was carrying her, like a child, to the house.

'Thank you, Mr Bideau,' Yves called as their neighbour reversed out in a cloud of dust waving a hand out of the window.

'Are you really OK, Mike?' His sister's face looked worried. She put her hand on his arm.

'Yes. Really. It was scary but we are fine… where are you going, Jacques?' His brother was moving back to the farm truck.

'Don't you worry. Get yourself cleaned up. I need to see if Grandpa and Grandma are all right. We were told that a bomb was dropped near La Rocque.'

'I'm coming. Stop!' He grabbed the door handle as the truck started moving, forcing Jacques to stop. 'I want to come'.

The truck bounced down the uneven track; Michael held tightly to the seat as he was thrown against the door on a sharp bend and then into his brother's shoulder as he turned left into the coast road. It took only minutes to reach the scene; Jacques brought the truck to a juddering halt in the middle of the road. In front was a crater, the width of the road, surrounded by rubble. Grey smoke belched from it. In the harbour to their right, two fishing boats were on fire, red flames leaping into the smoky sky. Two other boats were damaged, sinking, leaning into the water. Screaming, a high-pitched screeching noise out of control, broke the silence and Michael saw Mrs Ferrand, their grandparents' next-door neighbour, through the smoke, her face blackened, standing at her wrecked garden gate, pointing at the crater. Michael followed his brother who was moving towards her, feeling sick and dizzy.

'Richard! Richard!' she shouted, over and over. 'Richard! Richard!'

There was no sign of her husband, but the dog, peppered in gravel, blood staining its fur, was lying unmoving on the road on the edge of the hole.

He saw Jacques reaching out to touch her arm; she shrugged off his hand and repeated her calling.'Richard! Richard!'

Turning, his stomach churning in a fluttery panic, Michael saw his grandfather, his Poppa, stumbling down the garden path towards them and looked up for Grandma, relieved to see her pale face, mouth open, at the window.

'Poppa! Mr Ferrand…' he couldn't finish the sentence, afraid to suggest what he feared. His hands were sweaty over his mouth; dust and smoke pricked at his eyes. Poppa murmured into Mrs Ferrand's ear and she allowed herself to be led away, his arm around her shoulder, up his garden path. She turned once towards the smoke rising from the road, her faced creased and grey with misery, before the front door opened and Grandmother's arms gathered her into the house.

Michael was standing with his brother looking into the rubble-filled hole when Poppa returned, his shoulders hunched, his face lined and mouth turned down in a tight line.

'I heard gunfire too,' he said, his eyes scanning the harbour.

The three of them crossed the road together, skirting the crater and stood looking at the fishing boats; two had keeled over and were sinking into the high tide, one was still on fire. Another smouldered.

Two figures were sitting on a bench at the end of the sea wall, overlooking the harbour. Michael blinked hard and looked again. Slumped sideways, was a woman in a flowery dress, her hair falling across her face. The other was sitting with his head back, as if looking at the sky. Without saying anything, Jacques ran towards them, down the cobbled path from the road. Poppa grabbed at Michael's arm but he pulled away and followed Jacques. He knew they were dead before they reached the bench. There was blood staining the dress, the red flowers growing. He couldn't see any marks on the man until they stood over him. There was a hole in his temple; a trickle of dark blood had begun to spread across the shoulder of his white shirt. Bullet holes had splintered the back of the bench and gouged out holes in the granite wall behind. He was unable to make sense of what he was seeing. A couple, married probably, enjoying the evening sun looking out over the calm, rising tide, shot dead.

With hot tears running down his face, he turned back to see Poppa and a white-faced Mr Le Marquand from the Post Office, his mouth open, standing at the railing above him. Gulls screeched overhead and the sound of police sirens grew.

*

They arrived back at the farmhouse to see their father astride his motorbike, preparing to leave. He flung his leg back and pushed the bike back onto its stand as they pulled into the yard, strode over and wrenched open the driver's door before they'd stopped.

'Thank God. I couldn't wait any longer... what's happened... everything all right at La Rocque?'

'Don't worry. Poppa and Grandmère Cecile are fine. Shaken but unhurt. Two bombs and gunshots. I'm afraid Mr Ferrand is dead. And their dog. A couple by the harbour... shot...' Jacques told him.

'I'd better go...'

'No, Dad. Best not to... the police and ambulance are there. Poppa told me to... reassure you. They are looking after Mrs Ferrand. You can see them tomorrow. Let's get into the house. How's Mum? Come on, Mike...' Jacques put his hand under his father's elbow and raised his eyes at Michael, nodding.

Michael forced himself to smile at his father and grabbed at his hand, pulling him towards the open door.

Inside the kitchen, his mother was sitting at the table, her feet in a bowl of water, Amy kneeling by her chair with a towel in her hands, Yves collecting dirty teacups. They froze, faces pale, as Jacques repeated what had happened. Michael sat down at the table his thoughts swirling, his mouth dry.

Jacques stood with his back to the window, his face dark. 'It's started... the invasion. I knew it.'

A heavy quiet descended.

JULY 1ST 1940

On the first day of July, warm and cloudless as so many had been that summer, Michael was in the big barn looking at a pile of wood and discarded metal rings from an old barrel with the intention of making a cage for Dolly. Yves had agreed to help, but not today. He had driven off with Jacques soon after breakfast, intending to discuss the plumbers' yard possibilities with Bob. Their boss, Mr Huelin, had evacuated to England leaving no instructions and the keys on his desk.

The parrot watched him, perched on a cross beam, occasionally calling out to him. There were new words in her vocabulary. 'Come on, then,' was clearly articulated and there were a few other expressions which he was not so sure about, one unrepeatable, if he heard right. He sighed. Where should he start? Maybe it would be better to wait for Yves; he was the practical one. And anyway, he wasn't convinced that Dolly needed a cage. She was happy roosting in the hay bales. He glanced at his restored surfboard, leaning up against the back wall, and wondered if he would still be able to get out to St Ouen's this summer. Would his father think he was naïve or selfish for asking? Yves might be a better person to ask.

He had turned back to his task and selected some long struts when he heard the sound of the returning truck. Yves was slamming the door of the vehicle when Michael left the dark of the barn for the blinding midday glare of the sun. Jacques had remained sitting behind the wheel.

'Where is everyone?' called his brother.

Michael could tell from the expression and the sharp line of his mouth that something serious had happened.

'What? More attacks? Is Bob all right?

'No. Yes. I think so. We didn't see him. There's news. I bumped into John Coutanche in town before we got to the yard. Where's Dad? Mum?'

Yves had to shout loudly before his father appeared from the packing sheds and his mother poked her head out of the kitchen door.

'Come inside, Yves,' she called, wiping her hands on a dish towel.

Breathless, Yves blurted out what he'd heard as he ducked into the kitchen, followed by his father and Jacques. Michael was hard on their heels, straining to hear his brother.

'There's been an ultimatum… d-dropped this morning, early.'

'Dropped?' echoed his father.

Jacques dropped heavily into a chair and looked up at his father. 'John said that a canvas bag was brought to Mr Coutanche this morning. Dropped from a German plane; landed near the airport. It had red ribbons… streamers attached and landed in a field. A farmer spotted it falling. Thought it was a bomb.'

'After what's happened you can't blame him… John said the bag was brought into the breakfast room.'

Michael raised his eyebrows at the idea of a breakfast room but said nothing. Yves leant on the back of a chair.

'The document… papers were in German and none of the family could translate enough of it.' Yves paused, looking at his family. 'It was an ultimatum. They found a priest who speaks German and Mr Coutanche took the translation to the States assembly. John was waiting in the Royal Square for his father. I've never seen him look so… scared.'

'Did John have any idea… what it said? What the… ultimatum is?' asked his mother, her voice sounded as though she was having trouble keeping calm. She blinked rapidly.

'Demands… for surrender… we have to all show white flags. Other conditions… the document is being printed and published,' Jacques said as he rose abruptly, his chair legs screaming on the flagstones. At the open door, he turned back, a dark shadow in the doorway, frowning. 'I'll go back into town and find out more. We should have stayed and waited for news. But we wanted you to know.'

'Coming with you…' muttered Yves. 'Let's not go Mount Bingham way. Road still blocked.'

'Be careful,' shouted his mother as the brothers drove out of the yard in a cloud of dust. Michael slid into a chair next to his mother and put his hand out to touch her forearm as it lay on the table, her sleeve rolled up to the elbow. It was dry and soft and warm. She looked at him and put her hand over his. His father stayed standing, back to the window, leaning back on the sink, his hands thrust deep and tense into his trouser pockets. The quiet was broken by the sound of birds in the yard.

Surrender? What would that mean? He recognised fear in his breathlessness. There was an ache in his throat and a falling sensation in his belly. Mum looked blankly through the open doorway after his brothers.

'Where's Amy?' Michael's whisper broke the silence.

'Oh. In the tomato greenhouses, I think.'

Michael pushed his chair back, tripping over Lettie who was sitting outside the kitchen door, in his haste. Dolly eyed him from the top of the open barn door and flew after him as he jogged out of the yard and up the rough path to the greenhouses.

Hot air and the thick, earthy smell of tomatoes engulfed him as he stepped through the open doorway of the long greenhouse. Rows of bushy, fern-like plants stood in straight rows in the banked-up earth. Their tips touched the sloping glass roof. Red blobs, most half-hidden in the foliage, glowed in the bright light. The plants, supported by horizonal wire running the length of the house, were strong and alive with green, as always.

Hardy's words came back to him as he breathed in deeply: 'Yet this will go onward the same.' And yet. Something clutched at his stomach, a cold hand.

He needed to talk to Amy.

Standing in the suffocating heaviness of the hot greenhouse, he tried to put his confusion into perspective, into an order. He couldn't. He just knew he had to share with her. She would understand. She always understood. The greenhouse was empty.

'Amy! Amy!' he shouted as he backed out, looking up the rows of greenhouses, lined up, the sun glinting and winking on the sloping rooves as he walked up the path.

She appeared out of one near the end of the field, behind her two of the farm workers, Lucy and Judith, both young, married women living nearby.

Michael hurried up the sloping path towards them, rehearsing in his head how he would tell them what Yves had revealed. Desperate to appear calm, he stopped and swallowed, waiting for them, trying to moisten his dry mouth, quieten his pounding chest.

'Surrender… dropped this morning…' He found it difficult to form the words.

'What?' said Lucy, pushing forward, confusion in her voice.

'Jersey… to surrender… Mr Coutanche… we have to display white flags.'

Before he could get the full story out, both Lucy and Judith started to run down the field. He watched as Judith stopped and ducked into the first greenhouse, retrieved a basket and ran towards her bicycle, propped against the hedge near the house. She shouted something he couldn't hear to Lucy, who was running down the road, and looked back at Amy.

Calmer now, he took a breath. 'Yves and Jacques have gone to town. To find out the details.'

Michael saw himself in Amy's face, a smaller prettier version, but definitely him. People commented on how alike they were; he had never seen it before. They walked down to the farmhouse, side by side, Michael filled with questions he couldn't ask, Amy's arm gently bumping into his.

In the kitchen, their parents were seated at the table, a steaming pot of tea sitting between them. His mother got up to fetch more cups and the twins joined them, taking their usual places on the same side of the table facing their mother.

'Lucy and Judith have gone…' Amy said quietly and her mother nodded. She extended her hands to her children and they each took one of hers. Her hand was cool and smooth; his hot and sticky.

When Jacques and Yves returned from town later that afternoon, Michael was sitting on the rope swing hanging from the big chestnut tree on the field above the farm. His legs twitchy, he had been unable to sit still and wait and had excused himself to feed the animals. He had climbed the steep field with the parrot circling around him and looked out at the view from the highest point of the farm. The Le Bretons' land, neat green fields planted with potatoes or cropped by the dairy herd stretched in front of him, bordered by a copse of woodland to the east, Mr Bideau's farm to the north and scattered houses to the south.

Soldiers in green uniforms would be walking under these trees soon. Would they goose-step? He'd picked up the phrase from the newspaper.

Beyond the farm he had a hazy view of the sea: La Rocque, with the hooked harbour wall and a few tall masts; no sign of the bomb damage from here; Seymour Tower standing square and lonely among the black rocks and then, as his eyes shifted to his right, Icho, the squat white-painted Martello, only reachable on a very low tide. Le Hocq was now mostly uncovered, King's and Queen's rock guarding the pebbled beach. The tree-covered headland was the furthest landmark he could see, with Green Island hidden on the other side. Granny said that witches gathered on the headland. It used to make him shiver with excitement when he was younger. Now the group of dark green holm oaks, pushed into weird shapes by the wind, dropped cones on the beach.

The sky was hazy blue and there was no wind.

He saw the farm truck speeding up the lane as it turned off the main road, sending up a cloud of dust which rose through the overhanging trees as the blue of its roof flashed through the foliage. Michael twisted the rope using both feet to wind it as far as he could before letting it go. He closed his eyes and allowed the momentum to whiz him back, surrendering to the dizziness. The rope returned him, rocking, to the view spread before him and he watched his brothers get out of the truck. Amy, carrying Lettie, crossed the farmyard from the barn and they all disappeared into the house.

He wished it would all go away, that he could stop the clocks, turn back to those days when there was no shadow… just sunshine and Laura… the promise of summer. It wasn't fair; it wasn't right… He grabbed the knot and threw it at the tree trunk. It bounced off and caught him on the shoulder, giving him a push towards the slope as he turned away. He stumbled down the hill, picked up speed, jumping over tufts in the uneven ground, allowing the movement to blur his vision. Dolly squawked and followed. Breathing hard and feeling the sweat on his forehead, he slowed down and paused, blood pumping through his head, before entering the kitchen.

It was cool and dim out of the warmth and glare of the evening sunshine. The family was standing round the table, heads bent over a large news sheet, its curled ends weighted down by Jacques' hands on one side and Yves' on the other.

Michael leaned over the table, trying to read the bold black text upside down. It was a list of conditions and instructions, he realised. Amy glanced up at him as he squinted, his glasses steaming up, the words blurring and jumping on the page.

'It threatens "bombardment" if we don't surrender…' his sister murmured. 'Bombs? Does that mean bombs?' She looked up at their father who shook his head.

'The States have already decided to surrender. I was told that the bailiff was going to the airport, as instructed,' said Jacques. 'They were painting a white cross on the Royal Square when we left. What choice do we have? No defences…'

'White flags. We must put something out straight away… sheets? On the washing line?' Michael's mother had turned to his father, her face flushed, her hand twisted together in her apron.

'Can you do that, Hélène? I'd better get over to La Rocque and help Mum and Dad. I'll take the motorbike. Michael, could you and Amy go and tell Granny, get a sheet out on her washing line, or hang it from a bedroom window?'

Michael, pleased to have something to do, nodded and smiled towards his silent, immobile sister, as his mother left the room.

Jacques straightened up and the set of German conditions curled into a tight scroll over Yves' hand. 'I've got things to do… in town…' he muttered.

Michael saw Yves open his mouth and take a step towards his brother, but Jacques was out of the door and striding across the yard. Michael heard the truck door slam and the revs of the engine as it climbed up the narrow track towards the milking yard. Why was he going that way? Surely it was quicker to take the lane down to the main road.

Yves turned back, his hands on his hips. 'What's the matter with him? I'd have gone with him… s'pose we should put up a flag at the plumbers' yard.'

Was Jacques' behaviour connected to the stolen rifles? Had he already moved some of them from the hiding place in the old shed? Or was that what he was doing now? Did Yves really not suspect his brother?

'Come with me to La Rocque, Yves,' said his father, moving towards the open doorway. 'Then you can take the motorbike into town. I can walk home.'

Michael moved towards Amy who was gazing out of the window, biting her lip and rubbing one bare foot on top of the other, withdrawing into herself, as she did occasionally. He recognised the signs; he was aware that he did the same thing when he was anxious. But he needed her with him; he needed to know that she felt the same sense of panic, of fear… and he needed to know that they could both remain the same… that nothing would change. Not the most important things. How could he say that?

He let his mouth take over: 'Let's… take the dogs, Amy,' Michael said, putting his hand on her arm. 'And I expect Dolly will want to come. I wonder what Granny will make of her!' His words rang out in the room and sounded so ordinary… so ridiculous… so irrelevant. Amy nodded and gave him a crooked smile; he could see the tears filming her eyes. She understood.

*

Michael did not sleep well. It wasn't unusual; often he would wake in the night and find it difficult to go back to sleep. His mother said that he was like her, in that and in other ways. She called it 'sensitive' but he wasn't sure he wanted that adjective applied to him. Dreams, uncomfortable, unsettling, had flowed and spun through his brain. When he became conscious of the light as it seeped around his curtains, he lay still, feeling his pulse persistently beating in his temples and tried to recall the dreams. Nothing except heavy, fleeting shadows slid through his mind.

He pulled back his curtains, kneeling on the window seat to reveal another fine day, the kitchen garden still and lush below his window, the sky pale blue above. The height and direction of the sun, yet to rise over the hedges to light the rows of beans and lettuce, suggested that it was well before six. He focused on the brightening light of dawn, as his heart slowed, propped himself up on the wide window seat, his arms around his bent legs, and waited for the house to wake up. He didn't move when he heard his parents' bedroom door open and the heavy tread of his father descended the stairs, followed immediately by the lighter footsteps of his mother, her murmuring voice fading as the kitchen door closed with a familiar squeak. In the silence which hummed around him, he questioned his feelings. He wasn't angry like Jacques; nor was he excited, like Yves seemed to be about the new opportunities which had appeared for him in the two days since the Germans started arriving. Was it fear, this shortness of breath, the inability to articulate his questions? He'd never had trouble before; one of his teachers, Mr Green, who taught him biology, had told his parents at the last teacher-parent meeting, that he was always keen to 'probe, question and understand'. His father, showing a rarely articulated pride, said that Mr Green spoke of his 'sharp intelligence' and been emphatic about him staying on at school. Michael remembered the exact words and repeated them first to his disbelieving sister, who he thought might be jealous. He toned them down when Laura had asked about the meeting, not wanting to appear to be boastful or arrogant. Mr Green had suggested that Michael might want to study science at university, maybe think about medicine or becoming a vet. At the time, his heart had thumped and he had felt taller, more confident, capable of anything. How things changed… and so quickly. Now he was faced with the unknown, things out of control; he was being pushed away, dismissed as a child by many of his family. Except by Jacques. He was keeping a dangerous secret and that gave him a strength in a way, something he must cling to.

He took a deep breath, uncurled from the seat, feeling the wooden floor cool and solid under his bare feet, and dressed swiftly. He wanted to see these Germans who had invaded his island. His parents had told him to stay at home, help on the farm, but he was determined to find out more for himself. Amy's bedroom door was closed; she slept late if she was allowed. He tapped lightly and, getting no response, pushed it open and put his face around the door. A heap under a white sheet in the gloom of the curtained room did not move.

'Amy! Amy!'

'Mmmm. What's the matter? What time is it?' All he could see was a fuzz of fair hair; her words were muffled.

'About seven, I think... what about cycling into town? We don't need to tell Mum and Dad. See what's what?'

Amy sat up, her face even in the half-light, looked creased, her eyes widening and blinking.

'Not like you, Mike... to be a... rebel.'

'I just feel so remote out here. Jacques and Yves bring us news from town, but I want to see for myself... know what they're like. I don't see why we shouldn't. We aren't babies. Are you up for it?'

'Give me half an hour.' She swung her legs out of bed and stretched her arms above her head. 'It might be best to sneak off after breakfast... say we are going to help in the tomato houses.'

'Good idea. We could always tell Jude. She'd cover for us.'

It took longer than Michael had anticipated to get away. His mother had plans for them. She wanted help to get Granny's blackouts up before tackling their own, as instructed. And she was worried about Mr Bideau, who she hadn't seen since he had driven them back from St Helier on the day of the bombings. She'd walked over yesterday, she told Michael and Amy; it was very quiet around the farm and there was no answer to her knocking. He was probably out in the fields, but she thought it might be neighbourly for them to go over and offer some help. Maybe Amy and Michael could go, do a few chores, now that there was no school. Apparently one of the farm hands had told their father that he'd heard at least two of Mr Bideau's workers had evacuated.

Michael and Amy, having made promises to their mother that they would help that afternoon, watched her disappear round the side of the house with a basket of wet washing to hang outside, and cycled out of the farmyard in the glare of the mid-morning sunshine.

The lanes and fields were quiet, except for the odd tractor, followed by a crowd of calling gulls. Houses displayed their white flags of surrender but there was no other evidence of the invasion. Sheets were hanging limply out of windows or spread on yellowing lawns, weighed down with rocks. Michael laughed out loud as Amy pointed out a pair of huge, off-white bloomers pegged to a washing line in the garden of a small cottage at Five Oaks. The rushing air around his face felt good and he pedalled hard up the incline to the top of St Saviour's Hill, his calves burning. Waiting for Amy to catch up, he looked over the town; nothing had changed. Red and grey slate roofs, chimneys, white-painted and stone houses huddled together peacefully and silently.

Amy pulled in beside him, panting and smiling. 'You were quick up there!'

'Where shall we head to?' he asked, suddenly apprehensive. 'D'you think we'll be stopped if we go to the Royal Square?'

'Only one way to find out,' called Amy over her shoulder as she pushed off and freewheeled down the slope towards St Helier.

Michael followed and they slowed down as the road narrowed between tall houses with shops on the ground floor. Few were open; some were boarded up. Stray dogs sniffed around dustbins down the alleys. A few women, carrying baskets and bags of food, were out on the streets. Two men, flat caps pulled down over their eyes, gave them a curious look before putting their heads down and shuffling swiftly away.

Michael heard the sound of marching before they reached the Royal Square. Amy braked and turned to him, eyebrows raised. 'What now?' she asked.

'Let's dismount… try to get closer… what about the alley by The Peirson?'

Staying close to the row of shops, they wheeled their bikes round into Hill Street and down the cutting beside the pub. A small crowd had gathered, mostly men, some in shirtsleeves and ties, as if they had left their desks recently, some more smartly dressed and a few in overalls. Michael and Amy propped their bikes against the wall and squeezed their way to the front of the murmuring group.

A large white cross painted in the middle of the square glowed under the dappled shadows of the chestnut trees. Rows of soldiers, smart in their grey-green uniforms, were lined up outside the States building. Above them, rippling in the gentle breeze, was a scarlet flag, dissected by a black cross. In the centre, highlighted in a white circle, the bent, black swastika. Michael shuddered. A cold hand gripped his stomach. Now it felt real. The enemy was here.

As they watched, a column, four deep, was snaking in from Bond Street, presumably from the harbour. The sound of iron-tipped boots, precise and co-ordinated, rang out on the granite flags of the square. They lined up in front of the rows already there.

The men seemed to have been made from the same mould, upright with serious, blank faces only half-exposed under the rounded tin hats; no eyes. Rifles slanted precisely against shoulders. Michael looked hard at the soldier closest to him, about fifteen yards away, at the end of the row. He was taller, slimmer than the man next to him, but younger, maybe eighteen, close in age to Yves. Had he killed men? Had he fought in France? His face was tanned and smooth-looking. It dawned on Michael how sheltered he was, how inexperienced in comparison to the soldier, how young. As Michael watched, the man-boy tilted his head back slightly, allowing the sun to fall on his face. His eyes looked upwards towards the blue of the sky above the trees lining the square. What was he thinking? What must it feel like to be on foreign soil, on conquered land? Maybe he was thanking his lucky stars that he was here, in the peace and beauty of Jersey, instead of in danger on the battlefields. His face seemed ordinary, if you could disregard the uniform and the weapon, not threatening. And yet… he was the enemy. He wasn't ordinary. He was here to… to what? Prepare for an invasion of the mainland? To kill if necessary.

He glanced at Amy. She was staring at the rows of soldiers, a frown on her forehead.

She turned to him and met his gaze. 'Let's go. I've seen enough. It's real, isn't it? Seems silly, but until now…'

He held her eyes and nodded. As they turned away, he felt his plimsoll snag on something. At his feet, caught between two granite paving stones, a dull gold glinted. He bent to pick it up; a small, round, brass button lay in the palm of his hand. Engraved with letters. He held it up, close to his face. The words 'HOLD FAST', dark in the tarnished face, curved around the edge. On the reverse, a metal loop.

'Look, Amy!'

'What is it?' Amy turned back and took it from him. 'A button? Hold Fast?'

'What's it from? I've never seen anything like it.'

'I wonder if it's from a uniform. It could be a motto…'

'"Hold fast to that which is good…" isn't that from the prayer?'

Michael held out his hand, curling his fingers over the warm brass. 'Seems… appropriate, somehow.'

'A lucky charm?' Amy smiled at him. Michael pushed the button into the corner of his pocket.

They retrieved their bicycles and walked away, remounting when they reached the market where stalls were selling fruit and vegetables. It was quiet; only a few customers moving swiftly and filling bags. The usual chat and laughter of shoppers had been packed away, like some of the shops and stalls.

Michael peddled slowly side by side with his sister. He desperately wanted to tell her about the rifles, to ask her what to do, what she thought, if it would endanger the family, or protect them. He had never kept a secret from her before; even asked her what she thought about Laura when they started to spend some time together. Amy had laughed and punched his shoulder: 'And she likes you? Really? Can't think why? I s'pose you talk about poetry and things?'

He glanced sideways at Amy. Her eyes were screwed up against the sun. He couldn't tell what she was thinking.

He looked away and took a deep breath. 'We'll be all right… I know we will.' Amy gave him a small smile and nodded. 'Do you… Jacques…' No, he couldn't tell her. He wished that he didn't know. It was dangerous. And yet. If it came to it… he would fight. He'd fight for his family. But it wasn't going to come to that. The island had surrendered and all they could do was wait, follow instructions, hope for the best.

'What? What about Jacques?'

'Oh, nothing…'

'We can only… carry on as normal, I think. Don't you? Keep busy. There's always so much to do on the farm. And I'm determined to do some studying.'

'You're right. You are always right.' He was rewarded with a bigger smile.

They reached home late morning. The farmhouse was empty and their mother nowhere to be seen.

'Mum's probably gone to Granny's already,' said Amy. 'Why don't you go over to Mr Bideau's with the dogs and see what's what. I'll come over later, when I've helped Mum.' Michael nodded and whistled to Joe and Jenny who were lying in the shade in the yard. Dolly fluttered out of the open barn and circled the yard before settling on the kitchen windowsill.

The ride into St Helier had unsettled Michael: German soldiers in the Royal Square; the sound of metal-tipped boots marching; the swastika flying from the town hall. Could helping Mr Bideau bring back some sense of… normality? His fingers closed around the button in his pocket and he breathed in deeply. Here, in the quiet of Grouville, and the stillness of the farmyard, there was no evidence of occupation.

'Come on then, Dolly.'

The parrot flew to his shoulder taking up the familiar backwards-looking stance. He shifted her a little as her claws dug in and she nibbled his ear, crooning and purring like a cat.

Judith and Lucy were fanning themselves with dock leaves, taking a breather, in the dappled shade of an apple tree, as he walked up the path between the greenhouses.

'Hey, Mike. We could do with your strong hands over here!' called Judith laughing, causing him to blush.

He tripped over a tree root as he hurried away and crossed into the lowest potato field. Bob Moulin and David, casual workers who moved from farm to farm, were gathering the last of the crop in the far corner and Michael waved as Bob straightened up and eased his back with his hands. At the bottom of the field, he found the gap in the hedge and emerged into Mr Bideau's wheat. The crop, very dry and limp, didn't look as if it had been watered for weeks, though he knew that Mr Bideau had one of the new sprinkler systems which was pulled along by a tractor. The dogs, well-trained to keep out of the fields, stayed at Michael's heels as he walked around the edge and down into the dip where the farm buildings stood around a paved courtyard.

The house, with a grey, pebbled-dashed face, had its curtains drawn. Roses straggled over the door, petals reddening the paving where two lichen-stained stone pots held dead geraniums. A small, rusting threshing machine stood outside a new-looking barn, its large doors shut. It was very quiet.

'Mr Bideau!' called Michael, standing in the middle of the yard, while the dogs sniffed without interest at the yellowing weeds poking up between paving slabs. 'Hello! Anyone here?'

He pushed open the barn door and called again. 'Mr Bideau! It's Michael. Michael Le Breton.' Straw bales were stacked to the roof beams and barrels of potatoes were piled in front of them. A strong, stale smell, like that of a dead animal, hung in the air. He knew what it meant; the potatoes were going rotten. There were probably one or two at the bottom of the barrels, mushy, maybe more than one or two, he thought, trying not to breath though his nose. They should have gone off to be exported weeks ago.

He turned back into the yard and called again, his voice echoing off the walls. Dolly flew off his shoulder and sat on the tractor's triangular metal seat, pecking at the shining buttons on the dashboard. The front door of the house didn't look as though it was usually opened and Michael went into a small vegetable garden at the side to find another entrance. The side door was not locked; few people locked their doors, though more had developed the habit since the Germans came.

The dogs sat down outside in the shade and did not follow him into the gloomy interior. The door opened directly into the kitchen where there was a sour smell and a thin light, seeping through closed, faded curtains. On the table was an unfinished meal, over which flies buzzed, and a beer bottle on its side lying in a puddle of sticky liquid.

He hesitated, wondering if he should go back and find his parents. Something didn't seem right. He turned round and called to Joe, who did not move or even turn his head; he was getting deaf. Jenny pricked her ears up at her name, but did not respond to his call, lying down, her head on her paws, watching him.

He moved into the hall, calling, 'Mr Bideau. It's Michael.' The door to a living room was open, showing a glimpse of an empty fireplace and the back of a sofa. In the dark, he could make out a shape in a large armchair opposite the door.

'Mr Bideau. Are you ill?' He stood in the doorway and the shape did not move. His heart beating fast, he moved to the window, pulling back one of the heavy, velvet drapes with a metallic rattle and turned back to his neighbour.

There was a thick stick propped under his chin and, for a moment, Michael was confused. Mr Bideau was leaning back, his head resting on an antimacassar, as if asleep. And yet his face… A lump in Michael's chest leapt. The stick was a shotgun; the curve of the trigger shone in the pale light. The antimacassar was black and red. The bookcase behind his head was spattered with lumpy blood. Dark dribbles had run down the books and pooled on the floor, spreading like a gluey puddle, to surround two legs of a piano stool. The faded white and black teeth of the piano were flecked with rusty spots.

A cold wave rushed over Michael before heat forced its way into his face. He panted, his breath shallow. Turned and ran, ignoring the dogs which loped after him up the road and the parrot which flapped overhead. He crossed the fields, stumbling and panting, not stopping until he fell into the kitchen at home, relief flooding his head at the sight of his father.

'Mr… Bideau! Mr Bideau!' he gasped.

'What is it, Mike?' Is he ill?' His father put down the knife he was using on a loaf of bread.

'He… no… NO! He's dead… dead. He must have… shot… shot himself…'

'What? Oh my God! No! Are you sure?'

Michael nodded, his lips dry, his knees wobbly. 'His shotgun…'

'You stay here, Mike,' said his father as he moved towards the open door. 'No…no… can you go up to the stores? They can call the police and an ambulance. I'll go… are you sure he was dead?' He stopped in the door, his face dark with the light behind him.

Michael's heart was racing. He took a deep breath and nodded. 'There was blood. The shotgun was under… his chin. I… he was dead.'

*

A few days later, Michael was sitting at the kitchen table with a boiled egg growing cold in front of him. Looking at himself in the bathroom mirror that morning, he had seen a stranger, grey-faced, with dark patches under his eyes. He bit the inside of his mouth, tasting the tang of blood, and blinked at his mother who was sitting opposite. Tears darkened her eyes. He looked away.

'I… blame myself. I should have gone. You shouldn't have seen that.'

Michael picked up his spoon and held it over the egg before putting it down again, nausea gushing in this throat.

'You know he had been struggling since his wife died in May. He was so full of grief. And it… was hard for him.

I went over a couple of weeks ago; he seemed… sad, but he was working. Two of his workers evacuated before the invasion, he told me, but he'd found two replacements and seemed… hopeful. The police said that those two left this week, to work for the Germans. I don't know why he didn't ask for help. Too proud, maybe. But we should have asked… I should have gone over. I'm so sorry.'

Michael felt empty, and very tired. Suddenly he couldn't bear his mother's voice and her comforting tone. He pushed back his chair and left without speaking, banging the back door to deaden the sound of his mother calling.

The book of Hardy's poetry and *Tess* were the only things in the sagging canvas bag on his back when he rode out of the farmyard on his bicycle and down the hill towards the coast. The tide was low at Green Island and he walked across the wet sand and climbed up the tumbled rocks onto the grassy summit. At the highest point, facing towards the sea, out of sight of the beach and houses, he found a seat on a flat piece of granite. He was completely alone except for sea birds which swooped and called between the piled lumps of rock rising above a breathing, heaving, glittering sea.

He took out *Tess*, but the section of her revival at Talbothays didn't suit his mood. He smoothed the cover of the volume of Hardy poetry and thought again of Laura. He could visualise her small face listening intently in English lessons, fierce blue eyes and fair hair in a plait over her shoulder, a hand propping up her chin.

Looking down the index, his eye stopped on 'Penance'. On the first reading, the opening verse brought a picture of Mr Bideau, cold and dead in front of his piano, to mind:

Why do you sit, O pale thin man,
At the end of the room

By that harpsichord, built on the quaint old plan?
It is as cold as the tomb,
And there's not a spark within the grate...

He looked out to sea, and followed a gull lazily riding a thermal, free, unfeeling. His chest was fluttery and his jaw tense.

It was the second verse that brought tears, the reference to the *woman who lyred here/in the evenfall...* He had been told since the suicide that Mrs Bideau was the piano player and he wondered if Mr Bideau had missed the music as well as his wife. The silence in the house as he had entered was heavy and still. Was that what he had experienced every day?

...in loneliness bending wistfully,
Would wake each note
In sick sad rote
None to listen or see!

He thought of the warmth and the noise in his own house, of conversation, the wireless, and couldn't imagine what it must have been like for Mr Bideau to lose his wife and sit through an evening in silence. '*A dead man held on end.*' He couldn't remember where he had read that, but he thought it must be from a Hardy poem.

The last stanza described the '*chill old keys/Like a skull's brown teeth...*' and the memory of the keyboard, the blood-splashed ivory grinning at him, floated in his mind. Michael allowed the tears to run down his cheeks until he felt emptied and cold.

He fumbled in his pocket for a handkerchief. Felt the loop of the Hold Fast button. *Merde*. Hold Fast... to what? A thick, cold weight had settled on him and he couldn't see the future, as he once had. Everything seemed grey, meaningless.

Mr Bideau's funeral took place in Grouville Church where the tall, pointed spire rose from the rose and honey granite into a dazzling blue sky. Michael, who could not be persuaded to stay at home, waited, feeling light-headed, with his mother and Amy and a small group of neighbours outside the arched doorway as the horse-drawn hearse drew up. He was unable to take his eyes from the simple wooden coffin as it was lifted and carried into church by his father, Jacques, Yves and Bob Moulin. Michael's mother had tried to find information about Mr Bideau's family, searching through a well-organised desk in his front room. She knew there was a son, who had left the island to work in England years ago. She discovered letters confirming what Mr Bideau had told her. The son was in the navy, but his last letter was dated January, and sent care of the forces post, and she couldn't find an address, not that she would be able to send letters to the mainland. There seemed to be no way of contacting him, so the service was simple and short. He was buried in the graveyard, a green plot, looked after with reverence by the sexton, Mr Hammond. At the end of the row of gravestones which sloped up, away from the church and towards a field of cows, they watched the coffin disappearing under the dry soil shovelled by Mr Hammond and his son.

After the rector shook everyone's hand, the small group dispersed without comment and the Le Bretons walked home. There was nothing to say. Michael left his parents and siblings drinking tea and walked up to the cotil and sat under the big oak in the shade; the rope swing drooped above him. He fell asleep eventually, waking with the sun hot on his face and a pounding headache.

*

A few weeks later, on a warm day already promising to turn sultry and humid, Amy punched his shoulder at the breakfast table.

'The tide is perfect today for the Havre des Pas pool. Late morning. Come on, Michael. Come with me and Esme.'

Michael usually loved swimming in the pool. It was a sea-water lido with art-deco buildings that looked like a miniature exotic island linked to the coast road by a raised wooden boardwalk. It had been freshly painted in the spring and the white and turquoise changing rooms and tearoom were cheerful and bright. At low tide, it provided a sea-water pool on the beach; at high tide, a few inches of the wall showed above the surface of the water, enclosing a safe, clean area. Some of the locals, the older ones mostly, mumbled about it, in the way that parochial Jersey people did; they didn't like its vivid colours and the crowds of noisy youngsters who were drawn to it. They especially didn't like the way that young German soldiers had started using it, their tanned, healthy bodies on show.

Today he had no energy and no inclination to be polite to Amy's friend, but he allowed himself to be pulled to his feet by his sister; he couldn't think of an excuse quickly enough and he knew she was trying to cheer him up.

Esme met them outside the Marina Hotel, her face growing pink when she saw them. She was a pretty girl who Michael found rather irritating. She smiled a great deal and widened her big brown eyes, shaking her curls, giggling, whenever he talked to her. They left their bicycles propped against railings thick with white paint, rusting and peeling on the cross sections.

Amy skipped down the narrow boardwalk, her friend jogging to keep up. He lagged behind, looking at the groups of people already in and around the water. A beachball, its rainbow stripes spinning, was being punched into the air by three teenage lads, accompanied by splashing and screaming from a girl in the centre of their circle, wearing a red swimsuit. A courting couple trod water at the edge, their elbows touching and wet heads turned towards each other. Two young boys were throwing coins, diving to the bottom to fetch them, disturbing a woman in a flowery bathing cap, swimming back and forth across the diameter of the pool. A crowd of girls, descending arm-in-arm down the wide steps from the wooden decking, made little gasping sounds as the sea crept up their white thighs. Looking at the busy pool and the shining sea beyond, you might think that the occupation had been a bad dream. Michael stood still and envied them all. He couldn't forget what he had seen in Mr Bideau's room.

Amy and Esme found a vacant spot on one side at the top of the steps and were laying out towels when Michael joined them. He unrolled his towel on the other side of Amy to Esme and took *Tess* out of his bag.

Amy grabbed the book from his hands. 'Oh. Come on, Michael. We aren't here to read.' She met his eyes and smiled. 'Swim with us. You'll enjoy it.' He saw himself in her eyes and had to smile too. He must try to be more cheerful.

The girls had taken the precaution of putting on swimsuits under their clothes. Esme pulled her pale blue dress over her head, revealing a modest black costume, and carefully folded it on her towel, glancing at Michael with her dimples showing. He pretended not to see her and picked up the book from his sister's towel. Amy wriggled out of shorts and blouse and dropped them in a heap.

'Go ahead,' said Michael. He reached into his bag again. 'I'll join you.'

Using a faded blue towel around his waist, he struggled into his trunks, took off his glasses and ran into the cold water, avoiding Esme's upturned eyes, following the girls as they swam around the pool wall. They stopped to chat to some friends and he trod water for a minute, reluctant to talk, before overtaking the group and continued his slow breaststroke, averting his eyes from the whispering heads of the lovers. The cool, silvery water shimmered unnatural bright blue as he looked down. He hadn't swum in over a week. He'd almost forgotten how it made him feel: lighter, more relaxed. If only he was at Fliquet or Anne Port, where he would be by himself… why had he agreed to come? He was surrounded by people who were able to put the situation to one side and he found that difficult to accept. Didn't they feel anything? Or maybe, like him, they were only pretending to get on with life.

His thoughts were broken by a pulling on his legs and he slid under the water, a rush of noise filling his ears and a mouthful of salty sea catching in his throat. Annoyed, he kicked out hard and surfaced, flicking his hair out of his eyes. Amy and Esme bobbed away from him, laughing.

'I'll get you back,' he murmured without enthusiasm. They swam away to join in a game of water tag and he climbed out, heavily. On his towel, the skin on his back tightening in the hot sun, he retrieved *Tess* and his glasses and turned on his stomach. His wet head created a globe of shade on the open pages.

He read the section where Hardy's sad heroine, Tess, was beginning slowly to recover from her traumatic encounter with Alec d'Urberville, or rather, find a way to live with it.

Was that what he should do? Find a way to live with the shock of finding Mr Bideau's body? Not that he should compare his experience to that of Tess. She'd been raped, given birth in secret, nursed her weak infant, buried the dead baby without a proper funeral… he had been badly shaken, but that was all.

The noise of the swimmers and the lapping of the water against the steps faded into the background as he read of how Tess was welcomed by the milking community at Talbothays dairy. She joined in chat at the supper table and wondered whether souls can be detached from bodies. The attention of the scholarly Angel Clare was caught and he was drawn to her beauty and natural innocence.

Tess's response to hearing the music of a harp on a *typical summer evening in June*, was described in vivid detail. Hardy said that the atmosphere created the sense that inanimate objects seem to have been given human senses. Tess was described as a *fascinated bird*, and later as a cat, listening secretly and creeping towards the hidden Angel Clare. Michael felt a smile pull on his face. Angel, playing a harp!

The garden, as experienced by Tess, was damp and juicy, dazzling with coloured weeds which stained her skin. *The waves of colour mixed with the waves of sound.* He read the description twice, absorbed in its strangeness and sexy beauty, wondering if he was reading too much into it.

Angel asked Tess if she agreed that *…this hobble of being alive is rather serious…* Michael put his head down on the book and closed his eyes. Hobble? What did Hardy mean? Stumbling through life? Was that what he was doing?

He was suddenly aware that something had changed and he raised his head, the damp page sticking to his cheek. The swimmers were still and silent; the rippling surface of the pool had calmed. A middle-aged woman, standing on the wall, her shoes getting splashed, was pulling a small girl by one arm out of the water. He followed the direction of people's faces and saw a group of German soldiers, four of them, strolling down the wooden walkway, chatting and laughing. They were in uniform, carrying towels. One was in shirt sleeves, his grey-green jacket slung over his shoulder. They ignored the people around them until they reached the top of the steps, close to Michael. He did not move, his eyes on a pair of shining leather boots, a foot away from his face. They seemed happy, careless, oblivious to the suffering they were causing. Two young women, on the other side of the steps, leapt from their seated positions, pulled towels around themselves and ducked their heads as they darted away.

'Gut afternoon,' said the tallest of the German group, with just a slight guttural accent, to a family clinging to the edge of the pool, his voice precise and confident. There was no reply. The soldiers smiled and continued to stroll around the building. They moved around the back of the lido area where young men sometimes showed-off by diving from the railings into the sea. There was a deep, cold pool there, at high tide, if you knew where to look.

As the soldiers disappeared from sight, the tension was broken. Noise returned, this time more talking, less laughing. The beachball drifted on the surface of the water. People pulled themselves out of the pool. Amy and Esme slowly swam over to the steps and emerged dripping to join Michael who kept his head turned in the direction of the soldiers. A family left swiftly down the boardwalk; a child wailed.

Michael looked at the girls and raised his eyebrows. 'Shall we stay? They're only here for a swim. And it's our pool, not theirs! I don't think we should be scared away. What do you think?' Esme's face was troubled, but she shrugged her shoulders and looked at Amy who nodded and sat down shaking her wet hair like an amiable spaniel.

Michael and the girls sat and hugged their knees, watching the woman in the flowery cap who had taken advantage of the lull and was using a stylish crawl stroke to cross and re-cross the pool.

The noise of the pool had almost returned to its previous level when Michael saw four dark heads swimming away from the lido. They must have entered the water around the back and were swimming out to sea. He watched as two of them turned and slowly swam back towards the rim of the pool. A third turned on his back, kicking his legs and splashing in the face of the fourth. Before the pair reached the pool, the wall near them emptied, except for two young women, their eyes hidden behind round sunglasses, faces tilted towards the sun, arms on the top of the pool's rim, water lapping at their chests. One of the soldiers swam towards them, hesitating before getting close and turning to say something to his friend close behind him. There was a playful scuffle in the water before the two of them edged towards the women, finally touching the wall with outstretched arms. Their sleek heads rose together from the water, like a couple of curious seals, only a wall's width from the basking women. Michael did not hear what they were saying but one of the women turned to them and pushed her sunglasses to the top of her head, smiling.

He looked back at the other two soldiers; one was doing back stroke, kicking his way towards the lido, arms making perfect curves and entering the water with barely a splash. The other was immobile.

'Jerrybags,' a large ginger-haired woman seated quite close to him whispered to her friend, nodding at the women in the pool. Michael had heard the expression before; his mother had asked Jacques not to use it, saying that we shouldn't judge. The ginger woman gathered her towel and pushed a cardigan into a bag.

Her friend put her hand on her arm. 'Let's not allow them to spoil our day off, Dora, eh? Ignore them.' But Dora shook her head and tutted and the two women disappeared into the lido's changing rooms.

Amy frowned. 'I can't see what harm they're doing. The soldiers I mean. Just being friendly... maybe the women are afraid to ignore them...' her voice faded away. Michael wondered if she was being innocent. He could tell that the women were enjoying the attention.

One of the soldiers hauled himself out of the water and sat on the side of the pool, legs inside, muscular thighs spread. Tanned and broad-shouldered, his shining hair was pushed back and there was a wide, toothy smile on his face. His friend stayed on the other side of the wall but pulled his body half out of the water to talk to one of the women. Michael could see a dark, hairy chest and the flash of white teeth as his laugh rang across the water. When the shout came from the back-stroking soldier, who had flipped over and was treading water, the one outside the pool turned and waved, beckoning.

'*Hilfe!*' the shout was sharp, urgency in the voice. 'Jurgen! Tomas! *Hilfe!*' The seated soldier leapt up onto the wall and shaded his eyes before diving into the water, the other followed, kicking to keep up.

Michael scanned the sea for signs of the fourth soldier. Nothing. Just the splashing of two swimmers doing a swift crawl stroke away from the pool. And the head of the back-stroker, looking around, calling. He got to his feet and walked around the outside of the lido buildings, Amy at his shoulder and others following, to the railing behind it. He leaned on the railing close to where four green uniforms had been carefully folded on top of shiny boots. Clean white towels were hanging over the lowest rail. A woman standing next to him glanced at him before her hand darted out and she pushed one of the towels into the water; it floated for a few seconds before darkening and sinking. The woman smirked and walked away. A murmur and a ripple of laughter rose from those watching.

Michael raised his eyes. About a hundred yards away, where the bay started to curve away beyond the Marina Hotel, the three Germans were splashing. It was where the sea floor dips suddenly. If you're swimming there, you can feel the temperature of the water drop. He watched as one of the three dived down, reappeared seconds later shouting and spluttering. Two lifeguards from the lido pushed their way through the growing crowd and appeared next to Michael, in their red full-body swimsuits and white caps, red life-rings in their hands. A man next to him, a towel around his waist, grabbed the arms of one of the lifeguards.

'You can't be thinking of going in after them,' he hissed. 'They wouldn't save you. Leave them to it.'

The lifeguard, dark and serious, shook off the clinging hand and looked at his partner. They nodded to each other, threw their rings into the water below them and dived in, swimming strongly towards the floundering soldiers.

Esme started sobbing, noisily. Amy put an arm around her and her sharp elbow dug Michael in the ribs.

'Let's go,' she said under her breath. 'I don't think we want to watch this.' He looked back as he followed the girls through the crowd, but his view was obscured and all he could see was the back of people, in towels and swimsuits leaning over the rail.

They gathered their things swiftly from amongst the abandoned towels and clothes by the pool and, as they reached the end of the board walk, two soldiers, rifles over their shoulders, ran towards them down the road, and then onto the wooden walkway, boots clumping loudly. Michael and the girls stepped back as they passed and watched them as they disappeared, shouldering their way through the crowd.

Amy pulled at his arm and hissed in his ear, 'Come on… come on!' she said more urgently. Esme's face was creased and pale as she pulled the towel more closely around her damp shoulders and followed Amy, sniffing.

Michael felt as though he was sleepwalking down the gritty boardwalk. The black shadow of melancholy was descending again.

As the girls used the deserted bus shelter to change, he turned his back. He pulled on his shorts and shirt with difficulty, his body starting to sweat. A commotion drew his eyes back to the lido's buildings. A group of men in the water were lifting a limp shape towards the downward stretching arms of two German soldiers. Its head fell back and water streamed off the pale, long body as it was gripped and pulled roughly over the railings. It landed with a heavy thud on the wooden deck.

Michael closed his stinging eyes. He'd never been even close to death before and now he'd experienced two in as many weeks. He heard Esme's gasp behind him and forced words from his mouth. 'Let's go.'

When they reached the farm, he left his cycle in the front garden, ignored the pleas of Esme and Amy to come into the kitchen and, clutching his bag, slowly hauled himself up the stairs, feeling heavy and clumsy. On the landing he paused and looked at his reflection in the tall mirror. For the second time, he found it strange, changed, ugly and he turned away to the silence of his room and the loneliness of his bed, his eyes unfocused on the familiar cracks in the ceiling plaster. Cold gripped him and he reached into his bag, needing the distraction of reading. *Tess* was gone. He must have left it, alone on the concrete, as he picked up his clothes and towel. He pulled out the volume of Hardy poetry which Laura had given him and held it to his mouth.

How could it have happened so quickly? The German was warm and healthy and vigorous one minute and cold and dead the next.

A vision of a young man, limbs spread, eyes open, descending towards a pebbly seabed through waves of refracted light, drifted into his mind, the face white and set.

AUGUST 1940

Michael sat on the third step from the bottom and leaned his head against the wooden spindle, feeling his chin tremble. As a young child, he'd liked to sit on the bottom step to put on his shoes. Now his legs needed more space. Everything was bigger, more shadowy, unknowable. He had come down from his bedroom, in his bare feet, with the idea of saying good night to his parents and hesitated in the dark hall, seeing them in the light and peace of the kitchen; it seemed like another world. The back door was open to the warm evening. His mother was sitting still, her knitting limp in her lap as the grandfather clock in the hall chimed ten o'clock. His father, the *Evening Post* open on the table in front of him, was dozing, his chin descending to his chest in small nods, exposing a balding patch on the top of his sun-browned head. The gas lamp flickered and spluttered. A large moth flapped against the smoky globe. It was too much, too warm and cosy for Michael. He had backed away and sat down, feeling completely alone in shadows.

The quiet hummed.

He imagined his mother eying the black box which stood silent and sullen in the corner, as she had done earlier today. She loved listening to the wireless and resented the order prohibiting citizens from tuning in to any wireless programme other than German controlled ones. She missed the news on the Home Service, and *Despatches from the Front* and daytime programmes while she worked in the kitchen, such as *Housewives' Choice* and *Music While You Work*. His parents regularly listened to music programmes in the evenings; Dad enjoyed big band concerts and Mum loved orchestral programmes, such as *A Pocketful of Tunes* or request shows where listeners' favourites were played. Occasionally there were dramas or discussion programmes which the whole family had listened to. The ban was one of the reasons Michael spent more time in the evenings in his room. The other reason… he couldn't put it into words. Amy had been defiant about the order. How would the Germans know, she had argued. She said that some of her friends' parents didn't take any notice, but their father had decided that they were not going to risk it. He never took risks.

His father had blurted out a few sharp words a couple of days ago about Michael avoiding work in the garden and on the farm; now they were hardly speaking to each other; a barrier had grown and Michael couldn't work out how to break it down. He hated it. But he didn't know how to explain to his father how he felt. He felt alone. Too tired to put in the hours of physical work… unable to lift his arms properly. How ridiculous did that sound?

He listened as his mother coughed gently, the sort of cough which she used to get his father's attention. His father stirred and blinked.

'Cup of tea?' she asked.

'Mmmmm. Yes, please. Sorry, Hélène. I can't seem to keep awake.'

'It's not surprising, Paul. You've worked so hard to bring in Mr Bideau's wheat. I'll give you a hand tomorrow; the girls should be able to cope in the greenhouses.'

He heard water tinkling into the kettle and the soft puff of gas as she lit the range.

'We'll have to be more careful with our tea. Most of the stores are struggling to get supplies. That's what I heard at the stores. Nothing coming from England, and very little from France now.'

'Well, Mr Bideau's wheat will help with bread now that flour's rationed, but I'm not sure we can do much about tea. Let's keep it weak, eh? Just how you like it!' There was affection in Paul's tone and he longed to go in and see his father's smile and the creases around his eyes.

'Jacques has worked hard, hasn't he?' his mother said.

'He's done a good job. That old reaper machine of Mr Bideau's needed a bit of work before we could use it. I don't know where he's picked up his skills but he managed to knock a few things into place. With a bit of oil, she was up and running. Old Bideau's horse seems to have relished the exercise when we got her going. I think she must have been loose in the lower field for weeks. At least there was plenty of grass.'

'I know you hoped that Michael would help more. But he's still suffering. We need to be patient. Let's be careful. And working on Mr Bideau's farm after what he saw there wouldn't help.'

Michael gripped the spindle tightly. Maybe he should go back upstairs. Eavesdropping was never a good idea. But he stayed and waited for his father's reply.

'I know. I shouldn't have snapped at him.' Michael closed his eyes as the tears came and leaked down his face. 'It's hard to see him do nothing, when so many of us are exhausted. I just think he needs to get on with things.'

'Let's take it slowly. I'll ask for his help in the garden and greenhouses tomorrow. Or I'll get Lucy to suggest it. He likes her. We could do with a hand.'

'And I'll have a word… apologise.'

Michael heard his mother scape her chair on the floor as she sat down and he imagined the steaming tea being poured.

There was the snap of the newspaper.

'Listen to this, Hélène. Report of Yves' football match: "St Helier plumber, Yves Le Breton, played with skill and determination in midfield" …ummm… "the Jersey team was unlucky not to score more than one goal in the first half, with attempts from Emile Le Poidvin and Matthew Knowles…" The fact is, the Germans are strong, bigger and fitter. There's no mention of the Mourant tackle.'

Yves had told them at supper yesterday that there was one ugly moment when Peter Mourant had brought down a German striker with a clumsy tackle which could have broken his ankle. Jacques said that he'd loved it and had noticed, on the other side of the field, a group of officers, boots shining and caps badge glinting, who pursed their mouths and folded their arms.

'Yves is certainly thriving… despite everything. The plumbing business is going so well and there's a… confidence about him.' Hélène said.

Yves had expressed some doubts about doing some work for the Germans, but after discussing it with his parents he accepted their money and found the work satisfying. If he didn't do it, someone else would, their father had argued. They were paying him the going rate and Jersey's stuttering economy was going to rely on local businesses like his. Locals were less likely to embark on big plumbing jobs in the current uncertain circumstances, but working at the military headquarters and renovating some of the plumbing at requisitioned houses had tested his and Bob's skills. Michael had wondered if Jacques would rage at the thought of his brother working for the enemy, but he had nodded and said nothing. Michael envied Yves' sense of purpose. And Jacques' anger. Did he envy that? At least he was doing something. Michael was unsure what he was doing, but he was convinced that it was dangerous, subversive. And the rifles… had he moved them?

'More troops arrived this week,' said Paul. 'Look at this photo….' Michael knew what he was referring to. He'd collected the paper from where it had been delivered at the garden gate and skimmed through it while his father was still at work. There was a grainy photograph showing tidy lines of soldiers on the Victoria Quay, and more descending from a large troop ship. Another photograph was of King Street. A German brass band with trombones, trumpets and an enormous tuba were caught mid-stride, effortlessly marching and playing. Behind them was a group of officers saluting and behind them a group of women in headscarves, faces impassive.

'Bed?' asked his father, rustling the paper.

Michael retreated back upstairs on silent feet, mouthing, 'Goodnight'.

*

Hours later, Michael gasped into wakefulness, a sweat cooling on his neck. What was that? A deep rumbling was repeated. He pushed back the sheet and climbed out of bed. He parted the blackout curtains; a thin light showed plant shapes in the vegetable garden. The lane beyond was shadowy and still. The floorboards creaked as he moved to the door, opening it slowly to avoid the familiar squeak of unoiled hinges and crept along the landing, to the south-facing window with a view towards the coast. Leaning his hands on the wooden sill, he saw nothing but the dark land and the quiet outline of trees. Then flashes of white light momentarily gave glimpses of a silver sea and the booming sounds came again; he felt a vibration in the floor below his bare feet. No one else in the house stirred. His heart was loud in his chest.

Michael sat down on the window seat, yanked the heavy blackout curtain back into place behind him and drew up his feet. In the narrow space between the folds of black felt and the glass panes, he shivered and pulled his legs up resting his cheek on the boniness of his knees.

He and Amy had played hide-and-seek behind curtains when they were young; it seemed so long ago. The childish, breathless fear of discovery was replaced now by a heavier feeling. He couldn't see the end of the occupation. He couldn't see anything beyond a feeling of helplessness and emptiness. People said they'd be gone by Christmas and rumours whispered of a planned fight-back. But the Germans were building as if they meant to stay and fight. Trenches and barbed wire were scarring Le Hocq beach and Jacques said that fortifications and gun emplacements were being constructed around the coast. Jacques had seen the building work for himself, making notes, he said, to gather knowledge for the British. Yves was doing a job out at Noirmont, where construction was advancing quickly. He brought back tales of an ugly, tall, concrete observation tower going up.

Michael's eyes adjusted to the light and the grey land was paling. There were still pinpoints of stars in the clear skies, but blue was slowly returning, a deep, empty blue. He gazed out at the silver stripe that was gradually dividing the sea from the sky. Lights flashed but there was no repeat of the explosive noises which woke him. How could no one else have been disturbed? A snuffling sound and a ripple in the blackouts made him jump as a wet nose nudged his thigh and Jenny's shaggy head and shoulders pushed their way through the curtains. The dog panted with excitement and her paws scrabbled and slid on the polished wood floor, tail wagging as Michael rubbed her head before sliding back the curtains and swinging his feet back to the cool landing floor.

He straightened up to see a ghostly figure standing in the hall, a pale face in the grey light and a long white nightgown.

'What's going on?' his mother whispered. 'What were you doing in there?'

'Just watching the dawn coming up. Did you hear the noises?'

'The rumbling. Yes. What was it?'

'Sounded like bombs, a long way away...'

'Do you fancy an early cup of tea, or are you going back to bed?'

Michael nodded and followed her downstairs. They didn't light the gas lamp; the sky was peachy outside and the kitchen glowed in the dawn light when they pulled back the blackouts. He washed the two green cups from last night's tea at the sink and stood still staring out of the kitchen window when he felt his mother behind him, caressing the back of his head, as she had done when he was a child. He didn't move and felt a sob rising in his chest.

'I feel so lost,' he murmured.

'Lost? No. We are all here for you... look at me.'

Michael turned, his face creased and his eyes filling as she pulled him to her, warmth and softness enveloping him. He let his head come down onto her shoulder and couldn't hold in the spasms which shook his body.

'Let it go,' she encouraged. 'You'll feel better for a cry. There's no shame, and only you and me here.'

His body convulsed and he clung to her as she stroked his back.

'Why… what's wrong… with me?' he stuttered.

'You've had a rough time. Seen things that no one should see, particularly not children. Yes, you are still a child… a great big one, but still a child.'

Eventually he felt his sobbing subside and stood upright looking down at her. She took his head between her hands and looked into his eyes.

'You will be all right. You feel things deeply, like me… and my mother. She used to tell me it was a gift. I didn't know what she meant until I was older… until I had children of my own. I thought it was a curse… to feel so sad and empty at times. But the other side is the great joy you sometimes feel. You father loves you so much…' Michael felt tears again and he blinked them back. 'He doesn't understand… as I do.'

'I can't shake it. I don't want to… do… anything. I know that sounds… silly.'

'Not silly. I understand. Will you take some advice?'

'Tell me…'

'Try not to shut yourself away. It's hard but be with us. Get involved. Push yourself to work on the farm or the garden. And the pigs at the Bideau place need feeding… only when you are ready. You are going to have to do something about that parrot!' She smiled and made a face, imitating the bird. 'Pretty Dolly!'

'Oh, Lord! Have the animals been fed? How awful to forget them!'

'You have a sister. She cares… about you and the animals. Amy has been feeding them and taking the dogs out. She says Dolly doesn't like her and, to be fair, I don't think the parrot's keen on any of us, except you. Can't think why! She pecks and squawks and shouts!'

The kettle whistled and his mother made tea. Outside a band of orange expanded into a fiery horizon, fading to tangerine and yellow where it met the blue of the sky.

'Is it warm enough to sit outside?'

It was cool, but Michael fetched coats from the hall hooks and they slipped on shoes to sit on the bench under the kitchen window. They watched the dawn lightening in silence until the colours of the land seeped back around them.

SEPTEMBER 1940

Michael was woken by a gunshot. At least that's what he thought it was. Or was it in his dream? He waited, his thundering heart slowing. It was just getting light behind his thin curtains; he hadn't pulled the blackouts last night. He sat up and swung his legs out of bed, listening. There it was again. A shot. Close by. In the fields. He could see nothing from his window except the still kitchen garden. He pulled on a shirt and trousers and ran down the stairs as Amy and his mother emerged from their rooms.

Barefoot, he ran though the kitchen and out of the open door into the farmyard. Nothing. Then birds rising into the air, screaming. Michael dragged on a pair of wellingtons and ran across the yard to the low wall on the other side.

His father was standing with his hands in the air in the middle of his tobacco patch. There was a German soldier in the road by the fence with his rifle raised.

'*Ausgangssperre. Niemand draussen. Ausgangssperre,*' he repeated.

The German's head whipped around and stared at him but the rifle stayed aimed at his father. Michael raised his hands slowly, blood pounding in his head.

'My father.' It came out in a whisper. He cleared his throat and swallowed. 'My father. Just gardening,' he said pointing at the hoe which was propped up on a wheelbarrow. His father was still, silent and grim-faced. He felt his mother behind him and Amy grabbed at his arm.

'I think he's saying that Dad shouldn't be outside, because of the curfew,' she said in a low voice. "*Ausgangssperre*" is curfew.'

The soldier's head swivelled between the family and Michael's father. Michael could see the German's face clearly. It was pale. He was young. Slimmer than many of the Germans. His uniform jacket sagged from his raised shoulders.

'Jah. Curfew... *Ausgangssperre. Ausgangssperre,*' the soldier repeated loudly, nodding at the house. Why was this soldier alone? Michael glanced up and down the lane.

Amy squeezed his arm and he put his hands down on the top of the wall.

'*Garten,*' she enunciated clearly, pointed at their father's tools and mimed digging. '*Garten*'.

Michael felt the pressure of her arm against his. '*Garten... arbeit*'.

The soldier, staring at Michael and Amy, lowered the rifle and Michael heard the sigh of his mother's breath.

'*Gartenarbeit,*' repeated Amy.

Michael watched as his father lowered his hands and took a step back, towards his family. The soldier jerked his rifle up again and moved closer.

'*Halt,*' he shouted. '*Geh zuruck!*'.

The soldier's blue eyes widened and flicked between the members of the family.

Everyone raised their hands again and no one moved. Impasse. Wasn't that the word? What happens now?

The German's face suddenly relaxed. '*Zwillinge?*' The word meant nothing to Michael. A smile broke across the soldier's face, his teeth white. His eyes shone as he nodded, the metal helmet moving on his head. Too big for him.

'*Zwillinge?*' he repeated.

Michael looked at Amy and raised his eyebrows.

'*Ich bin Zwilling. Ich habe eine Schwester…*' the German trailed off.

'A sister,' said Amy quietly. 'I must remind him of his sister…'

The soldier moved closer towards them, Michael's father shuffling backwards ahead of him until he backed into the low wall.

'*Sister, jah… und Zwilling.*'

The soldier halted within a few yards of the family pointed his finger from Michael to Amy, a smile on his face. '*Zwillinge. Jah?*'

'Twins,' hissed Michael. 'It must be… he wants to know if we are twins.' He put an arm around Amy's shoulder. 'Yes. *Nous sommes…* we… *wir sind…* twins…' He attempted to repeat the soldier's word: '*Swilling?*'

'*Zwillinge,*' repeated the soldier. Michael and Amy in unison repeated it after him.

'I wonder if he's a twin, too,' said Amy smiling. She gestured towards him, her palm upwards. '*Zwilling?*'

'*Jah, jah. Meine Schwester ist Frieda…*'

He stopped suddenly and the smile dropped from his face.

'*Ausgangssperre. Niemand draussen.*' The words were softer than before and less threatening.

He looked around at the garden and smiled, as if he had suddenly realised the beauty in which he was standing. Examining a row of tobacco plants, he stepped among them, feeling the large fleshy leaves between his fingers, his rifle lowered.

'*Was ist das?*' he asked sharply.

'Tobacco plants.' Michael's father's voice was quiet and his jaw tense.

'*Tabak?*' questioned the soldier, making a gesture which looked like someone smoking a cigarette. Michael's father nodded. The soldier smiled again.

'Shall we offer him some?'

'I'll do it, Dad.'

Michael pointed to the edge of the field where tobacco leaves were drying on the make-shift frames constructed by his father. The soldier nodded and followed him, as he stepped in among the plants, shuffling down the neat row. Michael picked up a few of the largest leaves from the drying frame and handed them over. He mimed rolling and puffing on a cigarette. The soldier grinned and put the leaves under his arm, clumsily struggling with his rifle. He nodded at the family and then retreated back to the road, seemed about to speak, but turned quickly and walked off towards Le Hocq.

They watched him walk away, tin helmet bobbing along the top of the hedge, the metal caps of his boots tapping on the road.

'I didn't give him your best stuff, Dad. He got leaves which weren't ready yet.'

'He might come back for more,' his father sighed. 'Oh well, as long as they don't take it all!' The family filed into the kitchen silently.

Michael's father pulled off his boots and sat at the table.

'I know I shouldn't have been out before six, but I couldn't sleep. Sorry, everyone. He wasn't going to shoot me. Did you see how young he was? Just a boy, missing his family… I don't think he was older than seventeen.'

'He's the one who's on duty at the tower down at Le Hocq,' said Amy.

They all looked towards her.

'I've been down Le Hocq Lane a few times, on my bike. I wanted to swim a few days ago, but there's wire on the common. I asked him if I could. Practised my German… "*Ich gehe swimmen.*" But he waved me away. She lowered her voice and give a comic imitation of the harsh German accent. '"*Nein. Nein. Raus!*"'

Michael's mother gasped. 'It isn't funny. Keep away, Amy!'

'I'm not afraid of him.'

His father laughed but then become serious as he glanced at his wife's frown. 'You must keep away, Amy. Your mother's right. They are the ones with the guns. Don't forget that. And where did that German come from?'

Amy smiled. 'It's hardly fluent! "*Ausgangssperre*" is on the orders… about the curfew. Everything else is similar to English. And I learnt a few words in school. Our French teacher is a German speaker. I've heard that we're all going to learn German in school.'

Outside, the day was rising quietly; the sky a pure, clean blue, feathered with wispy white clouds. A cup of tea warming his hands, Michael stood in the yard doorway looking towards the East. The sun was a small white-hot ball in stripes of yellow, orange and violet, casting shadows in the vegetable garden.

Anger bubbled inside him, anger at the violation. He felt no fear when the soldier was pointing the gun, but a strength in his right to be here. They wouldn't always have the power. He would hold fast.

He turned back to his family and sat at the table. They talked about the weather; the second week in September had been warmer than usual, after the rain and wind of late August. But under the normality of the conversation, Michael felt the tension.

'There's so much to do with the two farms before the winter. I worry about it,' said his father. 'You've all been working so hard. It's not just me. Michael, you've been great.'

Michael felt a glow. He had been trying very hard. It wasn't easy but his mother was right to suggest that he push himself.

'I don't have to go back to school....' he said quietly.

'Yes, you do,' said his father firmly. 'You need your school cert. Both of you.'

'A few of my friends say they aren't going back. David Le Fallu isn't.'

His mother tutted and signed. 'He's bright, too, eh? His mother told me he wanted to be an engineer.'

Michael's thoughts slid away. What was the point? That black cloud was still drifting.

OCTOBER 1940

Michael turned his bicycle off the road towards Portelet onto a rough footpath which crossed Portelet Common in the direction of Noirmont Point. His frustration at being forced into having the company of Jonny and Keith, on what he had thought of as an important request from Jacques had not subsided throughout the long ride to St Helier, along Victoria Avenue, through St Aubin and up the hill towards Portelet and Ouaisné. Jonny bumped along beside him, keeping up a patter of words which he'd stopped listening to. No sign of Keith, though; his battered Raleigh had already held them up and now he was lagging behind again. He'd outgrown his bike and his long legs caught on the handlebars when he turned, if he didn't time his pedalling right. And he'd had to replace his tyre on the front wheel with rubber hosepipe, begged from a builder's yard. It was impossible to buy tyres; improvisation was necessary. Michael braked without warning and dropped his bike in the scrubby undergrowth. Jonny copied him.

'We'd better wait,' puffed Michael. He took a deep breath, turned away from Jonny and pushed his hands deep into his pockets. His father, keen to prevent him from becoming too isolated he thought, had suggested that he spend Saturday with his friends. They'd arrived in the farmyard after breakfast. Both lived quite close to the farm: Keith's parents had been evicted from the family home in St Helier, which was so near the field headquarters at Victoria College that it was wanted for officers' accommodation and the family had moved in with his grandmother who had a bungalow near Green Island; Jonny's father was a dairyman at Samarès Manor and his large family shared a tiny cottage that came with the job.

Michael had planned to follow Jacques' suggestion that he cycle out to Noirmont and sketch what he could see of the fortifications which were being built. His brother thought that collecting information about the defences might, at some stage, help the British authorities. When the boys had arrived, he considered changing his plans, but decided to go ahead. They'd been excited when he told them, though he didn't mention his brother's name, just suggested they could find out about what the 'Jerries' were doing by cycling to Portelet.

The wind was gusty; it had been a struggle getting up the hill and the boys were both panting. White and grey clouds scudded swiftly across a pale blue sky. The summer was over.

'What's happened to him? S'pect he couldn't get up the hill on those tyres,' said Jonny.

'Shall we walk for a bit? He'll see our bikes. I'm not sure we'll be allowed to get very far. Let's just see if we can spot what's happening.'

'Do you think it could be dangerous?' Jonny seemed to like the idea.

'Let's go down there and keep to the treeline,' said Michael, pointing to their left where a line of scrubby trees led towards Noirmont Point.

Followed closely by Jonny, he walked over the springy grass and wild blueberry plants. Both boys kept their heads down, bodies bent forward until they reached the cover of the trees.

After about ten minutes of silent walking, their path was blocked by a barbed wire fence. In the distance, where Michael knew the craggy headland fell away to the sea, he could see the top of a new concrete structure. He felt a surge of bile. His brother was right, not that he'd ever doubted Jacques' bitter descriptions of the way that the enemy was defacing the island. They were building what looked like a look-out tower.

Michael was wondering if he could climb over the barbed wire when he became aware that Jonny was looking curiously at him, expecting an answer.

'Sorry. What did you say?'

'I think we should go back for Keith. And… we can't go any further anyway.' Jonny's face had lost his usual wide-eyed look of boyish excitement. He looked scared.

'I… what if…?' Jonny mumbled, his pale, freckled face creased. He wiped his nose on his sleeve. 'C'mon, Mike… I can't.'

Michael had known Jonny since first school when they attended Grouville Primary together. They spent many afternoons on the Samarès Estate, helping with the cows or using the large gardens as a playground. Ancient trees with branches temptingly close to the ground had been climbed and the ornamental lake swum in, when they could be sure that the family was away from home. He'd been fun.

Recently he'd talked of nothing but planes and guns, uninterested seemingly in what the Germans were doing in Jersey, but wanting to discuss engines and bullets. And food, he always had a great deal to say about food. Michael had never seen him like this, like a small, scared boy.

Michael looked back towards the concrete building. He'd come back another day, alone.

'All right. We'd better go back for Keith.'

Jonny turned immediately and trotted back the way they had come, looking over his shoulder occasionally, stumbling and keeping his head low until they found their bikes where they had left them. Without speaking, they mounted and gained the lane quickly cycling in the direction of St Aubin, Jonny close on Michael's tail.

Before they came to the top of the hill, around a bend, in a narrow part of the lane, Michael's eye was drawn to something white, like a garment, caught in the hedge. In the field beyond there were more white patches, like drifts of snow. He braked and pulled the bike against the hedge. Jonny skidded on some small pebbles and fell, banging his shins on his crossbar.

'Idiot. What'd you stop for?' he muttered, picking himself and his bike up.

'What's this?' Michael pulled a damp sheet of paper from the prickles in the hawthorn hedge. A section was torn from the top. The other side was printed, like a page from a newspaper.

'"A message from His Majesty…"' read Jonny over Michael's shoulder. 'What? What is this?'

'Look…' Michael pointed. More sheets were scattered over the field where recently potatoes had been harvested, leaving rows of dying brown stalks.

Michael poked his finger at a smaller smudged line above the headline. 'I think this says… something… RAF? Yes, RAF. They must have dropped them!' His mouth remained open. 'The RAF. They dropped them from a plane. In the night, or yesterday. Jacques said that the RAF were dropping leaflets.'

'Why haven't the Jerries found them? Close to the fortifications at Portelet…' Jonny looked around frantically, but there was no one in sight.

'We should collect them!' said Michael, looking for a gate to get into the field.

'What? We might be seen…' Jonny hissed.

Michael folded the sheet in his hand and pushed it into his pocket.

'Let's do it before that happens.'

Michael crawled through a gap in the hedge, followed by Jonny, panting and sighing, gathering mud on their knees and blood on the backs of their hands. Michael took the right-hand side of the field and told Jonny to take the left. They quickly gathered all the sheets they could see. Ten minutes later they were stuffing a soggy mass into Jonny's saddle bag.

'Keith'll be waiting for us,' called Jonny as they set off again. 'I wonder if he ever made it up the hill from St Aubin.' Now that they were away from Portelet and the field of leaflets, his manner had become cheerful again. 'And he's got the food. I hope he hasn't eaten it. He wouldn't dare!'

Keith was a shy boy who worshipped Jonny, bringing him food that his Granny baked and following him everywhere.

As they reached the lane's junction with the main road which wound down to St Aubin, Michael braked sharply and Jonny collided with his back wheel, skidding on the pebbles and sand. '*Merde!*' he yelled. 'Not again, Mike!'

'Shhh. Look…' Michael pointed down the road. Ahead, in the middle of the road, there was a large black car, two German soldiers and Keith.

Smart in grey-green uniform, boots shining and wearing the peaked caps of officers, the men were each side of the boy. One was gesticulating, but they couldn't hear what was being said. Keith was gripping his bike's handlebars, which, even from distance, looked distorted, his head down.

The boys retreated quietly back down the lane and left their bikes in the hedge before walking back and peering around a stunted beech tree into the main road.

'What should we do?' whispered Jonny in Michael's ear. One of the soldiers had walked a few paces towards their hiding place.

'Shh. Keep still,' muttered Michael as his friend leant on his shoulder, pushing him forward. 'Get back!'

He dug his elbow into Jonny's abdomen causing him to double up and gasp. They froze, crouched in the hedgerow and listened. It was quiet and still. A few minutes elapsed before Michael glanced at Jonny and dipped his head towards the road. He put his finger to his lips and crept forwards, in an uncomfortable squatting position, keeping his head well below the hedge top. On his knees in the damp grass, he slowly extended his head until he had a view of the road. He could see the car, through the dusty lenses of his glasses, but nothing else. Just as he was about to return to Jonny, the car revved and drove towards him; he pulled back as a cloud of dust rose and he got a view of the gleaming side windows and a flash of Keith's ghostly face in the back.

'Was that the car?' Jonny had joined him. He nodded and the boys sat silently side by side. 'What now?'

'Better get home and see what my parents say…' He mounted and was off down the road before Jonny could argue.

The farmyard was silent and there was no response to Michael's shouts when the boys rode in an hour later, sweaty and dirty.

'Let's try the milking yard.' He remounted his bike and turned up the lane, pedalling off the saddle.

'Wait! I can't go any further,' yelled Jonny, panting. He followed Michael pushing his bike slowly up the steep hill.

The cows were in the yard, being herded into the shed for the afternoon's milking by Jacques' team, though his brother was nowhere to be seen. Michael climbed onto the top of the wide, metal gate and waved to attract the attention of Brendan.

'Hello there, young man,' the smiling Irishman waved back, leaning on the flank of a lazy cow to direct it to the shed. 'Come to give us a hand, have you?'

'Where's Jacques? Urgent!' shouted Michael.

'In the barn. You all right, Mike? I'll give him a shout, shall I? Jacques! Jacques! Your wee brother wants you.'

Jacques appeared almost immediately, a bucket in one hand and a rope in the other. 'What's wrong?' He addressed Brendan, but seeing Michael perched on the gate, dropped everything and pushed his way through the crowd of cows. 'What is it, Mike?'

Michael struggled to speak; he was panting and the dust in his throat was clinging to his words.

'They've... taken him.' He jumped from the gate into the yard and reached out to his brother. Jacques put out his hand and patted him on the shoulder.

'What are you talking about? Did you get to Portelet? Come on, let's go upstairs.' He called out to Brendan and Bob Moulin, 'Manage without me for a few minutes, lads?' And grabbed Michael's arm, pulling him up the steps and into his kitchen. 'Now. Deep breath. What's happened? You hurt?' He held his brother by both shoulders.

Michael shook his head. Looking down at his dirty hands he blurted out the story while Jacques listened blinking and frowning. '...Keith was in the car...' he finished. 'Where will they take him? We need... to tell his parents...'

'Where are the leaflets now?' asked Jacques sharply. Michael looked up at him, coughed and swallowed. 'What... about Keith...?' He coughed again.

Jacques filled a cup of water; Michael gulped it and wiped his hand across his mouth. 'Jonny. He was behind me…' He moved towards the door; his brother grabbed his shoulder.

'The leaflets?'

Michael pulled the sheet from his pocket and handed it to his brother. 'The rest are in Jonny's saddlebag.'

As Jacques unfolded the sheet, Michael felt into the bottom of his pocket and rubbed the button with his thumb. 'Hold fast,' he whispered.

'What did you say?'

'Nothing… what about Jonny… and Keith?'

'Let's find Jonny first and then we'll do something about Keith…'

Jonny was leaning on the gate when the brothers descended the steps and crossed the now empty yard.

'Hey, Mike. I thought I'd lost you,' Jonny shouted raising his hand.

'You'd better give me all those leaflets. Might be dangerous to have them…' said Jacques. 'Where are they?'

They put all the sheets into a sack which Jacques brought from the barn.

'Say nothing about these, eh?' He glared at each boy in turn as he took charge of the bag.

'What will you do with them,' asked Jonny.

Jacques didn't answer but ran up the step to his flat, dumped the sack and clomped down again, grabbing a bike from the shed.

'Right… let's find Keith's parents.'

They had to ask directions from a man who was pulling up onions in his garden before finding the bungalow. It was down a track off the main coast road at Green Island, a dull, cream, pebbled-dash building with a row of sheets and shirts hanging limply from a line across the front lawn. They let themselves into the yard, leaving their bikes out in the lane, setting off a large Doberman which was chained up outside a wooden shed, its door open revealing a clutter of tools and boxes. It barked and jumped, rattling the chain. Jonny retreated to the gate.

'God, that's a big dog,' he muttered.

The side door of the bungalow opened and a small woman in a stained overall rushed out, Keith's mother. She stopped abruptly when she saw them.

'Boys! I'm so glad to see you.' Her voice screeched at the dog. 'Belt up, Dennis. That's enough.' She bustled down the garden path and folded Jonny against her wrapped chest.

Jacques stepped forward. 'I'm Mike's brother… We need to talk to you… about Keith.'

'Come inside.' She turned back to the door and they followed her into a small kitchen, smelling of cabbage and damp clothes. At the table, his fair head down between his arms and his hands over his ears was Keith.

'He won't tell us what happened. Be quiet now, Janie… don't do that, Wilf!' She raised her head to address a baby crying in a playpen in the corner and a toddler who was pushing toys through the wooden bars. Keith's mother tutted, picked up the baby, pulled the toddler behind her and disappeared through an open doorway into a shadowy hall. They heard her shouting, 'Mother, I need your help.'

She reappeared almost immediately, closing the door behind her, and sat down and put an arm around Keith, who wriggled and pushed her away. A child screamed from behind the closed door and was ignored.

Jacques didn't stay. After hearing Keith's stuttering story, he left the boys, giving both Michael and Jonny a cold stare: 'Remember what I said…'

Apparently, Keith's wheel had skidded at the top of

the hill and he'd fallen into a ditch. The Germans' car had stopped.

'No, they didn't knock me off the bike', he muttered. 'One of them spoke good English.' He had offered to take him home. The bike fitted into the trunk.

'They brought you back here?' asked his mother, surprise in her voice. 'I didn't see them...'

'I said I was all right. They left me at the gate.' He looked around the kitchen, his eyes red and watery. 'I thought they might be arresting me. 'Cause of the tyres. Thought they might be tricking me... to get me into the car. But they were... nice.' His spotty face looked at his friends accusingly. 'Where did you go?'

Michael apologised, said that they didn't realise he was so far behind, told him that they had been unable to get to Noirmont. He gave Jonny a hard look and didn't mention the leaflets. As they left him, a cup of tea steaming into his face, grandmother on one side and mother on the other, the small children playing at their feet, he looked happier.

Michael and Jonny cycled down the lane now dappled with low autumn sunshine and parted with a nod at the back gates of Samarès Manor. Michael turned for home up the steep, narrow lane, overhung with trees dropping their yellowing leaves in the breeze. He took a deep breath and cycled hard, enjoying the pulling of his calf muscles and feeling stronger than he had in weeks.

NOVEMBER 1940

Michael was helping Yves with his washing up, the smell of fried onions lingering in the air, when Bob opened the door, crossing the room heavily and dragging a wooden chair up to the table.

'Is Willy coming?' He addressed Jacques, who was standing by the window looking out onto the plumbers' yard below, ignoring Michael and Yves, 'I haven't seen him for weeks.'

'I called in last week to tell him we were going to have a drink and game of cards here. He said he'd try. His wife might stop him. He's under the thumb.' He pulled out a chair and reached into a bag at this feet. 'Not the lad he used to be,' he muttered, setting a bottle of scotch on the table.

Bob smiled. 'Got any glasses?'

Yves turned. 'Oh! Jacques, where did that come from?'

'Better you don't know, Yves! Just thought we deserved it. Glasses?'

Michael reached up to a shelf over the draining board and brought a collection of mismatching tumblers to the table, putting them down next to a copy of the RAF newssheet that he and Jonny had picked up the week previously.

He'd seen most of the bundle burnt by Jacques, in the oil-drum he kept in the yard for rubbish and where he'd disposed of the rifles' crate. Michael remembered the shady corner of the shed where he and Jacques had hidden them. Were they still there? Jacques had talked of moving them again, suggested they might be safer here at the plumbers' yard.

Jacques must have put the leaflets he'd kept under his mattress. The copy on the table was flattened with the marks of the slats of the bed frame visible. Michael had nagged his brother until he had allowed him to study the newssheet carefully, after dark, one evening. Jacques agreed with Michael that the tone was optimistic; there were sketchy reports on the RAF's successful bombing raids over German cities and promises about coming to the relief of the islands. But Jacques' response was sceptical.

Jacques poured an inch of golden liquid into each of the three small glasses supplied and tapped one of the sheets with a dirty fingernail. 'It says here that Hitler's bombing raids have "stiffened their backs". What does that mean? Stiff backs, peckers up? It's all talk.'

Michael moved to the window at the sound of an engine turning into the yard. There wasn't enough light to see who got off the motorbike in the drizzle. But the two figures certainly weren't soldiers. A door slammed followed by the sound of work boots coming up the bare staircase. Rob and Willy entered, bringing a damp smell with them.

'Hey, lads,' said Rob in the doorway, his large open face lined with his wide smile. 'We've escaped from the wives for an hour or so. I've promised Willy's wife I'll have him back well before the curfew! What are we playing, poker? And is this your little brother, Jacques?' He gave Michael a friendly slap on the shoulder.

Behind him, Willy was taking off his boots. The room went quiet.

'Force of habit!' he muttered. 'We have a new rug at home.'

'What's this? Whiskey?' He glanced at Jacques. 'Don't tell me... I don't want to know. But I will have a little taste. Thanks.'

Six around the table was a squeeze; Yves brought a chair from the office and added more glasses and bottles of beer to the table and pulled a pack of cards from his trousers pocket.

'What's this?' said Willy, quietly bending over newssheet on the table. 'Where'd this come from...' He looked up and smiled. 'Someone at work said that he'd heard about them. I didn't believe it.'

Jacques turned the sheet and Willy squinted at it moving the oil lamp closer. 'I can't read that. What's it say?'

'Apart from a heart-warming message of sympathy from Their Majesties, which cheered me up no end... there's news of how the RAF is winning the war!'

'Are they?' Willy's moon face was like a large child's.

'Look at that... that should convince you...' Jacques stabbed his finger on a cartoon in the bottom corner of the sheet and shook his head. A burly, ugly figure, bare-chested in black shorts was depicted three times in action next to a punch bag on a stand with a spring near the base. In the first and second sketches, the fat man's massive hooks had caused the punchbag to bend both ways like a sapling in a storm. In the third, the punchbag had bounced back onto the boxer's head. His body was squashed into a squat figure; limbs distorted into concertinas and his chest compressed behind his distended belly.

Willy laughed. 'That's got him! Fighting back. Good news.' He looked around at the other men and frowned. 'What? Don't you believe it?'

'The Jerries here don't seem worried,' said Yves as he opened bottles. One fizzed over and Jacques had to pull the newssheet away from the spreading pool of beer.

Jacques lit a cigarette. 'Sorry not to share, lads. Limited supplies. Now, what can we do? We need to respond to the British efforts. Do something… Michael here's been trying to find out more about the fortifications, but it's not easy and there must be more we can do.'

Michael felt the heat in his face as the five men looked at him. Rob smiled and nodded.

There was silence. Willy coughed. 'Now look here! I told you I can't be involved in anything, Jacques. I have a family.' He nodded. 'It's all right for you. But I can't. I promised her. I thought we were going to play cards.' He downed the whiskey and wiped his mouth with the back of his hand.

Jacques leaned forward and tried to catch Willy's eye. 'Happy working for the enemy, are you? What about people who aren't being paid by Jerry? Have you heard about Bob Moulin's brother?' All the men looked at him. 'He won't work again. He took two bullets in his back when they machine-gunned the Esplanade in June. He's paralysed. Been in hospital ever since.' Willy's eyes stayed on the table in front of him, but Rob folded his arms and sat forward. 'His wife has recovered… walks with a limp. They have no income. Two little 'uns. She's had to move in with the in-laws. You wouldn't recognise her now.'

Jacques picked up his whiskey and gulped noisily.

'It's hard for people in town. Can't grow much veg. I took a box over yesterday,' said Yves quietly.

Jacques folded the news sheet and slid it into his pocket. 'I'll hide this. Latest orders say that anyone in possession will be imprisoned.'

'We have to hand in wirelesses by the 20th,' said Rob, rubbing his face. 'I'm not. Jude and me argued about it last night. I'll hide it in the shed. She'll never know. They'd never find it among the tackle and bait…' He bit his lip.

Yves moved to the corner and pulled up two floorboards in the shadows. 'Bob's! Shall we? Anyone object? Give us a hand, Mike.' On his knees, rear end raised towards the table, he reached down into the dark hole and handed the box to Michael.

Setting the wooden wireless upright on the table, Michael pushed the black switch down and twiddled the knobs. Nothing. He banged the top with his palm. 'What's wrong…'

Jacques stood up and reached over, clicking the on-off stitch up and down. 'Battery? Can we get another?' He fell back heavily in his chair, causing it to rock. The men shrugged. 'I'll get the one from the farm,' he said. 'Dad is bound to hand in the wireless. Haven't listened to it in months, anyway. No need for Jerry to have the battery, too.'

Yves picked up the pack of cards and shuffled. 'Are we going to play?'

'I can't stand it. I have to do something… *we* have to do something.' Jacques pushed back his chair and paced around the room.

'Count me out,' replied Willy. 'Game of cards? Yes, Yves.'

'Games? *They* aren't playing games. How can *you* play games!' Jacques' voice was shrill. He put both hands on the table edge and glowered at the men. Michael could see the frustration growing in his brother, his face darkening.

Yves paused in dealing cards and sat back. Quiet fell in the room. Michael's heart leapt at the sound of a loud thumping on the outside door downstairs.

Yves jumped to his feet. Jacques' head jerked up and he moved to the window followed by Michael who looked over his shoulder. Below them were two grey tin helmets, looking as if giant mushrooms had sprung up in the yard.

'Jerry soldiers,' muttered Jacques. Michael glanced at his face. He was pale and biting his lip. He spun back into the room, ignoring Michael. 'Let's get that wireless back into the floor. No need to advertise it. Give me a hand, Bob. Willy, deal the cards. Yves. You go down. Stall them.'

Yves didn't move, his eyes shifting from his brother to the door.

'Come on! Take your time!' Bob hadn't moved, so Michael helped Jacques who was fumbling with the floorboards.

Had Jacques brought the rifles here? He seemed nervous, why else would he be worried? What if they searched the place?

When Yves returned, followed by two German soldiers, rifles over shoulders, metal toes-caps snapping loudly on the stairs, the four men were sitting at the table, holding cards. Michael stood, pushing his shaking hands deep into his pockets, leaning back on the sink, where Rob had dumped the glasses and whiskey bottle.

The smoking oil lamp in the centre of the table illuminated the scratched, bleached surface, scattered with coins. Beer bottles glowed, like peat water in a puddle, and the chipped saucer was grey with cigarette ash.

Yves stepped back to allow the soldiers to enter and held out his hand, palm up, towards the table. 'C-cards. P-poker.'

The taller of the two soldiers, his thin face emphasised by shadows from the lamp, leant over the table and looked at each of the seated men in turn. Jacques kept his head down towards his cards, fanned out on his knees. Bob put his cards down in front of him and rubbed his hands on his thighs, his eyes darting from the soldier above him to the other, standing in the doorway. Michael held his breath.

Rob slowly stood and cleared his throat. His voice was unnaturally loud.

'Can we help you? We are playing poker. A few beers. Old friends.' He smiled and then lowered his gaze and sat down again.

One of the soldiers reached out and picked up a coin from the table, looking closely before dropping it with a clink. Willy flinched at the noise but was otherwise immobile. 'English money. You use German marks.' His voice was toneless. He looked around the room. 'Who live here?'

Yves stepped forward. 'Me and Bob run the p-plumbers' yard. We live here.'

'What do you want?' Jacques' question was gentle and clear and accompanied by a thin smile.

'We want… to… *wir suchen…*' He looked around at his silent colleague and raised his chin in a beckoning gesture.

Smaller, with a soft round face and pale blue eyes, the other soldier stepped forward smartly. 'We must search. We are looking for illegal items.' His English was good and the tone emotionless, the accent angular. He looked younger than Yves.

'Why?'

'Can you show us? Please.'

Bob rose quickly and his chair fell backwards. There was sweat on his forehead and the tendons in his neck stood out.

Jacques got slowly to his feet and picked up Bob's chair, smiling and nodding. 'Sit down, Bob.' His hand forced Bob to bend his knees and he sat on the edge of his chair and put his palms on the table. 'Yves. Show them the house… and the yard.' His voice was quiet and he raised his chin, hands folded across his chest and hands tucked tight into his armpits.

Bob's eyes were wide and unblinking.

Yves nodded and the soldiers followed him out of the

room. The light of their large torch flickered as they left the room and their footsteps faded as they descended to the yard. The outside door banged. The men sat still. Michael strained to listen, his heart beating hard in his chest, but the only sound was of Bob's laboured breathing and Rob gently tapping a coin on the table, until a glance from Jacques stilled his hand.

'What could they find? Why search here?' Rob's question got no answer except for head shaking. Time seemed to have stopped.

Running footsteps up the stairs and Yves burst through the door, smiling. 'They've gone. They looked in the sheds downstairs and the workshop.'

'Did they say what they were looking for?' asked Jacques sharply. He caught Bob's eye and shook his head, his lips narrow.

'Just poking around. I don't know.' Yves was standing in the corner, pushing at the floorboards covering the wireless with his toe. 'I mentioned that I was working at Les Landes on the bunkers. The one who spoke English was quite friendly. He said we were very young to be running a business.' Yves picked up his nearly empty beer bottle. 'Well, they've gone…'

'I think someone tipped them off.' Jacques dropped the words like stones, shaking his head. Michael's mouth was very dry. Tipped them off about what? He dared not voice the question. His shoulders were stiff with tension and his legs weak and he was worried that his fear would be obvious in his voice. He kept his head down.

Rob got to his feet and put his hands on his hips. 'About what? We have a wireless… not illegal yet. And they didn't find it, so we don't need to hand it in.' He nodded and smiled. 'All's well…'

Willy, who hadn't moved since the soldiers' arrival, got up and started pulling on his boots. He looked unhappily from Jacques to Bob. 'I need to get home. Rob? You ready? Oh, God, the motorbike. Thank goodness they didn't take it.'

'They stopped and looked at it. I said it was… essential for Rob's work. The younger one said he had one like it at home.'

The bike stuttered, revved and then purred out of the yard as Yves gathered the cards and neatly stacked them. Jacques patted the newssheet in his pocket. 'Don't finish all that whiskey tonight, lads! Come on Mike. Let's get you back to the farm. What are you looking so… worried about, eh?'

APRIL 1941

After morning milking, when the herd had been returned to the field, Michael and Jacques sat in the quiet stillness of the muddy yard for a breather. It was mild for April and a weak sun shone white behind a thin layer of cloud. Jacques had brought out a chair and was scanning yesterday's *Evening Post*. Michael, sitting on the wooden steps which led up to his brother's flat, was hoping that the lull in activity would give him the opportunity to find out more about what Jacques and his friends were planning. He had not been asked to any more of the meetings since November when the plumbers' yard had been searched by German soldiers. He was finding it frustrating. He had done as Jacques had requested, got as close to the fortifications at Noirmont Point as possible, this time without his friends, and sketched what he could of the structures which the occupying Germans, or rather the slave workers they had brought in, were building. The stubby tower covered in scaffolding, which he had observed on his first expedition with Jonny, had grown taller and was a fat, concrete funnel with rows of oblong holes facing out over the sea. What looked like the beginnings of gun emplacements had been started close to the tower. After handing over the drawings, Michael thought he might be included in the plans which he was sure Jacques' group was making. But all he got was a slap on the shoulder and a muttered, 'Thanks. Good work, Mike.'

Jacques snapped the pages of the newspaper and grunted. The *Evening Post* now had a section in German, with a separate front page: *Deutsche Inselzeitung*. He removed the insert and dropped it into the dirt of the yard, catching Michael's eye with a grim smile and grinding it with the heel of his boot before returning to his reading.

Michael had tried asking Jacques if he could be involved in what was being planned on a number of occasions over the last few months, without success. Since Christmas the farm had returned to a type of normality. Everyone was working hard as they prepared the ground for spring planting and cleaned out all the greenhouses. The growing of food was of increasing importance to both the residents of the island and the German soldiers; no imports came from France or Britain. Michael and Amy were back into the routine of school and they often went for days without seeing Jacques, who rarely came for supper at the farmhouse as he used to. Every time he had started a conversation with his brother about meeting the 'card group', as Jacques referred to it, he'd been fobbed off. That's why he had volunteered to help with milking at the weekend.

Jacques seemed engrossed in his reading. Michael cleared his throat with an audible cough. Where could he start? Could he ask about the rifles? Were they still hiding in the shadows of the padlocked outhouse which he could see from his perch on the step? Or, as he'd suspected months ago, had Jacques moved them to the plumbers' yard? And, if he'd moved them, why the padlock on the shed?

He cleared his throat again, louder this time.

Jacques looked up. 'What?'

'What's happening? Can I… come to one of the… poker evenings? I want to… help… do something.'

'Mike. You're still only fifteen. I can't drag you into any danger. Anyway, Dad's asked me to keep you out of it.'

'But I'm sixteen in August and aren't I already involved? Helped you with the rifles… did the drawings.'

'Yes. I know, and you did a good job, but I promised Dad. Tell you what… I'm going over to Willy's now, to try to get him a bit more involved. He could be useful. You can come along, just for the ride.'

'Great… yes. But can I ask you about the rifles…'

Jacques cut him off as he stood up, dropping the newspaper on the chair. 'Stop you there, Mike. Best you don't know.' He stamped heavily on the German section of the paper that lay at his feet, leaving muddy boot marks, and strode off towards the farm truck.

Willy lived with his wife and two young children at St Peter's, close to the airport. Jacques told Michael, as they drove through the lanes, that he worked with his father-in-law in his carpentry business and made a reasonable living, though money had become tight since the Germans arrived. 'Bloody Jerries,' he muttered as they turned into a narrow cul-de-sac.

They pulled up outside a small, pebble-dashed bungalow and knocked on the front door. Willy greeted them with a grin and beckoned them in. Following his brother into the dark hallway, Michael stumbled over a wooden train and caught a glimpse of a small snotty face peering down at him through the upstairs banisters.

'I need to speak to you. I haven't seen you since November, when we… played poker,' said Jacques quietly. Willy grabbed his arm, pulling him through an untidy kitchen and an open back door into a large rear garden, which looked as though it was being dug up for vegetable planting.

'That was too close for me… the search of the plumbers' yard. I can't do it again. What do you want to talk about?' Willy scowled. 'I thought this might be a social call… we could go for a pint. But that's all.'

'Hang on, Will. What's the problem? I'm not here to ask for anything,' said Jacques. '…Just hoped you might want to meet up again. I'm trying to get a group of us…'

'No…' There was a pause, his dark eyes fixed on Jacques. 'I've told you. I don't want to know. And I can't meet with the lads. Look… I've been offered work at the German military headquarters, on Mount Bingham. Missus says I should take it.'

Jacques frowned and allowed a pause to grow before speaking. 'You should take it. Can you refuse, anyway?'

'You know that I'm no collaborator, don't you? But I have a family. And I need the work.'

'I know. Pity… but think about it. Working in the German headquarters might be useful to us.'

'No, Jacques! I can see what you're thinking and the answer is no! I just want to survive this, look after the family. If you know what's good for you, you'd do the same. Just co-operate. Avoid trouble. We'll get through it. You too, Michael. You're far too young for this… resistance thing. And I'm surprised that you're using your little brother, Jacques. It's dangerous…'

'All right, Will. I get the message.' He held out his hand and Willy clasped it and nodded before turning to Michael. Willy's hand was damp.

'No hard feelings, eh? Take care.'

As Michael turned to follow his brother back into the house, he saw the faces of a woman and two children framed in the window of what must have been the sitting room. The light glinting off the glass gave them a ghostly look.

Jacques didn't speak until they were driving past the airport. He slowed down. The perimeter fence had doubled in height since the invasion and now had two layers of wire. Michael could see men in grey-green uniforms digging. 'Look at that… digging trenches at our airport! I can't just do… nothing, like Willy. Do you understand, Mike?'

'Of course I do! I feel the same. That's why I want to join your group. There must be something I can do.'

'I'll think about it, Mike. Stop nagging. It's just… I promised Dad. And it is very dangerous.'

'I know. And I can see why Willy can't do anything. Mum says that family come first… and his children are young. What if…' Michael couldn't find the words.

As they drove slowly down the road parallel to the runway, two small planes, marked with black crosses, took off in quick succession. Michael, turning and looking through the back window of the truck, watched them gain height, their wings tipping as they circled round, heading towards France. The engine revved and the truck sped up as two sentries with rifles over their shoulders started moving towards them.

'I need a drink,' said Jacques, turning sharply into the yard of The Star, opposite St Peter's Parish Church.

A few men sat outside the pub with lunchtime pints. Inside a group of elderly men were playing dominoes on a table in front of a fire flickering fitfully. The low windows, set deep into the thick granite walls, let in a grey light. The smell was of stale beer and damp. Two working men in donkey jackets stood at the bar and in one corner a young couple sat side by side on a high-backed bench. Michael noticed the woman's auburn hair, curling into her neck. The man and woman stared forward at their glasses on the table in front of them, saying nothing.

Jacques ordered a half-pint of Mary Ann ale and a lemonade. Leaning on the bar, he scanned the room. Michael had never been to The Star and he wondered if it was somewhere his brother drank with Willy, and maybe Bob. It was out of the Le Bretons' parish, but he didn't think that would stop Jacques.

The quiet of the bar was broken suddenly. The crash of the brass doorknob against the wooden panelling was followed by a raucous laugh. Three Germans strode in, officers by the look of their caps. One wore long boots and jodhpurs. He carried a cane and tapped it on his shining boots as he surveyed the room. With a slight movement of his head, Jacques indicated that he and Michael should move away and they shuffled towards the end of the counter. Michael kept his eyes forward, watching the soldiers in the mirror above the shelf behind the bar, where bottles of spirits used to sit before they were banned. The landlord, maybe used to seeing soldiers, or keen to show that he had complied with the regulations, threw the towel he was using to polish glasses over his shoulder and moved to serve them. They ordered three halves of cider and brought out packets of cigarettes, talking confidently. Michael recognised a few words, but nothing that made sense. The laughing one, who seemed to be the highest ranking, was short, overweight and florid. Sweat glistened on his forehead and he pulled his tunic down over a protruding belly, putting his peaked cap on the bar.

It happened very quickly. The laughing officer, looking around for an ashtray, had pointed at one on the table in front of the young couple and the youngest of the trio of Germans had moved to take it, smiling at the auburn-headed woman as he did so. The seated young man's hand darted out as if to stop him and their hands collided. The young Jerseyman withdrew his hand immediately and sat back heavily on the bench, a scowl on his face. Why did he do it? Perhaps it was just instinct, to protect something, something even as small as an ashtray, from his enemy. The woman sitting next to him drew in an audible breath and gave her friend a startled look, either of fear or contempt, Michael wasn't sure. The officer looked for a second at the man, pursed his lips and turned back to the bar, putting the ashtray down in front of his superior, who bellowed in amusement, throwing his head back.

Michael didn't see the young man move but heard the scrape of wood on stone, and then the flash of a blade and a lifted arm. The younger German lunged forward. There was a gasp and the Jerseyman collapsed to the floor, clutching his abdomen. The red-haired woman leapt to her feet but made no sound. After a moment's stillness, the barman lifted the wooden flap in the counter, knelt beside the groaning man and held the pot-cloth to his reddening shirt front. The three Germans stood looking down at the injured man at their feet. The fat officer had a smirk on his face.

Jacques slid off his stool, grabbed Michael's arm and pulled him down a dark, damp-smelling passage behind the bar. He pushed open a door into a walled yard stacked with beer barrels and gave Michael a shove before turning back to shut the door. The woman had followed them. She moved silently into the yard and pulled the door behind her, raising her chin as she came close to Jacques.

Jacques put his hands into his pockets; Michael could see a flush on the back of his neck. 'Will your… friend be all right?' he asked the woman quietly.

'Not a friend,' she answered firmly. 'He said he was going to supply me with some painting materials, but it turns out he's sold his stock to the Jerries. For more money than I could have paid him.' Her lip curled and she put her hands on her hips and shrugged. 'He'll be fine. Just a flesh wound. They're patching him up. I didn't want to get involved.'

She was wearing a pair of wide, dark trousers and a short-sleeved white blouse under an open trench coat. Michael noticed the slimness of her waist, pulled into a wide belt, before he realised he was staring. But she seemed not to notice him. She was watching Jacques with a little smile on her face and her head tilted to one side. Her eyes were dark; her skin very pale.

'No… better to keep away. No need to get involved in that sort of… incident. I'm doing the same, taking the back way out… do you want a lift anywhere?' asked Jacques.

'I have my bicycle, thank you.'

She made a move towards a wooden gate between two towers of beer crates. Jacques stepped towards her. 'Um… you said you were looking for painting supplies. Are you a painter… silly question really?'

Her nose wrinkled as she laughed and turned her eyes on Michael. Now he could see that her eyes were a shining hazel colour. She nodded, turning back to Jacques. Auburn curls bounced on her forehead. 'He's funny, your friend,' she said, directing the words, but not her face, to Michael.

'Brother…. he's my brother,' Michael muttered.

'Ah. Big brother taking little brother out for his first pint?' She smiled again, showing white teeth against her wide, red-lipsticked mouth.

'Not really… we…' Michael stopped, his eyes moving from Jacques to the woman. They were the same height, immobile, looking into each other's eyes.

The woman was the first to move. She pulled her coat closer to her body, folded her arms. 'A painter, yes. Well, it's not easy at the moment. I used to paint landscapes to sell to tourists. I still do, but they're gathering dust now. I'm trying to make a living helping my brother in his decorating business. We're struggling to get the paint… and the customers. And we won't work for the Germans; we agreed about that.'

'Must be tough…' said Jacques.

'We're coping, just about. It will be more difficult when the supplies finally run out. That's why I was meeting John Hill. Dead end, though.'

'Why won't you work for the Germans?'

The woman tutted. 'I am no collaborator. Might be the only thing I can do, refuse. Would you work for them… big brother?' It was the second time that day Michael had heard the word, 'collaborator'. Her eyes had angry fire in them, a challenge. Willy's eyes had seemed to surrender or ask for understanding when he had used the word. The woman was more… defiant.

'No,' said Jacques, taking his hands out of his pockets. 'But I don't… need to. I'm lucky. Running the dairy yard on our family farm. So far, they've left us alone.' A smile had transformed Jacques' face. Michael had rarely seen that recently. He looked handsome. 'But my brother, who's a plumber, has been doing some work for them.'

'How can he do that… hobnob with them? Help them, eh?' The indignation was bright in her voice. And the accent of a local, Michael guessed, this west side of the island, St Ouen's maybe. His grandfather had been talking to him about the different accents recently.

Jacques pushed at a lock of hair which had fallen over his forehead. 'I thought that too, until he told me what he and his mate do when they're working for them.'

'What do you mean?' she asked.

'They work very slowly, fit the wrong pipes and sometimes deliberately punch holes in ones they're fitting. I suppose you'd call it sabotage. They're brave, I think.' He paused. 'I probably shouldn't have told you that.'

A smile lit up her face. 'No, I'm glad you did. Good for him. I suppose there's more than one way to skin a cat!' They both laughed.

His brother held out a hand to the woman. 'My name's Jacques Le Breton and this is Michael. I don't suppose I could buy you a drink?'

She dropped his hand and the laugh came again. 'Maybe. But certainly not here and not now. I need to get back to work. I have to pay my way. I live in St Mary's. Rue du Rondin, right at the end, where it meets the road to Crabbe. Hazel Cottage. Avec parents. My brother and I are using an outhouse for the business.'

Michael couldn't suppress a breathy laugh. Not quite right with his accent guessing, but not far off.

'What's so funny, little brother Michael?' Her voice had an edge to it and a line appeared between her eyes.

'Sorry. I just thought, by your accent, that you might be from St Ouen's… but the way you said 'avec'… our granny was born in St Mary and she says it like you.' She was looking at him with a smile. 'Our farm is in Grouville…' His voice trailed away as he met Jacques' frown. He looked down at his feet.

There was a pause. She grinned. 'St Mary's. Yes. I am from St Mary's.' She turned. 'Oh, and my name's Lilian… Lily… Nichol.'

She turned away and strode through the open gate towards a bicycle leaning against the wall. Jacques raised his hand but she didn't acknowledge him as she buckled her coat around her waist and rode off.

'Lily…' Jacques was still smiling to himself, ignoring Michael, as he walked briskly towards the farm truck.

She was very attractive; Jacques obviously thought so. Michael hadn't seen him looking so… soft… so happy, for a long time. But what about Meg? Michael felt protective; he really liked Meg. She never talked down to him and they had their love of reading, and history, in common. He had thought, without voicing it to anyone, that Meg and Jacques might get married.

He jumped into the truck as Jacques revved the engine enthusiastically.

'How's Meg?' Michael asked without looking at his brother.

Out of the corner of his eye he saw his brother's head flick round to look at him. Then, with a scream of gears, Jacques pulled away from the pub.

MAY 1941

Michael was angry with Jacques, upset with himself and frustrated. He lay on his bed, his science homework waiting for him in his school bag, which he'd dumped on the window seat. His body was heavy and he was struggling to find the energy to do anything. Even his poetry books were gathering dust on the shelf. The signs were clear, he was getting melancholic again and he knew what to do; he must push himself, keep busy, work hard on the farm. He needed purpose. He'd thought he'd found purpose in Jacques' ideas, in defying the Germans, in trying to gather information that might be useful for the British when, or rather if, they attempted to liberate the island. But no. And now he was struggling again.

Since the incident in The Star and his foolish question about Meg, his brother had been distant and cold. He wasn't invited to any more card games and when he suggested that he could try to sketch some more of the fortifications, he had been told brusquely that his services were no longer required. He was sure that Jacques and the other men were planning something and wondered if Lily was involved too. One evening a couple of weeks ago, Michael had decided to confront Jacques and plead with him. He was desperate to do something useful. Jacques rarely came to the farmhouse for supper now and there seemed to be no opportunity to talk to him. Saturday evening was warm for late March and he'd walked up to the milking yard after supper. Jacques was running down the steps from his flat as Michael crossed the yard.

'Jacques. Can I talk to you?'

'Not now… I'm going out. Another time, Mike.'

Michael followed him to the farm truck, noting Jacques' smart slacks, clean shirt and his best jacket. His hair had been slicked back and there was a smell of soap as he turned and faced Michael, his hand on the open door.

'Can I come?'

Jacques' laugh had echoed around the yard. 'No. You can't. Don't be ridiculous, little brother.'

Little brother! That's what Lily had called him. He must be meeting her.

That was weeks ago and he had still not found the time or place to talk to Jacques.

Michael swung his legs to the floor and forced himself to the window. It was early evening and quiet. In the kitchen garden under his window, he could see the fair head of his mother bobbing up and down as she dug a trench for beetroot or summer cauliflower; he wasn't sure which. He could go and help her… but her questions, well-meaning as they were, wouldn't help.

He turned back to his room and sighed. Amy. She'd cheer him up. Maybe he should suggest a bike ride before supper. It could be the opportunity to talk to her about the rifles.

He knocked on her door as he'd taken to doing after walking in on her dressing one morning. She'd been very embarrassed. No answer. He was sure she'd come up to do homework. But he had fallen asleep… so where was she? In the greenhouses chatting with Jude, maybe. He ran down the stairs, found his old plimsolls by the back door and jogged up the path towards the greenhouses. The girls had sown tomato seeds in March and the green shoots were already appearing.

'Amy?' No reply.

Jude was walking down the path towards him, a basket on her arm.

'Hey, Mike! Bit late to help today!'

'Looking for Amy…'

'Ah… saw her earlier. On her bike. Looked like she was heading down to Le Hocq.'

'Really?' He couldn't think why she'd do that. It was still too early for swimming.

'Goodnight, Mike. I'm off now. Remind your mother that I'll be late tomorrow… helping my old gran move into ours.'

'Yes, of course. Is she not well?'

'She's fine. Tough old stick. She's been evicted from her cottage. Germans want it for some of the officers. She's livid… so I asked her to come to us. We'll cope. She's good company, gets on well with Rob too.'

Jude smiled at him, touched his shoulder as she passed him and walked briskly down the path. Nothing seemed to upset her. Michael wondered why he couldn't be more like that. She accepted things that couldn't be changed and was happier for it.

He turned and followed her down towards the yard, watching her as she waved to his mother, mounted her bike and rode down the lane.

He didn't want to go back to his room, or answer his mother's questions about his homework, so he went into the barn and fed Dolly. She wasn't much good for conversation, copying his words, 'There you are, Dolly,' as he tipped seeds from the tin into her bowl. But at least she made him smile.

A bike ride, fresh air and exercise, always did him some good, or so his mother said. He shut the squawking parrot in the barn and rode down towards the coast with the idea of going for a walk at Green Island. The tide should be out far enough for him get onto the rocks.

The downhill ride from the farm towards Le Hocq lifted his spirits. He allowed himself to go faster than was safe and the adrenalin gave him a rush of energy. They'd been studying hormones in Biology and he knew that both exercise and fear produced adrenalin to prepare the body for danger. It made him feel stronger, more alive somehow.

At the bottom of Le Hocq Lane, he braked hard as a procession of German vehicles, commandeered cars and imported jeeps, followed by two motorcycles, drove slowly towards St Helier. After watching them disappear around the corner and take a right turn up Ponterson Lane towards the inner road, he crossed the road towards the scrubby common above the beach.

It was very quiet. The low tide had exposed the rocks and fishing boats leant at different angles on the wet half-moon of sand below the bulk of King's Rock. There was no sentry in front of the tower. That was unusual; since August of last year there had always been at least one German soldier stationed at the tower. Apart from the barbed wire fence, he might be looking at the bay as it had been before the Germans arrived. And there was a gap in the fence, one section had been pulled back, as if someone had gone down onto the beach. He stood on the low wall and scanned the bay. Maybe the sentry had gone onto the beach for something. He could see no one; only the birds, geese in a gaggle beyond the boats, calling and paddling in the pools, and oystercatchers, circling over rocks, riding the warm spring thermals.

King's Rock had been a favourite for climbing in the summers before the occupation. He and Amy would race to the top, grazing hands and legs in their determination to win. Last summer, when they had a very warm spell in June, he'd climbed it with Laura, when the tide was out, just like this. They'd sat on the top, looked out to where the sea glinted before meeting the pale blue of the sky and talked about their concern for the future, the war in France. Weeks later her family evacuated to the mainland and he had not heard from her since. He missed her.

The exhilaration of the cycle ride dissipated into the heavy feeling of sadness that he was trying hard to shake off and he took a deep breath. Why not take the opportunity to climb King's Rock again? After another scan of the empty beach and the common, he jumped onto the shingle, his feet almost disappearing into the pebbles and began to wade through them towards the flatter, sandy area in front of the tower. As he got closer to the boulders, the enormous rocks which were tumbled under the high wall, he caught a glimpse of red, which stood out in the browns and tans of the rocks and sand. He stood still. Two figures were sitting opposite to each other on hip-height boulders. A woman in a coat and red hat, who had her back to Michael, was talking to a German solder, his helmet on his knees exposing a fair head of hair and a young face. The soldier who had raised his rifle at this father in their garden.

People talked disparagingly of 'Jerrybags', women who went out with soldiers. Michael's mother had told him not to use the expression, said that we had no idea of the circumstances. As long as they weren't harming the community. Michael wasn't sure he agreed; Jacques' argument was more convincing. He said that such women were selfish, selling themselves and making things harder for the rest of the Jersey people.

This scene looked perfectly natural. The two were talking, quite seriously; if it hadn't been for the green uniform, you might think that they were friends.

Then Michael caught sight of the woman's profile as she looked out towards the sea. A ripple of heat passed from Michael's face down to his stomach. It was Amy in her familiar red hat. His sister in friendly conversation with a German soldier. His legs felt leaden, yet he wanted to turn and run.

His face cooling in the breeze and the feeling returning to his legs, he turned slowly and walked back towards the common, his head down.

From the common they were not visible and, with a pang, he realised he couldn't leave them alone. And he wanted to hear what they were talking about. He turned and walked briskly to the tower, skirting it on the gently sloping grass until he was on the granite edge of the high wall above the boulders, about twenty feet above where he calculated that Amy and the soldier were sitting. They were still there, still deep in conversation. Amy had taken off her red hat, showing her frizzy fair hair with its plait over her shoulder, not as blonde as the German's, and was holding it on her lap, in a mirror image of the soldier with his helmet. Not even a murmur of their words floated up to him but the movement of their heads and the fact that their faces were turned towards each other indicated that they were still talking. What did they have to talk about? Were they talking English or German? Amy had learned the language quickly he knew, practising it at home on him.

He could get closer if he walked around the other side of the tower, down the slipway and climbed over the boulders towards them. He jogged around the tower, glancing across the road towards the pub, which was quiet. The evening was drawing in and he could just see a gas light flickering in the bar through the front window. It was light enough to pick his way down the slippery granite bricks which made up the slipway used to wheel boats down to the sea. He climbed onto the boulders and using both hands and feet, his head down, he crawled carefully towards where he had seen his sister. He was very cautious, keeping as low as possible; if Amy was still sitting in the same position as she had been, she would be facing him when he got near them. He found a large flat rock and crept onto it on his belly, raising his head slowly to see how close he was. Still quite a way away, though he heard a few words and a man's laugh. He stretched towards the neighbouring boulder. His foot slipped down into a crack and he gasped in pain as his ankle scraped against the rough surface, sending a jolt up his leg. He froze. He waited, listening, before grabbing onto another rock and hauling his foot out of the gap. He crouched uncomfortably, his back against the ridged edge of one of the larger boulders. A few minutes passed. He straightened up, raising his head. They had gone. He could see them walking towards the common. The soldier's helmet was on his head and Amy was pulling her hat down over her ears. As he watched, he saw his sister stumble slightly on the pebbles. The soldier put out his hand under her arm to steady her before dropping it and bowing slightly as she turned to smile at him. They moved out of sight towards the path leading up to the common.

Michael couldn't remember where he'd left his bike. If Amy saw it… he knew he should confront her about what he had seen, warn her… persuade her not to develop the friendship, or whatever it was. But he didn't want her to know that he'd been spying on her. So, she had a secret now… as he did. And they used to tell each other everything.

JUNE 1941

'Your father told me that you are hoping that you'll be out next week! Good news.' Michael's mother put a bunch of roses on Meg's bedside table and removed her jacket in the warmth of the sun-filled room.

'And I've brought you a book. I borrowed it from the library… poetry. I think you'll like it more than I did. It's quite difficult,' said Michael from the foot of the bed. He still couldn't really believe that Meg had been immobile in the plaster of Paris shell for nearly a year.

'Oh, Michael. Thank you! Maybe we'll be able to discuss them together as we used to when I get out of here. Or is your nose too much into those science books of yours to enjoy literature?' She didn't wait for an answer before turning to his mother. 'Those roses smell glorious! I have missed the garden. What a week it's been! I'm quite exhausted! Doctor Renouf told me yesterday that he is going to take off the cast on Friday. I think they want to keep me in for at least a few days after that. I haven't walked properly for twelve months and I can't imagine how weak my legs are going to be.'

'Do they have a physiotherapist here, or will you have to

go elsewhere for help with that?' She pulled the chair close to Meg and reached out to straighten her sheet.

'I don't know. I hadn't really thought about it. I'm sure they'll let me know. They are very kind and I don't like to bother them with too many questions. They've been rather busy as we had a visit from a group of German officers. That's what I wanted to tell you about. It was quite exciting!'

There was quiet for a moment. Michael studied Meg's face. Her eyes were shining and there was a glow in her cheeks. Exciting? Meeting German officers? He could see that his mother was uncomfortable with Meg's reaction; she tucked her hair behind her ears and licked her lips, glancing around the ward. 'Shall I… have a word with the matron while I am here? I think you need to know more about the rest of your recovery.'

Meg smiled and reached out a small white hand for his mother's roughened, tanned one. 'I'll talk to the doctor when he comes around tomorrow. Don't worry about it. I'm sure my father has spoken to him already. I saw them talking in the hallway when he was here on Tuesday.'

'I know it's traditional not to bother the patient with details, but I really think you should be consulted and informed. You are an adult, not a child… just because you're a woman…'

'Hélène!' Meg's musical voice was gentle and calm. 'Please don't get cross with the men. They like to think they are in charge, and I suppose they are. I promise you that I am happy to wait and do as I am told. It has always been my way and look at how things have turned out. I am better and ready to go home. It won't be long before I can go back to work, if my job still exists.'

'Things have changed so much, Meg, as I keep telling you. I think you might be shocked. But I don't know about insurance companies. I'll see what I can find out or set Jacques onto it.'

The colour came again to Meg's cheeks and she turned her head away.

'What is it? What's going on between you two?' She lowered her voice, glanced up at Michael. He pretended interest in the poetry book still in his hand. 'I know he hasn't visited you as much as you would have liked, but he's been busy with work… and he isn't comfortable here. He says he finds it claustrophobic, though I think it's because there are so many women. And he feels helpless… you know what men are like.'

Meg sighed and gripped his mother's hand pursing her lips.

'Things will be different when you are out of here.'

'Hélène… you need to know that the last time Jacques visited, back in February, he told me that he thought we weren't well-suited. I haven't heard from him since, not that he was ever good at letters. I think things are over between us, though he didn't say that directly. We were talking… well, he was talking and I was listening mostly… about what he'd like to do… I assume you know… I think he's planning to 'disrupt' the Germans as much as possible.'

Michael's mother looked at him again and then back to Meg. 'I think it's better that we don't know too much. I worry about him and his friends, but I'm glad they are doing something, at least. Someone has to. I think I'm too much of a coward.'

'I'm not sure they should be doing anything. We'll all be safer and things will be less dangerous if we comply and wait for liberation. It will come.' Meg smiled.

'You might be right about safety, and that sounds very practical, but is it morally right?'

'You sound like a romantic novel. I should know; I've read enough of them in here! I've not seen the worst of it, I realise, but the Germans seem to be very decent and polite.'

Michael knew that Meg was being shielded from what was happening, but 'decent' wasn't a word he would use. Polite, yes. Many people thought they were polite, but that didn't make them decent.

'The officers who came on Monday were very well-mannered… impressive. We'd all been warned to be on our best behaviour.' A tinkling laugh showed her small white teeth. 'As if we could misbehave! Matron had the orderlies pulling out all the bedside tables and sweeping under the beds on Sunday evening. They weren't happy at the extra work. And she inspected all the beds herself.' The excitement had returned to Meg's voice.

'Did they come into the ward? Did they come into your room?' asked Michael.

'They did. Three of them. I heard them in the big room and then they were shown into here by matron. Their uniforms were very smart and their boots polished. They all took off their caps and put them under their arms. The one who spoke to me was tall and tanned and his English was very good. So polite… and good-looking!' Her eyes shone.

Michael felt heat rising to his neck.

'Oh…What did he speak to you about?' asked his mother.

'He asked me why I was here. I was quite nervous, and I'm not sure that I explained things clearly but he listened to me and nodded and said he hoped I would recover very soon. He seemed so decent, so confident.'

Michael's mother opened her mouth. There was a pause. 'Well, you'll have plenty of opportunity to decide about them for yourself, once you are out of here. Things are different. I think you've been lucky… not lucky to be in hospital, but fortunate to be well-looked after and… kept away from things.'

'I read the papers, Hélène. I do know what's happening. It just seems to me that they aren't all bad and we should try to live as peacefully as possible with them. They could have treated us badly.'

'Don't forget that the paper is censored, Meg. And they do treat some people very badly…'

'You are talking about the construction workers, aren't you? Mrs Le Ruez's husband was saying that they are kept in camps… but aren't they criminals? We need protection from them. Hard labour is a better punishment than just locking them up, surely…'

'Let's not talk about this now…' Michael's mother got to her feet. The smile on her face was fixed. 'We're going to meet Paul at the plumbers' yard. He's helping Yves with a few things. Sends his love, of course…'

'I'm so pleased Yves is making a go of the business. It must have been hard. Give him my regards… and to Jacques too. Do you have to go so soon?'

*

The plumbers' yard was tucked away off La Motte Street. The double gates were ajar and Michael and his mother walked into the courtyard where the farm truck was parked. Through large wooden doors, open to the sun, they could see his father and Yves working on shelving constructed from pallets. Yves was up a ladder hammering struts into a crumbling brick wall.

'This wall might be damp, Dad. I hope we're doing the right thing.'

'You just need somewhere to store the pipes and arrange them by size. I don't think a bit of damp is going to harm.

Let's get this one finished and I'll leave you and Bob to organise the rest.'

His father turned as they entered the workshop. 'Ah, there you are! How was Meg?'

'Meg seems very well and is hoping to come out of hospital next week. What a great job you've done here! What is this place?'

Yves backed down the ladder and stood smiling with his hands on his hips.

'It was completely unused. Full of rubbish. Old tools and materials. I've thrown away truck-loads of the stuff. It's perfect for storage of long pipes. And for the soldering irons.'

'Where's Bob?'

'He's out on a job.' He paused. 'Do you want to see what I've done with the flat?'

Michael's father stepped towards them. 'Can you see it another time, Hélène? I need to get back to the farm.'

'Of course.' She took her husband's arm. 'We'd better go,' she said. 'I should get back to the tomatoes… All right, Michael?'

'Let's go Mount Bingham way,' she said to his father as he backed the truck out of the yard. 'We might get some crab from the shack on the old quay.'

'Let's hope the Weighbridge isn't too busy.'

Passing the Royal Square, they turned down Conway Street, under the German flags rippling in the wind on the Town Hall. German uniforms mingled with the shoppers and they were directed by a couple of soldiers to turn right near the Weighbridge, rather than left.

'What's going on?' his father muttered as he followed the sweeping arm of the sentry and crawled down Commercial Street behind another farm truck, tomatoes glowing in stacked baskets in the back. 'I suppose it's another of their marches.'

At the junction with the Esplanade and Castle Street, the truck in front halted. The driver got out and walked towards the seafront, as if to find out what the blockage was. Michael followed his father as he too got out of the truck squeezing between the vehicles in the queue and the wall of the warehouse. More vehicles waited in front of them, stopped by a row of German soldiers facing towards the Esplanade. As they watched, they saw a line of soldiers walking the width of the road, rifles in their hands, coming from the harbour. Behind them was a crowd of people moving slowly, following the soldiers. They were close together and, at first, it was impossible to see them as individuals; they appeared to be a grey and brown mass of rags. As they approached, Michael began to make out faces, pale, lined like leather, mostly looking at their feet. He gasped and moved closer to his father as the procession came alongside them.

Brown eyes, large in a grey face, framed in stringy hair, met his and a hand reached towards him. The head was covered in a black shawl which hung down across thin shoulders. He was sure it was a woman, the only one he could see. A dirty hand clutched a small red carpet-bag. A soldier blocking vehicles from entering the Esplanade pushed the woman back into the mass of moving creatures and she was pushed forward again by a soldier behind her clutching a rifle. She stumbled, dropping her bag. As she groped for it on the ground, she fell. Hauled to her feet by the soldier, she was poked in the back by his rifle and moved forwards, swallowed up in the group.

The only sound was the tap of iron-tipped boots on the asphalt; bystanders were still and no one moved after the last of the prisoners, an old man, leaning on a stick, limped away. The red bag lay in the dust at the side of the road, close to Michael's feet.

'More "foreigns",' muttered a man in a Homberg standing next to them. 'Poor buggers.'

His father shook his head and, grabbing Michael's arm, turned away from the Esplanade. They walked in silence back to the truck. 'They are being treated like animals. But I am glad you didn't see that,' he said to Michael's mother as they got in beside her. 'It's not right. It's not human.'

'There was a woman… did you see?' said Michael, talking across his mother as she sat between them. 'How can they expect her, or that old man, to do manual labour? She was so small…'

'I don't believe it…' muttered his mother.

They waited in silence until the traffic started moving. Turning left onto the Esplanade, Michael looked for the bag. It must have been run over by a vehicle and was gaping open. He caught a glimpse of a shawl or scarf and the corner of a book before his father accelerated away.

Michael leant his head back against the worn leather, pulling away from his mother's warm arm against his own, to lean against the door. Tears swelled under his closed lids. Once again, he could see Meg's flushed cheeks and excited voice. 'Decent' she had called them. No. What they were doing was *in*decent. The islanders were having it easy in comparison to the prisoners. The Germans may be polite and well-mannered, but there was no reason in the world to treat people like that. He had to do something. And he had to talk to Amy. The young German she had become friendly with was one of them and what they were doing was unforgiveable. She needed to know; she must keep away from him.

OCTOBER 1941

Since Michael had confronted Amy about the German sentry, there had been a change in their relationship. With high colour in her cheeks, she had told him that they had only been chatting because he had allowed her onto the beach and she had, out of politeness, asked about his sister, the twin he had told them about in the garden. She was shocked to hear that his sister had been killed, last week, in an air-raid which struck the hospital where she had just begun work as a nurse. Amy related this, a tremor in her voice, without looking at Michael, before rushing off upstairs and slamming her bedroom door. He had stood quite still in the empty kitchen and tried to imagine what the German soldier might be feeling. Losing his sister... he couldn't contemplate it. And being so far away from home. But he was part of an enemy who used foreign workers as slaves...

Amy no longer came into his room during the evening to talk about homework. Michael had tried to apologise, but it was clumsy and she had shaken her head and raised her eyebrows in that maddening way she had when she felt that someone was being stupid or slow to understand. She spent time that summer with Esme who often came to the farm before cycling off with his sister, their baskets piled with swimming kit and a picnic. They no longer invited him to join them and sometimes he felt lonely. But he told himself that they were naïve and he had better things to do. He had persuaded Jacques to let him attend more meetings at the plumbers' yard and listened to their plans to disrupt the Germans. Nothing was in place yet, but there had been talk of setting fire to the enemy's storage depots and stealing supplies. Lily was outspoken at the meetings; Michael watched her as she suggested she might be able to use her cover as a decorator to get access to German-occupied buildings. She was brave and he would be too.

One October evening, after he'd finished his maths homework, he left his room to go up to Jacques' place at the milking yard to ask if he could attend the next meeting. He noticed Amy's room was empty with the door wide open. The house was quiet; his mother and father had walked down to Granny's, saying they'd be back for a late supper.

'Amy,' he called. No reply.

Her room was untidy as usual, the bed unmade and clothes thrown in a heap on the chair by her desk. His eye was drawn to her window seat. She'd been drawing and he could see a bright coloured mess of paint tubes, a large sketchbook, open to a landscape, and a thick red notebook, stuffed with bits of paper, possibly her diary. Curious to see what she'd been painting, but wary of interfering again, he advanced further into the room and called again: 'Amy!'

He'd have liked to see what she'd written in her diary, and what she regarded as keepsakes, those bits of paper poking out. But he would never do that. Had she met the German soldier again? He didn't think so. She knew it was dangerous and cared what others thought about her. No, she was too sensible… and yet she had been secretive. Was she aware of what the Germans were doing, how they were treating the foreign prisoners? He had not spoken of what he'd seen, the group of pathetic men, and the woman, being marched along the Esplanade. His parents hadn't said anything either and he felt sure that Amy didn't know. He disapproved when his parents kept things from them, after all they were sixteen, but he had been unable to find the words to tell her, and there had been so little opportunity. The German soldier must be aware of what was happening. Could he support such inhumane behaviour?

He moved closer to the window. The picture was an unfinished sketch of Le Hocq. She'd included the tower and the wire framing the common. The sea beyond was stormy and the sky heavy with cloud. In the doorway of the tower was a shadowy figure. The drawing was very good. She'd always been talented in art, but he had never seen her work so detailed, the shadows so real. He turned the pages. There was a painting of the harbour at St Catherine's on a summer's day, a colourful scene with boats in the foreground and the expanse of a blue sky behind the breakwater, diminishing as it extended out to the horizon. No evidence of occupation.

Michael knew that Amy had spent some time with Lily at her studio, an excuse, he thought, for Jacques to take her and to see his new beau. But Amy must be learning from her. He could see a new confidence in the landscapes, a sense of perspective, which had not been there before. Behind the St Catherine's picture was a pencil sketch of a young man. He hadn't seen any portraits of Amy's. It was a head and shoulders and the subject was looking directly at the artist. He was young with wide eyes and sharp cheekbones. His hair, probably fair, though difficult to tell with the light pencil shading, was short and pushed off his forehead. With a pang, he realised it was the German soldier. She must be still seeing him.

His hands fumbling, he turned the pages back to the drawing of Le Hocq. His mind was racing. What should he do? As he put the sketchbook back on the window seat, his hand touched a small package, something wrapped in blue tissue paper, which had been hidden underneath it. It had been folded carefully and he took time to open it, heart beating. Should he be doing this? What if it was a present from the German soldier? Of course, it was more likely that it had been given to her by someone else, Esme maybe, for her birthday. But if so, why was it wrapped up and hidden. A small gold charm nestled in the creased paper, an oyster shell with a minute shining pearl in it and a loop to attach it to a charm bracelet. Amy didn't have a charm bracelet.

'Michael?'

He turned to see Amy standing in the doorway and a flush rose to her face. 'What are you doing?' Her voice was shrill. She moved quickly to him and grabbed the charm and tissue paper from his hand. 'How dare you come into my room… and snoop?'

Michael opened his mouth. 'I just saw your pictures…' He indicated the sketchbook. 'They are so good… I couldn't help but see… I'm really sorry.'

Amy's face was pale and she frowned and bit her lip. Her voice was gentler. 'I need to tell you something… I need to tell someone. Promise you won't tell Mum and Dad?'

'You've been meeting that German, haven't you?'

'I can't hide it any more. It's just a friendship, but I feel so guilty. What would Dad say? And I can't bear to think what Jacques would do, if he knew… he's so… angry.' She turned away from him and sat down on her bed. Michael perched on the edge of the window seat and waited.

'After you saw us on the boulders, I didn't see him for weeks. You were right… I tried to avoid him. But then I met him on the lane near the farm. He was going to meet his transport on the inner road, he said, but I think he was looking for me… He talked about Frieda, his sister, again and I was so sorry for him. It made me think… about how the Germans lose people too. You… tend to think that the bombing of Germany is a good thing… but it destroys people.

'When I saw him again, about a week later, he asked if we could go for a walk when his duty was finished. He was… so sad. I couldn't say no. I couldn't see the harm in it. I asked Esme to join us, but at the last minute, her mother needed her for something and we went alone. We just walked in St Catherine's woods. We talked… his English is improving and I understand a bit of German. Between us… we managed.

'He's finding it difficult to be patriotic, I think. He struggled to express himself, but he's not a Nazi. He did say that he believed, at first, in Hitler's… vision. But he's been disillusioned, he says by the violence. Not that he's seen very much, but he was in France for a short while and said that he couldn't believe what had been done to the country and the people. He's devastated by Frieda's death. She loved painting; isn't that an incredible coincidence? She was a nurse, in a hospital. It seems so wrong doesn't it?'

'All war is wrong.'

Amy looked up for the first time since she had started speaking, her eyes bright with tears. 'Yes, yes. That's exactly it…'

'What about that?' Michael nodded at the blue package, clasped tightly in her hand.

'He gave me the oyster charm a few weeks ago. He'd bought it for his sister, before her death. So I feel… sort of… honoured to have been given it. I couldn't refuse, could I? We've walked and talked, that's all, I promise. He loves the island. I've shown him some places he hadn't been to. We cycled up to the north coast… one time I said I was going to Esme's.'

'But he is a German, Amy, the enemy…' Michael said quietly.

'I know, obviously… but… he's also just… like us… His name's Kurt.'

'No, he isn't like us.' Now was the time to tell her. He licked his lips and met her eyes. 'You must know what the Germans are doing. I don't just mean occupying the island… do you know how they treat the "foreigns"?'

'Actually, yes, I do. I'm not as naïve as you think. And we've discussed it!' There was defiance in her voice. 'He was stationed at the German underground hospital that's being built in St Peter's Valley, for a short time. Guard duty only, but he saw things he didn't like. He said the prisoners were treated very badly… says he didn't know before. I said I didn't believe him, that he must have been aware… but in the end… I think he was just ignorant. He'd been told that they were criminals. He didn't even think about the rights and wrongs. He said when he saw them he couldn't believe it. They were marched into the tunnels in the mornings, in rags and without shoes most of them. The guards beat them often and, there were old men, and women too. He found out later that they were kept at a camp near St Ouen. Walter, that's his friend, persuaded him not to make a fuss… because it would only cause trouble and nothing would change. Apparently one of the soldiers who questioned the prisoners' treatment was beaten. Kurt… cried when he told me… I believed him.' Her face was wet with tears and her nose was running. 'What shall I do?' Her face was creased and her eyes desperate for help.

Michael sat down next to Amy and put his arm around her shaking shoulders. He felt her relax against him. 'I don't know… but maybe don't tell anyone else at the moment. I can't tell you to stop seeing him and I don't know if I believe his story about the prisoners… but I… admire you… for being sympathetic. But I worry… people won't understand.'

'I've told Lily. I had to tell someone…'

'But no one else… we'll figure it out. Be careful!'

Michael produced a handkerchief. Amy wiped her eyes and nose and smiled at him. 'So like you to have a hankie in your pocket!'

FEBRUARY 1942

It was one of those unexpectedly bright, sunny February days when Michael cycled out to Gorey to have tea with Meg. After a dull winter, not cold enough or clear enough to be enjoyed, there was a hopeful quality in the low, white sun. January had been grey and breezy with heavy clouds slow-moving across an invisible sky. The optimism expressed by the family during Christmas and at New Year celebrations for a quick end to the occupation had faded into stoicism. Michael occasionally had good days, when he felt useful and content with his family. But most of the time, he couldn't shake the emptiness which had grown since the beginning of the occupation and the disruption to his happy life and it deepened beyond his control when he witnessed the deaths of Mr Bideau and the German soldier. Today, as he cycled at speed, a warm wind rushing in his ears and sun flashing through the newly green branches of the conifers lining the coast road, he felt lighter, ready for spring which was pushing its way of out of hedgerows and trees. Daffodils and early blossom, and the fresh green flags of the season were brightening the island.

In a basket, swinging from his handlebars, he had a bunch of narcissus, their bent necks shaking miniature yellow heads, a batch of his mother's scones in a red biscuit tin and book of poetry he borrowed from Meg before Christmas. He steered off the road onto a track across Grouville Common. Mounds of sand and piles of stripped undergrowth scarred the landscape where the Germans were digging to make concrete for fortifications. Although much of the coastal path was fenced off, where the railway line was being extended towards Gorey, he was able to bump his way across towards the narrow rocky footpath that followed the curving line of the wall all the way round to the harbour. The tide was going out and the sand looked wet and clean, sloping up to the wall where it met a tumble of boulders and pebbles and cones dropped from overhanging trees. He had to concentrate on where his wheels were going as the path was rough and tyres precious, so he didn't see the two German soldiers sitting to his right on the wall with their legs hanging over the beach until he was nearly behind them. He braked quickly, to avoid getting too close to them and skidded in the sand. One of the soldiers was on his feet and facing him as he picked himself up and righted the bicycle.

'Good afternoon,' Michael said, his head down, moving away. 'Sorry…'

'Hello. Are you the twin? Amy's… twin?' The voice was gentle and the soldier's smile friendly. He wasn't wearing the helmet Michael was used to seeing him in at the tower His fair hair stood up from a tanned face, his eyes very blue. It was the face from Amy's sketchbook. Michael felt obliged to stop.

'Oh, yes, I'm Michael. And you are… often on duty at Le Hocq…' He smiled and started to move again. He couldn't mention Amy. Didn't want to discuss her… didn't want to know…

'Walter,' the soldier said, addressing his companion who had stayed sitting but was now facing the path. 'Remember.

I told you about the family I shot at… by mistake. This is a twin. Amy's brother.' There was something about hearing the German saying Amy's name that made him feel… strange, as if something cold was creeping up his neck.

Walter got up and nodded. He was taller, broader and older than the other one, and had large ears, very short dark hair and round glasses. 'Ah, yes. The tobacco was good! It is hard to find now.'

Michael nodded and pushed his bike down the path; the younger soldier was blocking the way. 'Excuse me. I need to get to Gorey. Do you want to see my papers?'

'Oh, no. No need. Pardon me.' The soldier stepped to one side and waved Michael on. 'It was good to see you.'

Michael walked a few paces before he mounted his cycle again; glancing behind him, he could see the two men watching him ride off.

The path became firmer and smoother as it met the public gardens planted between the road and the wall. It had been a tourist attraction before the occupation and the team of volunteers from the village had kept up the tradition. It was too early for the dahlias and geraniums which brightened it in the summer months but it had been dug over and a few groups of daffodils were gathered under the trees and larger shrubs. Michael sped up, manoeuvred around a group of elderly men and passed a lone German soldier sitting on a bench and smoking, his legs outstretched and his eyes closed to the warmth of the sun.

Above the harbour towered Mount Orgueil Castle, its medieval ramparts and tall walls, solid in the spring sunshine. From the flagpole on the highest tower fluttered the red and black of the German flag with the black swastika in the centre. Below, lining the quay along the small harbour, was a row of Georgian cottages, dwarfed by the castle above them.

Michael identified Meg's pale yellow house, among the pastel colours of the buildings, three from the end nearest the sea; he could see troughs of red tulips on the front window sills.

She answered the door promptly, a wide smile on her freckled face, and embraced him warmly.

'Goodness me, how tall you are getting! It's only a few weeks since I saw you, but I swear you have grown. Or maybe it's me! I know I'm rather a dwarf.' She continued chatting cheerfully as he propped his bike against the wall and brought his basket inside. 'Thank you. You know how I love spring flowers. Oh, and what are these?' She opened the offered tin and sniffed, closing her eyes. 'Mmmm! Yum! Has Hélène been able to get real flour?'

'I think she traded some vegetables for some from a neighbour.'

'Come into the kitchen and I'll make us tea. I think I've got some jam that will be good with those, though our butter ration has already gone! Dad has to have his toast in the mornings.'

Michael followed her to the back of the house, where the kitchen opened into a small courtyard. The soaring lower walls of the castle were visible behind, through the open windows, framed in bright floral curtains. The room was feminine; ruffled fabric had been hung to cover shelving under the scrubbed, pine work-surfaces, and there was a row of shining copper pans, lined up, their handles all facing the same way, above a shiny black range.

'Isn't it a lovely day? It always makes everything better, doesn't it? Spring sunshine, I mean. Now, how are you? You look very serious…'

'I met a couple of Germans on the front. One of them was the one who Amy knows. The one I told you about. I don't know if she still sees him but it's unsettled me.'

'There are quite a lot of soldiers around Gorey billeted in the guest houses. They even wanted to use Aunt Yvonne's next door, but she said it would be impractical as she's taken in some elderly couples.'

'It must be difficult for you.'

'No. It's fine. I find them well-mannered, on the whole. I've even lent one of them some books. He was so interested in Mont Orgueil. I found him one day just staring up at it and trying to translate a reference book that he'd found in the library. It was a really old book; I found some more accessible ones in Aunt Yvonne's collection that she keeps for tourists. We had a chat. I found him quite cultured and very serious about history. He has little round glasses, a bit like yours, and looks quite studious, older than most of them.'

'Oh, that sounds like the man who was with Amy's… friend.'

'It probably was Walter. I've seen him with a younger friend, Kurt, he's called. I think they are in the Old Bank House Hotel.'

'Walter… yes… that's what the other one called him.'

Meg had set a teapot and china cups on the table. She cut two scones in half and scraped a thin layer of strawberry jam on top.

'I need to be careful with this. It's going to run out before the new season.'

'I… I'm surprised that you're… friendly with the Germans. How do people round here react?'

'I wouldn't call it 'friendly', just courteous. I think it makes things easier for everyone. I wouldn't socialise… go to a bar or anything, if that's what you want to know. I know many people would disapprove of even talking to them… Jacques would…' Her face clouded for a moment before she smiled again. 'I think there are a number of Germans who don't want to be here, don't want to be aggressors. Walter talked about his family when I saw him last week. He misses them terribly; he has a small child. I… see them as individuals, just men…'

Michael licked crumbs from his bottom lip. 'But… they are occupying our island and I can't understand the way they are treating the prisoners, the "foreigns"…'

'I know and I agree. Since I got out of hospital I've realised. But… what I cling to is that… well, it's not all of them. I know Walter finds that situation almost intolerable, but they have no choice but to do as they are told. I suspect that if they were encouraged, they might…' She stopped abruptly, biting her lip. 'More tea? Now weren't we going to talk about poetry?'

'What were you going to say?'

'I've said too much already. Now… how did you get on with the Metaphysical poets?'

Michael smoothed the cover of the volume he'd put on the table beside him. 'I found them quite hard, to be honest, and there are some poems which I didn't understand at all.'

Meg nodded and smiled. 'I know they are challenging, but I'm sure you are capable of it. Did you try the ones I suggested?'

'It took me a while to work out the arguments, but I loved 'The Flea'. I could visualise the man and the woman… arguing. He's… persuasive and funny, in using a flea to… try to seduce her, but I liked her reaction – killing the flea!'

'Yes. It's dramatic isn't it?'

'And I love the way Donne changes his tune to win at the end. He uses her action of killing the flea, which she thought would win her the argument, against her to… counteract her fear. He suggests that just as the act of killing the insect was easy and insignificant… irrelevant, not dishonourable, so her 'surrender' to… sleeping with him… will be… harmless.'

Meg blinked and flushed. 'Oh, my goodness. You are good at this! This is so exciting. I've never been able to share my love of poetry with anyone and now…'

'Reading Donne has made me realise how important it is to understand background and culture. I had to look up some history in one of our Encyclopaedia Britannica to find out. Religion is important now, but the rules, particularly surrounding relationships, were so much stricter then, when he was writing, weren't they? And the poor women… they had it worse because they were looked down on for relationships outside marriage. I suppose they still are, but it's not connected with religion. I'm sorry, I…' He addressed the comments to the book of poetry under his hand and felt warmth creep up his face. He'd never discussed anything like this with anyone.

There was a pause. He daren't look at Meg.

'I can't help but think about Tess… do you know the novel?' He continued without waiting for an answer. 'Angel Clare destroys her because of his belief in the need for… purity. She suffers so much and is so faithful. She even forgives him.'

'Michael.' Her voice was very soft and, at the note of emotion in her use of his name, he glanced at her face. 'You are a sensitive and thoughtful young man. Don't apologise. Have you considered how men's judgement of women is relevant in our situation? I'm not sure things have changed so very much since the seventeenth century!'

'No. What do you mean?'

'People condemn women who go out with Germans, call them 'Jerrybags'. I'm sure some of them are… loose in their morals, but are their actions so very bad?'

'Well, yes… they are the enemy. Jacques thinks we should make things uncomfortable for the Germans, not pleasant.'

'Jacques... well! I don't think he's wrong and his heart is in the right place. I would... trust him with my life, but can we really judge, when we don't know? What if one of these women had a family that was struggling? Going out with a German might mean that they are better fed. What if they just want a bit of fun or friendship? Is that so bad? What if the women are working against them in secret, but pretending to be friendly or to go out with them?'

Michael's mouth opened and closed. Quiet settled in the kitchen and a butterfly flickered against the window. 'It's hard... to know what to do and what to think... isn't it?'

'But people will tell you what to think and what to do. No one can tell you what to... feel. I think you should trust your instincts, keep an open mind. Think about individuals, not types. They aren't just the enemy; they are a collection of men, mostly young, mostly scared. I try to see them like that... to look below the uniform.... oh, that didn't come out right, at all.' Meg's giggle made Michael smile.

Michael felt into his pocket and pulled out the Hold Fast button, putting it on the table in front of him. 'I found this... look, it says, "Hold Fast"...'

Meg picked up the button and held it close to her eyes. 'Oh, yes. "Hold fast... to that which is good." What's the next line?'

'"Render to no one evil for evil..." I think.'

'"Strengthen the faint hearted... support the weak... help the afflicted",' Meg went on.

'"Honour all men",' Michael said.

'"Honour all people",' said Meg with a smile. 'Let's not forget the women!'

'It's not easy though, is it? To "honour" the enemy? How do you do that?'

'I don't have all the answers, Michael. But I do know that we must "hold fast" to the good that we see. Help people in need. And there are plenty of people in need. We can all do our bit to help.'

'Are you thinking of the "foreigns"?'

'I wish you wouldn't call them that. They are men, and women, who are being brutalised…' She stopped abruptly. 'Anyway… back to the Metaphysicals. Did you know it was John Donne who wrote, "No man is an island."'

'Really? I didn't realise that.'

'I think he was writing about connections and how we are all part of the same world. "Any man's death diminishes me because I am involved in mankind". I've always remembered that. It's so relevant now, and not because we are an island, but because there is so much death, so much cruelty, which is affecting us all, diminishing us…'

The small round face opposite him was frowning, looking down at her hands on the tablecloth.

A sharp double tap at the courtyard door made him jump. A dark shape through the clouded glass. Meg got up quickly, looking slightly flustered.

'It'll be work. We are so busy at the moment. I'm expecting some papers.'

She stepped out into the yard and pulled the door closed behind her. Michael could hear a murmured conversation. He flicked through the book in front of him and tried not to listen. He re-read 'To His Coy Mistress.' It wasn't one recommended by Meg, but his eye had been arrested by the title after thinking about the seduction scene of 'The Flea'. He'd like to talk to her about it but was worried that she'll think him too interested in relationships between men and women. His face heated again at the thought. It was more than that. He'd enjoyed the rhythms and rhymes which he felt helped create the sense of time passing and the need to grab things while you can. The famous line *Time's winged chariot* had stood out and made him think about how time was passing. How easy it was to lose things… before you appreciated them. Mr Bideau, the rifle under his chin, and the drifting of the drowned German towards the seabed moved through his head again, like clips from a film. Were people just waiting for liberation? Should we take control and not just allow things to happen? And what does that mean? Was Jacques' way of action and resistance the way to go? Or was Meg's more passive way safer, better? And was she passive? He was beginning to suspect that she wasn't.

Meg returned, tucking an envelope under a vase on the sideboard and dangling a set of keys from her finger.

'It was Jim… from work. I'm going up north to the Le Marquand farm first thing tomorrow. He's brought the company car. I'm being trusted with it. Fancy that… a woman too!' Her laugh tinkled around the room again and her voice seemed unnaturally loud as she shook her curls and smoothed her dress. 'Now, where were we? What shall we discuss next? Or have you had enough of the Metaphysicals for one day? What about looking at some of the Romantics? Have you had the chance to read "The Ancient Mariner"? What a story!'

Michael felt a change in the atmosphere. He wondered if the visitor had really been someone from work. Why didn't she invite him in? She'd been different before the visitor, more serious, talking to him as an adult. Now he felt he was back in a lesson. She was the one in charge, the teacher. His own sense of who he was, or could be, which had bloomed when he was talking about Donne, when he had found the courage to voice some of the issues he'd been mulling over for months, was shrivelling and fading, bending in breeze which had blown in with the visitor. He had hoped that his black mood was lifting. It was still there. He needed clarity, answers, but who do you listen to? Who do you trust?

'Michael?' He looked up into Meg's frowning face. 'What's wrong?'

'Nothing... I'm fine. Just thinking... yes... "The Ancient Mariner". What was he thinking when he killed that bird?' He smiled as he looked for the poem in the index. 'Ah, here it is. What do you think it's about? Is it a warning?'

Meg sat back and took a sip of tea. 'Oh, that's cold... shall I make a fresh pot? That'll give me time to think of a good answer to your difficult question!'

He watched her deft movements as she measured tea into the pot and took the kettle from the range using both hands and a thick red square which usually hung on the oven handle to protect her from the heat.

'It's a warning, yes,' she said, her back still towards him. 'A warning against interference with nature but it also suggests that thoughtless decisions and selfish actions can have far-reaching consequences.'

Her face was serious as she put the pot down on the raffia mat, scorched and flattened from use. 'Isn't poetry fantastic? One can always see something in it relevant to one's own situation.' She smiled and sat down. 'Don't you think, Michael?'

'The wedding... keeps being mentioned. It goes on regardless. Could that suggest that the poet thinks that people don't heed warnings and continue to enjoy life regardless of the dangers?'

'Well. I hope he wasn't suggesting that we should all be miserable and expect the worst! It's complex, and maybe this isn't the day to pull it apart, but I think it has many themes; it's about blame and guilt and learning from mistakes. And that's worth thinking about, isn't it?'

Michael examined her face; she was frowning again and her eyes were narrowed and unfocused. 'No one has the answer, either to the meaning of the poem, or life itself and certainly not to our situation… but I do believe that we have to be careful about blaming and making assumptions.' There was a pause. The ticking of a clock was loud in the warm room. 'For what it's worth, I think the most important thing is humanity… I mean treating everyone with dignity and consideration… and I think that standing by, if you know of cruelty, and doing nothing, is as bad as being cruel. Honour all people. Maybe that's the most important thing.'

Meg picked up the 'Hold Fast' button and pushed it into Michael's hand. The clock struck, a gentle but insistent pinging. Five o'clock. Outside, the courtyard had lost the stripe of sun which had warmed the back wall and drawn his eye upward to the castle walls.

'Goodness me! Look at the time. I don't suppose you have a light on that bike, do you? You'd better go. But let's do this again. I enjoy it so much. I hope you aren't doing it to be polite, are you?'

'No, of course not. You are the only one I can talk to about books… and poems, since… Laura…'

'Ah, yes… the mysterious Laura! I was hoping you'd tell me more about her, but it will have to wait. Do you want something else to read? Shall we go for something a bit lighter, this time?'

She was out of the door before Michael could respond. He picked up the cups and teapot and took them over to the sink, leaning his hands on the cool white of the porcelain, craning his neck to see if he could see the top of the castle wall; it curved slightly away from him and the effect was of a bulging power sticking its self-satisfied belly over the small house.

'Oh, you needn't have done that! Dad likes to do the washing up. One of his jobs.' Meg was back with an armful of books. 'I couldn't decide, so I thought I'd bring them all: *Rebecca*, I love… not light reading, and sort of gothic, but fascinating. *Of Mice and Men* you may have read… another sad but sort of uplifting tale about… love and suffering. Yes, I know, not light either. Why are all the best books sad? And I've brought two more American novels… I'm quite into them… by F. Scott Fitzgerald.'

She dumped the books on the table and opened her arms. 'A hug, I think!'

Michael felt her arms around his neck and he gently folded his around her waist. Her head touched his chest and she felt small, smelt of lavender.

'Meg… I want to do something… show some sort of resistance…'

She cut him off. 'Resistance is dangerous. I know that Jacques is involved, but you are very young. Maybe you could…'

'What? Tell me…'

'I'll think about it.' She smiled as she looked into his face, her hands lightly touching his cheeks. 'Off you go. When will I see you again?'

'Could you come to the farm? I know Mum would love to see you too. She was a bit jealous of me coming today. She's rather busy though. She wanted to finish preparing the kitchen garden today for planting.'

'Well… it is a little uncomfortable for me… because of Jacques…'

'I… why did you…?'

'Not now, Michael…' her voice was sharper and he knew not to pursue it.

His return cycle ride was quiet in the growing gloom.

There were no soldiers or old men along the coast path and a cold wind rushed in the trees, sounding like the sea which was far out and grey in the distance. Spring, which had lifted its head for a few hours, seemed to have retreated.

AUGUST 1942

Michael jerked upright, his heart pounding. In the silence of his bedroom, he saw a faint light around the blackout curtain and guessed that it was around five o'clock. He waited, lying down and drawing the sheet up to his chin, sweat drying on his forehead, his pulse slowing. What had woken him? The remnants of a dark dream lingered, but he couldn't remember any details. He turned on his back, took a deep breath through his mouth, tried to relax. Something caught on the back of his throat, something acrid. Smoke? Surely not? He slipped out of bed, welcoming the cool of the morning air on his damp face, and crossed the room barefoot, opening his door to the dark landing.

A dark shape rose from its customary position outside his parents' room and moved to his side. A wet nose touched his hand. 'Shh. Let's not wake anyone yet, Jenny. We'll check outside.'

The dog followed him down the stairs, her claws clicking on the wooden steps. In the kitchen, Michael drew back the curtains and a pale light showed the breakfast plates set on the table, the pots on the draining board covered in a bright yellow tea towel. He opened the back door. There was no sign of anything on the farm on fire. No sign of smoke. He sniffed and walked into the vegetable garden where runner beans reached over the top of their frames and hung their long pods among the clustered leaves. The smell was slightly stronger here, so it must be coming from the west, but there was still nothing to see. No need to wake anyone.

He wondered if Jacques and his group were involved in something, something he hadn't told Michael about. German stores had been sabotaged in the last few months, but he'd denied any involvement. Said that he was working too hard on the farms to plan anything like that. And they all were. The whole family was harvesting the cereal crops which the Germans had demanded that they plant in the spring. The authorities had recently published one of their formal declarations: that all cereal crops must be in, and registered, before September 5th. They were trying to meet that deadline, both on their farm and on the Bideau farm next door. Paul didn't think it possible, but they were using all the help they could beg and everyone was working long days.

There was a fuss last week when most of an oat crop in St Lawrence was stolen from a barn. Rumours abounded, as always, but the general consensus was that it was the 'résistants', trying to thwart the Germans. Was Jacques involved in that? Michael had talked to his mother about it. She said that maybe it was better that they didn't know. She admired those who risked German wrath to display their opposition and yet, she'd said, her job was to protect her family. She would not get involved. V signs on the road were popular and news was passed on using illegal wirelesses or homemade crystal sets. She'd heard that some postmen looked carefully at letters delivered to the Germans and discreetly removed anything they thought might be the work of those who ingratiated themselves with the enemy by naming anyone who didn't abide by the orders. Betrayal was worse than defiance, Michael thought. Some people had betrayed neighbours for little more than jealousy or long-held hatred, apparently. He found such attitudes difficult to understand. People were far more complex than he had ever imagined. He shivered, his feet wet with dew, and turned back into the house.

Last night's *Evening Post* lay on the table, open on a report of the inquest into the death of Denis Audrain, who had drowned in May when he and two friends had tried to escape from the island. The boy's face stared back at him; the photo looked as though it has been taken at a wedding or other family occasion. He was smiling, his hair neatly slicked back. The shoulders of a smart suit and tie were visible. The other two boys had been sent away, to France or Germany. Michael sighed and closed the paper. They were his age. Were they brave, or foolish?

He filled the kettle, lit the range and was spooning tea into the pot when his mother appeared silently in the doorway.

'Michael,' she said, a smile brightening her sleepy looking face. 'You're up early.'

'I think it was that smell. Can you smell smoke?'

She wrinkled her nose and sniffed noisily. 'Oh, yes… have you looked outside?' She moved towards the door, reaching down for her shoes.

'It's fine, I think. I've been out and looked. It's coming from the west. No reason to panic.'

She turned back and nodded at him. 'You're a good lad. What would we do without you?'

'Less of the "lad", mother… not only am I seventeen, but I'm now much taller than you!'

'When have you ever called me "mother"?' Hélène laughed as the kettle whistled. 'I'm just glad to see you cheerful. I know you're still finding things… difficult, but I can see that you're not as down as you were.'

'I wish I could be as… composed as you. I can't accept what's happening – the cruelty to the workers… Jude said that she saw another group arrive yesterday. In a terrible state, she said. And the damage the Jerries are doing to the island, the… arrogance, rules and regulations, punishments for trivial things… rationing. And then they put on concerts and plays, football matches! I can't make sense of it.'

'Well… I don't "accept" any of it either. And I don't feel composed. But I do try to keep going, stay calm. We will survive this…'

'This sounds like a serious conversation!' Paul stood in the doorway, dressed for work.

'Good morning. I was going to bring you tea in bed, Paul. You deserve a little spoiling. Michael got up when he smelled smoke… went out to have a look. Did you smell it?'

'Yes. I opened a window. But I think its way over to the west. Thanks, Michael. Where's that tea then?'

They sat at the table and talked of what needed to be done. Paul was going to take as many men as he could over to the Bideau farm and get in as much wheat as possible while the weather held. He'd registered the crops as though Mr Bideau was still running the farm and the authorities still hadn't realised that it was vacant. Paul had hoped to persuade someone to move in, but he'd not found the right person yet. Until then, he was determined to keep it going.

'At least it provides us and our neighbours with more cereals and those pigs are useful. We could have one for Christmas. Maybe trade some of it…'

The back door opened abruptly and Hélène and Paul jumped slightly. Jacques was grinning at them. 'Good morning! I'm glad to see there's tea going?' He took off muddy boots and left them outside the door. A waft of smoke entered the kitchen with him.

'That big house at Les Silleries, the one the Germans took for billeting men, is on fire!'

'Is that what I can smell?' asked Michael.

'I can see it from the milking yard… at least, that's what I think it is! And hope it is!' The grin had not left his face. There was a grey smudge on his forehead and dust or dirt on his trousers.

'Oh Jacques, I hope you haven't…' said Paul.

'Me? Now why would I…?'

His father interrupted. 'Don't be flippant, Jacques. And don't you dare endanger this family. We know that you are involved in things… but you must keep us out of it. And be careful.'

Jacques nodded. 'I'm sorry. You're right, of course. But I can't help being a little pleased when things don't go right for them.' He slurped his tea and got up, yawning. 'Morning milking…' he called as he disappeared into the yard.

'Right… breakfast. I've got some eggs and can throw some tomatoes in, if you're interested.' Hélène put the blackened frying pan on the range. 'I'll get a bit of cleaning and washing done before I join you over at the Bideau place. Will you call Amy, Mike? We'll all be needed today… the pigs will need feeding…'

St Peter's Valley, Jersey

DECEMBER 1942

He leans forward, gathers himself, staggers towards a row of spiky black trees, stumbles across stony ground, invisible under his feet, keeping the damp sack pulled tight around his shoulders. The roofs of a small farmhouse and outbuildings are silhouetted against the greyness, windows dark, unseeing; he crosses a grassy verge and follows a track into a farmyard. Relief shoots warm into his throat when the metal ring handle on the barn turns and he falls into the dusty shadows, retching, spitting porridge-like phlegm onto the concrete floor.

Out of the wind, the quiet rings in his ears and a shuffling, vermin probably, rustles at his feet. His eyes adjust to the gloom and the flowery smell of apples guides him to a row of barrels along one wall. His mouth fills with saliva as he pulls off the lid of the nearest one. His hands grope in the straw and memory flashes: a fairground in the city, a lucky dip. He closes his eyes and, just for a second, he can sense home, but it is so far away that the cloud dissolves. The moment is gone. The apple sits snugly in his palm; his teeth sink into the flesh. Juice dribbles down his chin and he sucks at the sweetness. He's not tasted an apple for so long, not since a silent lad, holding the hand of a woman in boots and a headscarf, threw one at his feet months ago. He'd managed one bite before it was wrenched out of his hand by the tall Spanish prisoner, the one everyone avoids. This apple is sharp and crunchy and no one will take it.

The sharp sound of a dog's bark cuts into the silence. It's outside but not far away. Dogs scare him; one of the guards sometimes brings an Alsatian on a thick leather leash, a black wolf. It curls its wet, pink mouth back over yellow teeth and shakes its glossy coat. Sometimes it catches rats in the huts.

He throws a few apples into the sack, grabs a jacket left on a hay bale and runs. The barking increases as he emerges into the farmyard and the metallic clatter of a chain reverberates around the buildings. As he runs up the path, a voice bellows at him from the house. 'Oi, oi! Hey, you, bâtard. Out of my barn! I'll set the dog on you! Bâtard… foreign muck…' He can't understand what's being said but the tone is clear. He's scared what will happen if the dog is released from the chain, and he doesn't stop running, clutching his sack and the jacket, until the stabbing pain in his side forces him to slow down and he leans on a fence. Deep breaths tear at his chest. Acid stings his throat; he swallows it down and waits until his breathing has slowed before moving again.

The roads glitter and bulbous clouds roll off the moon. They won't look for him in the dark. He walks, alert to noises, passes houses and herds of ghostly cows, steaming like fat wraiths, before they dissolve into the gloom. The fields and trees and clusters of small dwellings are familiar, not very different from those of his own village near Orel, though here granite houses have an upper floor and steep shingle roofs, with more living space than the low, whitewashed houses of his home village. There, shallow thatched roofs, green with damp, reach out over small dark windows and narrow doors. That was before most of them were destroyed by the advancing Germans, blown into piles of rubble and wood and twigs. What's left now? Who is left? He shakes his head, dismisses the thoughts which distract him from his mission, to survive, to live.

In a moonlit garden, behind a stone cottage, he finds a row of turnips, the tops of their purple bulbs and limp green leaves lined up behind a hedge. He sits, taking shelter from the wind against the sagging side of a padlocked shed, looks up at the dark windows of the house, nibbles a peppery turnip. The warmth inside is barred to him. Are there families, warm in beds or gathered around a fire, eating bread and soup with chicken and carrots? A memory of his grandmother's stew, steaming and thick with parsnips flashes into his head. He swallows down a hard lump of turnip and turns his head away. He inhabits a different world. He isn't invisible but he can't share their lives. Occasionally, when being marched back to camp, they'd been offered things by people they passed; he'd acquired his trousers from a woman who reached out and pushed the clothes at him. She was wearing knitted red gloves, darned with black wool on the fingertips. Once, he had been given half a loaf of bread. The old man's eyes, sunk deep behind blue-veined lids, had not looked up when he had broken off a chunk for him; he had sucked on it and later vomited it up on the floor of the hut.

Their pity isn't enough.

He buttons up the tweed jacket which sags from his thin frame and, gripping the sack with his upper arm, pushes his hands into the pockets.

He keeps walking; the wet of the grass verges numbs his feet, seeps into the sacking he tied around them yesterday. His anger swells as he thinks of how he's been treated, worse than a cow or a guard dog. Rage gives him the energy to keep walking, to ignore the cold and the pain in his feet and the ache in his stomach.

He's never going back.

He finds the cellar by accident when night thins to cold grey. After climbing steadily up a road overhung with trees, he steps through a gate into a field and the moon reappears above distant water, silvers the wrinkled surface. A narrow track descends, then widens into a farmyard where pieces of machinery crouch and a house, windows blank, stands silent in the darkness. Worried about dogs, he creeps down an alley between the side of the building and a wooden barn and crouches down to make himself small. No dogs. At his feet, a wooden door leans at an angle in a low brick structure. It opens towards him revealing a pitch-black space. Cool air moves below him and gusty, wet wind pushes at his back. He allows himself to drop into the dusty hole and the trapdoor bangs shut behind him. The dense black around him is thick with metallic cling and the gritty lumps shift beneath him as he scrabbles with numb fingers and aching legs, pulls himself onto his knees and gropes for his sack. A coal cellar. He's escaped one grave to lie in another one. A cold hell. But it's dry, and safe – for now, at least. A powdery tickle coats his dry throat as he takes a deep breath and rolls onto his side, his head on the rough sleeve of the jacket, the sack clutched to his chest and his knees under his chin. Closing his eyes makes no difference to his vision. He blinks; his lids fall and a ripple of warmth relaxes his shoulders.

He's not going back.

*

The land was still dark when Michael slipped out of the house, pulling on the old overcoat inherited from his father and a hat knitted by Granny, and climbed up to the high cotil. Bare trees were silhouetted against the luminous, empty blue of the vast sky. Bands of vivid orange and gold stretched thin on the horizon in the east, the colours intensifying as the edge of a fiery sun gaped between cloudy, grey drifts. He watched, sitting on the large knot of the rope swing, legs dangling, as the fields slowly emerged from the night and the browns and greens, blurred by misty dampness, were revealed. The quiet and stillness was broken quite suddenly as a chorus, a crowd of birds, blared their noise in the trees and thick hedgerows in the corner of the field. His father would identify the calls and put names of birds to the musical sounds, but Michael heard the squealing, shrieking and repetitive tick-tocks as a discordant accompaniment to the appearance of the winter sun.

He used his feet to twist the rope round and round until the tautness stopped him. He raised his feet and span back, out of control, causing the fields and trees to blur, until the rope rocked back into position and he looked down the hill at the awakening farm buildings below. Nausea swept over him and he blinked at his feet until stability settled again.

It was one week before Christmas, the third since the Germans came. Jacques was insistent that the islands had been abandoned, sacrificed even, but Michael still believed that the British government would do something soon. His brother Yves, using a hidden wireless for information, kept him informed of the political situation, but news was sparse. They knew that the Battle of El Alamein in North Africa had been a success for the allies and that General Montgomery was considered a national hero. They knew the battle of Stalingrad was continuing and Hitler was refusing to retreat despite enormous losses and impossible conditions for the German army. Occasional rumours about British commando raids in France lifted people's spirits, but no end to the occupation was in sight.

Two incidents closer to home meant that some islanders believed that this would be the last Christmas under German occupation: rumours of raids by commandos on Sark and Guernsey and the bombing of a convoy of German ships by the RAF off Noirmont Point. Islanders were cheered by the sight of a damaged ship limping into the harbour and learnt that two others, and some French barges, had been sunk. Michael saw smiles and furtive thumbs up among the workers on the farm. But the food situation was getting worse. No imports from England; only occasionally from France, and most of that produce was consumed by the German forces. As farmers, they were lucky, they grew most of what they needed, but they still had to plan carefully and work hard. And they all missed sugar, chocolate, tea and proper soap.

What would the new year bring? More of the same? He was tired of the relentless cheerfulness of his parents and Amy. She seemed to spend any free time she had with Esme. Or the German soldier. He wasn't sure what she was doing. He hardly saw Yves now, and when he did, all he talked of was the success of the plumbing firm. Jacques was up to something again. Michael was resentful that he was reluctant to include him. If only he could pin down his own feelings… about defying the Germans, about Amy's friend. What he felt most strongly about was the treatment of the imported slave labour. And what could he do? Meg talked about his ability to feel. She seemed to think he was 'sensitive', whatever that meant. At least he had her to talk to. Maybe when he saw her again, he'd find the courage to talk about this… heaviness.

With the sky lighter and the birds singing loudly, he descended to the farm, avoiding the muddy track and keeping inside the field. At the bottom, a small holly tree, growing under a bare hawthorn caught his attention. Its prickly leaves shone glossy in the morning light and blood-red berries were clustered along its branches. They'd been looking for holly with berries this week, to decorate the front room. How had they missed this tree? He gathered a few branches, snapping the tough stems with difficulty and sucking his fingers when blood beaded on their tips. He could come back for more with gloves. Mum'd be pleased. But his mood did not lift, even when he opened the kitchen door to the smell of bacon and the sight of Amy and his mother sitting at the table.

Michael accompanied Amy to feed the hidden pigs on the Bideau farm after breakfast with the now familiar soupy feeling in his stomach and pressure in his head; over two years since the death of Mr Bideau had not lessened the shock and the images of death had not faded. The romantic teenager, who had moped over Laura's family's evacuation and read sentimental Thomas Hardy poems, had been chased away at the end of the long, hot summer of 1940. What did he feel about it? Who had taken his place? He was unsure about himself and so much of the new life in which he felt trapped.

He had only begun shaving regularly in the last few weeks and in the mirror this morning, as he rubbed soap into a lather on his chin with the brush, he looked closely at his face and felt detached from it. He didn't like it. His eyes were more grey than blue and had shadows of the same colour beneath them. His eyebrows were wiry and darker than his thick straw-coloured hair which would never lie flat. His nose was too long, ears too big and cheekbones prominent, almost skeletal, in his pale face. People said he looked like Amy, but he couldn't see it; she had sea-blue eyes and peachy cheeks. Her lips were fuller than his and she smiled often. And she wasn't short-sighted. The spectacles made him look older, like his father.

He was existing in a kind of numbing fog, unable to see clearly and insensitive to what was happening around him. He had been trying to be more sociable, to get involved with family and friends; occasionally a stab of feeling flashed, but those moments were brief and rare. He should talk to Amy, but she was too happy, too content and he didn't want to be a pessimist.

His father was going to kill one of the Bideau pigs for Christmas, sharing it with neighbours and bartering joints, a bottle of wine from one family, dried fruit from another to make the cake. They were supposed to have registered the pigs, which would mean the Germans taking a percentage, but since the farm technically did not belong to the Le Bretons, his father had argued that they weren't breaking any regulations. The pigs were kept in the barn, behind a wall of haybales in the big pen, fed on scraps and vegetables. The litter, born in July, was now old enough to be slaughtered. Amy disagreed; she'd grown attached to the ugly creatures and felt that this particular family was her own. She'd tried to convince Michael to support her argument that they could have something else for Christmas, as they walked over to the Bideau farm after breakfast. Jenny followed them out of the yard and ran on ahead, sniffing in the hedgerow.

'They're still too young and anyway, I don't like pork. Roast chicken with all the trimmings would be great. Turkey, of course, would be best, but as we can't get those now, one of the chickens, with Grandma Cécile's special stuffing, and apple sauce and roasties. Don't you agree, Mike?'

'You do like pork. Who doesn't? You ate it last time we killed a pig. Mum's crackling is the best. And her gravy. You are too soft because you think those piglets are yours.'

'Pretty Dolly! Pretty Dolly,' murmured the parrot from Michael's shoulder. He reached up to smooth her feathers and felt the bird tremble under his hand. She didn't like the cold weather and was unsettled. He had the strange feeling that she knew how he felt and her behaviour was an echo of his own emotion, but he choked the idea back and told himself not to be so wet. He had been unable to stop her flying out into the yard when he had opened the barn door to collect the buckets of scraps and vegetables cuttings, and she'd followed him into the house, hooking herself onto his shoulder.

They skirted the fields of winter wheat, planted by the Le Bretons and neighbours in September and showing in bright green, feathery rows, and crossed into the lane which dropped down into the valley. The Bideau farm appeared as they began to descend. The farmhouse, empty and quiet, with paint peeling off the window frames and weeds around the door made Michael's stomach tighten and he slowed his pace.

'All right, Mike?'

'I… I… wish that I could shake off this feeling… when I come here. Why can't I get rid of it? It's been so long.'

He could see that Amy was struggling to find something to say. He'd asked the question many times before. He pushed his hands deeper into his pockets and forced his mouth into a smile.

'Sorry. Let's go and see your pigs. Jenny! Where has she gone? Jenny!' The dog bounced out of the field and ran ahead of them down the lane. Amy and Michael followed.

*

His body rises to the surface. Above him a pale frame of light glows around the trapdoor through which he dropped in the dark. He watches it brighten; a thin light reveals the heaped coal and black walls of his refuge. There's a shuffling near his left ear and he sits up, the pain in his buttocks deepening. But he's used to rats; a white flick of a tail disappears into a corner. He wobbles upright and reaches for the trapdoor. Just out of range. He fumbles in the coal, heaping it up under his feet. His fingertips push at the wooden door. The hairy jacket hangs heavy and the pockets bulge with apples, swinging into his abdomen as he reaches up. He drags a pallet from the corner of the cellar and balances it on the top of the coal heap. Now he can push harder, at least at the base of the hatch; it's at an angle in the brick wall. Taking a deep breath and standing on his toes, ignoring the sharp pull of pain in his feet, he launches himself forward and the hatch swings open. The light stabs white in his eyes and he falls back into the crumbling blackness, cold air stinging his nostrils. He pulls the jacket close around him and hunches his shoulders against the chill. He wraps his arms around his folded legs, gazing up into the blue square above him. Last night, in the light of a misshapen moon, he'd tumbled into a cold hell. Above him now, just out of reach, is a glowing blue heaven.

He tries again, building his stack of coal and pallet step, and hauls himself through the hatch, landing in the wet grass on his knees. There's a stiff breeze pulling at his jacket, forcing its chilly fingers into his shirt collar, flapping his trousers against his bare ankles. The freezing brightness pushes at his eyeballs. He flattens himself against the wall of the house, edging towards the farmyard. He can hear a dog barking in the distance but here there is no life, either human or animal. He creeps around to the front of the house. It's large and symmetrical, like so many he's walked by, though this one is grey, with an uneven surface. He peers into a window using his hand to shade the glare of the sun. It's shadowy and still. Armchairs face an empty grate and books are stacked up on shelves. A piano, its white keys grinning at him, stands in one corner. His grandmother had owned a piano; he had wanted to learn to play, but his father had told him there was no money and it was a waste of time. Father had sold it after her death.

He moves around the corner of the house, through a gate in a wall and looks into a kitchen window. There is no evidence of food, but there's a dresser and a door to what could be a scullery or pantry. The door does not budge when he puts his shoulder to it, so he pushes at the window frame. It holds firm. The glass is icy on his forehead.

The kitchen garden is a mess; it hasn't been tended to for a long time. Brambles, their fruits brown, have grown over the weedy soil and raspberry bushes straggle into the hedge. The winter sun lights up a row of scrubby plants, leggy and drunkenly leaning into each other. Sprouts, bright green balls, cling to the stems. The outer leaves are bitter, but the savoury green of the inside is tasty.

The barking of the dog is louder. He stuffs another sprout into his mouth, and moves back towards the farmyard, pushing himself between two prickly bushes so that he is concealed but can peer over the garden wall. The sprout bulges his cheek. The yard is empty but he can see the track winding upwards through brown winter fields. Two figures, one taller than the other, are walking towards the farm and a dog, black head bobbing, is bounding in front of them. He crouches down, hugging his knees, crunching and chewing. It was stupid of him to think that the farm was abandoned. The sound of voices reaches him but they make no sense; he speaks very little English and only a few words of German. He risks another look. Now the barn door is open and he can see the two, their backs towards him, looking at something inside. A grey bird is sitting on the shoulder of a tall young man and the girl, young woman really, has her hand on the head of the dog. They are dressed in winter coats and boots; the girl wears a red hat, a knitted shapeless one, and a thick rope of a plait emerges from the hat at the nape of her neck and lies between her shoulder blades. They disappear into the barn and he looks around. He is trapped. Could he climb the wall at the back of the kitchen garden? He waits, not wanting to move. The green den is sheltered from the wind and only his feet are cold.

The dog is sniffing at the barn door and following a trail around to his coal cellar. It barks, gallops across the yard into the kitchen garden. It's large and shaggy, with a waving tail and it leaps up to his face. Pushing it off, feeling his elbow crunch against its jaw, he runs away towards the back of the garden. It follows, yelping and nipping at his hand, jumping around him. His fingers scrape against the brick, feet scrabble for a hold and pain shoots through his toes. He drops down as his knees crumple, his side tight against the wall. His hand finds a stone among the stinging nettles at his feet and he grasps it, his other arm over his head. He feels the dog's breath on the back of his neck and expects pain; the barking increases.

*

'Jenny! Come on, girl!' Amy called as they crossed the yard and stood at the gate of the kitchen garden. Jenny was standing over what looked like a black heap of old clothes in the nettles under the back wall. She yelped and snarled; her tail down and a ridge of black fur raised on her neck. A movement and a flash of white eyes made Michael gasp. The dog jumped again at the thing and he could see a sleeve protecting a filthy face below a tangle of brown hair. Half a brick was in his hand.

*

The two youngsters are at the gate, their mouths open and their faces alike and pale. He can easily run from them. Or knock them down. The boy is tall, but quite slight. Not a fighter. They are little more than children, a couple of years younger than him, maybe sixteen or seventeen. But he wants food and warmer clothes and boots. And pity. He needs pity.

The last time he spoke was to the old man. His voice is husky. 'Ich… I… please…Ich bin…' He raises his head from the earth.

The boy's face shows fear, the same expression he'd glimpsed on the woman who gave him his trousers. Disgust too. He steps back and turns to the girl. He hears the word 'foreigns'. It's a word the locals use about them. He's heard it muttered when the work party march down the road; he's heard it shouted in anger when he's stolen from houses. The barking dog edges nearer; its teeth are close to his face and there's saliva on a long red tongue.

The girl steps forward and is pulled back by the boy. His brow is furrowed. She shakes him off, calling to the dog. It retreats and she holds its collar when it pulls, rearing up on its back legs, and barks again. Her serious face speaks words which don't hurt, don't instruct, but make no sense.

He could try the wall again. He gets to his knees and glances over his shoulder. The girl grips the top of the gate, red mittens hooked over the wooden slats. She says something that sounds like a question and frowns and bites her lip. He gets to his feet, wiping his face with his jacket sleeve. A loud screech causes him to cower and he throws his arm in front of his face as the grey bird swoops around his head. The girl laughs like the tinkle of a piano and the bird flies to the boy's shoulder, its beady eyes shining and sharp beak open.

*

'Jenny! Jenny! No! Down!' The dog backed off a few paces and the man raised his head and lowered his arm. He whispered something. Michael could hear a ragged breath and see the whiteness of his eyes rimmed with red.

'It's one of the "foreigns". It must be.' Michael had seen a group of the Todt workers a few weeks ago being marched down a road towards a building site, guarded by Germans with rifles. He had watched and pitied and felt helpless. He knew of a family who had helped one elderly man, letting him sleep in an outhouse for two nights, and feeding him before he disappeared again. It was risky; punishments were severe.

'He's scared of the dog. I don't think he'll hurt us.' Amy stepped forward and shook off Michael's retraining arm. 'Jenny! Jenny! Come here.' The dog turned to her call and Amy grabbed her collar as she retreated back to the gate.

'He's got a brick in his hand. And he's desperate, hungry. Be careful!' Michael grabbed at her arm again, speaking quietly.

Amy kept her eyes on the man still hunched against the wall and spoke clearly. 'The dog won't hurt you. He's just protective of us. We can get you some food.'

The man moved to his knees, one hand still on the broken brick, his head flicking around, as if searching for something.

'Are you hungry?' Amy mimed putting something into her mouth.

The man moved again slowly, onto all fours and then to his feet. They were wrapped in muddy sacking, tied with bits of twine.

A rush of air accompanied Dolly's scream. Michael drew in a quick breath, and a laugh escaped Amy as the man ducked and threw both arms over his head. The brick fell out of his hand and he dropped to his knees again.

Dolly circled around the man and floated back to Michael's shoulder, cocking her head on one side and nibbling his ear.

'Come,' Amy said, pulling Jenny out of the kitchen garden and beckoning to the man. He hesitated, looking back towards the wall behind him, then limped towards them, pulling his jacket around his thin frame. His eyes were fixed on Michael and his chin lowered. He stood at the gate, shoulders hunched, the jacket sagging off his shoulders, ragged trousers exposing thin brown ankles, scratched and lumpy. Blood oozed from the rags on his feet.

'Shall I fetch Mum or Dad?' said Amy, moving closer to Michael and speaking in a low voice.

'Yes, yes. We haven't any food here for him. Or shall I go?'

Amy looked down at her wellington boots. 'You'll get there quicker, I think.'

'But I don't think I should leave you with him. What if he panics… I don't think he understands English. We could try a bit of German.'

'Let's get him into the pig pen; it's warmer there and hidden.'

Michael smiled at the man and took a small step towards him. '*Wir hilfe… kommen sie mit uns…*'

The man blinked and nodded. '*Ich bin… hungrig.*' The voice was gravelly. He took a step into the yard and winced, grabbing at the gate.

'Hold on,' said Michael, raising one hand. 'Amy, aren't there some old boots in the barn?'

Dolly flew to the tractor as he ran across to the barn, landing on the steering wheel. When he returned a few minutes later, a battered pair of boots in his hand, the man was sitting on the ground, his back to the wall, his hands over his face. Amy was stoking Jenny's back. Michael put the boots down next to the man's feet and stepped back. 'Try these.'

His head jerked up and he grabbed at the boots, smoothing the hard leather with bony hands. He pulled them on, fumbling. Michael watched, embarrassed at the man's difficulties, wanting to help, but not knowing how.

The man got up and shuffled forward, laces trailing, the boots too large.

'Can I help?' Michael stepped towards him and the man gasped, flinching and stumbling backwards against the garden wall, falling awkwardly. Michael knelt and took his arm. A smell, like rotting potatoes at the bottom of a barrel, and something like manure, was thick in his nose and throat and he gagged and held his breath as he helped him to his feet. The man was taller than him, but the arm under his hand was fragile and the grimy face, now he was closer, looked younger than he had expected. Michael pointed at the laces and got down on his knees to tie them. When he looked up, as he got to his feet, he saw that the man was crying, the tears striping his face through mud and black dust.

'Come on.' Amy's voice was urgent. 'We can get out of the cold in here.' She walked over towards the barn and the man followed, his eyes moving between his heavy boots and Jenny, who was straining at Amy's hand on her collar and growling.

He was reluctant to enter the barn and Michael had to pull aside the bales and show him the tunnel before he stepped out of the wintery sun and into the gloom. He stumbled with caution, glancing around him when Amy pulled the barn doors shut behind them, leaving them in a grey semi-darkness, but followed Michael through the archway of hay and into the pigpen at the back, a high window allowing light to seep down. The fat sow was lying on her side on a pile of hay, her six offspring rooting around the floor. The man sank down onto a bale and stared at the animals, his face creasing into a half-smile and his mouth opening to reveal yellowed teeth.

Amy secured Jenny's collar to a rope attached to a ring in the wall and started emptying the baskets of foraged vegetation and scraps for the animals. Chubby piglets scampered over, snorting and squeaking around her boots. The man's blank, black eyes were fixed on the animals and the scraps and his forehead was creased into dirty lines.

'I'm Michael. This is Amy.'

The man's head jerked up and his mouth opened and closed. He blinked; a breathy, hissing whisper escaped his chapped lips. Michael leaned closer to him and a meaty, stale, sour smell rose as he coughed and cleared his throat.

'Michael,' he repeated putting a hand on his chest. 'Amy.' As he raised his hand to indicate his sister, the man flinched and drew back, his shoulders hunched.

'It's… all right…' Michael looked up and raised his eyebrows at Amy.

The man coughed again and again, a deep racking cough that caused his shoulders to shake as he bent over his knees. He spat out something brown into the straw at his feet.

'I'll go now,' said Michael. 'I'll run. I wish we'd brought the bikes…'

He turned to go, and the man raised a hand and opened his mouth. This time the hissing was louder and the scabby lips parted.

'Konstantin. Konstantin,' he repeated and tapped his chest. 'Konstantin.'

Amy smiled. 'Konstantin? You are Konstantin?'

He nodded; his head drooped, and he sheltered his head with his hands, as if in mourning. Michael felt the beat of a pulse in his head and the prick of tears. Pity.

He licked his cold lips. 'I'd better go'.

He was aware of the man watching him as he left, moving fast and leaving the barn doors ajar. Dolly flew to him, squawking, as he emerged into the sharp light of the morning sun and followed him as he jogged up the road, a sense of purpose lifting his feet.

JANUARY 1943

New Year's day was stormy, with a gusty wind that had seen off the early rain, as Michael and his mother walked over the ploughed field to the Bideau farm. His wellington boots sunk into the turned earth, making the going hard work. He wrapped his duffle coat more closely around him. His mother had her head down against the wind, her hat pulled down over her ears and the basket on her arm swinging against him. He breathed in deeply, feeling alive and hopeful in a way he hadn't for some time. Last night's celebrations had been muted in comparison with those before the occupation. At the turn of the year from 1940 to 41, people had muttered about how the new year would bring an end to the suffocating life they were leading. When 1942 dawned, there was a burst of optimism again, rising like a wave, and the island had felt different: fewer German soldiers and many seemed unhappy; fewer sports events and races, though there had been an increase in foreign workers, building fortifications and underground tunnels. Snow in the middle of January, reduced rations and the drunken behaviour of soldiers in St Helier, among other things, put an end to the good cheer and the wave of optimism broke swiftly, what surfers would call a dumper, causing a murky cloud of sand, leaving a ghostly froth behind. The rest of 1942 seemed like a struggle for survival: food shortages; hard work on the farm; Michael's dark cloud of sadness. Jacques' brooding.

Throughout this year's Christmas and New Year celebrations, Michael felt a new focus, Konstantin, and that had changed everything. Last night's family dinner with just Granny as a guest had had a kind of forced cheerfulness. Grandmère Cecile and Poppa were too anxious about the curfew and regulations to attend and their car had been commandeered. The Le Bretons had played card games as usual, allowing Granny to win. Distracted and strangely nervous, Michael's thoughts often turned to Konstantin, alone at the Bideau farm, wondering if they should have risked bringing him over for the meal. But that would have meant Granny being told the secret and his father had insisted that only the immediate family should know. He felt his mother's anxiety about the situation too; her usual happiness at feeding people had disappeared.

The traditions of New Year's Eve seemed to be a burden, rather than a pleasure. One of the family's precious chickens, killed and plucked by Michael's father, accompanied by roast potatoes and a mound of winter vegetables, had been followed by plum pudding and custard. The plums had been preserved after the glut of August and though only potato flour was available, no one had commented on the relative toughness of the dessert. The remains of the dinner were wrapped under muslin in earthenware dishes currently swinging from his mother's arm and a stone bottle of cider gurgled gently. Not that Konstantin couldn't fend for himself; he seemed more than capable now that he was stronger, but Michael found an unexpected excitement in the prospect of seeing him smile at the food.

It was nearly two weeks since Michael had run into the scullery where his mother was washing sheets and blurted out his news.

He was pleased in a way that Konstantin had come to them. He would be able to make reparation somehow for not being able to help the woman he had seen in the procession along the Esplanade… her pathetic bag… lost to her. It haunted him sometimes at night; the woman's sunken eyes, accusing him.

They'd hidden him at first in the secret pig pen, constructing a sort of hay room out of bales at the back of the barn. Konstantin had kissed his mother's hand when she showed him, then lay down on the rough bed she'd made with an old mattress covered with blankets and fallen asleep almost immediately. Michael had sat down and watched him, moved by the thinness of his legs, stick-like in the filthy trousers, and by the gaunt, shadowed face. His stillness made him anxious and he'd knelt at his side to check his breathing, sitting back on his heels when a sour, animal smell emanated from him.

Konstantin slept and ate, at first vomiting up much of what he devoured and suffering from stomach-ache. The family had learnt to only offer small quantities, despite his ravenous appetite, and to mash food, keeping it bland and nutritious: eggs, potatoes, soup. He turned away from them when eating, as if embarrassed at his manners or his appetite. They'd brought him a bowl of warm water and he'd turned it black, cleaning his face and hands slowly, but shook his head and frowned when Michael's mother mimed taking off his clothes. Underneath his stolen jacket, blackened with coal dust, they could see layers of tatty shirts. His trousers, baggy and exposing his thin ankles, were dusty and worn at the knees. They looked like something a farmer might throw out at the end of a hard winter.

A few days later, they brought the tin bath from the farmhouse to the barn, a bar of coal tar soap taken from Mr Bideau's scullery and a pile of towels. His father had half-filled the bath with buckets of hot water carried across the farmyard from the kitchen range. His mother had shooed Amy out and told Konstantin, speaking slowly and using her hands to indicate what she wanted, that he must bathe. He had not spoken since he'd told Michael and Amy his name. He had nodded and sniffed at the soap, tested the water with his hand. He had shrugged off the jacket and pulled the ragged shirts over his head. On the white rails of his collarbone, hung hairless grey skin over a row of ribs. He had pulled back his shoulders and lifted his chin as they left him alone.

When they returned half an hour later, he was asleep, curled up under layers of towels. The cool water was scummy grey and the remains of his clothes were folded neatly beside the boots Michael had found him. A bony foot, like that of a small dinosaur, poked out over the mattress, its sole criss-crossed with lacerations. Michael's eyes had pricked with tears. How could anyone treat a man like this?

Jacques' reaction had been to question him about what had happened and where he had come from originally; how he was treated, what the Germans were building. He got little response, other than frowns and headshaking and his mother had laid a hand on Jacques' arm and suggested that he should wait. He had nodded and undertaken to get false papers for him. Yves, practical as always, brought clothes from his own wardrobe, which hung on the man's frame like those on a scarecrow.

On Christmas Eve, he had spoken for the first time. They had brought over a jug of tomato soup, bread and apples. He'd just started to eat fruit and seemed to be particularly fond of apples, though he was missing a number of teeth. They talked to him, asking how he was feeling, without expecting a reply. It was a way to fill the silence. Michael hoped it was comforting. His mother told him that it was Christmas Eve and they were going to midnight mass. He had raised his eyebrows and blinked rapidly.

'Christmas. Do you celebrate it? Are you Russian? Orthodox Christian?' she asked.

'Yes.' His voice was gruff and he whispered something Michael could not quite catch.

'Konstantin. That's your name, isn't it?' she asked quietly.

He had nodded and turned his head to Michael. 'Yes. Russian. Yes.' His eyes were very dark, flecked with light, and he found it difficult to look away.

He was sitting on a hay bale spooning tomato soup into his mouth. A dribble of scarlet smeared his chin. 'Thank you,' he said, wiping his mouth with the back of his hand.

Michael had brought him a book, *Christmas is a Time for Giving*, given to him for Christmas, aged nine. Konstantin had smiled and kissed Michael's hand, something they had all tried to stop him doing. He had pored over the book, laughing at the illustrations and pronouncing the words under his breath, when Michael read them to him.

He was quick to pick up the language and they had learned a little about his life in the last few days. He had responded to a question Michael had asked him a few times previously: 'Where is your home?' They had learned that he came from Orel in Western Russia. He had been taken from his village by a troop of soldiers, along with all the other young men, though he had no idea where they had ended up. He was eighteen when he had been taken and he thought that was about three years ago, though he wasn't sure. He had been moved from place to place, doing physical work, showing them by miming digging and using a pickaxe. He had spoken of his father and cried when he mentioned his 'Babushka' who they thought might be his grandmother, but they had not found out much more than that. Michael's mother suggested borrowing a Russian dictionary from the library but his father reminded her of the dangers they faced if anyone found out what they were doing.

Konstantin had been surprised to learn that he was on an island; he had thought he might be in France, had thought that the boat journey, hours in the dark hold of a cargo ship was up a river; a man had died next to him. He had never heard of Jersey or the Channel Islands.

They had moved him into the Bideau house a couple of days ago. His father was worried, as usual, but it seemed to be the right thing to do. Konstantin couldn't stay in the pigpen and the house was empty. Michael had argued that it was better if someone was living there, if the Germans discovered it. His father had countered the plea with the fact that, if they did visit the house, and found him, it wouldn't be good for any of them. They all knew what happened to people who had helped the escapees: imprisonment, deportation. But what could they do? They couldn't turn him away. His father said they should wait until he was less weak and his wounds healed and then they would think about how he could move on.

It was Jacques who had come up with the idea of passing off Konstantin as Mr Bideau. He was far too young and looked much darker and thinner to be the man in Mr Bideau's passport and German ID, which they'd found in a desk in the hallway, but Jacques knew someone, he said, who might be able to help. He'd taken a photo of Konstantin's head and shoulders on a Brownie camera he'd borrowed from someone. The family agreed to accept Konstantin as Mr David Stanley Bideau. Stan was suggested by Amy, very English, close to his own name, and it was perfectly acceptable for him to be known by his second name. He had grinned when they asked him and nodded.

When they arrived at the farm, it was quiet. The kitchen was clean and there was no evidence of Stan's presence. He'd worked hard to clean the few rooms of the house that he lived in, sweeping and tidying, setting traps for the rats which had moved into the kitchen, clearing out the larder. He was meticulous in washing up and putting away food. A pot-cloth was folded over the warm lid of the range.

Michael opened the back door and saw him at the far side of the kitchen garden with his back to him, clearing brambles and weeds, in shirt sleeves and a wide belt pulling in an old pair of Yves' trousers. He watched him for a few minutes, feeling a warm sense of satisfaction in his quick movements, his brown forearms, the way he was gaining strength. There was a little leap in Michael's chest. He was doing something useful and it felt good.

'Stan!' His head jerked up and the shadow on his face passed swiftly into a smile, a lop-sided smile, showing a missing tooth, and healing lips. He looked younger than he did two weeks ago. Michael felt the leap again, and smiled back.

'Hello, Meek.' Michael had tried to teach him to say Michael or Mike, but 'Meek' was the closest he got. 'I am…' he indicated the jumble of dead foliage. '…How do you say it?'

'Gardening?'

'Gardening. Yes.' He seemed to relish the word. 'We have… gardening… too in Russia. Bad plants to kill.'

'Weeds… you get rid of the weeds to plant… vegetables and flowers.'

'I plant to eat and… roses. I like roses.'

He pointed to the back wall and Michael saw that he'd trimmed the rambling rose that climbed it and had tied its leggy branches back to the nails.

'What is colour of rose?'

Michael frowned trying to visualise the kitchen garden when Mr Bideau nurtured it; he remembered beans on a tall wigwam with red flowers dancing on a windy day, and lettuces, rows of tightly curled leaves, and a strawberry patch, covered in netting.

'I don't know. We'll have to wait for it to bloom.' Would he still be here in May or June? Leaning on a spade, squinting in the low sunlight, Stan could easily pass as a Jersey farmer, his dark looks suggesting French ancestry.

'Bloom,' he repeated as if tasting or kissing the word.

Michael's mother was standing behind him. 'I've brought you some food, Stan. Shall I put it in the kitchen?'

Stan turned his head. 'Amy!' His sister had been in bed when they had left, but Michael knew that she'd follow them as soon as she was up. Stan always seemed to have a wider smile for her.

'Hello, Stan! How are you today? Happy New Year! Do you wish each other that in Russia?'

'I am well, thank you. I show you…'

Stan strode over to Amy, took her by the shoulders and he bent to kiss her three times on her bright cheeks.

Amy stepped back from Konstantin, giggling and pulling off her hat, her hair, fuzzy and static in the sun, curled around her face. She pushed her plait back over her shoulder and laughed in Stan's face. Michael felt a cold hand grip his stomach, a flutter in his throat. Was he jealous of the attention?

'Will you eat now, Stan? Or shall I put it in the larder?'

Her voice sounded too loud, shrill, brittle and he knew that she disapproved of Stan's behaviour.

Stan's face was serious and his tone formal as he turned to Michael's mother. He was always very respectful with her. 'Thank you. I finish work first. Weeds…' He turned his back to Amy and indicated his work. He was showing off. Was he flirting? His mother moved closer to Amy, putting an arm around her shoulders. Amy shrugged her off.

'I… just wanted to wish you Happy New Year. But I see you are busy. I could help you with the digging!' Amy's voice was excited, dangerously enthusiastic.

'Let's all help,' said his mother. 'Before it rains again. We could clear the brambles and weeds from the big bed… make a fire.' She took off her coat and rolled up her sleeves, looked up at the low-hanging grey clouds. 'It is threatening, so we'd better get going.'

Michael picked up a rake and handed his mother a spade. They began to drag the weeds and brambles into a pile. Amy laughed as she pushed clumsy hands into the enormous gloves Konstantin offered her and squatted down to gather the debris.

They had built a bonfire and were fanning a reluctant flame when Jacques appeared at the gate. 'Goodness me! Good work going on here! Happy New Year, Stan!'

Stan stepped forward and, before Jacques could move, he was kissed noisily on both cheeks. The third kiss surprised Jacques so much he stumbled and muttered, 'Steady on, old chap…' Amy laughed out loud.

'Appy New Year, Jacques!' Konstantin seemed pleased with himself, laughing, apparently enjoying Jacques' discomfort, before returning to the fire.

The fire smoked and smouldered and the damp weeds curled and crackled. Stan built it up with dry leaves from a sheltered corner of the garden before it took. Through the heat haze, from the opposite side of the fire, Michael watched Stan's face wobble and distort, as he stared into the heart of the fire, unmoving.

'Are you all right, Stan?' Jacques stepped closer and grasped his arm. He nodded hard, pushed the back of his hand across his face and blew out his cheeks.

'Yes. Yes.' His smile was thin and he turned and forcefully rammed the fork into the earth at his feet. 'I remember... I... no...' Michael moved around to Stan's side and reached out to his shoulder. Stan had broken down before, crying and clamming up, always returning into the hard shell of silence and coldness. Stan shook his head and moved away from him, dragging the fork from the earth.

'Why don't we just finish burning this pile and leave it for the day?' Jacques suggested.

Stan did not respond but started digging up a row of shrivelled cabbage stumps. Jacques, without speaking, took the fork out of his hand, and put his arm around Stan's shoulder, roughly pulling him into an embrace. Michael watched, frowning as Stan's head dropped and collided with Jacques' chest. He'd never seen his brother so gentle, so intimate. A stab of envy made him blink hard; he'd have liked to be able to comfort Stan. A moment of stillness settled and hovered until Jacques patted him on the back and he moved away, wiping his face on his sleeve.

'Sorry... so sorry. One day... I tell you...'

'No need,' muttered Jacques, raising his eyebrows at his family. He began to load the fire with more weeds. His voice, cheerful, broke the mood: 'I bring good news. My friend has made contact with the doctor. He is able to get Stan's ID, identity papers, and will try to do the passport. I don't think it will take long.' He spoke slowly and waited for Stan to nod after each sentence.

'Doctor? For ill people?'

'Yes. He's trusted by the Germans because he's a medical man. But he's able to sort out false papers. I don't know him, but my friend Bob does. He works with Yves. I had to tell him.'

'Yves,' Stan said, nodding. 'Good man, Yves.'

Michael thought that he had not understood all that Jacques said, but it didn't matter; he was pleased to see some cheerfulness return.

'What about that lunch now?' his mother said. 'And I brought you some cider. From apples.'

'Cidre… yes – we have too. Babushka, grandmother. She make.' Stan's face was transformed with a smile.

'Your grandmother… Babushka…'Amy began, trailing off as Konstantin's smile faded and he bit his lip. 'I'd love to know…'

'Let Stan have his lunch, Amy.' Jacques' tone was light but his face serious.

Stan followed Michael and his mother into the kitchen, disappearing into the scullery as she unpacked the basket and he fetched a plate and glass from the dresser. When Stan returned, his hair was wet, pushed back from face. He stood with his hand on the back of a chair, looking at the food on the table with a smile.

'I think we should leave you to eat. Maybe Amy and Michael will come by later for that English lesson.' He didn't answer, but pulled out the chair, its feet scraping loudly on the flagstones and, with his elbows on the table, tucked into the cold chicken, noisily feeding slices into his mouth.

'Slow down; you know what happens if you eat too fast,' said his mother. As if she was not there, he turned his fork, mashed the potato, and shovelled it in, his head close to the plate. With his left hand he grabbed at the glass of cider, sniffing it before gulping the golden liquid and nodding to himself before replacing the glass and leaning down to the plate again, his bare forearm protecting the food. Michael felt a twinge of disgust. Immediately swallowed it down. After what he'd been through… Stan had every right to eat as if the food might be his last.

'Be careful with that… a little at a time,' said his mother with a laugh. Stan didn't seem to hear her. She nodded at Michael who grabbed the empty basket and shut the kitchen door behind them. Amy was feeding the bonfire from the pile of garden rubbish. A smell of smoke and decay hung in the air.

FEBRUARY 1943

The burnt, bitter smell of coffee made Michael wrinkle his nose when he opened the door to Stan's kitchen. There had been no reply to his knocks. On the range sat a battered French pot, small-waisted with one black arm on its hip. Coffee was one of the things that Stan said he missed most but they hadn't been able to buy it for over a year. Michael's parents had experimented, when it became scarce, with roasted wheat and acorns, at the suggestion of one of the farm workers, but they gave up after a few unsuccessful attempts and usually stuck to tea, though that, too, was becoming expensive and rationed. His mother, who seemed determined to make up for what he had been deprived of, passed over her coffee pot and a bag of dried-up acorns to Stan, with apologies. Michael found it difficult to understand why anyone would want that strong bitter flavour, coffee or acorns, but it was becoming a familiar smell, not homely, but comforting in a way; it meant Stan was still there.

'Stan!' He waited for a reply before going to the bottom of the stairs and repeating the name. Nothing. The kitchen garden was empty, tidy, ready for seeds and plants, which Paul had promised him. Dolly was sitting on the back of the tractor seat in the muddy yard and she cocked her head at him. She refused to accompany Michael into the house and seemed to have taken a disliking to Stan, screaming if he got close to her and flying off. Stan said that she hadn't forgiven him making his first appearance like a scarecrow. The word 'scarecrow' he loved; he had laughed about it when Michael had used it. 'Scare crows?' he had asked separating the two words. 'A man for fright-ing crows?'

'Frightening,' Michael had corrected gently. 'And not a man… a mannequin… um… a model… a doll….' He could see that Stan was becoming more confused. His face was screwed up in concentration. He tried again. 'In a field… we dress up a figure… made from branches… to look like a man, so that the birds don't eat seeds or crops.'

Stan had muttered something that sounded like 'Chewcha' and he had nodded. 'Yes. I understand. We have in Russia.'

'Where is he, Dolly?' Michael asked. The bird cocked her head again.

The door to the barn was ajar and he left the parrot hopping up and down on the seat without waiting for an answer.

Stan was sitting watching the pigs, his back to the entrance to the pen. His broad shoulders were hunched forward and he was wearing an old Jersey of Paul's. Jacques had cut his hair a few days ago. It was thick and dark brown on the top, but the back of his neck was white and exposed above the ribbed edge of the sweater. Michael ran his hand over the back of his own head and wondered if he should have a shorter cut. Stan was very still and Michael was reluctant to disturb him. He seemed at peace, self-contained, solid. He cleared his throat and Stan was on his feet, legs apart, hands slightly raised, defensive, his eyes narrowed and mouth pursed. When he saw Michael, his face cleared immediately and he laughed; his whole body relaxed and he put his hand into his pockets and smiled, a full, creased transformation, with his head on one side.

'Sorry! I didn't mean to frighten you,' said Michael moving further into the barn.

The piglets had grown into tubby porkers and were now separate from their mother, who had a pen, which Stan helped to build, in the copse of oak trees behind the kitchen garden. She could fend for herself there, though they still took her vegetable peelings occasionally. Stan found the piglets funny, he told Michael, imitating their rooting by wrinkling his nose and shaking his head.

Michael's father was talking with a few neighbours about swapping some of the piglets for things they can't get hold of. It was tricky because they were all wary of anyone who could be suspicious of Stan at the farm; he had told those who were interested that they were hidden in an old barn at his place. Amy had argued, as Michael knew she would; she wanted to keep the pigs. She'd given them all Russian names, and she and Stan visited the animals most days, laughing over their antics and trying to identify who was who.

Stan sat down again. 'Is this Ivan or Oleg?' he asked poking one of them with his boot.

Michael laughed. 'I don't know. You'll have to ask Amy. I can't tell the difference at all.' He sat beside Stan and felt the warmth of his shoulder against his own, a solidness that did not move. He glanced at Stan's profile; there was stubble on his jutting chin and he was almost unrecognisable since they'd discovered him in the kitchen garden nearly three months ago. His cheeks were still pale, but his grey pallor had faded and the lines weren't drawn so deeply around his hooded eyes.

He followed Stan's eyes to the pigs which were moving and snuffling. The pen seemed less crowded than usual. Was there one missing? He counted and recounted as the pigs moved around. One of them was squeaking and pushing at a pile of straw that had collected in a corner of the pen.

'Stan… I can only see four of them. Has one escaped?'

Stan turned to him, his lips pressed together and his shoulders up in a shrug.

Piglets scattered as Michael moved across the pen. Pulling aside armfuls of prickly straw, he gasped at the sight of a small dead pig, lying on its side, its head twisted unnaturally backwards. 'Look here, Stan! What's happened?'

Stan was standing next to him, shaking his head, pushing at the pig with his boot, his foot leaving a dirty mark on the pink flesh.

Michael turned to him and followed as Stan moved away without answering, skirting the pigs and leaving the pen, stumbling through the tunnel of hay bales to the barn door. Amy was walking down the road towards the farm, her red hat bobbing. She lifted a red-mittened hand and waved. 'Amy is going to be upset…' Michael muttered. 'Can you… distract her… talk to her… while I move the pig? Or will you?'

Stan's face was set in a way that Michael had not seen before. He looked older, harder. 'Is only a pig. We must eat it.' There was no arguing with his tone. He spun on his heel and disappeared into the barn, while Michael walked across the farmyard to meet his sister.

'Why didn't you wait for me, Mike?' she shouted as she opened the big five-barred gate.

'I thought you were seeing Esme today.' He had reached her and helped her push it back, replacing the heavy metal ring over the gate post. 'I was sure you said you'd be meeting her.'

'No, that's tomorrow. Where's Stan? I thought I saw him with you a minute ago.'

'Here I am, Amy.' There was a big smile on his face as he shut the barn door with a bang and turned to her. 'I was feeding pigs.'

Michael waited for some indication, some explanation about the missing pig, to prepare Amy for its loss. Stan kept his face averted, smiling at Amy. There was no way that she wouldn't immediately notice, if she went in the barn. What was the point of pretending? Maybe Stan was protecting her. He knew she'd be upset; he was putting off the moment, or maybe thinking of a way to soften it.

'Good morning, Stan. What about a walk? We can cross the fields, stay away from the roads. I'd like to show you one of the beaches… do you think it would be safe, Mike?'

'Maybe we should ask Mum or Dad?' Stan was smiling at Amy's lit-up face and Michael didn't want to put a dampener on things. 'Or just take the bikes. What about that little bay behind Mont Orgueil; Petit Portelet, I think some people call it?

'Not near Gorey. It's beautiful, but I wonder if we will be able to get down there. Aren't there soldiers stationed at the castle and around Gorey?' Her face had fallen and her brows were drawn together.

'You're right. When I visited Meg, she said there were lots billeted in Gorey Village. It would be stupid… maybe going out at all is dangerous.'

'Who is Meg?' Stan asked.

'Oh, a friend. She and Jacques used to… be close. She's… we read together.' Michael blushed and looked down at his feet. How ridiculous it sounded. 'She doesn't know about you.' He hadn't seen Meg since before Christmas and the pile of borrowed books was gathering dust on his window seat.

'I don't think there is any wire on the beach at Fauvic. I know it's not... hidden, but if we are confident about Stan being Mr Bideau, having the right papers, we shouldn't worry, should we?'

'If that's the case, why not Petit Portelet?'

'Well... I like Fauvic and it's closer.'

Stan was smiling again. 'I would like to see beach and sea.'

'Let's do it then,' Amy was rubbing her hands together. 'We'll need to borrow a bike for Stan...'

'Bike? Bicycle? I find... come.' Stan set off towards an old shed opposite the barn and showed them a rusting cycle among a jumble of crates and farm machinery. One of the tyres was flat, but there was a pump attached to the crossbar and Stan swept off the cobwebs and set to work to blow up the tyre.

'We'll be lucky if it isn't a proper puncture... God, are you sure we should be doing this, Amy? What if...'

'Don't spoil things, Mike. Look at him. He's so excited. We need to get our bikes, and maybe something to eat for lunch. Stan... we will go and get our bikes and come back. All right?'

The twins set off up the road, followed by Dolly fluttering and calling.

'I think we should tell Mum or Dad, just in case,' said Michael.

'In case of what?' Amy was laughing at him. 'We are seventeen! Where is your sense of adventure?'

He couldn't spoil her mood and her happiness was infectious. Beside the road, as they ascended out of the bowl in which the farm nestled, daffodils were just beginning to show yellow heads. One or two were already out, blowing their luminous trumpets in the still, cool air of spring. There was a damp smell, of new life. At the top of the incline, Amy started to jog and Michael lengthened his stride, breaking into a run, as his sister looked across at him, a challenge on her face as she quickened her pace, flopping heavily in her black wellies. Dolly screeched and took off from his shoulder, flying low behind them as they matched each other, stride for stride, until the mud at the field entrance brought them to a stand-still. They grinned at each other and picked their way around the field, out of breath and laughing.

In the farmyard, Jacques was sitting in the truck, the engine running, as if he was just leaving. He wound down the window and leant out.

'Have you been at Bideau's place? Everything all right?'

'Yes… but…' Michael moved close to the open window of the truck as his sister, who had waved and smiled at Jacques, disappeared into the kitchen. 'One of the pigs in the barn is dead. Stan said he killed it… he moved it so Amy didn't have to see it. I haven't told her yet.'

'She lives on a farm… we eat animals. It's ridiculous. You mustn't make a fuss.'

'But why kill it? We were going to fatten them up.'

Jacques dismissed Michael's concern with a wave of his hand. 'I am going over there later. I'll have a word.'

'We were going on a bike ride… with Stan. He's found an old bike. We thought we'd show him Fauvic. It's quiet…'

Jacques turned off the engine and frowned. There was a pause and Michael waited for the disapproval or refusal. It would be a relief in a way; he didn't feel confident about Amy's plan.

Jacques' eyebrows lifted and he nodded. 'It might be good for him. He has his papers; remind him to carry them. Take the quietest paths and stay off the roads. I'll go and see him about the pig later. We can't afford to lose any of them.'

The truck stuttered into life again and Michael opened the yard gate.

'Don't just stand there! Get the bikes out!' Amy was shouting from the kitchen door. 'I'm getting some lunch together.'

Michael, hand in his trouser pocket, sought the Hold Fast button, rubbing it between his fingers. He felt a lightness in his stride as he crossed the yard to shut Dolly in the barn in case she decided to follow him.

It took only ten minutes before they were pushing the bikes over the field and riding them down into the Bideau farmyard. Stan was still working on the old bike and he sighed and shook his head as the twins peered around the open door of the shed.

'Kaput.' He straightened up, hands on hips and a dirty streak of oil under his nose, across one cheek.

Amy frowned and tutted 'Are you sure?'

'See… many holes.' He showed them the ancient tyre, bald and thin, and the inner tube which he'd removed, perished, useless.

'My friend used a piece of hosepipe…' Michael said looking around the shed.

'We haven't got time for that now.' Disappointment was thick in Amy's voice.

'We go two on one?' Stan's question was hopeful.

'You mean share a bike?'

'Oh yes, let's try! I could ride on your crossbar, Mike.'

Amy handed over her bike to Stan who looked huge as he grasped the small frame and tried to raise the seat. Michael helped his sister onto the crossbar in front of him and wobbled around the yard, skidding to a halt as she fell off. 'I'm all right! But let's try me on the back.'

It was hard work with the extra weight, Amy balanced on

the metal flap which he used to strap boxes to if he needed to transport things. Her legs stuck out both sides and he could feel her hands clinging to his saddle under his bottom when he sat. It wasn't ideal, but she wouldn't be suppressed today.

'It's fine. What about you, Stan?'

Looking tall and lanky on the small frame, he had raised the saddle and was poised to leave, one hand in the basket attached to the handlebars where she'd stowed the picnic bag. 'Mmmm… what's in here?' His green-brown eyes twinkled at Michael.

'Leave that alone! It's our picnic,' giggled Amy.

'Pic-nic?' Stan repeated slowly.

'Food… lunch.'

'Picnic…' he repeated. 'Funny word!'

'It is when you think about it,' said Amy.

They found paths all the way from the farm to Fauvic, crossing only one road. Once, they made a wrong turning, but Michael's instincts and years of solitary bike rides, meant that he realised quickly and looped back. At one point they had to dismount and push their way down an overgrown track, but finally the path widened and the dunes above Fauvic spread ahead of them. They rode until their wheels clogged on the gritty sand and they were forced to leave them and walk. Amy extracted the bag from the basket and led them through the rough grass and sandy mounds pushed into wave-like shapes by the winter wind, towards the abandoned and crumbling Round Tower. The tide was high but only reached half-way up the sandy expanse and the dry sand seeping into their shoes was dusty and littered with pinecones and tufts of Marram grass. To their left, in the distance, rose the bulk of Mont Orgueil Castle. To their right, two more Round Towers marked the coast, before it curved away, out of sight towards La Rocque. Michael thought the first of the towers was occupied by Germans but from this distance, about half a mile, he couldn't see any movement.

Stan was smiling like a child. He hadn't spoken on the ride and he was looking out at the horizon, his hands laced behind his head and his chin raised. He took off his boots and socks and walked towards the sea. Amy dropped the bag. 'Wait for me!' She followed him until the dry sand darkened near the water's edge and then paused, looking down at her feet as if wondering whether she should discard her boots too.

Michael sat down and watched as Stan, head bent and hands lifting his trouser bottoms up his skinny shins, stood, his feet disappearing into the sodden sand, until water swirled around the top of his feet and he backed away.

Michael drew up his knees and wrapped his arms around them, breathing deeply and feeling his chest expand and rise. The anxieties sank into the softness of the creamy sand and he felt a tingling warmth surge through him. He leant back, propped up on his elbows and spread his fingers feeling the fine grains under them shift and settle as he relaxed. Above him, catching his eye with its red beak and legs and flash of white underbelly, flew a lone oystercatcher. As he followed its flight over the dunes towards Gorey, it cried loudly, repeating its sharp, high-pitched peep. He straightened and stretched his legs and his eyes were drawn back to his sister and Stan. She had linked her arm into his and they were laughing. He smiled; things seemed… right… balanced in a way that he had not experienced since… If only he could hold onto the feeling.

'We're starving.' His sister was standing over him, blocking the warmth of the February sun, and he shivered.

Stan threw himself down beside Michael.

'Cold. Sea is cold.' He was drying his feet on his socks, the sand clinging and reddening the skin. Amy threw him the tea towel in which she had wrapped their lunch and she laughed as it landed on his head.

'We have bread, cheese, tomato, pickle and... your favourite, Stan... apples!' she announced triumphantly. They sat and ate quietly, looking out on the silvery sea, the sun low in the February sky on their faces, until a barking behind them made them all turn and look inland. Michael's heart leapt in fear. The German guards used Alsatians. He relaxed when he saw a small terrier digging in the sand not far away and two boys appeared and shouted to the dog. He raised a hand to them and they waved back and continued to wade their way through the soft sand along the coast.

Stan had frozen; he sighed and whistled under his breath as the boys disappeared over the curve of a dune.

The low sun moved behind a rolling grey cloud.

'We should go,' said Amy, gathering the remains of their meal into her bag and brushing sand from her trousers. 'It's getting cold.'

Stan went straight to Michael's bike and lifted it. 'I ride Amy.'

They wheeled the bikes onto the firmer ground and Stan indicated that Amy should sit on his crossbar. He hardly wobbled as he moved off quickly, Amy laughing and clinging to his arm. Michael had to shove the picnic bag into the girl's bicycle basket and rush to catch them up. As they bumped along a stony path between the hawthorns, their lichened, sharply-angled branches showing signs of new green life, he felt strength in his legs. He lifted his chin and breathed in deeply. This was the challenge he needed: responsibility, helping Stan regain his health, friendship.

*

Stan feels Amy's warmth and weight against his chest, as she wobbles on his crossbar between his outstretched arms. Frizzy curls, escaping from her red hat, tickle his chin. There is a fluttering in his abdomen. Shallow breaths dry out his mouth. He runs his tongue around his lips, works up some saliva, swallows. This peace is temporary. Insubstantial. A dream he can't have and doesn't want. He won't allow the family to hide him and feed him, as if he is some sort of pet or charity case. He is stronger now, ready to fight back. And he will find a way to do it. Killing the piglet was... a test... of his resolve, of his grit.

He'd been ridding the barn of vermin and it came to him, the impulse to kill again, as he collected the two stiff grey bodies from the scattered straw. Paul had brought rat poison and they'd been careful to use it well away from the pigs, but rats were rife in the barn; he had to collect the bodies most mornings and had been dumping them around the back of the house. When he'd turned one over with his boot this morning, one of the piglets had snuffled at the corpse and he had picked up the squirming creature, tucked it under his arm and, grasping its wet snout in one hand, had wrenched the head back. A crack and a sagging. Nothing else. So easy. And he felt nothing.

The family are kind... too kind. The boy is getting too attached, the girl too friendly, coming to the farm too often. He trusts no one and they shouldn't trust him.

Amy tips up her chin to meet his eyes, so close to his, and giggles. She smiles too much. Stands too close. Held onto his arm on the beach. She is leaning on him now, trusting him. He squares his shoulders, pulls away from her. No one should trust him; he is not part of their world, their little island. Who is he? He is no longer a slave of the German machine and just a number. But he isn't Konstantin, the Russian peasant farmer's son, dreaming of escape to the city, chasing the music of his grandmother. Everything has changed.

Stan. They call him Stan. That is not his name; it's theirs, their pet name for him. He hates it. What is he? He will find out.

Jacques is the one who he must talk to. Anger, frustration, energy; they are obvious in Jacques' face and his words. He must be involved in some sort of resistance, action against the Germans.

He'll bide his time. He will have revenge.

*

APRIL 1943

It was an overheard argument about the rationing of petrol which led to Michael's attendance at a meeting of the group which he secretly thought of 'les résistants', though they would never have called themselves that. As he put on his plimsolls outside the kitchen door, on the first day of the Easter holidays, he heard Jacques' raised voice coming from the barn. Dolly flew out screeching and circled the yard before landing on his shoulder.

'Poor Dolly,' he murmured to the parrot who bent her head to rub her feathers against his cheek. 'What's going on?'

The low morning sun created a slab of light cutting into the gloom of the barn. As he moved closer, he could see his father, broom in hand, his back to the door, facing up to Jacques.

'....need to reserve fuel for the farm,' his father was speaking calmly. 'Rationing is getting more difficult'.

'I realise that. I'm not stupid. But I'm only going into town, meeting the boys. We need to discuss... things.' Jacques' tone was angry, the words spat out, as if he had already made his point and was tired of repeating it.

'Such as...?'

'Dad. You know what we do, try to… defy the Jerries. We can't do much, but I feel we have to do something.'

'And it's dangerous… there've been arrests.'

'Are you saying that I can't use the truck this afternoon because it's dangerous. Or because you don't want me using up our petrol ration?'

'Look, Jacques. Please calm down. And lower your voice. I am worried that the day will come when we can't get our potatoes or our fruit delivered… the petrol ration is very tight. And what happens then? How do we sell them?'

'I think you're being too cautious. We haven't run out yet. And if we do, what about using the horses? I know that's what some farmers are doing, getting the old carts out.'

'Yes, but I've heard that horses are being commandeered, like cars, because the Germans are struggling with petrol too… but I am worried about what you boys are doing too. There've been arrests, haven't there? What's that lawyer's name? Ogier? Advocate Ogier, I think, and his son, arrested for espionage. I know that you've been snooping around the fortifications, making sketches… that's what *they* were doing. There've been arrests of people in possession of a wireless, too. Have you still got that one at the plumbers' yard?'

'Lots of people have hidden crystal sets… I can't do *nothing*! I'm willing to take risks. All I want is to use the truck for one afternoon. And be back before the curfew. I need to pick someone up or I'd take my bicycle. I want to talk to the boys about stepping up the V-sign campaign. We could do so much more.'

'All right. I understand. But be careful…'

'Thanks, Dad. I will.'

Michael moved away from the barn door, walking across the yard to the five-bar gate and turning his back. He'd never persuade Jacques to allow him to go to the meeting if he thought he'd been eavesdropping. Dolly flew off his shoulder and landed on the kitchen window sill. He could see her cocking her head and tapping on the glass, probably trying to attract the attention of his mother as she cleared up the breakfast things.

'Are you going to let me out, Mike?' called Jacques. Michael turned to see Jacques collecting his bicycle from where it had been propped against the fence. He moved slowly and fiddled with the gate catch so that Jacques couldn't ride out of the yard without stopping.

'How are things going, Jacques? I'm on holiday for a couple of weeks. Ready to do… whatever… help the lads… It's been ages since I've been to a meeting.'

Jacques grinned. It was good to see him cheerful. 'Did you hear what I was talking to Dad about?'

'Well, yes. Couldn't help it…'

'All right. Come with me. Meeting at the plumbers' yard. I'll come here for the truck at three.' He lowered his voice. 'We have to pick up Lily from St John's. Don't tell Dad…'

'Great. Thanks. I'll be here.' He swung open the gate and waved as Jacques rode out and up the lane towards the milking yard.

Michael turned his face into the weak spring sunshine and felt his shoulders relax. Before Christmas, before Stan had come into their lives, he'd felt lost, powerless and useless, like a piece of driftwood washed up on an unknown beach. But the tide had turned. He now had purpose, had helped to bring Stan back to life. That's how he thought of it. And now he'd be able to get involved with les résistants. Pushing his right hand deep into his trouser pocket, he found the button: Hold Fast.

*

Lily's friendly greeting as she swung herself up into the front of the truck and her warm shoulder bumping against his added to Michael's glow of well-being. She was wearing a large green sweater over paint-spattered navy trousers, her hair held back with a brightly coloured scarf.

'It's good to see you, Michael. How's school?'

'Just started the Easter holidays, so it's good! I could do without the German lessons, but apart from that, it's all fine. Thank you.'

'German lessons? Oh, Lord.'

'You never know when it'll be useful,' said Jacques. 'Keep at it, Mike.'

A column of German vehicles travelling quickly in the opposite direction to them as they drove down the St John's main road brought a pause in the conversation. A shiny black Chrysler, with a swastika flag fluttering on the front of the bonnet, was escorted by motorcycle outriders and followed by a number of commandeered farm lorries, painted dark green, and three open-topped solid-looking Kübelwagens. Michael had learned the word from Keith, whose interest in the war had shifted to military vehicles which had been imported to Jersey on barges, presumably from France. He felt his pulse quicken.

'Bastards,' muttered Jacques as the last Kübelwagen swished past.

Michael pushed his hands underneath his thighs and tried to breathe noiselessly through his nose to calm himself down. Lily's hands, he noticed, were tightly clasped in her lap. He wondered what Jacques would have said if they'd been stopped and questioned.

They drove the rest of the journey in silence and arrived at the plumbers' yard just as Rob cycled through the open gates. Yves and Bob's kitchen felt crowded; there were two men who Michael hadn't met before and no one introduced him. One was middle-aged, squat and dark-haired, dressed in a faded tweed jacket, twisting a flat cap in his hands. The other was younger, taller than most of the men, and better dressed, probably doing an office job, thought Michael. He stayed near the door as Jacques and Lily took chairs at the table which seem to have been reserved for them and was grateful when Yves caught his eye across the room and beckoned him towards a stool next to his seat.

'Right,' said Jacques, as the murmuring in the room died down. 'Let's keep this brief. The less time we are here, the less likely it is that we'll be discovered. Who's got the cards? I'm not sure we'd be able to keep up the pretence of playing poker if we were raided, there are more of us now, but you never know.'

Yves leaned forward and scattered a pack of cards and a few coins on the table.

'How're the V signs going, lads?' asked Jacques.

The younger of the two new men spoke up, his voice educated. 'Me and a couple of friends painted some signs on the roads out at St Ouen. It's harder than I thought to paint when it's dark! Just hope they were Vs!'

There was a wave of laughter before Jacques held up his hands for quiet. 'Good work, Emile. I painted some on those German signs in St Peter's Valley… lucky not to get caught. I didn't wait until dark! Is that it? Anyone else?'

There was silence.

'We need to step things up, lads. There are signs, I think, that the Jerries are struggling. Three German suicides in the last few months. Can we all aim to be involved in the V signs campaign before we meet again?'

There was murmuring and nodding between the men.

'Good. Now… anyone any other ideas, before I make a suggestion myself?'

'Has anyone heard about the Jersey Democratic Movement?' asked Emile. 'Someone I know at work mentioned it.'

'I've never heard of it,' said Rob. 'Sounds political to me.'

Jacques nodded. 'I've heard a little bit about it. I don't think I'd be interested. Seems to be about persuading people that the island should have closer ties to England after the war and do away with our States departments, basically removing our self-governing status. Why? I think we'll need more power, not less. And anyway, we should be thinking about the here-and-now, not what might happen after the war. We need to do what we can to oust the Jerries, or at least unsettle them, show we've not given in. Be ready for liberation. What do the rest of you think?'

The rest of the men started talking at the same time. Michael couldn't make sense of their response, but the gist of it seemed to be in agreement with Jacques.

Lily's clear voice cut into the noise and all the men turned to look at her. 'What about trying to get more of the Jerries questioning what's happening here and now?' She pushed a curl of auburn hair behind her ear, lifted her chin and looked around the circle of men, her eyes wide and challenging. Michael, admiring her confidence, felt himself nodding slightly, he wasn't sure why.

Jacques tilted his head and looked at her with a slight smile.

The older, dark-haired newcomer folded his arms and spoke for the first time. 'Sounds like pie in the sky to me… how on earth can we do that?' He shook his head and tapped his booted foot on the floor.

'Let her speak, Geoff,' said Jacques frowning at him. 'Do you have ideas, Lily?'

'Do any of you know about Lucy Schwob?'

Most of the men shook their heads. Geoff shrugged his broad shoulders.

'She's a photographer… and writer. I met her just before the occupation. She came to an exhibition I'd got some paintings in. She was… interested in my work and she told me about hers. Her work sounded quite… outlandish. She was part of the surrealist art movement in Paris before she came to Jersey. Called herself Claude Cahun then. Her work is… unusual… and she was too, dressed like a man…'

'What? We don't want to get involved with… queers… what's all this about?' Geoff cut in sharply, gesturing towards Jacques with his palm up. 'Didn't think we were here to discuss this… tosh.' He laughed and looked around for support, but the group showed no signs of agreeing with him.

Lily turned to him. 'Let me finish… if you don't mind.'

'Pipe down, Geoff,' growled Jacques. He nodded at Lily.

'My brother told me recently that Lucy and her friend, Susanne, I think she's called, have been writing anti-German leaflets. They are in German… based on BBC reports of Nazi crimes…'

'And how does this… help?' asked Rob.

'Apparently, they make the stories into poems, sign them from "*Der Soldat Ohne Namen*".

'The soldier without a name,' offered Michael quietly, pleased to be able to make some sort of contribution.

'Yes, Mike… that's right.' Lily's smile and nod in his direction made him feel good.

'I don't get it at all,' muttered Geoff.

'They distribute the leaflets – throw them into windows of German cars or buildings where soldiers are stationed, slip them into soldiers' pockets, put them into cigarette packets. Get themselves invited to events or parties to distribute them secretly. Germans like culture, or pretend to, so they have been able to get into places others might not.' Lily paused and looked around the circle of serious faces. 'It's dangerous. I admire them.'

'I still don't get it…'

Jacques glared at him. 'For God's sake, Geoff… just listen, will you?'

Geoff shrugged his shoulders and tutted.

'I think their idea is to suggest to ordinary soldiers that there's a conspiracy, a group of Germans who don't want to support the Nazis. To create unease.'

'Brilliant,' nodded Rob, 'but so risky.'

'We've no idea what the result of the campaign will be. And I'm not suggesting that we do the same thing. But could we do something which might contribute to the plan… stir up unrest, somehow? Find a way to get some of them to question the occupation. If nothing else it will help if, or when, the British decide to try and liberate us.'

Jacques smiled. 'Great ideas, Lily. Now we just need to think about how we could do that. Is it really possible?'

'Well, I may have contact… with a German soldier. A friend of a friend, let's say. We might be able to start there.'

Michael's stomach lurched. Was she talking about Amy?

'Really?' said Jacques. 'And do you think we'd be able to…"turn" this fellow? Sounds like a very long shot.'

'Worth a try though, don't you think?' Lily looked around at the men.

Expressions varied: blank, dubious, surprised. No one spoke. Geoff muttered something that Michael couldn't make out and looked down at his feet.

'Who is he, the friend?' asked Jacques.

Lily glanced at Michael, her eyes widening before she looked back at Jacques. 'The friend is a 'she' actually. I need to talk to you about that, Jacques… maybe after the meeting.'

She was. She was referring to Amy and her German friend. Why else would she have given him that look? Michael had been so involved in helping Stan, as Amy had been, that he'd pushed the incident with the soldier, Kurt, to the back of his mind. Amy had said that she'd told Lily… and she'd been up to the studio recently. Did Amy still see Kurt? He had no idea.

The noise of people talking across each other intruded on his thoughts and he looked around, trying to hear what the men were saying. Lily was leaning towards Jacques, her hand on his forearm, talking quietly into his ear while he nodded, his mouth a thin line.

'Let's discuss Lily's idea at the next meeting, when we've all had time to think.' Jacques' voice silenced the room again. 'But now I want to tell you all something before we finish today. I should have said something ages ago… Bob and I acquired something before the Jerries came.'

The sinking feeling hit Michael for the second time that afternoon.

Jacques cleared his throat and glanced at Michael. He raised his eyebrows at Bob, who folded his arms and put his head down. An image of the rifles, as he'd last seen them, over two years ago, tucked into their tarp, hemmed in with barrels and tools, beside the rats' nest, flashed into Michael's mind. Did Jacques have a plan to use them?

'We have five rifles.' Jacques' tone was matter-of-fact.

There was a second of taut silence.

'What? Bloody hell! Where…? God, no! How have you…' The men's reactions were mixed, all talking at the same time.

'Now you're talking…' said Geoff loudly, a grin on his face. 'Where are they?'

Michael bit his lip. Five rifles? He must have kept one.

There were six in the crate. When did he move them? Where did he put them?

Yves jumped to his feet, his chair falling backwards to the stone floor with a clatter.

'Jacques? How did you...? No!' He swivelled round to face Bob. 'You stole them? From the NAAFI supplies, that day... You... bloody fool. You've put us all in danger. And our families.'

'Yves... mate...' Bob shook his head and shrugged. 'Where have you kept them, Jacques?'

Geoff leaned forward. 'Yeah. Come on! Where are they?

Jacques was looking around at the men. He hesitated, his eyes on Geoff's eager, dark face. 'It might be best if I keep that to myself. For the time being...'

Emile puffed out his cheeks and loosened his tie. 'Well, that's made things a bit different. I... this is not what I...'

Yves leaned on the table, glaring at his brother. 'I can't believe you did this, Jacques... painting V signs, our dodgy plumbing work, is one thing, but... guns... I don't think I want to be involved with this. What about the rest of you?'

'Don't be so wet, Yvey-boy.' Geoff's voice was thick with mockery. 'Come on, Jacques. Where are they and what are we going to do with them?' He sat back and grinned.

'Yves. Will you sit down?' said Jacques. 'I'm sorry I didn't tell you. The fewer people who know, the better... don't you think?'

Yves sat heavily, elbows on his knees, head down between his hands.

Michael licked his lips and looked around at the others: Rob's mouth was open, his eyes fixed on Jacques; Emile on the edge of his chair, his hand over his mouth; Geoff, still grinning, nodding; Lily, sitting back, a small frown creasing her forehead, arms folded. Jacques must have told her earlier; she had showed no surprise.

Jacques got to his feet. 'Why don't we call it a day? There's a lot for everyone to think about before we meet again.'

'Hang on, you need to tell us where they are.' Geoff stood up, glaring at Jacques.

'No… I don't think so,' said Jacques quietly. 'I need to drive Lily home, before the curfew, and Mike. Let's go…' He moved to the door swiftly and disappeared from sight, his boots clomping on the stairs.

Michael laid a hand on Yves' arm as he got to his feet and gave him a half-smile as he caught his brother's eye. Yves raised his eyebrows and nodded at him. What would he say if he knew that Michael had been involved in moving the rifles? And where was the sixth gun? Michael turned away quickly and followed Lily's green sweater down the stairs.

Lily sat between the brothers on the journey back to St Mary's. No one spoke until Jacques turned into St John's Main Road, the truck crawling behind a farm cart piled up with tools, crates and barrels pulled by a slow-moving shaggy black horse.

Jacques turned and glanced at Lily. 'Well? Do you want to tell me about this friend who knows a German soldier?'

Lily raised her arms and pushed her hair more securely under her scarf, bumping Michael's shoulder with her elbow. 'Sorry, Mike!' She seemed to be hesitating, reluctant to speak.

'Or do you want to wait… maybe when Michael's not with us?' asked Jacques.

'Oh, no. Mike's fine. It's just a bit difficult… you aren't going to like what I have to say…'

'What do you mean? You've got me worried now…'

Michael knew what she was going to say, willed her not to say it. He feared Jacques' reaction and the effect it might have on his sister. But it had to be said. His pulse quickened again and he took a deep breath, spoke quickly, without looking at his brother. 'It's Amy. She's… friendly… with a German soldier. He's called Kurt.'

Out of the corner of his eye, he saw Jacques' head flick towards him, heard a gasp escape, wanted to get the words out before his brother's temper kicked in. 'He's the one who shot at Dad in the garden, does the guard duty at the tower…' The warmth of Lily's shoulder against Michael's steadied him. He licked his lips and looked across. Jacques was hunched over the steering wheel, his knuckles white, his mouth open. 'I couldn't tell you… Amy swears it's only friendship.'

'Only friendship? You're more of a baby than I thought. They don't want friendship… randy buggers. I'll kill him!'

'No, really… I think she's sorry for him…'

'What?' Jacques' voice was cold. 'Sorry for the enemy? What? Don't be ridiculous!' He slammed his palms into the steering wheel and the truck juddered.

Lily put out a hand to Jacques' thigh. Michael looked away as she spoke calmly. 'Jacques. Please. It's not like that. I know. Trust me. She's talked to me. I believe her. He's young and Amy needs fun and… friends.'

'You knew? And didn't tell me! No. No. She won't be a… Jerrybag!' He spat the words out. 'Fun and friends! This is a war. He's an enemy! No. I'll kill him!'

There was silence. Jacques' eyes were fixed firmly on the cart in front as it turned off the road into a field.

'No, Jacques. You won't kill him,' said Lily, her hand gripping Jacques' leg. 'But we can make use of him… turn him. Spread unease. Don't you think?'

Jacques made a noise in his throat, not quite a grunt. 'You are both naïve… think too well of people.'

'Maybe, but I'm a good judge of character, too. And I'm serious about talking to him.'

'All right… you've made your point. I need to think…'

There was surely going to be another outburst. He waited, but it didn't come. As the truck started to pick up speed, Lily turned her head towards Michael, raised her eyebrows and nodded almost imperceptibly. She approved, maybe even admired the way he'd talked to his brother. The glow she'd caused gave him confidence.

'Jacques… I'd like to be involved, if you'll let me. Talk to him…'

'I said I need to think! Leave it for now, Mike,' Jacques snapped.

Out of the corner of his eye, he saw Lily's hand reach out again to Jacques' thigh.

JULY 1943

'You're very quiet today,' said Meg as they walked slowly up the steep path which ran behind the row of houses and small shops opposite Gorey harbour. Michael leaned into the warm wind which was combing the grasses and shaking the feathery Queen Anne's Lace in the hedgerow. He had suggested that they stroll and talk instead of sitting indoors, thinking that it might be easier to talk to Meg when her serious face wasn't scrutinising him closely across her kitchen table. And he really needed to get a few things off his chest. She was the only person with the time to listen to him without judgement, to whom he felt he could say anything. He took a deep breath and sighed, shrugging his shoulders out of his thin jacket. The exertion of the climb had made him perspire; his armpits were damp. Hooking his fingers into the collar he threw the jacket backwards over his shoulder.

'I think I'd like to tell you something… even though I probably shouldn't. A family thing. But I need to…discuss it and I don't know who else to talk to.'

Michael didn't look at Meg, but out of the corner of his eye, he saw her sideways glance as they got to the top of the slope and turned right towards the gravelled track which led towards Mont Orgueil Castle and the narrow road to Le Petit Portelet.

Meg touched his arm and nodded towards a low granite wall. 'Let me get my breath back and enjoy the view.'

Michael spread his jacket over the rough stones for her and they sat looking out at the expanse of grey-blue ocean and the hazy distance, beyond which was France, invisible today. During the last few weeks, France was looked towards and sighed over every day: hundreds of allied planes regularly flew west high over the island and the booming sounds of bombing had been heard. Today was quiet, except for the noise of the wind, rustling in a stunted hawthorn tree, its twin twisted trunks forming a V shape through which the harbour was visible below.

'Look at that,' he said, nudging Meg with his elbow and pointing at the tree. 'Is that a good omen, do you think? Nature is on our side!'

Meg laughed and then turned to him. 'I hope you haven't got involved in the V sign campaign, Mike. It's so dangerous!'

'Well, I have. But I don't want to talk about that…'

'Go on. I'm listening.'

Michael felt the same tightening of his throat and flutter in his stomach as he had when he told Jacques about Amy and Kurt.

'We've been… hiding an escaped prisoner.' The words rushed out. 'On the Bideau farm.'

'Ah. I have to admit that I know about that…' said Meg, softly. 'Or rather I guessed.'

'What? How?'

'I've been helping a few other escapees, taking messages, finding hiding places. With the company car, I can visit farms and the Germans don't suspect a quiet, mousy woman like me!'

Michael's mouth dropped open. 'I didn't know. But…'

'Honour all people, Mike. Isn't that what we spoke about. When I was asked, I couldn't say no. I know the doctor who helped with your chap's papers. And of course, I knew about Mr Bideau and the empty farm. I didn't say anything because you just never know… who to trust. And I thought you were too young to be involved. But I was wrong about that…' She smiled at him.

On their left, across a parched bit of common land, the massive vertical stone wall of the castle reared up towards the medieval crenelations. Michael could see two German soldiers standing guard in the shadows of the ancient wooden doors in the arched entrance, rifles on their shoulders.

'The thing is that I'm worried about him. Stan we call him. He's actually Konstantin. He's so… bitter and aggressive sometimes. The rest of the family don't seem to have noticed or aren't concerned. He's… really… nice, sickly nice, I think, to Amy and to Mum. But I've seen something else. I don't think he cares… about anything, except maybe revenge. He killed a pig, for no reason… Does that sound odd to you?'

Meg's face was thoughtful. 'I've met a couple of escaped slave workers, but only briefly. They've been very badly treated. One was Spanish. He was very thin, hardly spoke. The other was a boy, looked about fourteen but it's so difficult to tell… he cried when the farmer's wife showed him a barn he could sleep in. I didn't see anger, just… sadness, exhaustion. We can't imagine what's happened to them.'

'Mum says that Stan's damaged… mentally.'

'Yes. He must be. How can he trust people? What's happened to him must change everything.'

'I see that, but I'm worried that he'll so something… dangerous. Puts us in danger.'

'What your family is doing is very risky. But do you have a choice? Help the afflicted… that's what you're doing. Hold fast. That's all we can do.'

Michael took a deep breath, exhaled and nodded. He pushed his hand deep into his trouser pocket, feeling for the button, smoothing it between his thumb and finger. The castle drew his eye upwards to the newly constructed towers rising from the top, the black and red flag, the figures with rounded helmets on the battlements.

Meg put her hand on his arm, squeezing gently. 'Why don't we just walk towards Le Petit Portelet, see how close we are allowed to get. I used to love going down there for a swim on a high tide. Bit of a climb down. It's fenced off now. Such a pity.'

Meg linked her arm through his as they turned their backs on the view of the harbour and glittering sea beyond and climbed the last steps to the road.

'Miss Vibert!' The call came from behind them. Michael looked over his shoulder. Meg spun round. A German soldier was waving as he approached them, panting from the climb up the same path they had used. Michael recognised him as the friend of Kurt's who he'd met on a previous visit to Gorey; Meg had said that she chatted with him occasionally.

'Hello, Walter!' she responded. 'I wish you'd call me Meg. This is Michael, a young friend. I think you might have met before.'

Walter stopped a few feet away from them, took his cap off and dipped his head in an old-fashioned bow. He was sweating and red in his thick uniform; he wiped away a trickle from his temple, as a farmer might, after planting his seed potatoes.

'Yes. I have had the pleasure of meeting Michael, with Kurt.' He turned to Meg. 'How are you, Miss Vibert? It is a while since we met.'

'I'm well. What about you? You've lost weight, I think.'

'Rations cut again. But is good for me, I think!' He pulled at the front of his jacket which was hanging loose around the belt and smiled. 'I am doing guard duty at the castle today. I am pleased to explore it. If I am allowed.'

'Oh, I hope you are able to.'

'I have read much about it. I thank you again for the book. It is so interesting.'

Michael studied Walter's face, an ordinary, middle-aged man, with an interest in history; a family man according to Meg… who knew nothing of their secrets.

'You are a student, Michael, I think,' said Walter, taking off his spectacles and polishing them with a grey handkerchief he had pulled out of his pocket.

'Yes, I enjoy history too, and literature. But I hope to study science after… when… it's all over.' He wanted to say more, wanted to tell the German that he was optimistic, that Jersey was British and would be again. But what would that achieve? He felt the slight touch of Meg's shoulder against his arm and smiled at Walter.

Walter pushed the metal arms of his glasses around his ears, adjusted them on his nose and nodded. 'When it's over… yes,' he murmured, glancing over to the castle. 'I go now. I must not be late. Goodbye, Miss Vibert. *Auf Wiedersehen*, Michael. I will like to talk again.' He took a step backwards, replaced his cap and gave his formal bow before turning and walking away, briskly, towards the castle.

'Poor chap,' muttered Meg. 'He's not cut out to be a soldier.'

Michael drew her arm through his. 'Let's go. I wish we could swim at Petit Portlet…I feel so much better after talking to you. Stronger. I'm not sure why. And I almost feel sorry for him, for Walter.'

SEPTEMBER 1943

A warm, still Saturday in early September. Michael was hoping that Kurt might be tempted by the weather to take a dip off St Catherine's breakwater. With Jacques and Lily on either side of him, he leant on the white railings which ran along the length of the long granite arm of the pier, narrowing into the distance, reaching out towards France. It had been built about a century ago, Granny had told him, to create a harbour for the Royal Navy to counter a possible French invasion. But it was never completed because of the shallow waters at low tide. It was a tourist attraction, or it had been before the invasion; now, over three years into the occupation, you were more likely to encounter solitary fishermen rather than pleasure seekers. Old men and young sat patiently on the wall or slipway hoping for bream or plaice to supplement their diet. Michael used to enjoy cycling to the end of the breakwater after he'd been swimming at Fliquet, but this summer he'd found less time for such pleasures with his responsibilities for Stan and his involvement with Jacques' group, and anyway, much of the East coast was inaccessible to residents of the island, guarded and fenced off.

In August, as he'd taken a cycle ride to St Catherine's, with the intention of noting down details of the fortifications in the area, he'd witnessed some of the young German soldiers swimming and fishing. He'd spotted Kurt, Amy's friend, and Walter, the older soldier he was billeted with at Gorey, watched them talking as they walked back along the wall, before stripping off and jumping into water. Jacques and Lily had been pleased with his report, saw a potential opportunity to get at Kurt but two previous trips this month to St Catherine's had been futile.

'I think that might be him.' Michael's excitement rose. He pointed to a fair-haired German soldier, walking slowly down the slipway below them, a white towel over his shoulder.

'Shh. Don't point,' muttered Jacques, laying a hand on his arm. 'Are you sure?'

'Yes, that's him. And he's alone!'

They watched Kurt. He stopped, looking out to sea and then down into the steely blue water, as it moved gently against the granite wall. He sat, pulled off his boots and socks, before unwinding a bandage from around his foot and looking closely at it. He peeled off jacket, shirt and trousers. Moving awkwardly on the uneven surface, the foreshortened figure, looking like a pale, malformed animal, piled his clothes and shoes against the wall behind him. He limped back to the edge in a pair of grey undershorts and dropped into the water. His gasp, as his head reappeared from the white splash he'd created, reached the trio above him.

'Perfect,' said Jacques, his eyes on the wet head of Kurt swimming away from the wall using a rapid breaststroke. 'We'll be there when he gets out… Lily, are you ready to do this?'

'Yep. We're lucky he's alone. I'll go now,' she said, hoisting her bag onto her shoulder.

'What's the plan?' asked Michael.

'Just wait and see. We can move a little closer. Come on.'

They followed Lily until Jacques stopped directly above Kurt's clothes, about twelve feet below them, and watched her walk away before she turned back down to descend the sloping slipway, her red hair glowing. She sat down with her feet dangling over the water, not far from where Kurt had entered the water.

After about ten minutes, Michael could see Kurt had turned round and was heading back. He nudged Jacques, whose eyes were closed against the rising smoke of his cigarette.

'Here we go,' muttered Jacques.

They watched as Kurt struggled to haul himself out of the water onto the slipway, glance in Lily's direction and hobble across to his clothes. He sat with his back to the wall and pulled a towel around his pale torso.

The voice of Lily carried up to them. 'Good morning,' she said turning and smiling in Kurt's direction.

'Good morning,' the soldier responded, rubbing at his chest and head with the towel.

'Is the water very cold? asked Lily getting up and moving closer to Kurt. 'I brought my kit but I haven't decided whether to go in or not.' She was standing quite close to him, one hand on her jutting hip and the other clutching her shoes. 'Oh, my goodness, you've got goose pimples… it must be cold.' She laughed.

Kurt's face was turned up towards her. 'Excuse me… my English is not good. Did you say *goose… purples*?'

Lily thew back her head and laughed again before crouching down beside him and reaching out towards his bony shoulder. He flinched and she drew back her hand. 'I'm sorry. There on your chest… goose pimples. We say that, I don't know why, when the cold makes your skin… sort of…

bubble. Like that.' She reached out again and touched his upper chest. 'What do you call them?'

'Ah, I see. We say, *die Gansehaut. Ganse*... are like ducks. Gooses, do you call them? So we have same word. *Haut* is "high"'.

Lily sat down beside him with her back against the wall and legs outstretched. Her grey skirt had risen above her knees. 'Geese. Yes. Strange that the words are so similar, don't you think?'

Kurt was struggling into his shirt, his words muffled and inaudible to Michael and Jacques as he dragged it over his wet head.

'No, I'm not. I've decided. It's too cold. No *Gansehaut* for me!' She pulled up her knees and curled her arms around them.

'Oh. I like the cold water. I swim here... many days,' Kurt said, pushing his arms into the sleeves, and leaning forward. Lily reached out and helped him pull it down over his damp back.

'Yes, I think I've seen you before. My name's Lily.' She held out her hand for him to shake; he hesitated and then took it. 'Oh, my goodness. You are cold.'

Michael could see that Kurt was uncomfortable with Lily's attention. He hoped she knew what she was doing.

'Are you an athlete? So many of you Germans are very fit and strong.'

Kurt had grabbed his trousers, holding them over his upper thighs. 'No. I like to swim and play football... but no athlete.'

Lily had slid closer to him, her thigh only inches from his. She stretched out her left leg and touched the top of his right foot with her pointed toe. He moved it away quickly.

'Sorry. But your foot... that looks painful... is that a blister?' she asked.

'Oh. Yes. My boots…' he said indicating them with his head.

She picked one up and examined it. 'Can't you get new ones? These look ancient. How long have you had them?'

'There are no new boots in Jersey.' He smiled at her.

'Not even for soldiers? I am surprised.'

'Things are not easy. Not only for you Jersey people…'

'I know… and you'll catch your death if you don't get dressed…'

'I put trousers on…' he said getting up, turning his back to her and dragging the damp wool over his legs. Lily giggled as he hopped around.

'She's good at this,' said Jacques in Michael's ear. 'Flirting…'

They watched Kurt stuffing his arms into his jacket sleeves before he sat down again next to her. They both looked out over the gently rocking water and said nothing. She reached into her bag and retrieved a tin. 'Can you roll a cigarette?'

She opened the tin and showed him the contents. Roughly cut slivers of thin paper and what looked like tea leaves. Lily giggled again. 'Yes, it's lavatory paper! Can you get cigarette papers?'

'No. We have no tobacco.'

'Ah, well, this is grown by a farmer. You know him, actually, and I think you've had some of his tobacco… he's surprised you haven't been back for more.'

There was a pause in the conversation.

'I believe you once shot at him for breaking the early curfew…' said Lily.

Kurt turned to look at her. 'You… know the Le Breton family?' he asked.

'Oh, yes, very well. Don't worry, but if you look above you, you'll see more familiar faces.'

Kurt's pale face tilted up towards Michael and Jacques. He jumped up and glanced around him as if he was expecting danger. Lily got to her feet and put her hand on his arm.

'It's only Jacques, and Michael, Amy's twin. Hey, come and join us, boys. And bring your matches…'

After cigarettes had been rolled and lit, the four of them sat against the wall, the smell of smoke sharp in Michael's nose.

'So how's life in Jersey for you?' Jacques' tone was friendly and there was a smile on his face.

'Oh. Jersey is beautiful,' said Kurt. 'We are… glad to be here. You are lucky to live here.' He nodded and looked at Lily.

'Well, not so lucky at the moment.' Jacques' smile hadn't wavered. A crackle of burning tobacco turned his cigarette end red and he closed his eyes and tipped his head back as the smoke drifted up.

A few seconds of quiet. Michael saw Kurt's shoulders pull forward.

'Look,' said Lily. 'It's Kurt, isn't it? We don't want… we only want to help.' She had her hand on his arm again. 'We know that things are difficult for you… as much as they are for us. Maybe we can help each other.'

'Help?' Kurt's eyes flicked between Jacques and Lily.

'Tell me, really, are you happy? Wouldn't you like to see an end to this war, to this… situation?' Lily's voice was soft, persuasive.

Kurt sucked on his cigarette and tucked his other hand under his armpit, shaking his head slightly.

'You could do something about it,' said Jacques quietly. 'We know that there are many German soldiers who would like this to end. Your food situation is as bad as ours. And things aren't going well in France, are they? And Italy…'

Michael could see that Kurt was becoming very uncomfortable. His shoulders were hunched and he'd drawn his legs up to his chest. He wondered if Jacques and Lily were going too far, too quickly.

'Look,' said Lily again. 'Will you think about something?'

'Could you distribute leaflets among your colleagues?' Jacques was up on his haunches now, squatting and looking seriously at him.

'I… I don't understand,' whispered Kurt.

'We think you would be better off surrendering.' Jacques' statement was blurted out.

Kurt stood quickly, grimacing as he forced his bare feet into his boots and directed his answer to Jacques. 'Surrender… no! What are you talking about? Germany will never surrender…' His voice faded and he scratched his head.

Lily got to her feet and took a step towards him. 'All you would have to do is slip pieces of paper into colleagues' pockets. No one will know it was you. We are going to distribute them too. They will make soldiers think.'

Michael rose slowly, his back to the wall. He could feel the rough granite on his tense palms.

Lily brought out a bundle of folded sheets of paper from her bag, glancing at Jacques before she offered them to Kurt. 'We want your troops to question what's happening…'

'No! No. Stop. This is not right. How can you talk to me like this?' He held up his hands, refusing to take the papers.

'Listen,' said Lily, extending her hand towards him again. 'What is written here might make soldiers question what's happening, think again.' She unfolded one of the papers and read: '"How long do you want to stay here and starve? The war is lost. We call on you to surrender." Surely you recognise that the war is lost. You must want to survive and go home.' She smiled into his face.

Kurt frowned and backed away, shaking his head.

'Do you know what mutiny is?' Jacques' voice was low and deep. He reached out and his hand closed hard around Kurt's wrist.

'*Meuterei?*' muttered Kurt under his breath, wrenching his arm free. He pulled back his shoulders and straightened his jacket. 'No. No more. I go now.' He picked up his damp towel and discarded socks and began to limp away from them.

'I know about you and Amy,' Jacques called after him. 'Stay away from her. How dare you!' The words were spat out. 'If you say anything... about our conversation... she will know what you are really like... how you use our women.'

Kurt stopped, a look of horror on his face. 'What do you mean? I respect her... Amy is my friend.'

'You stay away from her.'

'Don't threaten me. I know things... secret things,' Kurt mumbled.

'What? What did you say?' Jacques shouted as Kurt turned again and walked quickly back up the slipway.

What secrets could Kurt know? Something Amy had told him? Was it just an empty threat? Michael's mind raced and blood thumped in his ears. What if he knew about Stan? No. He'd have reported it, surely. Except... he knew that the family, including Amy, would be in trouble if he did. Serious trouble. And would she have told him?

Jacques stood looking after Kurt. Michael noticed the muscles in his jaw tensing and his hands curled into fists, until Lily put a hand on his shoulder. 'Let's stay calm. Not draw attention to ourselves,' she said quietly.

Jacques nodded and turned, looking from her to Michael. 'Not a great success. Can't win them all...'

DECEMBER 1943

As he pulled back the heavy blackouts, a glaring light flooded into his room. He blinked at the white garden below. Snow had not fallen in Jersey since... he couldn't remember. But he recalled building a snowman with Amy in the milking yard and the strange sight of a white beach below pale, wilting grasses in the sand dunes at St Ouen's. The sky was a watery blue and the sun was already restoring some of the garden green, but under the trees the shadows were silver-blue. In the past he would have rushed into Amy's room and woken her with the news. Not today. He pushed up the sash window, decorated in the stars of Jack Frost. Kneeling on the wide window seat and sticking his head out, he breathed in the achingly cold air, until the cold crept down his pyjama jacket collar making him shiver.

He pulled the window down and drew up his legs onto the window seat, wrenching the curtains shut again with a clank of the metal rings, creating his secret space. His legs were now too long to stretch out into the width of the seat and he laid his face on his bent knees, staring at the conifer opposite, its branches drooping with snow. It was yesterday's uncomfortable confrontation with Stan that was weighing him down, creating that familiar hollow ache of unhappiness.

He'd decided that the only way he would be able to give Christmas presents this year was if he made them and thought he might consult Stan, who seemed to be able to turn his hand to most things. He had found him sitting in his kitchen, with the coffee pot at his elbow and the *Evening Post* spread on the table in front of him. He had asked Michael's help with a few articles, showing a particular interest in the report of a woman who was arrested for throwing horse manure at a column of German troops. He had smiled and nodded approvingly but grown angry when Michael had explained that the report ended with the statement that she had had her three-month prison sentence doubled after she had appealed through a court martial.

'Why they do nothing?' He was not addressing the question to Michael. His head was down and he was scanning the paper for more information.

'Who? Why do who do nothing?' Michael asked. Stan's head came up and he frowned.

'Jacques, his friends… they do nothing.'

Michael felt defensive of his brother. 'Well. They do. They've been collecting information on fortifications… sent some of it to England with escapees… And they've painted V signs. Maybe something more serious, sabotage possibly, but Jacques won't tell me what.'

Stan made a dismissive sound and sat back in the chair. 'It nothing.'

'What would you do?'

'Kill. Just kill. Many.' Stan's dark eyes were cold and unblinking and Michael felt his stomach drop. An image of the dead piglet, floppy and distorted, on the barn floor flashed into his head.

'No… you wouldn't…'

'Yes. I will. When it possible.'

But… that's suicidal and…' He could see that Stan had not understood. 'It would be very dangerous. If Jacques and the others were involved, they would be sentenced to death… or sent away. There are so many troops with weapons. And anyway, Jacques wouldn't just kill in cold blood… I mean, without provocation…' Had he lost Stan again? How could he explain provocation? 'Jacques would only… defend his family. They call what they do, "acts of defiance". Do you understand?'

'I understand that they do nothing. They will never… they don't have courage… is right word?' The chair scraped loudly on the flagstones and he glared at Michael. 'And you, you just child.' He turned and marched out.

Michael stood in the silence of the cold kitchen. When Stan had first recovered, just less than a year ago, Michael had felt drawn to him; he'd somehow filled a gap in his life. Hiding him had given him a feeling of achievement and, when Stan's health had improved and he'd smiled over learning new words and shown pleasure on the short trips they made, he'd felt a warmth that had eluded him since Mr Bideau's death and the drowning of the soldier. Or was it since Laura left? He hadn't felt the sense of danger which his father warned him of, but he'd been careful, understanding the risk. To be called a 'child' hurt. He'd felt as if he was the older one when he was helping Stan and he'd loved the sense of responsibility. Stan didn't appreciate what he did. His mother always excused Stan's outbursts and silences, his lack of gratitude, telling Michael that he was seriously damaged by what had happened to him, but he found the moods difficult. And now he was confused. How could he say that Jacques lacked courage?

The low morning sun had risen high enough to peep into the window and he felt a little warmth through the glass on his bare feet. He should have followed Stan yesterday and challenged him. Defended his brother, his brave brother.

He took a deep breath and decided to put Stan out of his mind for the day. Amy had said yesterday that she hadn't visited for a while, so he'd leave her to it, keep out of the way and focus on Christmas presents. Maybe Jacques would have some ideas and he could talk to him about Stan too. Stan and Jacques had seemed friendly at one time though he couldn't remember the last time his brother had been at the Bideau farm, at least not when he was there.

He pulled back the curtains and crossed the cold floor to his bed, resisted the temptation to get back under the bedclothes, and quickly dressed from the pile of clothes thrown across the end. His socks had a hole in one heel and he found a clean pair, dragging them over the others. Two sweaters: an old one of Yves' fitted perfectly over his own Jersey, and his warmest trousers. A splash of cold water on his face from the bowl on his chest of drawers and a dry brush of his teeth completed his ablutions.

The grandfather clock on the landing, ticking softly as always, told him it was just after half past seven. Jacques would probably have finished the morning milking; it might be a good time to catch him. He hesitated at the bottom of the stairs, hearing his mother humming in the kitchen and the noise of pots being moved around. She'd probably be making soup. He'd go out of the front door to avoid her questions and, anyway, Dolly might hear him if he went out of the back door. Maybe Jacques would have some breakfast he'd share; he sometimes came home with a few bits of meat which he'd traded with friends for tobacco or butter that he was still making in the dairy. Bacon Michael dreamed of. They'd always had it for breakfast before the occupation. Now it was a treat and he knew that of the three pigs left and still hidden on the Bideau farm, his father was thinking of killing one for Christmas.

He shrugged on his coat in the hall and his only pair of boots, wearing thin on the soles and pulled his woolly hat down over his ears. He pulled the front door closed behind him and stood enjoying the still white of the garden and the way that the winter sun, behind the leafless trees, threw spiky shadows across the field.

The dairy yard was deserted when he arrived, breathing deeply from the brisk walk up the lane. Milking was over; the yard was slushy and muddy with cow prints. The milking shed doors were shut.

'Jacques!' The sound bounced off the stone buildings. No reply. He ran up the wooden steps to his brother's rooms. The door was not locked but the room was empty. A warm pot and the bitter lingering smell of burnt acorns, Jacques' substitute for coffee, hinted that he'd not long gone out.

Michael sat on the top step and looked out over the quiet dairy yard. The sun's weak light shone in his face. Maybe he'd try to carve something out of wood as Christmas presents. Yves had made animals last year; Michael's miniature cat, with its tail curled around its neat haunches, just like Lettie, sat by his bed. He couldn't compete with Yves' figures. What could he make? There might be some old crates or planks in one of the sheds. He could make a small side table or stool for his mother.

From his vantage point he could see the old shed where he and Jacques had hidden the rifles before Jacques had moved them to the plumbers' yard. Or some of them. Was the sixth one still in the padlocked shed? He'd like to know. Jacques was still hesitant about telling him things, not allowing him to get involved.

'Jacques!' he called again. A few crows rose from a leafless tree in the lane, cawing and swirling black in the white sky.

The shed door rattled at his push, but the padlock held firm. He circled around the back and swept away a few cobwebs from the cracked window, put his face close to the glass and used his hand to shade out the sun. A ray of light from a crack in the brick wall fell on a small barrel which used to contain screws and nails, and he could see the outlines of tools, but his view of the corner where they'd stashed the rifles was obscured. Surely Jacques wouldn't have left one here; it would be hidden in his flat.

The little barrel would make a good table. He could sand it down and paint it; his father would have some paint somewhere. He stamped down straggling brambles and forced his way around the back of the shed to get a better look. The hole in the back wall was small but the crumbling bricks started to give way when he pushed at them with his boot. He gasped when a large rat dashed out, his neck prickling as he backed into the branches of a snowy shrub. He took a deep breath, told himself not to be silly, and looked around for a stick. Crouching down, he waved the stick around inside the hole, hoping to disturb any other vermin before trying again. His stick met the tools piled up and, as his eyes had adjusted to the light, he could see the draped edge of a green tarpaulin, like the one they had used. It could still be there, the sixth rifle, shrouded and decorated with cobwebs.

He straightened up. He'd like to know, get into the shed and find out. And he'd like to reach the barrel. If he tried to make the hole in the shed bigger, he might damage it further; the roof sagged dangerously. Tentatively, he moved a few more bricks and pushed his arm in. He could almost reach the barrel, no higher than his knee. Perhaps he could knock it over and roll it towards the hole. It might just fit through. Using his stick in one hand and reaching with the other, his cheek against the damp brick, he blindly groped towards the barrel. He heard it fall, pushing other things with it, and groaned. Kneeling in the slushy snow and putting his face to the hole, he saw that the barrel, on its side, had rolled back into the stacked tools and dragged the tarp down. Above its folds a long thin tube was exposed…

Michael scrambled to his feet, his heart racing. Even though he had suspected it was there, it was a shock. Had he imagined it? The silence of the empty dairy yard hung heavy in the cold of the shadows. He got back on his knees and pushed his head into the hole, awkwardly turning his shoulders which prevented him from going further. Now he could see the long nose of the rifle and the shining top of the metal trigger.

He squirmed back out into the cold of the morning and carefully filled the hole with the old bricks, pricking his hands as he pushed brambles over it and hauling rotten branches into place to cover the path he'd made round the shed. He stood in the sun thinking, licking at a scratch on the back of his hand, the metallic taste sour in his mouth.

'Jacques!' He shouted. 'Where are you?' The only reply was the harsh call of the crows in the tall trees of the lane.

His mother, both hands around a cup of tea at the table when he pushed open the kitchen door, looked surprised to see him. 'I thought you were still in bed! First day of the holidays. You always have a lie in. Did the snow tempt you out? Isn't it beautiful?' She got up and took another cup from the hooks above the range. 'Are you all right, Michael? You look a little pale. You must be cold… warm your hands on the range. I had to get it lit to make the soup and I've managed to make some bread – with the potato flour. We have so little fuel. Tea?'

Michael nodded and stood with his back to the warm range feeling the heat on his thighs.

'What have you been doing? Look at your wet knees! Surely you are too old for snowmen! And anyway, there's not nearly enough snow for that… Michael… what is it?'

'Mum… would Jacques? I…' He wanted to tell her; he wanted the comfort of her knowing what to do.

'What is it, love? Is something wrong… it's not Stan is it?' There was fear in her voice.

'No. No. I was just walking… I slipped in the snow. I'd like some tea… please.' He couldn't tell her, not about the rifle and not about Stan's threats.

Fortified by his mother's warm bread, Michael opened the barn doors to find Dolly perched high on a hay bale looking down at him. He had stopped trying to find a fastening for her cage that she couldn't undo, but she was safe in the barn and she could burrow into the bales if she was cold. 'Poor Dolly', she squawked, flying to his shoulder and nibbling his ear.

'Stop that! You know I don't like it!' Michael gave her a gentle push and she sailed out of the open door and around the yard, landing on the kitchen window ledge and tapping with her beak on the glass. He could see his mother knocking from the inside and shooing her away. She had never made friends with the parrot and said she was sure that the bird disliked her and annoyed her on purpose. Michael set about cleaning out the cage and filling her food and water trays. Dolly climbed into the cage of her own accord at night, seeming to like the security and slept on the perch, before freeing herself in the morning. There was no sign of Lettie and he hadn't seen her for days. His mother said that she was perfectly capable of feeding herself and that she kept vermin down on the farm; just as well as they'd been unable to get cat food. He'd found her once in the barn at the Bideau farm being fed by Stan on scraps that were meant for the pigs. He'd felt a strange sort of jealousy that Lettie had gone to Stan as she purred and rubbed herself against his legs.

'Michael! I'm off to see Mr Bideau. Are you coming?' Amy's voice rang out, as usual enjoying the subterfuge of his false name. 'Mum says she's too busy, but she's given me some bread and a few potatoes to take over.'

Michael hesitated. Should he ignore yesterday's conversation? Was it too soon to go back to the farm?

'Well?' Amy face appeared around the barn door. 'Come on!'

She'd think it odd if he didn't go with her. And Stan was always different with Amy, softer somehow. He smiled and nodded. 'I'm starving. Think Mr Bideau might offer breakfast?'

He waited until Amy reappeared, an old scarf of their mother's wound around her neck and hair tucked into her red hat. A basket hung over her arm. 'Let's take the road route. Dad says we should be careful about using the footpath between the farms and, in the snow, it would be more obvious.'

'Do you think it's still dangerous to have Stan on the farm? He's been there a year now and his papers haven't aroused suspicion. Maybe we've got away with it. He's Mr Bideau now.'

'You can't be too careful, though, can you? It would only take one false answer or one soldier thinking that his accent is odd… or someone betraying us.'

'Who would betray us? Anyway, hardly anyone knows about him. I wonder if the Germans can tell the difference between him and us? His English is so much better, but not perfect… but then, their English isn't that good.'

'Some of them are much better than others. Kurt's English...' She stopped with her hand over her mouth and looked at her brother.

'I wondered if you were still seeing him.' Michael thought of the unsuccessful attempt to turn Kurt at St Catherine's. Somehow, he'd imagined that it might make a difference to Amy's relationship.

'You know we're only friends. He's like another brother and he misses his sister... we talk of her... sometimes. I think she must have been a little like me. She painted too. He said he'd like to show me the picture he brought back after her funeral, but obviously I'm not going to his billet. It's in Gorey, in one of the guest houses.'

'Just be careful, Amy. Not everyone would accept your friendship...'

'I know. We are careful... Now let's talk about Christmas!'

They walked up the snowy lane, pausing to look at the view towards France before turning right at the top. There was a haze on the horizon and the coast of France wasn't visible, but the stillness of the cold, blue morning was beautiful.

When they reached the farm, Amy disappeared into the barn to see the pigs in their secret home and Michael hesitated, standing with the basket in the middle of the yard. There were no footprints visible in the snow; presumably Stan was in the house. He walked around to the side door and found him in the garden, digging onions. He glanced up when Michael opened the gate and returned to his task without greeting him. Michael knew that his mood had not lifted. 'Shall I help?' he asked. 'I could grab another spade.'

'No. Is all right. I need one onion.'

'Look Stan...' The Russian raised his head, one foot on the top of his fork. 'I don't want us to fall out... we are friends, aren't we?'

Stan shrugged, then shook his head. 'I am grateful. Your family are kind…'

'It's not about gratitude. We are friends,' he repeated, wanting confirmation, wanting some warmth in return.

'I not know… I used to have… friends. They dead, I think.'

'We are your friends… all of us.' Michael could hear the pleading in his own voice.

Stan's tone in contrast was calm and flat. 'Best not to have friends. It hurts.' He shrugged again and bent to pick up the onion by its limp green top.

'Come on. That's just silly…'

'Silly… what is that? Stupid? You call me stupid?' He spat the words out. 'You stupid. You and Jacques, your weak brother.'

'No! He's not stupid and he's not a coward! You can't say that.' Michael felt his pulse racing.

Stan made a dismissive sound with his mouth and pulled the fork out of the ground, turning away from Michael towards the back door.

'He has a rifle! That's how much of a coward he is!' Michael shouted at Stan's back. There was a moment of complete stillness before Stan turned. Their eyes met; Stan's were cold and glittering. A tight smile creased his face. Michael clamped his mouth tightly shut. He shouldn't have said that. Why did he say that?

'There you both are… what's the matter? Did I hear shouting?' Amy was standing by the garden gate, unwinding her scarf, looking from her brother to Stan.

'Hello Amy! I'm so glad to see you,' said Stan. 'How are you today? Do you like snow?' His voice was full of syrupy sweetness and the mask of his face was alive with a big smile. 'We have so much snow in Russia… This is nothing. Come in. I make pancakes. Fresh eggs today.' Without looking at Michael, he took the basket from him and, slipping his arm around Amy's shoulders, he guided her to the door.

Michael took a deep breath and exhaled noisily. He'd seen two sides to Stan: the affable one who Amy responded to in her natural, friendly manner and something uglier, unpredictable, dangerous. Who was the real Konstantin?

FEBRUARY 1944

Towards the end of February, the mild, rainy weather gave way to cold with a gusty north wind bringing sleet and snow flurries out of grey clouds which raced across an icy blue sky. Michael decided to use his Saturday morning to cycle to La Hougue Bie to see for himself what the Germans had done to the neolithic mound and chapels. Jacques said they had built a bunker into the side of the mound and were using it as a vantage point to look out towards the French coast. It might be useful to have some more detailed sketches of the place and how it was guarded. He joined the main road north towards St Saviour and put his head down, pedalling hard against the wind. When his name was called, as he approached La Hougue Bie, he was surprised to see the two German soldiers who had stopped on the opposite side of the road. It was Walter who greeted him, smiling and beckoning to him in a friendly way. Kurt's face was impassive and he kept his foot on one pedal as if he was keen to move off. So Amy's friend had not said anything, even to Walter, about what had happened at St Catherine's in September; if he was still angry and upset about what Jacques and Lily had suggested, at least he'd kept it to himself.

Michael wheeled his bike towards the men, fixing a smile on his face, wondering if he could use the connection to find out about what was happening at La Hougue Bie.

'Hello,' said Michael. 'Is it cold enough for you? We don't get much snow here… but at least its stopped raining.' Walter propped his cycle against a five-barred gate, climbed up and took a seat on the top, struggling with a large khaki-coloured cape. It looked cumbersome but would keep the weather off far better than his thin raincoat, Michael thought.

'We are better equipped than you, it appears,' said Walter, turning to Kurt. 'Let's take a break… maybe Michael can help us out…'

'Help you out? How?'

'We have been given a… special job. Haven't we, Kurt?'

Kurt nodded, biting his bottom lip.

'A special job? Are you able to tell me…?

'Oh, yes. No secrets. We have been told to look for papers… um… how you say… *Flugblatter… die Broschure?*

Michael felt a tingling at the back of his neck. His voice was shaky. 'L-leaflets, maybe?'

'*Ja. Ja.* Leaflets. Dropped from airplanes by French… we have to collect… you understand? Have you seen leaflets? In fields? Our officer says they have false news… And we are to search houses and farms.'

Kurt spoke for the first time, turning to Walter and muttering in a rapid German that Michael couldn't understand. Michael breathed out slowly, allowing his shoulders to fall. Not Jacques' leaflets then.

'Speak English, Kurt. It is rude to speak German. I do not think we give away secrets.'

'No. No, I haven't seen anything,' said Michael, gripping his handlebars and shaking his head, tensing his jaw to keep his voice level. 'I have no idea about such things… um… did you come from La Hougue Bie? That's where the Command Post is, isn't it? I expect you're interested in the mound, aren't you, Walter? The passage grave. Did you see it? I think that's what it's called.'

Walter nodded and grinned. 'It is interesting... fascinating. Prehistoric, I think you say.' His face collapsed suddenly and he shook his head. 'But... we have... damaged it. The mound, not the passage, thank God. I am so unhappy... war is... terrible. It destroys.'

In a moment of stillness, Michael could hear the insistent tic-tic of a robin's call from the hedgerow. There was something hopeful almost, in Walter's words. If some of the Germans recognised the awful situation, maybe Jacques and Lily's campaign was possible. The men in front of him were just men, as Meg had said.

Hold fast to that which is good ran through his head, in Meg's voice.

'Walter... what do you think is going to happen?' he asked quietly.

Walter looked up and glanced at Kurt before replying. 'Peace will be negotiated and we will all go home in the spring! And you will get your beautiful island back!' He threw back his head and laughed. Then stopped abruptly. Michael followed his gaze upwards. High above them, just visible in the low clouds, black bird shapes moved across the sky, hundreds of them in neat formation. A humming sound, quiet, but persistent.

'Are they British?' Kurt's voice was strained.

Michael couldn't take his eyes off the aircraft. There was a fluttering in his belly.

'I think so... heading east... to France and maybe Germany.' Walter's voice was quiet and emotionless. '*Auf gehts*, Kurt.' He jumped off the gate and moved to his cycle.

'We have a job to do, Michael. Whatever happens, we have to do our job. We have no choice.'

'No… no one has a choice,' said Michael, moving out of the way of the two soldiers.

Walter threw his leg over his saddle and adjusted his cape. 'Back to work. Leaflets… we search. *Auf wiedersehen,* Michael. We have to look everywhere. I hope we do not disturb your family… you live in Grouville, I think.'

The little flutter of excitement turned to nausea in Michael's stomach. Search the farm? And the Bideau place? He forced himself to raise his hand as Kurt and Walter cycled away from him. How much time did he have? What was the best thing to do? Warn Stan? Warn Jacques? His head buzzed, his mouth dry.

Keeping well back, he followed the two Germans back down the road towards the farms. They turned in at the gate of a cottage, a small-holding, set back from the road. The building was squatting, half-hidden behind a row of stunted trees. There was a scrubby patch with a couple of dilapidated sheds, henhouses maybe, Michael thought, though no chickens or livestock were in sight. From behind a dripping black hedge, he saw them wheel their cycles up the path. An elderly woman, her ghostly face seeming to float in the small gap between the door frame and the peeling front door, nodded and stepped back to allow them into the house. He was pleased to see that they took off their caps before they entered and wiped their boots on the mat in the porch.

He remounted and pushed off, peddling hard. With the wind now behind him and the help of the downward slope, it wasn't long before he turned into the deserted milking yard.

'Jacques! Jacques!' A dull echo bounced off the barn wall. Dropping his bike in the wet grass, he vaulted over the gate and ran across the yard towards Jacques' flat. It was empty and quiet. He clomped back down to the yard and sprinted over to the shed. The padlock had gone, the door sagging, secured only with a brick. Michael ducked into the gloom groping his way between the boxes of old tools towards the corner where he had seen the rifle. In a dusty green heap, lit by a thin shaft of light, the tarpaulin lay, like the discarded skin of dragon. Relief, a warm glow, flooded his head. He took a deep breath and backed out into the wet yard.

He knew that Stan was always on the lookout, prepared to answer questions if the farm was searched, but he felt responsible. He needed to warn him. The quickest route was by bike on the road, but there was the danger of meeting Kurt and Walter again. He swung open the gate and wheeled the bike into the yard and left it blocking the bottom of Jacques' stairs. If his brother did return soon, he might realise that something was wrong.

Around the back of the milking shed, he squeezed through the hawthorn hedge and ran awkwardly along the edge of a ploughed field, ready for spring sowing, the rows of raised soil dusted with snow. He climbed over a fence and into what had been a small wood until most of the trees had been chopped down for firewood. Stumps tripped him and clinging brambles grabbed at his feet, darkening his boots and wetting his trousers. When he reached the first of the Bideau farm fields, where a flush of green was showing, the oat crop which he had helped to plant nearly three weeks ago, he was breathing heavily. Keeping to the edge, mud heavy on his boots, his calves aching, he moved quickly around two sides of the field and through the gate onto a rough track. The farmyard lay below him. He glanced back up the hill towards the road, but all was quiet. If the two Germans were searching other places before reaching here, he had time, but he didn't want to take the risk of being seen.

Michael trotted down the track and into the silent farmyard where the tractor sat between two ancient rusting machines. Where was Stan most likely to be? The barn was shut.

He heard the piano as he reached for the kitchen door handle and froze, hand outstretched, the memory of Mr Bideau's blood splashed on the white teeth of the piano vivid. Single notes, as if the player was searching for something, tentative but deliberate. Michael took a deep breath and opened the door, careful to make no noise. Louder now, through the open door into the sitting room, the notes moved up, then down the scale. Behind him, in the kitchen garden, a blackbird pinged out a single repetitive sound. There was a moment of quiet and then a tune he didn't know started, slow at first, rhythmic and repetitive, building up to a quicker pace, making him think of dancing, folk dancing, girls in bright colours with ribbons in their hair, a village green, crowds of people, families and small children. The music stopped abruptly. He waited, unsure what to do. The piano came to life again; this time the tune was familiar, though slow. After a few bars he identified it as 'Für Elise', a tune Amy had learned, and played over and over, when she was having piano lessons, before the occupation.

The tune was being played with what he could only describe as tenderness. Amy had never made it sound so beautiful, so liquid. So moving. The piano was a little out of tune, some of the higher notes slightly flat, but there was a softness to the performance and he didn't want it to end, didn't want the ugly warning he brought to kill the moment. When the music ended Michael felt empty; the silence rang in his ears and the stale smell of cooking filled his nose.

Konstantin did not move from the piano when Michael walked in, calling his name. Stan's broad shoulders, straining the seams of one of Paul's old shirts, were hunched, his head down. His dark, wavy hair was tousled and curling over his collar. Was he remembering home and the grandmother he had spoken of; he wouldn't want Michael to see his emotion.

'Stan,' he said again, reluctant to intrude. 'I met Germans on the road. They are searching… you need to…'

There was no indication that Stan had heard and the silence felt taut.

Suddenly Stan was on his feet pushing back the chair which tipped backward with a wooden clatter as he turned to Michael. There was something animal and intense in his eyes, a coldness. A frown furrowed his forehead and his lips were drawn back from yellow teeth. He was almost unrecognisable. Fear, a cold hand, squeezed Michael's chest.

'You… should be ready… I met two German soldiers, sent to search farms and houses. I just thought I'd warn you. I must go.'

Stan's face softened and he nodded. 'Yes. Go. I am ready. Thank you.'

Michael turned to leave. His mother was right. She was always right. Stan was damaged and unhappy. As he left through the kitchen garden gate, he looked back to see Stan standing in the doorway, watching him, a frown on his face and his arms folded.

*

Is this it? Is this his chance? To get revenge. To kill. To satisfy the itch. He feels no fear, only a tingle of excitement. The Le Breton family expect him to continue the farce, to produce his papers, play the part of Mr Bideau. He knows he should prepare, go over his story as they have suggested: he works alone on the farm since his wife died; occasionally his neighbour, Paul Le Breton, helps out.

What he really wants to do is sharpen a knife, keep his pitchfork handy…

The Le Bretons think they know him, believe he'll protect them and their secret. They have been wrong to trust him. He hardly trusts or understands himself now. He feels… no, he feels nothing. Feels no gratitude or loyalty.

Only with his grandmother and with Anya had he felt anything. Anya… that was a lifetime ago and in another country… A cloudy memory of the orchard in spring, wind swirling white blossom and Anya smiling, drifts into his head. She holds his hand and they walk towards the river. A picnic: his grandmother's fresh bread, cheese, last year's apples from the barn store. Stan closes his eyes, leans his head on the door jamb and he's there, propped up on one elbow on the red blanket. Anya lies on her back, dark curls framing her pale face, pulling a green cardigan close around her against the gusty April wind. He bends to kiss the parted lips… but he can't recall the moment, the sensation has left him.

Opening his eyes, he's back in Jersey, a cold wind blowing into the kitchen through the open door. Outside, the last leaves of kale are curled and green against the turned earth and the autumn raspberry canes need pruning.

*

Michael glanced up the track leading from the yard towards the road as he jogged past the front of the farmhouse and turned into the passage next to the barn. He'd keep out of the farmyard, circle around the buildings. Still no sign of Kurt or Walter. Moving quickly, he didn't see the little brick structure, concealed by brambles and undergrowth, until he tripped over part of it, painfully banging his foot, and falling into the wooden door. He picked himself up, cursing under his breath.

The coal cellar. Stan had told them that he'd hidden in a coal cellar before they found him; this must be it. A good hiding place. He imagined Stan, frightened, cold, hungry, falling into the darkness, over a year ago now. How Stan had changed from the skinny, silent victim to… to what? And how Michael had changed too. He felt more powerful, less fearful, and yet… Was the worst yet to come? He was sure that Walter's comment about a negotiated peace was a pipedream. Things were more complicated.

He examined his hands, both grazed from his fall, one smeared with blood, and wiped them down his trousers. His foot felt bruised, like it had when Jacques had nearly run him over… before the Germans came.

They were surely on the way now. He limped back to the corner of the barn and peered around towards the road. At the top, outlined against the white sky, a figure, just one, in uniform. He ducked back and took a deep breath before looking again, keeping low. The figure hadn't moved. He was sure it was one of the Germans, probably Kurt, not the sturdy figure of Walter. The arms were raised. He was watching the farmyard, through a pair of binoculars. Michael sat back against the side of the barn. He could do nothing; he must go home. One more look. The figure had gone. The track was empty.

APRIL 1944

Easter Monday's sunshine brought crowds to the football match in St Clement's. Michael followed his mother and Meg as they edged their way towards a corner of the field where there were fewer people and spread a tarp under a tartan picnic blanket. He had persuaded them to come; he was 'a sub'. He probably wouldn't get on the field… only if there were injuries. His mother had teased him and said she hoped that he would not, that she didn't want him to get a black eye, like Yves, or a broken leg, like one of the lads in the last match. Yves had sported his black eye with pride; purple for the first week, fading to sickly yellow. Michael could see him with a few of his teammates in the opposite corner of the pitch, some doing sprints, and wondered if he should join them. Most of them were standing in small groups chatting, arms folded, keeping an eye on the German opposition who appeared to be doing a more co-ordinated programme behind the crowd, off the field near to their transport trucks. In neat rows of four, and in unison, they were stretching to one side and then the other, legs apart, hands above their heads. Tall, mostly fair. Dressed in black shorts and white tops, they looked sharper and more professional than the Jersey lads. No matching kit there; some wore baggy shorts, others working trousers under vests or woollen undershirts. Yves' frayed, cut-down shorts hung to his knees below an old white cotton shirt with the sleeves rolled up.

He sat down on the rug, listening to the conversation between Meg and his mother, keeping his eyes on the German team and Kurt who was warming up with them.

'... gorgeous day! Did you get to mass, yesterday, Hélène? I was so disappointed when I woke to that heavy rain battering the daffodils, but by the time I was ready for church, the sun had come out and it felt so much more like Easter.'

'Oh, yes. St Clement's was decorated beautifully and the church was full. There was a feeling of... optimism, I thought.'

'Spring always makes me feel hopeful. And we've been there before, haven't we, hoping that the end of the occupation might be in sight?'

'I know, but seeing the crops growing, potato harvest in full swing and tomato seedlings in the greenhouse, I can't help it. And the rumours and allied planes. It can't go on much longer surely. Do you think that the Germans might be worried? I know you talk to one or two who are billeted at Gorey.'

'I talk with Walter occasionally. He's quite... reticent about that sort of thing. You know, I admire him. He's not interested in the war, but he's not going to be disloyal. We talk about Jersey – history mostly. And he's told me about his family, how he misses them. He so rarely gets letters. He didn't say so, but I know he's hoping there'll be an end to it as much as we are.'

'What are you looking forward to most, Meg, when all this is over?'

Michael turned to look at Meg when she did not reply. She was frowning and biting her lip.

'I… it's silly… I know, but I'd like things to go back to how they were… with Jacques, I mean.'

Michael felt a squeeze in his chest. Did Meg know about Lily? He thought not. He watched as his mother put out her hand and grasped Meg's fingers which were clutched on her lap.

'Well. Let's wait and see…' she said, quietly. And then with a note of cheer in her voice: 'I'm looking forward to proper bread, with a crusty top, smothered in butter and jam! At least we had some coffee substitute in our rations this week. Better than the acorn stuff that Paul made.' She made a face and glanced at Meg, whose smile had returned.

'What about that red wine we were allowed? I was looking forward to it so much. Father and I saved our cheese and I baked some biscuits to go with it. It was awful! Vinegar would have been better! I think I'm most looking forward to some good French wine, a burgundy with some smelly, ripe brie! What about you, Michael?'

'So many things… friends coming back. And chocolate… real chocolate.'

'Oh, yes, and scented soap,' said his mother.

'Mmmm! What a joy it will be to have a bath and get out smelling of lavender or something… floral. I put some of my dried lavender in my bathwater this week, but it didn't have much effect. I suppose that could be because I had to use father's bathwater,' Meg said, laughing. 'Things will get better. I know it!'

A whistle shrieked and the referee, a German officer, clad in black trousers and shirt, ran onto the pitch, followed by the two teams. The Jersey team pushed forward a tall, lanky fellow, with a mop of ginger hair.

'That's Rob Marett, isn't it, the captain?' asked Meg.

'Yes, Judith's husband. She's one of the girls who works in our greenhouses.'

'Oh, yes, I know him. Didn't he have a tough time because of the fishing regulations? I hope things have improved.'

The referee tossed a coin and the German captain gestured with his hand towards the end of the field closest to where uniformed officers were watching, then turned to Rob and held out his hand. Michael saw Rob hesitate before shaking the offered hand as his team spread out across the field.

'Jude says that it is easier now, though there are still ridiculous limitations on when and where they can fish… Oh, goodness me! That looked painful.'

Yves had been brought down by a tackle on the other side of the field and was picking himself up out of a muddy patch. Michael stood up, wondering, hoping, he might get to play.

'Poor Yves… Oh, I think he's all right. Are you sure you want to play, Mike? It looks quite rough.'

'I'd like to beat them… but I don't think my football is good enough, really. They are so strong and seem very organised. I can't see us scoring against that line of defenders.' He sat down again and rummaged in the picnic basket bringing out an apple.

'Michael…' Meg's voice was low. She looked around. 'Can I ask you to do something for me?'

'Of course!'

'Can you give a message to one of your team, at half-time?'

Michael stopped eating and looked at Meg.

His mother shook her head. 'Meg… should you…?'

Meg glanced at her. 'Michael's been trustworthy over

Stan for more than a year, hasn't he? He can give a message to one of the footballers.'

'Of course I can,' said Michael. 'What do you want me to say?'

'It's just a simple message I want you to give to George Le Brocq. Do you know him? He's the goalkeeper. Tell him that I'll be up tomorrow to collect the apples he promised me.'

'I can do that. What does it mean?'

'No, Michael,' said his mother. 'Don't ask Meg. She won't tell you! Better that way. Just have a chat with him about the game and give him the message, as casually as you can. No need to whisper or see who's listening. Make it sound like an ordinary message.' Hélène patted his shoulder. 'Maybe you should go over to your team now. In case you are needed. Easier to go with them at half-time.'

Michael stood up, pushed the apple core into a corner of the basket and tucked his shirt into his old trousers. 'What I'd really like is to get on for the last few minutes and score the winner!'

There was a cheer from the German spectators.

'Oh, no! I don't think George had a chance to stop that! What a shot! See you both later.'

Running around the edge of the field, as the German players shook hands with each other and the Jersey lads gathered in a huddle in the middle of the pitch, Michael felt a surge of energy and a warmth in his face. He'd love to join them, have a go, show some opposition.

MAY 1944

In the copse of freshly-greened beech and birch trees, behind the concealed pig pen, Konstantin watches. He waits, in the cold shadows. Maybe this time the German boy will come down to the farm. He's ready. A bright shaft of sun lights up the overgrown passage between the two buildings and a slice of the silent yard. During the past few months, he's seen the figure almost every week, silhouetted against the grey sky, at the top of the track, binoculars trained on the farm. He's pretended not to notice, gone about his routines as usual. Keeps a pitchfork and a sharpened scythe just inside the barn door. Until now, the soldier hasn't ventured down the track. This morning, as he crossed the yard from a visit to the barn to collect eggs, he'd glanced up and seen the familiar figure beginning to walk down to the farm, alone. Not quickening his pace, he continued into the house and dumped the eggs in the sink, excitement buzzing in his head. He stumbled through the sitting room and into the unused, damp-smelling dining room, pushed up the sash window that he'd been oiling for weeks and squeezed through, falling into long grass and nettles at the other side of the house before running back towards the copse.

It's very quiet. He waits for the sound of boots on the concrete of the yard. He has no plan and no weapon. Why didn't he keep the pitchfork in the kitchen garden? Or take a knife from the drawer? But he's calm and focused. Here's his chance.

A movement in grass. A fat tabby he's never seen before is creeping along the barn wall; a thick abdomen suggests pregnancy. Her head and tail down, she's hunting. Pounces, arching her back, shaking her head. She trots away, a large mouse or rat in her mouth, around the corner. Out of sight. The yard, or what he can see of it, is still empty.

He squats down, edges on hands and knees down the gap between buildings to get a better view. The soldier is at the gate, fumbling with the catch. So young, thin, no match for him. He watches as the German swings open the gate and stands, scanning the yard and house before moving towards the barn, his hand on the sheathed knife at his belt. He pulls open the barn door and moves cautiously into the gloom.

Here's his chance. He leaps up and runs, booted feet as light as possible, into the barn, barges into the German's back before he can turn at the noise. Pins the man against a stack of straw with the weight of his body. Kicks into the back of his right knee. It buckles. A boot between the shoulder blades and he's face down on the concrete. Both groping for the knife.

Konstantin snatches it, kneels on the German's back, wrenches his head back with a fist in his hair. Holds the blade to his throat.

'Steh auf!' *The words are snarled. He wants to see his face, wants to see fear.* 'Steh auf! *Up! UP!*'

The German gets to his feet and turns his eyes on the knife, his face white, mouth open.

A surge of heat rushes through Konstanin and he smiles. 'Arschloch! Schwanz! Schwein! Abschaum!' *He yells in the German's face, the words of abuse he remembers from his imprisonment.* 'Abschaum! Abschaum!' *Grabs at the front of his jacket, spits in the sweating face. Raises the knife.*

*

Michael heard shouting and his pulse leapt as he and Amy reached the gate. The yard was empty, except for a fat tabby cat, licking her paws by the kitchen garden gate, the barn door open.

'Stan! Are you here?' called Amy, running towards the barn.

'Wait!' Michael dashed after her. She wrenched open the barn and a slab of sunlight fell on Stan and Kurt, frozen, eyes wide. Stan had twisted Kurt's arm behind his back, forcing him forwards and onto his knees.

There was a loud moment of absolute silence. Michael's legs were shaky, unmoveable. Amy gasped. When she spoke her voice was strangled, thin, scared. 'What? Stan? What are you doing?'

Stan shook his head, pursed his lips. 'He watch farm… German soldier. I was afraid.' Light glinted off the blade in his hand which he brought out from behind his back and held up in front of his face.

Michael stepped forward. 'Put the knife down, Stan. Give it to me. He's… only doing his job. He has to search… let him. It's fine. I promise.' He held out his hand to Stan who shook his head.

'No. Stay away. I keep knife.'

Stan grabbed Kurt's collar and hauled him up to stand with his back to him, his arm tight round his neck.

'Oh, God,' sobbed Amy. 'Don't hurt him, Stan. I… what shall we do, Mike? Please let me talk to him.. Stan… please.'

Stan shook his head. 'No. I am in charge.' His voice was cold, his face wooden.

Amy's voice was stronger: 'Stan… I know this soldier. He's harmless. He… I don't think he wants… trouble. He has no weapon now… look. Will you put the knife away? You are scaring me.' A long moment of stillness.

'Go home, girl. And you, boy. I deal with him.' Stan tightened his grip. Kurt's eyes were closed, his hand curled into fists.

'Please, Stan. Don't hurt him. He wouldn't say anything. He's… my friend.' Amy pleaded. 'What are you going to do?'

He shook his head, sneered. 'Go away. Leave. Or you will see…'

'I am going nowhere, Stan,' said Amy taking a step towards him. 'Look, Stan. What do think will happen if you hurt him? If he disappears?'

Michael stepped up to stand with his sister, taking her arm. 'They'll find you, Stan… and us. We'll all be in danger – all of us. We've come this far. Please don't do this.'

'Kurt's not like the others, the ones who hurt you,' said Amy softly. 'He's told me he's ashamed… of the way foreign workers are threated. Do you understand, Stan? They aren't all like that. He won't say anything. He won't betray us.'

'All the same… all German the same.' Stan's voice was quieter.

'No…no. You're wrong. But think of us, the family.'

Amy moved suddenly, pulling her arm out of Michael's hand, grabbing at Stan's restraining arm. There was a scuffle, the bellow of a hurt animal. Michael lurched forward, tried to pull Amy back, saw the knife raised before Stan tumbled forward onto his knee, trying to shoulder Amy away without moving his arm from Kurt's neck. The German twisted out of Stan's grasp and was out through the open door, his boots ringing on the flagstones. The knife hit the floor with a clang. Stan yelled and screamed, his teeth bared, words which Michael had never heard before '*Gavno! Muduk!*' Then, looking at Amy, softly, with a curl of his lip, '*Blyat.* Bitch.'

JUNE 1944

'Mike. MIKE.' The voice hissed in the darkness. A knife glinted. 'Mike!' Laura needed him… wanted him; her face, pale, unsmiling, quivered. 'MIKE!' There was a humming he couldn't identify. He struggled out of the clouds of sleep and a dark figure put a warm hand on his shoulder. He sat upright. Bad dreams had dogged his sleep since the incident with Stan and Kurt.

'What? What's the matter?'

'Can't you hear it? The… humming.' Amy sounded excited. It was the most animated she'd been for weeks.

It wasn't humming; it was a droning noise.

'What is it?'

'Allied planes, I think. There must be hundreds of them.'

The wooden floor was cool on his feet as he moved to the window and pulled back the blackout curtains, looking up into a sky turning grey. Dark shapes, in symmetrical formations moved across the leaden expanse. A stuttering burst of anti-aircraft fire, probably from the gun emplacements on the north, was followed by sustained shooting and spouts of light shot up into the dark.

'Maybe it's started! The allied invasion. What do you think?'

The last few weeks of hectic activity had been discussed endlessly at home and on the farm. Bombing in France, usually at night, had been heard, with explosions visible in the dark. Every day allied planes, and sometimes German ones, flew over the island. More leaflets, usually in French, had been dropped. The Germans were behaving differently too; they were less relaxed and fewer were seen in town and at the Havre des Pas pool. Many were involved in the daily manoeuvres and exercises. Farmers had been complaining of trampled crops and damage to fences and hedges. Jersey people were excited, nervous. Michael couldn't feel hope, not yet. The dread of Stan being discovered, Kurt betraying them, was a weight in his stomach every day. But it had not happened, not yet.

The family had discussed moving him, finding another place to hide him, the day after the incident, over two weeks ago, when Michael had blurted out his fears to their parents early in the morning, after a restless night. Yves brought Meg over to the Bideau farm and the family sat around the kitchen table. Stan was withdrawn, quiet, his eyes flicking between Michael's parents' and Meg's and Jacques' faces, on the edge of a chair, like an animal poised for flight. He was reluctant to meet Michael's eyes and he turned away from Amy when they entered the kitchen. There was a bulging sack and a pitchfork by the door.

Meg was calm. She smiled and reached out to pat his shoulder. He flinched but looked up at her and leaned forward, folding his arms on the table in front of him. As she talked, he fixed his eyes on her.

'Well, I think if Kurt had decided to tell anyone about what happened, the Germans would be here now… or yesterday, so let's be optimistic. Moving Stan is possible but might be as dangerous. They are on high alert, stopping cars, questioning people who are moving around. Why not grit our teeth and act as if nothing unusual has happened? He's played the part of Mr Bideau successfully so far.' She turned to Stan and smiled at him. 'Konstantin, what do you want to do?'

Stan didn't take his eyes from her face, but rubbed his hands together, scratched at his neck. Wiped his nose on his sleeve. He shrugged his shoulders and shook his head, as if trying to clear his head.

'I…s-sorry…' he stuttered. 'I was wrong… I not want trouble for you…' He looked across the table at Michael's mother and father, opening his eyes wide and turning his palms up, as if pleading. 'You tell me… what I must do.'

Michael glanced at his sister. Amy was very pale and still, her eyes fixed on Stan's face, a deep frown on her forehead. Was she also thinking how different Stan had looked and acted when Kurt had escaped? Was that the real Konstantin? Full of rage and hate? Michael had guided her home, with his arm around her shoulders, as if she were a traumatised child. She had refused to talk about it, only nodding when he had consulted her about telling their parents, her red eyes evidence of a sleepless night.

'So… if we all agree, let's try to act as if nothing happened.' Meg looked around the table in her searching, thoughtful way. Michael nodded and smiled at her, noticed the way her eyes stopped on Jacques' face.

'Meg's right… it's better that he stays,' said Jacques. 'You'd better put those things away.' He gestured towards the bag and pitchfork by the door.

Michael had not seen Stan since. His father and Jacques went to the Bideau farm to help with the potato harvest, and had said that Stan was working hard, but he avoided the place.

Amy slid onto the window seat next to him, her pale face angled upwards, straining to see the planes. 'The beginning of the end… it must be the beginning of the end… finally.'

Churchill's famous words after the victory at El Alamein had been circulated by those who listened to the BBC World Service on hidden wirelesses: 'It is not the end. It is not even the beginning of the end. But it is, perhaps, the end of the beginning.' Since then, after news of allied victories, or German setbacks, people talked of 'the beginning of the end.' But most of the excitement ended in disappointment.

'Let's not get our hopes up, Amy.'

'I know. But this… looks so… big. Look at how many planes are heading for France. Hundreds!'

'It's frightening. Think of all that… destruction they'll cause. All those deaths.'

'I know… but… aren't you just a little bit excited?'

'I'd like it all to end. I'd be excited to get our island back… for the Germans to go.' He paused. 'Have you seen Kurt recently?'

Amy sighed and there was a silence, broken by more anti-aircraft fire.

'No… not since… Stan threatened him. He hasn't been at Le Hocq. Two other soldiers are there most days. It's been nearly three weeks…' Amy put her head down on her knees, her eyes fixed on the darkness outside the window.

'I saw him last week. He was on a bike, with Walter, heading up the St John's Road,' said Michael.

Amy sat up and looked at him. 'How did he look? Was he all right?'

'He was fine, I think. He must have seen me… Walter raised a hand. I was with Jacques in the truck.'

'Mike… I wish I knew what was going to happen. It's so unsettling… I've been feeling nervous. This time last summer, I was… happy. Kurt is, was, so easy to talk to. Now… things have changed so much. I didn't think it could be so difficult. I thought it was simple… you are friends, or you aren't. It's much more complicated.' Michael waited. What could he say? 'And Stan. He's become so aggressive, even more unhappy… he was like an… animal… when he found Kurt.'

'Everyone's tense…' His response felt thin. He wished he could comfort her.

'I think it's more than that with Stan. There's something in him…'

'I know. It must be desperate for him too. He's worried about being discovered. Maybe he worries about us too; I'd like to think he does, but I'm not sure.'

'What will happen to him, do you think? I suppose he'll get back to Russia, when this is all over. He doesn't know if any of his family are alive, you know. He still doesn't talk about them, but I don't get the impression that he's close to his father. And he's never mentioned a mother or siblings. Just the grandmother… maybe he'll stay in Jersey…'

Michael and Amy talked until the sky lightened and still the planes passed overhead.

Jacques barged through the back door as the family sat down to breakfast. Michael's mother had surprised them with bacon and fresh eggs. She'd saved the bacon from the pig that was killed last week, hiding it in a meat safe at the back of the potato cellar. 'I knew there'd be something to celebrate!' she had said when the smell had called Michael and Amy to the kitchen.

'Any of that for me?' asked Jacques. There was an unnatural glittering in his eyes and his lips looked sore and cracked. He pulled out a chair with a scraping of wood on flagstones.

'Too late, Jacques! I only had enough for four. I can do you eggs. The hens are laying well at the moment.'

'Thanks. But I can't stay, actually. Well, what about the planes? Did you hear the noise last night? And I saw more going over as I was walking down.' He spoke quickly, his eyes hooded.

'It must be the start of a big attack. What else could it be? I wonder when we'll get any news. I might go and see what I can find out.' Michael's father drained his mug of tea. 'I'll take the truck.'

'I think this could be it! We'll soon be free of them.' Jacques stood up again and bounced on his toes around the kitchen, as his father left. He punched Michael playfully on the shoulder. 'I was going to meet with a few friends at Yves' place this afternoon, if I can use the truck. Want to come, Mike?'

'Oh… yes. After school?' Michael wanted to know if his brother was planning anything, wanted to know about the rifles. In a sudden rush, it became clear; he wanted to stop his brother using the rifles, wanted to keep the family safe. Would he be able to do that?

'Well. I'll get back to the milking. Pick you up later. All right?'

Amy spoke as the door slammed and the dogs' leads swung on their hook. 'I suppose we do have to go to school, Mum?

'Of course you do. Nothing's changed. There'll be news later if anything important has happened. Go on, both of you.' She stood and started clearing the table. 'There are cold jacket potatoes you can take for lunch; we've eaten all the bread… and there are plenty of apples.'

The morning's lessons dragged. Michael normally enjoyed science lessons, but Mr Russell was distracted, they all were;

apart from copying out some formulae from the text book and working slowly through some problems, they didn't achieve much. Rumours started to circulate just after lunchtime. Jonny raced back from his lunch at home saying that he'd heard that there'd been a big assault on the beaches of Normandy. British, American and Canadian soldiers. His father had heard from a neighbour... no details, but surely this was it, he said, the big push! There were cheers in the playground. Girls were hugging each other; the boys made do with slapping each other on the back. Michael, in the shade of the big chestnut tree, listened to the chatter and laughter and looked around at the smiling faces around him. His chest was tight and he took a deep breath. He had so many questions circling in his head, none of them fully formed and none of them answerable. Stan's future? Laura? Freedom? Food?

Jonny poked him in the ribs with an elbow and put his mouth close to his ear.

'Mike... let's skip school this afternoon... celebrate.'

Michael leaned away from him; bunking off with Jonny was the last thing he wanted to do. 'Tempting... but...'

'Bloody hell, Mike. You used to be fun. What's happened?' Jonny walked away and Michael watched as he chatted with Keith. Both of them turned to look back and him and then moved away towards the bike shed. What's happened? He'd have liked to answer that. Jonny seemed so untouched by everything. He'd like to tell Jonny about Stan, about Meg's work with escaped workers, about Jacques' activities and the hidden rifles. The secrets massed like black clouds in his head. That's what he was really looking forward to, an escape from secrets... and normality. Would things return to what they were? Would Laura come back? She'd be the one to share his thoughts with.

Jonny and Keith were missed in arithmetic. He shrugged his shoulders when Mr Le Cornu tapped his cane on his desk and asked if he knew where they were. The day ended with an English lesson. Unlike Mr Le Cornu, who had insisted on testing the class on their recent work, threatening and shouting at those boys who had refused to concentrate, Miss allowed the class time to talk about the situation and asked them what they were looking forward to most, once the occupation was over. The day ended with her reading aloud to them from The Hobbit and Michael allowed himself to get lost in visions of Bag End and Gandalf.

His parents were in the kitchen with mugs of tea when he and Amy arrived home.

'It's all true,' said his father as they drew up chairs. 'I heard it myself on the World Service. There was a "communique"... that's what they called it... it said that today allied naval forces had landed on the north coast of France. It was very brief... no news on whether it was successful for not.'

They sat in silence for a couple of minutes. Michael could hear the grandfather clock in the hall ticking and birds outside tweeting and calling.

His mother reached out and put a hand on Michael's hunched shoulder. 'It's good news...'

He looked around into her smiling face. 'I know, and I'm happy... really. But what's going to happen here? We saw lots of Germans on our way home. There was a large group marching down the road near the school and cars and motorbikes passed us all the way. Most of them were carrying rifles and wearing helmets.'

'We have to wait, Mike,' said his father. 'Let's hope they'll surrender. It certainly doesn't look like that at the moment... I agree. Maybe they'll send British troops here. Things aren't over yet. We have to be prepared...for an attack.'

He looked across at Amy's pale face. She was very still, her eyes fixed on her hands clasped on the table in front of her. Who was she worried about most? Kurt or Stan? He reached into his pocket, felt for the comforting coolness of the button. Hold fast.

'Shall we go and feed the animals, Amy? Has Dolly been in the barn all day, Mum?'

'Most of it, yes. You know she doesn't like me, Mike. I went in to fill her water bowl and let her out. She flew around the yard, shouted things and tried to sit on my shoulder.'

Michael smiled. 'She's just affectionate.'

'The things she said didn't sound affectionate. I can't repeat them, but she was cursing. Who's taught her that? And she pecks my ears…' Mum was smiling and glancing at Amy. He wasn't the only one trying to distract her.

Michael sat on the yard gate and waited for Jacques. He strained his eyes towards the coast of France but the horizon wasn't clear and the sky and sea merged in an expanse of blue-grey. Jacques was smiling widely when he skidded to a halt beside Michael. They were lucky to have the motorbike; so many others had been requisitioned.

'Let's hope we won't be stopped. I'll take the back lanes…' His voice was lost as he revved and moved off at speed. Michael grabbed his belt and felt the cool rush of air in his hair.

The kitchen was already hazy with cigarette smoke when Jacques ran up the narrow stairs ahead of Michael and into Yves and Bob's flat. Rob and Emile were seated at the table. Yves, who'd locked the door to the yard behind them, dragged a couple of chairs forward and they joined the group. Rob had brought a bag of beers and Emile was pushing him to say where he'd got them from.

'Couldn't possibly tell you! Hello, Jacques, Mike – have a beer before they're all gone. Let's drink to… victory?'

The bottles were raised. 'Victory… finally!' said Jacques.

Michael took a swig of warm beer. He wasn't very keen, but today wasn't the day to refuse and he gulped the bitterness down and looked around. On the table was a copy of the *Evening Post*. He leaned forward and read one of the headlines: *The Invasion Starts*.

'Can I look at that?' he asked.

Jacques passed him the paper. 'Go ahead. You'll see that they're playing it down. I'll be back in a few minutes. Just need to see a man about a dog!' He left the room and his boots tapped as he ran down the stairs.

Michael read the brief article. Jacques was right. The subheading was *Many Parachute Units Destroyed* and, at the top, the source was identified as 'Berlin 6th June.' According to the article, the *long expected attack* by *the enemy*, consisting of *heavy bombing attacks, air-borne troop forces* and *navel landing units* had been dealt with by the defence forces of the German army, with many parachutists killed or taken prisoner and battleships and landing craft destroyed. It ended by stating that the fighting was 'in full swing'. What did that mean? Was it good news or bad? How could you ever know?

'Doesn't look good, does it?' Bob nodded towards the paper and frowned.

'But it's only the Germans' version,' said Michael. 'There's nothing here about the hundreds of British planes we saw. They must have inflicted a lot of damage…'

'Or they were destroyed by German guns… I'm worried…'

'Don't be ridiculous, Bob,' said Jacques, as he returned with a bag under his arm which he put under the table. 'They'd never tell the truth. We'll get more from the BBC later. Apparently, the King is making an announcement.'

'The fight-back has started. That's the most important thing,' said Yves. 'It won't be long.'

Michael dropped his eyes to the newspaper again and read the message to the people of Jersey from Oberst Heine:

PROCLAMATION

To the Population of the Island of Jersey

Germany's enemy is on the point of attacking French soil.

I expect the population of Jersey to keep its head, to remain calm, and to refrain from any acts of sabotage and from hostile acts against the German forces, even should the fighting spread to Jersey.

At the first signs of unrest or trouble I will close the streets to every traffic and secure hostages.

Attacks against the German forces will be punishable by death.

Der Kommandant der Festung Jersey

Jacques was tapping the paper. 'That's more interesting. They're expecting fighting here. And they'll get it!'

'What do you mean? It's just threatening… they know we can't do anything,' said Rob. 'They have all the power.'

Jacques smiled. 'Do they?' He looked around at Bob and raised his eyebrows. 'I wonder if we should have a little… fun while we can. It's time we took control. Time to use the rifles!'

Bob put down his bottle and frowned, looking steadily at Jacques. 'Oh, no, pal. Punishable by death, it says. You know I can't get involved. I've got my mother to think of. We need to sit it out.'

'What do the rest of you think?' There was a silence in the room. Michael looked around at the men, his pulse racing. Yves' mouth was open and his face flushed. Bob was frowning and biting his lip, Rob blinking, his hand over his mouth. Emile was perfectly still and keeping his eyes fixed on Jacques.

'Well. The rifles have been in the attic, here, for… nearly four years. Just in case.'

In the attic? Since when?

'What? No. I don't b-believe you.' Yves stuttered and shook his head. 'Here?'

'Calm down, Yves! Lest said, soonest mended. Isn't that what they say? Or is it "what the eye doesn't see the heart can't grieve over"? I thought it best you didn't know.'

'That t-t-time…' He couldn't get the words out. His face was red.

'When the Jerries searched? Lucky, weren't we? And if you'd known, think how you'd have felt, showing them around?'

Yves sat down and covered his face with his hands. 'Oh, bloody hell. All this time…'

'As I said, better you didn't know. And when I told you about having the rifles, there was something about Geoff that worried me. I don't trust him. So I decided not to say where they are.'

'Funny you should say that about Geoff. I feel the same. Weird bloke. Asked me about black market stuff. Seemed too… keen for information. Not that I had any,' said Rob.

'Well. I can trust the rest of you, I think! I'll have to, now! Let's think. Would it be best if we left them where they are for now, or should we take one home each? For defence… just in case there is fighting,' said Jacques.

'How many have you got?' Rob asked.

'Five.'

Michael looked at Jacques' eager face. He lied well. Where was the sixth?

'Bloody, bloody hell! All this time! Who else knows about them?'

'I told Lily… she won't say anything. She wanted to take one. I thought it might endanger her family. So, I said no.'

Had Jacques thought the same about his own family when he had hidden them in the shed? Michael's chest felt tight. What was he planning?

'You… should have told me, asked me. I live here!' Yves looked up and frowned at Jacques, his face grey and set. Michael had never seen him angry. 'What if…'

'Calm, down, Yves. I just thought it safer not to tell you. Do I need to keep repeating it? Look. Let's all sleep on it… talk about it again, with Lily and the others here. Emile. You've been very quiet… what do you think?'

Emile stood up. He was tall with very dark hair which flopped over his forehead and eyes. He pushed his hands deep into his trouser pockets. 'I think you should have told us earlier, Jacques. We could have used them… in that raid on the stores. I'd have felt safer with a gun, wouldn't you, lads?' He looked around for support, but no one met his eyes or replied.

Jacques sighed. 'Maybe I should've told you. But… there was never a right time. I never wanted to just… kill them. I know that it'd be suicide to do that. They were for, *are* for, protection, or special circumstances. I'd kill to protect my family, wouldn't you all?'

Emile sat down again, his face creased. 'What about the fire? That could have killed some of them. That wasn't about family. That was dangerous.'

'We made sure the place was empty, didn't we? Sabotage is different. Make life difficult for them, that's what we agreed. But things have changed…'

'Everything we have done puts us in danger,' said Rob. 'We take risks all the time.'

'Well, I vote we back off now and wait. Let's not do anything stupid,' said Bob.

'But the Germans are… worried, aren't they? Twitchy. They're less predictable; we need to be on our toes,' said Emile.

'Yes, and this latest news must unsettle them more. I think we should plan for some sort of action. Lily's very keen to continue to try to get soldiers to mutiny, isn't she?' said Rob. 'Can we try again? More of them might be persuaded now.'

'Why's Lily not here?' asked Yves.

'I'm not sure. You know she had her bicycle requisitioned… and the buses aren't reliable now that there's so little fuel. I suspect she just couldn't get here. I should have ridden over… but I brought Mike instead.' Jacques turned to Michael. 'What about you, Mike? What do you think?'

'Me? Yes, I want to do something, but the rifles… I don't think we should use them. Can we distribute leaflets to the Germans? About British advances. Who prints them? I'd help with that.'

'Great. Anyone else?' Everyone except Bob nodded. 'Lily has some contacts for printing stuff. Why don't we meet in a few days with some ideas and I'll talk to Lily.'

'And we'll make a decision about the rifles then, too?' said Yves. 'Now I know they're here, I'm nervous! Maybe we should move them…'

'Yep. Don't worry. They've stayed hidden for nearly 4 years; no reason we can't keep them there a bit longer. Shall we say Friday? Now… let's be optimistic and raise a toast to all the lads fighting in France.' He reached into the bag under the table and brought out a bottle which glowed like gold in the light of the oil lamp. 'I saved this for a special occasion. Here's to the boys! Ever tasted whiskey, Mike? You are in for a treat…'

JULY 1944

On a warm, blustery July morning, Michael was collecting eggs when Stan arrived at the farm. Despite his mother's attempts to keep the hens in the run beside the barn, they managed to escape and often hid their eggs in the cabbage patch or below the loaded, flowering bean frame in the kitchen garden. His mother was particularly worried about the hens which they relied on for eggs. Granny had told her that hens and ducks had been stolen in the parish, according to Mrs Le Brun on one of her weekly gossip visits. Mrs Le Brun was the source of local news updates and kept abreast of all sorts of useful information, probably because she was such a nosy woman. According to Mrs Le Brun, Granny had said, the culprits were hungry German soldiers whose rations had been cut again. She'd told Granny a dramatic tale – swore she had seen a dark, uniformed figure in her neighbour's garden. Woken by a squawking in the middle of the night, she had pulled aside her bedroom blackout curtains and seen the thief.

Michael's list of jobs now included clearing a space in the barn so that they could be locked in at night, but he was putting it off again. The Friday after the meeting when Jacques had revealed that the rifles were hidden in the plumbers' yard had come and gone. There had been no meeting, at least not one to which he had been invited. He was preoccupied, wondering how soon he could get up to the milking yard to talk to Jacques, on his hands and knees reaching under the beech hedge, when Stan appeared beside him.

'Michael!' he said. Startled, Michael jumped and sprang to his feet. It wasn't a greeting. More like an order. He found Stan's tone difficult to read; he sounded annoyed or anxious.

He hadn't seen him since the Normandy landings, over a month ago, rarely taking him provisions or checking up on him now because he didn't need as much help as before and anyway, he felt uncomfortable with him.

Stan's flat cap was low over his forehead, so that he couldn't see his eyes, but the lower half of his face was serious, the mouth thin. Perhaps he was lonely. Michael felt a lurch of guilt.

'Hello, Stan. I haven't seen you for a while. How are things on the farm?' He forced a smile and hoped his voice sounded friendly.

Stan made a grunting noise and spoke slowly, as if he were thinking about his words. 'Yes. Good on farm. Wheat crop is strong. We must thresh very soon. So much rain and now sun. But I am angry most of it will be taken by Germans.' He pushed back his cap and pulled up the corners of his mouth. Not quite a smile in the tanned face.

'You must be busy. I know you've been helping Dad too. What about your kitchen garden?'

'I come to talk. Not of gardens. I help.' He reached forward abruptly and took the basket of eggs from Michael. 'Can we talk?'

'Mmmm… what about a cup of tea? Only nettle tea, I'm afraid… but it's hot and…' As soon as he'd said it, he wished he hadn't. The thought of him sitting at the kitchen table, made him feel shaky. He wanted him gone; it was better that way. He couldn't trust him.

'Yes, tea… please.' He turned and walked towards the back door. Michael's feet dragged but he had no option but to follow him.

Dolly was sitting on the window ledge by the door as they approached. She took off and flapped around Stan's head, whistling and calling. 'Poor, poor Dolly'. He ducked and tried to bat her away with his hand. 'Pizdets! Pizdets! Get lost!' The parrot screamed and flew up to the barn roof.

'She's harmless,' said Michael, clenching his fists. 'I know she's a pest sometimes, but I'm… fond of her,' he said, leading the way into the kitchen.

'Pest… yes… like rats.'

Michael glanced at his face as he filled the kettle. There was something animal in his features. Where was his mother? She could always find something cheerful to say to Stan. 'No! Not like rats. She… she's a pet. I rescued her. She'd been abandoned.'

'Pet? No… pest. Pest, not pet!' He grinned, an empty, gap-toothed smirk, and nodded, pleased with his mastery of the language and sat down heavily on a chair resting his forearms on the table.

When he and Amy had found him at the abandoned Bideau farm, with torn feet and desperately hungry, barely able to stand, they hadn't hesitated, none of them had, even though they knew the risks. He needed help. Michael had pitied him, helped nurse him back to health, regarded him almost like a member of the family. It gave him hope, purpose, confidence. But now Stan was a different person and Michael found it hard to like him.

Recently, Amy, playing the piano in the back room, had stumbled her way through 'Für Elise.' It had brought back to mind that aggressive animal face that Stan had turned to him when Michael had heard him playing Mr Bideau's piano.

And it was worse than that. He feared for the family: the risk in hiding him had been real throughout those eighteen months, but now, since the confrontation with Kurt, the danger felt nearer, as if a black bag was hovering over his head, about to suffocate him. He licked his lips and kept his voice level. 'Stan. Are you being… careful? About being seen. Talking to people? Did you hear what happened over at St Ouen?'

'No… what?' He was alert. Pulled back his shoulders and fixed Michael with his dark eyes.

He busied himself with cups, not wanting to look at him. 'Mrs Gould. In St Ouen. She'd been hiding a Russian, a worker like you. I heard from Meg… Mrs Gould was arrested and now she's been deported… sent to Germany, I think. I worry… that they'll discover you.'

'I worry too.' His voice was cold, breaking over Michael's thoughts like a wave. 'I have knife if German comes back. But now… with fighting soon… I want rifle.'

But Kurt had not come back. Kurt had not betrayed them. If he had, they would have all been arrested weeks ago. The last time any of them had seen him was when Michael had passed him cycling up the Queen's Road, with Walter.

'What do you mean? What fighting?'

'Jacques has rifle. You tell me. I want rifle. Paul say British soldiers come soon. Maybe fighting.' His eyes, glittering, bored into Michael's.

What had he done? How stupid he'd been to tell Stan about the gun. He shook his head, rubbed at his nose. 'What? No! I… didn't mean it. I… lied. We… aren't allowed weapons. Everything was handed in, at the beginning of the occupation… I was just… trying to tell you that Jacques is strong… has tried to… do stuff.'

There was a second of quiet in the kitchen.

Stan slapped his hand down in front of him on the table. 'No! He has rifle. I need rifle.'

'No… no. No rifle. Look… I understand. Things are d-difficult. We are all waiting… hoping… hoping… there'll be an end to all this. But we can only… wait. The Germans might surrender. We must be patient.' How could he calm Stan? How could he calm himself?

Stan got to his feet, the chair scraping and screeching on the flagstones. Michael's heart pounded and lurched in his chest. He felt the hard edge of the range against his lower back, forced himself to meet Stan's eyes.

'No… they will fight,' Stan said, determination hard and steady in his voice. He turned away, slamming the door behind him. The dogs' leads rattled as they swung wildly on their hook. Michael watched him stride past the window. Bile bubbled sour in his mouth and he moved on shuddery legs to a chair, picked at a loose piece of cotton on his worn shirt sleeve. When would all this be over?

'Michael?'

His head jerked up. His father was standing in the doorway, eyebrows raised. 'Oh, Dad… I… I…' He covered his face with his hands and shook his head, not trusting his mouth to make words. Paul's hands on his shoulders were gentle and his touch so tender… tears pricked and fell. His father sat down next to him, pulling Michael towards him, so that his head collided with his father's chest. The warmth and strength of his shoulder, the familiar earthy smell, the softness of the threadbare shirt choked him. He gulped down the thing rising in his chest and took a deep breath. 'Sorry. I… don't know what's wrong… just felt… I don't know. I just… I want this all to be over.' Now was the time to tell him about Stan's visit, his threats. About the rifles, the fear he had that something bad, really bad, was going to happen.

His father said nothing but held onto him. His whole body started shaking and Michael allowed himself to bawl, until his pulse slowed and the convulsions died into twitches and sniffing.

'I'm sorry…'

'You're tired. And worried. And we're all… frustrated. Things will get better,' said his father. 'We have to be patient now. Things are turning. Sit it out, eh? Wait. There's nothing else we can do.'

'It's just that I am so worried about… everything, but mostly… Jacques. He's involved in something dangerous, I know he is. Amy… seems so unhappy. And Stan… what if…'

'We can't dwell on "what ifs", Mike. Come on now, pull yourself together. We've come this far and we'll get through it. Jacques can take care of himself. He's strong and determined. And he's doing what's right, what he believes in, eh? We have to trust him and we have to trust Stan.'

His father gave him a quick squeeze and dropped his arm from Michael's shoulder. 'I'll make tea. That kettle is about to whistle. What do we have? Nettles? Chamomile? I think we both need chamomile.' He disappeared into the scullery and Michael wiped his eyes and nose on his sleeve. Outside a blackbird sang in the willow tree; inside the weight of silence whirred in his ears. His father didn't need this panic, these weak tears; he needed Michael to be strong, pull his weight in the family, help with his grandparents.

A British bomb had fallen at La Rocque last week, blocking the inner road. No one had been hurt and there had been only minor damage to a garage belonging to Mr

Le Marquand, but his grandparents had been shaken by it, Grandmère Cecile hysterical, according to his mother. The bomber must have been aiming for the gun emplacement; leaflets had been dropped from planes warning locals to stay away from German fortifications, but that wasn't possible if you lived so close to one. His mother had suggested they moved into the farmhouse, but Poppa had refused to abandon his garden.

'This is the chamomile, isn't it?' Paul was standing in the doorway holding up the jar of flower heads looking like tiny dusty pom-poms.

'Yes. Let me do it. I feel better now. I'm sorry, Dad.' He got up and took the jar from his hand, turning away so that he couldn't see his face. 'I'll cycle over to La Rocque later this morning. I've found plenty of eggs which I'll take. Mum said she was going to make a pudding to take over. Apparently, carrageen moss makes a sort of milk jelly. Another Mrs Le Brun recipe, she said.' He was babbling and aware of the false cheer in his words. But it helped to pretend and he felt less shaky as he spooned the chamomile into the teapot.

'Well, that's kind, Mike. But I don't think we should worry so much about them. They're capable of looking after themselves, though your Grandmère does like a fuss made of her, as you know!'

Michael put a cup of golden tea in front of his father and sat down opposite him, welcoming the burn on his cold hands as he grasped the cup tightly.

'What's going to happen, Dad?' he said quietly. 'The Germans seem so jittery and the food situation is getting worse. I feel as if… we've been forgotten.'

'Let's keep calm. I don't think anyone can make predictions! But what I am certain of is that we can get through this. Look after each other, eh?'

Michael let the steam from his tea moisten his face and the soft herby smell filled his nose. He put the cup down again without taking a sip, raised his eyes to meet his father's and put a smile on his face. 'Of course we will.'

A sharp tap on the windowpane made them both jump. Dolly's bright eyes peered at them and his father laughed. 'She'll crack that glass one day! Mad bird!'

Michael took a deep breath. 'I'd better get on… she needs feeding. And I'm supposed to be building a hen run… in the barn. God knows what Dolly'll make of sharing her space.'

But he sat on, his eyes on the scrubbed table, his vision blurred.

OCTOBER 1944

Michael had already fallen off his bike once in the dark, grazing his knees on the rough coastal path close to Grouville Common. Now his front tyre bumped hard into a hole and he skidded across what he'd thought was the turning into Rozel Harbour. He stuck out his left leg and felt the prickle of undergrowth before he toppled into a ditch, his front wheel spinning close to his face. Shocked by the bite of stinging nettles up his arms, and alarmed by the loud ticking of the wheel, he jumped to his feet, climbed up onto the grassy verge and pulled his bike out and back onto its wheels. The darkness under the overhanging trees was thick, although splinters of the half-full moon were visible above him, as grey clouds rolled over it. He waited, listened, blinked until he could see the cloudy shape of the hedge and the grey glimmer of the road. Slowly, keeping his bike on the grass bank, he crept down the slope. The trill of crickets repeated and repeated and the strengthening wind hissed in the hedge, but there were no other sounds. There were guards in the harbour; he'd seen them on his last recce, sitting outside one of the fishermen's huts, but his target was out of their range at night: a sign, a pale square on the opposite side of the road. He crossed swiftly, propped his bike against a field gate and shrugged the rucksack off his back, wrenched out a can of black paint and one of his sister's thickest brushes. *Zutritt Verboten* – access forbidden – was almost obliterated in his large V sign and dripping capitals: BRITISH VICTORY IS CERTAIN. He grinned, clicked the paint lid back on and wrapped the brush in a rag before stuffing them into his bag. And he believed it. It was certain, but when it would happen was less clear.

The journey back was uneventful, though he had to pedal hard against the wind which was gusty and cold. A storm was on its way. He took the quietest tracks and footpaths and cut across the Bideau farm to avoid the road which was often used by a patrol after curfew. He had intended to wheel his bike around the back of the barn, not cross the farmyard, just in case Stan was still around, but as he pushed it through the long grass in the orchard, he paused. Voices, angry voices, were coming from the barn and he could see a flash of light, from a moving torch or a lantern, through the partly opened door. His father's truck stood in the yard, doors gaping open. Leaving the bike leaning against the coal cellar trapdoor, he crept silently towards the barn and looked around the door.

With their backs to him, Jacques and Stan were bending over a lumpy shape, partly concealed under the mess of a scattered hay bale. As his brother squatted down next to it, shining a torch downwards, Michael realised that it was a body. Face down. His stomach lurched and he couldn't control the gasp that escaped his open mouth. Two pale faces spun round. Then Stan's iron grip grabbed his arm, twisted it up his back, before he was able to splutter, his head down, searching for relief from the pain in his arm: 'It's me! For God's sake!'

Stan pushed him towards Jacques' gaunt, shadowed face.

'Bloody hell! What are you doing here?'

'I was...'

'Never mind. Help us now...' Jacques turned from him and crouched down again over the body, brushed straw from the back of the pale head, grasped the rough grey wool of the shoulder and rolled the body towards him. It flopped heavily. Open eyes in shadowed sockets. Boyish full lips. Kurt. A wave crashed in Michael's head and his vision blurred.

The black spread eagle above a breast pocket. Empty knife sheath. Dark stain, a hole, above a shiny belt buckle. Smell of urine. Wet trousers.

He felt the weight of Stan's silence next to him. Jacques got to his feet. Cleared his throat. Didn't take his eyes off the body. 'Right. Barrow. Shovels. Fetch them.'

'What... happened?'

'Now! Go. Haven't time. Go with Stan. Move. Move!'

Michael stumbled out of the barn into the yard on shaky legs, felt the wind snagging at his breath and bent over, retching and coughing.

He heard the clatter of tools in a metal barrow from the tool shed followed by the dark shadow of Stan, a cone of light from his torch moving before him.

'Take torch.' Stan's voice was husky.

Forcing air into his lungs and feeling a sharp pain in his chest, he grabbed the torch and followed the Russian back into the barn, held up the light. The shovels clanged and rang on the concrete floor as Stan tipped the barrow sideways. Without speaking, Jacques crouched and lifted the shoulders. Stan's large hands pulled up the shins and the body sagged between them as they swung it into the well of the barrow. A steel wristwatch glittered on an arm which drooped over the side. The head jerked backwards and the eyes looked up, blank, stony-cold.

'Let's go.' Jacques picked up the tools and gave Michael a shove towards the door. Stan followed wheeling the barrow into the yard before using a fireman's lift to load the body into the back of the truck. Jacques lifted the barrow in on top.

Once again Jacques roughly yanked at Michael's arm, pulling him towards the passenger door and he fell into the dark cabin, wedged between his brother and Stan.

Michael's dry mouth struggled to form words. He glanced at the frowning profile of his brother to his right. The word came out in a whisper; 'W-what?'

He felt rather than saw his brother shake his head.

Fitful moonlight, as dark clouds scudded across the low sky, showed the outlines of hedges lining the narrow roads and they met no vehicles as the truck rattled towards the coast. Stan was silent and still, leaning away from Michael, his head turned to the side. Michael fumbled into his trouser pocket, pulled out the Hold Fast button and gripped it tight in his palm.

At the bottom of Le Hocq Lane, Michael was flung against Stan as Jacques wrenched the steering wheel to the right. He was heading towards the marsh. What were they going to do with the body? Surely not bury it in the marsh? The truck bounced and bumped over the rough ground, branches scraping its sides as the path narrowed. Jacques braked suddenly under a drooping chestnut tree, its leaves curling and rusty, and turned off the engine. In the ticking seconds that followed, before any of them moved, the first fat drops of rain pattered against the windscreen. Michael slipped his hand into Jacques' jacket pocket, pushed the button to the bottom. Hold Fast.

'Right!' Jacques' voice was firm and steady. 'Once we've got him into the barrow, you carry the shovels, Stan. In front, with that torch, Michael. Keep it low so we can see the path.'

'Where?' Michael's voice was strained. He cleared his throat. 'Where are we…'

'The beach. Not sure which side of the tower yet. Out as far as we can go. Dig. Roll stones over it. You can help us down as far as the common. Then the moon will give Stan and me enough light. You drive the truck home. Too public here. We have to move quickly, tide'll come in. Come back for us later.'

Stan climbed into the back of the truck and rolled the body down into the waiting barrow with a thud. Jacques adjusted it, crossing the arms over the chest, almost tenderly, before covering it in the stiff folds of a green tarpaulin, the one they'd used to conceal the rifles. Pulled his cap down tight on his head.

The path through the trees was rough and muddy; crawling roots crossed the track and more than once Jacques had to right the barrow and pull the body back. The gusty, wet wind tore at Michael's jacket. Rain dripped down his collar. Now that he could no longer see Kurt's face, he felt stronger. He could do this. He had to do this. Had to help Jacques. Maybe everything would be all right. With the body buried and the tide washing rocks and sand over the grave, it would never be found. And… if it was, how could it be linked to them?

His mind wouldn't focus. But questions raced… What had happened? Who had done it and why had Kurt been killed?

The common was empty. The tower, lit by a cold moon, over which heavy clouds moved, was unguarded. The rocks and sands exposed at low tide stretched away until they met the glitter of the sea in the distance. Stan, two shovels under his arm, followed Jacques, bent over the barrow pushing it across humps of low-growing Marram grass and piles of seaweed thrown over the wall by yesterday's high tide. Michael put the torch down and he and Stan moved the wooden Xs, topped with barbed wire and Jacques descended the stone slipway with the barrow. Michael watched as his brother struggled over the patch of pebbles close to the wall, followed by Stan with the shovels over his shoulder, and then turned and ran back into the marsh.

*

Jacques' forehead glistens with the effort of pushing and keeping balance. He pauses on a patch of damp sand, lowers the barrow, pants, pulls his shoulders back, his eyes shut tight.

'I take now.' Stan steps in front of him and pushes the shovels into Jacques' arms. Black cloud drifts off a white, gibbous moon and the rocky landscape of Le Hocq sharpens in clarity. They set off again, keeping the bulk of King's Rock on the left, Jacques leading, down a shallow channel of shimmering water, rumpled with wind waves, which winds its way down, though mounds of rock, slippery with vraic, towards the invisible sea. The water rises cold over Stan's boots and seeps up his trouser legs. He picks his way with caution, disturbing the dark water beneath his feet.

Why the memory comes at that point, he has no idea. Maybe the silver of the moon on water. Maybe the rain. Why did he meet Anya that night by the river? They ran from the sudden downpour, he remembers that… her cold hand in his, her dark hair stuck to her face. And her laugh. He can hear her laugh.

'Stan! STAN!' The hissing of his name makes him stop and look up. The moon is covered and he can only make out an outline of Jacques, who has halted. The channel has deepened

between two piles of jagged boulders, the water over their knees and lapping at the underside of the barrow.

'Right. Listen!' says Jacques. 'I think we must carry the body now. I'll take it first. I'll be slow. Stay close and take these'. He hands over the shovels. Stumbling at first to find grip with his feet, he heaves the dead weight over his shoulder, grunting with effort. The wind tugs the tarp into his face and he wobbles.

'Help me, Stan… help me!' he shouts, his voice scattered by the wind, which is strengthening, pushing at them. 'Help me!'

Stan steps towards him, uses both hands to steady the body, tucks the tarp under it and stands firm while Jacques finds a secure footing, hoists his burden higher and turns towards Stone Beach.

The journey is slow, Jacques takes small steps until he is out of the channel and onto an area of relatively flat rocks where they swap jobs again.

Stan's eyes become more accustomed to the dark and, raising his head briefly from the dark tread of Jacques' boots, he makes out the rearing bulk of the Stone Beach rocks, still a long way off, the top of the stack outlined against the racing grey sky. He grips the tarpaulin-rolled legs and forces himself forward, feeling the weight shift and flop with every lurching step. Not so far now. Not so far now. He whispers the phrase to himself, breathing heavily, legs shaking. The rain lessens to a damp drizzle. A patch of sand allows respite from the fear of rough rocks. Momentum drives him forward, adrenalin surges through his body. Suddenly he trips over a rock, disguised in seaweed. It brings him to his knees and he collapses. The body falls forward.

'Shit!' he shouts into the wind, going down on his knees.

And Jacques is over him, a tight hand on his arm, wrenching him to his feet. 'Let's rest,' he says. He bends over, hand on his thighs, breathing in and out, trying to summon strength. He watches as Jacques wraps the body tightly and heaves it over his shoulder, stumbling backwards but regaining his balance. He stands with legs apart, waits for Stan.

Stan picks up the shovels and leads the way now, feeling lighter, energised, back into water, shallower as it curves over soft sand between fields of sharp stones and pebbles.

They reach Stone Beach as the hunchbacked moon shows itself again and throws a ghostly light on the granite rock rising from a stretch of sand and grit, littered with rounded boulders.

'Here. Yes. This is it.' Jacques drops the body and it falls, thumping on the sand like a dead sea creature.

He wants it over now. Wants to run. Or lie down on the wet sand, curl up, shut his eyes. Wait for the cold of the tide. But Jacques hands him a shovel, peels off his jacket and moves towards the big rock, selecting a place under the granite shelf where sand and small rocks gather in waves and humps. 'Under here. Let's dig. We can roll rocks over it.'

They dig. And dig. The sand and grit are heavy; the hole shifts and collapses. They pull out boulders, half-buried, bracing their legs on the unstable ground, roll them to one side. Hands bloodied, they rest, breathing heavily. Stan feels the burn in his lower back and thighs, sits on the pebbles, his arms around drawn-up knees, his head down.

'Come on.' Jacques nudges his shoulder with a boot. 'We can't stop.'

Sweating, the chill of the wind stinging his face, he begins again, the clang of metal hitting rocks echoes back at them from the towering granite face above. They dig until a curling swirl of water smooths the sand at the lip of the hole, the first sign of the tide turning. Jacques throws down his shovel and grabs the body under the arms, nodding at Stan to hold the feet. They shuffle across the stones and watch it fall into the hole. It rolls out of the tarp and becomes a boy lying in a grave. He's seen many of them. This dead boy looks up at the rain-filled clouds. Jacques grapples with the tarp that's flapping in the wind and climbs into the grave, tucks it over the body and covers the dead face. He reaches out a hand up to Stan.

'Help me out.' Jacques' face, small below him, smeared with sand and water, is pale and frowning. 'Come on. Help me.'

He freezes. Feels the sand sink beneath his feet. A shallow wave churns white over the edge of the hole.

'Help me! For God's sake!'

Stan reaches towards him, grabs his arm. It slips out of his grasp and Jacques falls back, steps onto the body with a crack of shattered bone. Then he jumps, clawing at the pebbles and sand, using his knees, then rolling out into the shallow water.

'Come on,' he shouts. 'There's not much time. The tide's coming. We must cover it.' He picks up a shovel, throws it down again. 'Rocks! Get rocks!' With water eddying around their ankles, they began hefting rocks and rolling them into the hole. The body disappears.

'Help me with this big bugger here,' he calls, indicating a large oval boulder. 'Come on! Push.' Jacques puts his foot to the stone gesturing for Stan to do the same. They force it to the edge and pause, panting. 'Right. Last heave!' shouts Jacques. He steps closer to the grave and pushes as the edge gives way. Stan steps back but Jacques sinks and falls forward with the boulder as it topples over the edge.

A yell of pain comes from the darkness of the hole. He can't see Jacques. Daren't step closer. The water cold, invisible, swirls around his ankles.

Jacques' voice is muffled. As if he's face down. 'Hey! Help! Help!' Only the empty black sky above him.

A wave of water sloshes up his legs. Pushes him onto rocks. He falls forward, bashing his knees. He won't die like this. Fear surges through him. Heat gives him strength. Water hits him in the face, blinds him with stinging sand. He gasps, coughs. The water recedes and he takes his chance, pushes himself onto his heavy feet and out of the shadows of the rearing rock as clouds roll off the moon. To his left, on the witches' headland, silhouettes of the spiky, deformed pines. To his right the pyramid of King's Rock. He stumbles towards the dark outline of the firs on the common, his legs moving slowly as if under water.

He's going to survive.

*

It was past midnight when Michael woke, stiff, cold and confused, behind the steering wheel of the truck. He allowed himself only a quick switch-on of the torch to look at his watch. He'd need it at Le Hocq. He blinked, rubbed his eyes and stretched his legs. Rain dribbled down the blurry window, but the worst of the storm had abated and the farmyard was grey and shadowy under the moon, and the wind tugged at the trees behind the house.

He'd followed Jacques' instructions, collected the truck and decided to drive to the Bideau place to wait, rather than risk his father seeing him and questioning what he was doing. And he'd collect his abandoned bike and rucksack at the same time. He'd tried to get into the house, thought of making himself a warm drink, maybe changing his damp clothes, but the farmhouse was locked.

The barn smelled of pigs and, when he raised the torch, a dark patch glistened amongst the scattered straw where Kurt had lain. Had he died here? Where was the rifle? Was it Jacques'?

He'd dragged a bale of hay from the heap to cover the stain on the floor and returned to the truck, folded himself into the driver's seat, turned off the torch. Two hours and he'd return. The rain glittered and battered the windscreen and the truck rocked in the strong wind. He closed his eyes, tried to imagine Stan and Jacques battling the storm on the beach…

The truck shook and coughed when he turned the key, but spluttered into life on the second go and he manoeuvred the vehicle up the track out of the farmyard without headlights, the wet dark of the road guiding him between the raised verges.

When he reached Le Hocq, he pulled the truck onto the common, as far into the shadow of the tower as he could, shielding it from any passing traffic or patrol. He'd half expected the men to be waiting, hoped to see their silhouettes emerge from behind the tower, or climb up onto the wall when they heard the purr of the engine. But there was no movement. Michael waited, scanned the beach. The tide was half in. As he got out of the truck, the wind, coming in directly from the sea in salty gusts, pulled the door out of his grasp and the metallic bang startled him. He glanced around, moved quickly onto the wall, pushed aside the barrier and peered over, hoping to see something move in the shadows of the beach. Nothing.

He jumped down onto the pebbles, shone the torch up and down along the length of the wall, illuminating briefly the trees waving and leaning over from the common. He flicked the light up towards the incoming tide, its waves folding and splashing white, switched the torch off and on. Surely, they'd see it.

Nothing. He shivered. He was late. They'd walked. Or something worse had happened. No. Best not to think of that. He drove slowly up Le Hocq Lane, looking into doorways, expecting the two figures to emerge.

He drove into the miking yard, ran up the steps to Jacques' flat. It was dark and empty. The smell of cigarettes and stale beer lingered. On the table, two chipped glasses with dregs of red wine in the bottom. Michael sat down heavily on one of the wooden chairs, and put his head down on his folded arms, closed his gritty eyes. Waited.

NOVEMBER 1944

Meg looked small and pale sitting across the table from his mother in the kitchen, her hands around a cup of grassy-smelling nettle tea. It was raining again, battering the east-facing window, throwing itself against the glass in angry bursts. Four weeks of wet, greyness and stinging cold since Jacques and Stan had gone.

At night, wind howled in the chimney while Michael lay awake, clammy and nauseous, imagining them rocking in that tiny, old boat, fighting the waves. By day, he felt shaky and weak, blamed himself. If he had only got there on time, would they have taken the boat?

'So… still no news then?' asked his mother.

Meg looked up, blinked and licked her lips. 'No. Sorry, Hélène. I… I've heard nothing since… George… told me he'd met someone who helped them drag out the old rowing boat. I… suppose no news is good news.' Her smile was weak. She sipped her tea and grimaced. 'I wish I could get used to the bitterness of nettles… still, it's hot. Won't it be great to have real tea again? All that talk of Red Cross parcels… I wonder…' She lapsed into silence and put down her cup.

Michael cleared his throat: 'I know I keep asking this, but what do you think their chances are? And why haven't we heard?'

Meg bit her lip, patted her hair, pushed a few curling strands back under the floral scarf holding it off her face. 'I wish I knew. I… I don't think we can do anything except wait. George knows that we are all desperate for news. I don't know how he finds out, but… well, he told me about the four who got to France last month. Let's hope…'

'And he told you about… the others too.' Hélène's voice cracked. Michael's pulse quickened and blood flooded into his face. 'The ones who d-drowned. Oh, God, Meg. I can't. I can't…' Tears rolled down her face and dripped off her chin.

Meg reached out and covered his mother's trembling hands with her own. 'No news is good news, Hélène,' she repeated more quietly this time. She got up and walked to the window. 'When will it stop raining?' Her shoulders were tight as she leaned over the draining board as if looking for a way out, shaking her head.

'I'm sorry, Meg. I know you are worried about them too…'

'Yes. But… let's just cling to… hope. We have to… pray and…' Her voice faded.

A fist of fear leapt in Michael's chest. 'You've heard something… What are you not telling us?' He sprang to his feet.

Meg spun round. 'No,' she said softly. 'I promise there is no news. It's… something else.' She twisted her hands together. 'I…'

Hélène moved to her and took her by the shoulders, 'What is it, Meg? I'm sorry. All we have thought about is Jacques… and Stan, of course. Is something wrong at home?'

'Last night. We were targeted… by… by tar-daubers.' She looked up at Hélène and glanced at Michael, her mouth a tight line and her brow lined. 'They must think we're… collaborators.'

'That's terrible,' muttered Michael.

His mother was angry. 'What? How could they think that? And how can they do that to people? Haven't we all suffered enough? How's your dad? He must be upset.'

'They smashed our front window. It frightened both of us. We were asleep.'

She sniffed and wiped her nose on a small handkerchief which she pulled out of her sleeve. 'They ran away. I looked out of the upstairs window. Two lads, quite young, I think. In the morning, I found the tar. Black sticky stuff on the front door. I couldn't get it off. It's awful, Hélène… people will think…' She broke off and sobbed in Hélène's arms. Hélène held her, stroking the back of her head, as if she were soothing one of the children, until the racking sobs subsided. Her voice was muffled as she spoke into his mother's shoulder. 'I had to take Dad to Auntie Yvonne's next door. He was so scared. It's not fair, Hélène. Just because I talk to Walter.' She pulled back and smiled weakly. 'I'm all right. Really, I am. I'm just… tired. I couldn't sleep afterwards. I sat up and read. I didn't really think they'd come back… they're just boys. I'll be better after a good night's sleep.'

'Come and sit down. Mike'll make us some more tea. Shall we go for chamomile this time? We could all do with a bit of calm.'

Michael, filling the kettle at the sink, watched his father cross the yard, his head down, a bucket in one hand and an axe in the other, his yellow sou'wester glowing in the gloom of the morning.

'Why don't you come and stay with us for a bit? Would

your dad be happy to stay with Yvonne? Maybe just for a week or so?' said Hélène.

He turned to see Meg smiling at his mother, a spot of colour bright in each cheek.

'Oh, Hélène! You are so kind. I don't deserve you! That would be wonderful. Dad said this morning that he would stay next door for the foreseeable anyway. I wasn't sure I could face the house alone. Not now.'

'That's settled then. You can go over and collect a few things later. Thank goodness you've still got the company car. And I'll make up the bed in the spare room.'

'Thank you. I can't tell you how grateful I am.'

As Hélène loaded the range with a few logs from an almost empty basket, the back door swung open revealing Paul, dripping, his arms piled with wood, struggling to get his muddy boots off. 'I broke up some of the old fence we took down last year. Pity it's wet, but it'll burn, eventually.'

'Good timing, Paul. We're down to our last few,' said Hélène, dragging the basket to the door and helping him drop the wood in. She handed him the dogs' towel from the back of the door and took his sou'wester and coat, making a trail of drips as she whisked them into the scullery.

He stood in damp socks and smiled at Meg, rubbing the towel over his head. 'Hello! How are you? No news?'

'Sorry, Paul. Nothing, I'm afraid.'

'Meg is coming to stay with us for a while. Those boys who've been daubing tar and painting swastikas have damaged the house.'

'Oh no! God help us! That's awful. Why would they do that?' Paul sat down at the table.

'I think it's because I know Walter. You know, K-Kurt's friend. We talk… about history. I suppose they've seen me sitting by the harbour chatting to him. People get the wrong idea… I saw him last week. Only for a few minutes, in the bus shelter. It was raining…'

A flush was staining her neck and she rubbed at her nose. Michael sat down opposite, the range warming his back as the flames burned orange and spat through the glass door.

'Amy's been worried about Kurt, I think,' said Michael.

His mother nodded. 'She's very quiet. Pretends she's studying, goes to her room in the evenings, but I think she's pining. She hasn't seen him for months.'

Meg's words came out in a rush: 'He must have deserted. Walter said he thought Kurt might have done; he's been very unhappy for a long time, questioning why they're here, what's happening in Europe… I think he's right. I've heard of a few…'

There was silence for a few minutes in the kitchen. Michael watched his father. With his finger, he was tracing the pink ghost of a ring of red wine on the scrubbed table. Where Jacques usually sat. His summer tan had faded to a sickly yellow, the lines around his mouth deep. He seemed diminished.

Where were Jacques and Stan? Had they made it to France? Were they lying in hospital beds in St Malo unable to send word? Or maybe they'd made it to the beaches near Portbail? It was the closest to Jersey. His parents had pored over a map of France many times in the last few weeks, pointing out possibilities, wondering where the currents might have dragged the boat. There was no way that they would have aimed for England; it was twice as far as the nearest beaches of France. It was a faint comfort to know that Jacques wasn't alone, that the two of them could row together, or one could bail out, if the sea was rough. Or… he didn't want to think about the alternative, the turbulent sea on that night last month, the rocks around Le Hocq. But

Jacques knew them well, and anyway, if the boat had come to grief, it would have been washed ashore by now. But why had Jacques decided to go? There was no hint when he'd told Michael to come back later. Something must have happened for him to take such a big risk. Had they not been able to bury the body? But if that was the case, it would have washed up before now. His father had said that he wouldn't have wanted to endanger the family by telling them that he was planning to escape and that Jacques knew they would have tried to stop him. He was always impetuous, said his father. But he didn't know what Michael knew.

'Shall I make the tea?' Meg's voice broke into his thoughts.

The kettle was puffing steam, droplets spitting on the range. Michael rose, shaking his head. 'I was miles away. Sorry!'

'Then I'll wash these cups. I'm not here to be waited on!' Meg took the half-empty cups to the sink. 'I think the rain is stopping. It's definitely brighter than it was,' she said.

As he poured the boiling water on the dusty chamomile heads, he saw his mother reach out and cup his father's cheek with a look of tenderness. His throat closed up and a tightness pulled at his chest. Everything had changed. Yet nothing had. They must still drink tea, help friends, scavenge for firewood. And, according to last night's paper, the Amateur Dramatic Club was putting on a comedy. A comedy? What was there to smile about?

JANUARY 1945

'This is it.'

Amy had stopped in front of a small, white-painted house, set back from the road, surrounded by shrubs and the wintery remains of a kitchen garden. A few curled cabbages, their yellow outer leaves insect-eaten, were lined up beside the pert green ferns of parsnip tops. She rested her bike against the low wall and waited for Michael and the panting dog to join her.

'Hazel Cottage'. A faded wooden sign was attached to the slatted gate. He rubbed his hands together, trying to create a little warmth in his numb fingers.

The rain of December had given way to sunshine and iron-blue skies in the first days of the new year. Cold had pushed its way into his neck, despite his tightly-wound scarf, and reddened his cheeks, as they'd cycled up the St John's Main Road. Turning left at Haute Croix, they'd pedalled through St John's, passing the squatting stone parish church, where a stripped Christmas tree lay on its side in the graveyard, and then passed through farmland, edged in spiky hawthorn hedges and into the scattered houses of St Mary.

'She's probably in her studio, over there.' Amy pointed to a sturdy brick building, almost concealed by shrubs and trees, in the shadow of the house.

Michael followed her up the stone path. It was months since he had seen Lily but he could summon up her shining auburn hair and the smile in her eyes. Would she want to help them? Would she shake her head at his suspicions like the family had?

Amy tapped on a blue-painted door and listened, her head close to the door frame, cocked to one side.

'Lily!' she called. 'Lily! It's Amy? Are you there? She doesn't always hear, she's so wrapped up in her work. The first time I came, Jacques had to bang with his fist before she answered!'

Amy had visited the studio a couple of times and her enthusiasm for Lily's paintings and admiration for the woman was clear in her shining eyes. Michael had noticed once, after she'd returned home from Lily's place, that she'd tried to tame her frizzy, fair hair into curls and had put on her mother's only pair of heels, looking at herself over her shoulder in the landing mirror, until her brother's laughter sent her back to her own room, slamming the door behind her.

'Lily! It's Amy. Are you in the studio?' She knocked again and raised her voice.

They waited in the silent gloom and sour-smelling leaf-mould of the shadowed garden.

Amy knocked again before clicking down the metal tongue of the latch and pushing open the door.

'Lily! It's Amy!' she repeated.

Michael followed her into a large storeroom, smelling of turpentine, damp and wood. Through high windows, shafts of sunlight lit up a wide ladder of shelves, with a few rusting paint tins gathering cobwebs. In the middle of the floor, brown paper had been torn back from an opened cardboard box, like the dry petals of a large square flower. Michael recognised it immediately. A Red Cross parcel. His own family had collected theirs from the harbour earlier in the week and Hélène had been rationing the luxurious contents ever since.

'Lily!' Amy was pushing her way through a set of faded red curtains.

Lily's bright head emerged from a pile of blankets on a faded sofa. She struggled to her feet, revealing a man's paint-stained shirt over baggy trousers. Her feet were bare. 'Has something happened? You've had news?' She raised her eyebrows and smiled.

'I'm afraid not. Nothing's happened.'

'Oh.' Disappointment flattened her mouth. 'I was hoping… Sorry. I was asleep. Gorged myself on the chocolate from Red Cross box and stayed up most of the night painting that.' She nodded towards an easel angled towards the light. The oil painting was a head and shoulders portrait of Jacques. Michael gasped and Amy's cold hand touched his as they stood side by side and looked.

Michael was drawn to Jacques' dark eyes, the left one shadowed in a deep socket, looking straight at him, as if challenging him, pleading with him to understand. Lily had captured the tilt of his head and his full mouth, closed below a narrow nose. A strong square jaw, 'the Le Breton chin' his mother had called it once, pointing out the likeness between Jacques and his father. Large ears, and his mop of black curls, pushed back, a widow's peak neatly forming on a high forehead.

'Oh, Lily! It's… so good. You've really caught his likeness, his glance!' Amy smiled. 'This is how he was, before the occupation. This is the big brother who my school friends all fancied!'

'It's the face in my head when I'm thinking about him. And it's the one who'll return to us.'

Michael glanced at Amy and stepped towards Lily. 'Lily… there is something we'd like to talk to you about.'

'Why don't I make us some tea? Real tea! I'm trying to ration it, but I can spare some for friends.'

As she busied herself with the kettle and washed cups in the sink, Michael walked around the studio looking at the water colours leaning against each other, unframed. Most were landscapes: St Ouen's from the sand dunes in autumn, white grassy-topped mounds in the foreground, the wet beach almost indistinguishable from the rough sea, a wide faded blue sky crowded with grey, orange-edged clouds; Rozel harbour, the L-shaped quay reaching into dark, churning waves; Mont Orgueil Castle, painted from the beach near Fort William, its medieval bulk towering over the little houses lining the harbour. Michael looked closely, located Meg's house, window boxes each side of the blue door a blur of silvery green. On each painting, not dominating, but painted with accuracy, was evidence of the Germans' fortifications: a gun emplacement; a bunker; a set of barracks. Marks of occupation.

'Here we are. Find a seat.' Lily put down a tray of cups on an upturned crate and pulled up an old wooden chair, nodding towards the sofa. 'So, what did you want to talk about?'

'Well. It's… difficult. But I… we… want to ask you, about Jacques.' Michael didn't look at Lily until he'd accepted a chipped mug and sat down, steam dampening his face.

'Go on,' Lily held his eyes and nodded encouragement.

'I… we need to find out what happened to Jacques. I

can't believe he'd just disappear… leave without telling anyone. Amy agrees with me, but everyone else seems to have accepted the story.' He paused. 'I wanted to know what you think.'

Michael wished he hadn't brought Amy with him. If she wasn't here, he might have been able to share his secret with Lily. She might be able to connect the disappearance of Jacques and Stan with the death of Kurt. But Amy still believed Kurt would come back and he couldn't tell her, couldn't describe what had happened, how he was involved. And he was ashamed… of his brother and Stan. There were still too many gaps. If he could talk to someone…

Lily put down her teacup and ran her hands through her hair, pulling it off her face and pushing it behind her ears.

'Well. I found it hard at first. We'd planned things… the campaign, the leaflets. But Meg's information seemed so… plausible too. He'd talked about escaping, trying to get to England, many times. And to France, since D-Day. I can understand why he didn't tell anyone of his plans; it's so dangerous… though I like to think that he could have trusted me… we made a pact to tell each other everything…' she broke off, biting the inside of her cheek, rubbed her sleeve over her eyes. 'Why don't we talk to Meg again? It can't do any harm.'

'She's staying with us at the farmhouse,' said Amy.

'No time like the present then… I assume you have your bikes. I managed to get some new tyres just before Christmas. I had to swap them for a painting, but at least I'm mobile again. Give me a minute to dress more respectably and tell Mum and Dad where I'm off to.'

*

His mother was darning socks and sitting in a comfortable silence with Meg before a small fire in the front room when Michael and Amy entered, glad of the warmth after the chill of the late winter afternoon. Lily, in a trench-coat and dark trousers, her long red hair restrained in a green paisley scarf followed them, hesitating in the doorway.

Meg rose to her feet, the skirt she was hemming falling to the floor, a flush in her cheeks. Michael looked from one woman to the other, wondering what each was thinking about Jacques.

'Hello, Lily,' Meg said in her clear, polite voice, stepping forward and holding out a hand. 'How are you? I haven't seen you for a while. Not since… Jacques… left.'

'Meg'. Lily moved into the room and clasped the outstretched hand with both of her own. The difference in their heights was striking 'It's good to see you. I'm well, thank you. Trying to keep cheerful, as we all are. How are you?' She looked closely at Meg. 'You look tired'.

'Isn't everyone? I'm not too bad, all things considered. I've certainly had a wonderful Christmas here, thanks to Hélène, and the whole family. Haven't eaten so well in ages. But I'll be out of their way this week and back to work. I'm sure I've outstayed my welcome.'

'Mum, this is Lily…' As Michael introduced her and the women shook hands, he noticed a streak of black paint across Lily's thumb.

'I've heard a lot about you… all good. Amy so admires…'

Amy stepped forward, blushing. 'Mum. Please don't be embarrassing! Shall I make some tea? Are there any of those biscuits from the box left?' She was out of the door before she'd finished speaking.

'Michael. Take Lily's coat. Why don't you sit down?'

'Thank you. I'm so glad to meet you at last, Mrs Le

Breton.' She shrugged off her coat and handed it to Michael with a grin, sitting down next to Meg and crossing one knee over the other, in a way which his grandmère would not have approved of. 'What tiny stitches!' she said, peering at the sewing which Meg had picked up and smoothed across her knee. 'I'm really clumsy with a needle. My mother despairs of me!'

Meg smiled at her. 'But you're handy with a paint brush, I've heard. I'd love to see some of your work.'

Sitting together on the sofa, they looked so different, Michael thought: Lily so confident, colourful and chic in her mustard yellow jumper and blue and white silk scarf; Meg, small, ordinary looking, and yet... brave and determined.

It had been a long time since Meg and Jacques had drifted apart and Michael continued to feel sad about it, hoping that maybe, in time, their relationship would be restored. But he could see why Jacques was drawn to Lily. If only Jacques were there...

Once tea had been poured, Michael, sitting on the floor at his mother's feet, his legs stretched out towards the fire and his back against her chair arm, changed the atmosphere, determined to ask his questions.

'Meg. I hope you don't mind, but... well... I... we... wanted to ask you a few things. About Jacques, about his departure. I can't make sense of it and... well, I just thought that you might help me understand.'

Meg put down her sewing and straightened her back. Her face looked drained of colour, the freckles peppered across her nose. She blinked and swallowed. Dabbed at the corners of her mouth with a white handkerchief.

'I know it's difficult, Mike, but I have... told you all I know. George Le Brocq told me, from someone he won't name, who helped them, as I said... that Jacques and

Konstantin had taken the rowing boat, the old one which had been hidden in the pub garage. They were last seen rowing beyond Stone Beach. No trace has been found. George has promised to let us know if he hears from France.'

'Yes. But Meg… would Jacques really go without telling any of us? He'd planned a campaign with Lily, to try to get German soldiers to desert, or refuse to fight if the British came. They'd planned… other stuff too. So I can't understand why he would suddenly leave?'

Amy was sitting with her hands between her knees, her head down. 'Do you think that's what's happened to Kurt? He's deserted?'

Meg gasped, coughed. She licked her lips and stretched her hand as if to touch Amy's shoulder, drawing it back before she made contact and smoothing her skirt tight across her knees. 'Amy… I don't know. Could be. Maybe. We… we all have to be patient. I agree, Michael, it's not like Jacques to give up… to go. He'd talked of escaping, when the Germans first came, but you're right… it's difficult to believe.'

'And Stan? I don't see why he'd go.' Amy sat up, looking at Meg. 'He knew that this will soon be over. He was safe at the farm. Kurt knew about him and didn't say anything; the danger was over. And besides, he was scared of the sea. I don't think he could swim. Michael's right. None of it makes sense.'

A silence descended on the room. Red and orange glowed in the fireplace. A tube of ash shifted and settled. The grandfather clock in the hall ticked softly and a dog barked in the yard. Meg was twisting her top lip, pulling at the skin with her teeth. Michael, Amy and Lily were staring into the fire.

Meg cleared her throat. 'I…' She exhaled out audibly. 'There's something I haven't told you.' She looked at Hélène and then at Amy. 'Something I couldn't tell you…'

'What, Meg?' Michael pulled up his legs towards his chest, wrapping his arms around his knees, and turned to her. 'What is it?'

'I haven't been completely honest.'

Michael's chest gave a leap and the blood rushed to his face. He knew it. Meg was hiding something.

'I knew there was something else. Meg! What? We need to know! Is it bad news?'

'No. Not bad news, I promise, Hélène. There is no news about Jacques since he left the island.'

She took a deep breath and glanced at each of the family in turn, her eyes lingering on Amy before meeting Hélène's wide stare.

'It is true that Jacques took the boat. But Konstantin wasn't with him. He's still here. And…' She blinked and put her hand to her mouth. 'Oh, God. This is so hard!'

Hélène gasped. 'What? Meg…Why…?' The words were stuck in her throat.

Michael got to his feet and stood in front of the dying fire, legs planted apart, his stomach churning. Had she not told the truth because of his involvement? What did she know? Maybe this was the time for him to tell the family what he knew. Too many secrets.

'Meg. I need to say something. I…'

'I think I need to finish what I have to say, Mike. Konstantin told me everything.'

'Did he? So, where is he?'

'He's in a safe place.'

'But why? I don't understand.' Michael rubbed his hands over his forehead and through his hair. If Stan told Meg about his involvement…

'I… wish I had told you the whole truth earlier. I thought it was for the best that you believed that they'd both gone.

You don't need to know where Konstantin is... it's safer for you and...'

His mother cut her off. 'Look, Meg. You aren't making sense. We all took risks to hide Stan. Why is it safer that he's not here now?'

Before the question could be answered, Michael heard the kitchen door slam and the voices of his father and Yves.

'Hang on, Meg. That's Dad and Yves. I think everyone needs to hear this,' said Michael.

The chill of the hall felt like a cool wave against his flushed cheeks as he opened the door of the front room. 'Dad, Yves!' he called. 'Can you come in here?'

The room felt crowded when the men entered, the cold draught of their movement causing a flame to leap and hiss in the grate. They stood just inside the door, taking off their coats.

'What's going on, Hélène?' said Paul, 'Family meeting? Something happened?' His eyebrows shot up as his eyes lighted on Lily. 'Oh. Hello! You must be Lily. Pleased to meet you!'

'Paul.' Meg's voice was strong, determined and her face was pinched. She sat on the very edge of the sofa, her hands twisted in the lap of her tartan skirt. 'I was just saying... I need to explain something... about Jacques leaving the island. About why he left. This is not going to be easy for any of you to hear. And I'm so sorry...' Glancing again at Amy, her voice faded. She cleared her throat. 'But I have to tell you.'

A log fell forwards and a shower of sparks landed on the tiles in front of the fire. No one moved. Michael's throat was dry.

'In October, the night Jacques left, Konstantin came to me in the early hours of the next morning. He was very scared, hurt, cold, soaked to the skin. He'd been in the sea. He was crying. He'd walked from Le Hocq. It took me hours to get the full story out of him. I had to piece it together. He and Jacques had had a big argument the night before. He'd gone to Jacques' place to talk about Kurt, who he'd seen watching your farm from the road and he was worried. They argued about what to do. Jacques talked about killing Kurt. Konstantin said that he'd never seen Jacques so… angry. Angry about Kurt's friendship with Amy and angry that Kurt could hurt the whole family. Jacques produced a rifle – Konstantin thought he must have stolen it, hidden it – and Stan followed him into the truck. They argued as they drove down to the coast road. Jacques planned to drive to Gorey – he knew Kurt was barracked there. Apparently, there was a bit of an accident near the marsh at Le Hocq because they were driving without lights – it was well after the curfew – and they ended up in a ditch. Anyway, Stan said he managed to calm Jacques down and he thought that would be the end of it. They pushed the truck out of the ditch and Jacques dropped Stan back at the Bideau Farm.

'The next day he turned up late at night at the Bideau Farm. He was drunk, Stan said, though God knows where he got whiskey from, and led the way to the barn and revealed… Kurt's body.'

Amy gasped. 'No… no… he wouldn't…' She turned to her mother who reached out and took her hand.

'I'm so sorry, Amy. Jacques told Stan that he'd confronted Kurt earlier. He was hiding near the road and watching the farm, just as Stan had told him. He'd forced him into the truck, shot him, right there in the truck… taken the body to the barn when it got dark.'

Amy sobbed and gulped into her mother's shoulder. 'No… no!'

'This is so hard… but you need to hear the truth.'

His father's voice was cold and emotionless. 'I don't believe this. Go on Meg. What did Stan tell you about what happened next?'

'He told Stan to fetch a barrow and two shovels; they were going to bury the body on the beach.'

Why did Stan not mention Michael? Would he want to protect him?

'Which beach? Where? This is not true.' Amy blinked and leaned towards Meg, tears and mucus shining on her face.

'Le Hocq. I think it is true. Stan said they put the boy in the truck and drove to the marsh, wheeled it in the barrow down behind King's Rock and dug behind a low granite wall. I assume he meant the wall protecting the place where fishermen used to keep live lobster. You know of it? What's it called?'

'A nourrice,' said Paul.

Amy covered her mouth with both hands and tears overflowed her staring eyes, fixed on Meg's face. A frown deepened on her forehead.

'So… they dug a hole?' Michael struggled to imagine the dark beach at night, digging in the sand, stone and grit.

'Stan said that it was very hard work. It felt like they were digging for hours. They rolled many boulders into the hole… over the body. His hands were blistered and bleeding when he came to me. The details made me believe him.'

His mother lifted her head. Lines deep on her forehead. 'I can't believe Jacques would do this…'

Meg nodded. 'He's not… violent. Angry… but not… but, I think to protect his family…'

Amy gasped. 'It's my fault…'

'No, Amy, no. None of this is your fault.'

'And then… he took the boat?' Yves spoke for the first time and Michael noticed beads of sweat on his forehead.

'Yes. Made Stan help him. They had to break down the garage doors and move the things which were hiding it. He told Stan he must go with him, said that they'd be in great danger if they stayed. And be more use if they got to France. They could join up and maybe come back to help liberate the island.'

Meg paused and looked around at the circle of faces.

'The tide was coming up. Jacques wheeled the boat down the slipway and into the big channel towards Stone Beach. Konstantin was scared. You know he hates the water. He thought about going with him, nearly did apparently, but backed out. He regrets that now, he says.'

'So, he saw Jacques row off, on the tide?' said Hélène, looking at Paul who had not moved from his position behind her chair.

'Yes. There was a bit of moon. He said he saw him rowing strongly. He lost sight of him when he'd got as far as Stone Beach.'

'And he came to you, eh?' Paul's voice was quiet. 'Why didn't he come to us?'

'I think he was scared and he knew that it would be hard to tell you about… what Jacques had done. Just as it is hard for me to tell you. It's… it's out of character. Jacques had a temper… he never stopped being angry, but I never thought he'd do this.'

Lily sat forward on the sofa. 'I've seen him angry too. But I'm surprised. It seems an odd story, doesn't it? I can imagine Jacques trying to escape, but I didn't think he'd ever kill a German. He's too clever. He'd never take the risk.'

'I hid Stan at home for a couple of days. More than once I nearly came to tell you, but I didn't know how. I was a coward… and I thought maybe you'd all be safer if you believed that he'd gone too. I found a family in Trinity to hide him. He's been in their attic ever since.'

His mother was shaking her head and looking into the dying fire. 'So, he was alone in the boat? Jacques left alone. Would he have any chance? Paul? What do you think?'

'He's very strong. Knows the currents and rocks around the coast… I think he could have got to France. I know we'd all like to hear from him, but it'll be hard to get a message to us.'

Michael's face was flushed. He moved away from the fire and back again. 'I just can't… see Jacques doing that. Killing… Or am I the only one…?'

'I agree with you, Michael.' Lily's voice was strong. 'You probably don't think that I knew Jacques well. I haven't known him as long as you all. But I think I did. We… spent a lot of time talking. He was calmer than when I first met him. We spoke about waiting… being safe.'

'I know it's very hard to accept. I've struggled with it too. But he was very protective of you all. If he thought you were in danger, I believe he could have done anything.' Meg stood up. 'I think I ought to go home. You need time to… talk about this.'

Hélène stood and embraced her.

'Thank you all. For having me here.' Her voice had a tremor in it, but she cleared her throat and continued: 'I must go… get Dad back into his own bed.'

Yves' voice was gentle. 'I f-found some glass for your window, Meg, and Dad and I painted over the tar marks. The house looks fine now.'

'You are a dear boy! And Paul. So kind. Thank you.' The tears dribbled down her cheeks. She wiped them away with her handkerchief and sniffed. 'Look at me… so silly,' she murmured. 'Right. I'll pack up my things.'

'Let me help you, Meg. I'll come with you.' Hélène, keeping an arm around her shoulder, guided her to the door. 'Amy, come with us.' She looked back over at Paul and Yves. 'Perhaps one of you could drive over to Gorey later, to pick me up.'

'I'll be there,' said Yves.

Michael stood in front of the dying fire as his family departed. When only Lily remained, he sat down and put his head into his hands. What Stan had said fitted in with what he knew in many ways… the body in the barn, the burial on the beach. But he still found the idea of Jacques killing Kurt to be implausible.

He raised his eyes to Lily's face. Her green eyes were large with tears. She shook her head and a drop trickled down her face.

MARCH 1945

There's no running this time, but Konstantin feels the same empty, hollow tremble that haunted him over two years ago when he escaped the grave of his slavery. It's like hunger... And something else... he doesn't know what.

He's being led, in the dark, by Meg's cool, dry hand, up the steps of the cellar. Another cellar. This one's dry and coal-free. Lined with shelves of boxes and files. It's a relief to be heading upwards, out of the suffocating prison of the cellar where he's been for two long days. Behind him is another woman; he can smell her musky perfume. He didn't remember the face which flared in the light of a match, but the name, Lily, he knows. She told him that they'd met before, with Jacques. Jacques. The name, whispered into the dark like a secret, is a blow to his chest. He hopes she can't see his panic. He recalls a conversation with Jacques about Lily; he'd been jokey about their relationship, making a crude remark about her legs. Jacques had frowned at him. He wished he hadn't said that. Stupid.

If they knew... but he can't change anything. The lies have been told. It doesn't matter anymore. He must be calm. He must escape again.

At the top of the wooden steps, Meg opens the door into the dark insurance office. She guides him around furniture, but he bumps into a desk or table which solidly pushes at his hip. He feels a cool breeze as she opens the door to the street.

'Shall I lock up?' Lily's whispering voice behind him.

'Key in the lock...' Meg's low response.

There's the purring sound of an engine, distant, but growing closer. Meg pulls him back and closes the door. They stand close together. He can hear their breathing and feel his own, hot on his lips. He feels his pulse racing and reaches up to wipe sweat off his forehead. His hand brushes a softness and Meg steps away from him with an intake of breath. 'Sorry,' he mutters.

The growl of the engine is receding.

'All right?' Lily's question is calm and soft, her voice low in pitch.

'Right-oh.' Meg's voice sounds falsely cheerful. 'Let's go.'

Meg grasps his wrist this time and the door opens into more blackness. He waits for his eyes to adjust, but nothing changes and he blinks hard. He feels Meg pulling and follows her. Behind him the metal click of the key in the lock and Lily's hand is on his upper arm. They move swiftly and silently down the pavement and around a corner. The dark presses on his eyes as he strains to see. A moon, very white and not quite full, slides out from a dark cloud between two tall buildings ahead of them and he recognises the back of the Le Bretons' farm truck, pulled into an alley in front of them. The dent in the back bumper, scratched blue paintwork.

Michael's voice: 'Everything all right?' His face in shadow under a cap. He's waiting behind the truck and he opens the back as they approach. 'There's a tarpaulin. Get under it. Just in case.' He touches Michael on the arm as he climbs into the truck, but gets no response. The earthy, dryness of potatoes is familiar. His hands find the weight of folded canvas and he sits down, his back to the cab window and pulls it over his body. He can't put his head under, not yet, not unless it's absolutely necessary. Confinement brings breathlessness, panic.

The truck doors shut with thin metal clicks. He can't bear the thought of going back. He won't go back, won't be tethered again like an animal. He'll run and wait for a bullet in the back. He wonders what happened to the old man who slept on the shelf under him; he hasn't thought of him since he ran. He can't still be alive.

He has to focus on survival. Why are they risking everything for him? They'll be imprisoned for breaking the curfew, hiding an escaped prisoner… probably deported. Maybe worse. He doesn't deserve it.

Meg told him that two women have been sentenced to death for circulating propaganda.

The driver, probably Lily, he thinks, has to turn the key twice before it fires. She's being too cautious. He knows the truck; he's driven it often enough. She revs and the vehicle slowly pulls away.

'If we get stopped, Stan, you have two options.' Meg from the passenger seat, calmer now. 'You can hide under the tarpaulin, or you can jump out and run. We'll try to create a diversion, whichever you decide to do. We are going to pretend that Lily's going into labour. She's stuffed a cushion up her jumper.'

'Labour?' he doesn't understand.

'About to give birth… we are going to the hospital.'

'Ah. Yes… good story.'

'Do you understand?'

'I understand… Sorry.'

'Stop apologising. We know.'

No. They don't know. They'll never know. He'll never tell.

'Let's just take it one step at a time.' Lily's voice.

'I don't want trouble… for you.'

'We are all in trouble. We are going to hold our nerve and keep to the plan.' Meg. Still so calm.

'All hands crossed.'

'Fingers…' He knows it's 'fingers'. He'd hoped to hear them laugh at his mistakes. Not this time. He swallows down the sourness rising to his throat.

The trunk bumps and shakes on the cobbles of back roads. He feels it scrape something on the left-hand side and hears the scream of metal on stone. The truck stops.

'Merde! What did I hit? I can't see. Shall I put on the headlights? Just for a second.' Michael's driving. He imagines his serious face concentrating, eyes behind his spectacles straining in the dark, his tall body leaning forward. Still a child.

'No!' Meg and Lily answer him at the same time.

'We're in one of the streets parallel to St Saviour's Road. They're narrow. Just keep going, slowly.' The truck moves again. He closes his eyes.

'Please God…' he whispers. God. He went to a service, just once, with the Le Bretons in the cool of the granite church. The ancient building was beautiful. The smell of incense, the singing voices seemed to give the family strength. But he didn't see God. He saw ghosts. His father… grandmother…

'If you turn into Highlands, we can cross into Les Varines.' Meg again.

'But that's crossing Mont Millais.' Michael's voice is hissing, tight with tension.

'Can't be helped. We have to cross a main road somewhere. Stop before the junction. Anywhere here and I'll get out and take a look.'

The truck slows to a halt and the passenger door opens. He holds his breath. He lets it go, the warmth bouncing back to his chin from the canvas.

There's a sharp tap on the driver's window and a whisper as Michael winds it down. 'It looks clear and quiet. Creep up to the junction and I'll wave you across.'

'Wouldn't you be better getting in? It might be quicker. We could get away from Mont Millais straight away.'

There's the door click again and the truck moves more quickly this time.

'It does seem very quiet,' says Lily. 'Saturday night was a good time to choose. There'll be some patrols, but most of them will be drinking or sleeping. And that new brothel on King Street has just opened…'

'I know where I am now.' Michael's voice. 'I planned the route from here with Yves.' The tension has gone from his voice and Stan opens his eyes again.

'Stan… there's a bag of food for you. Hélène packed it and some warmer clothes. Can you see them?' Michael again. Hélène. Why is she kind to him?

He pushes off the weight of the tarp and crawls on his knees until he encounters a soft pile of material. He feels a woolly sweater and the oilskin of a fisherman's jacket. Under them is a small rucksack.

'I have them. Thank you… you are very kind… I am not…'

'That's enough.' Lily's firm tones. 'We mustn't get emotional.'

He doesn't feel emotional. He can't remember the last time he was moved about something. He's learned to pretend.

The truck is moving faster now and the road is smoother. It is very quiet. He shrugs off the thin jacket he's got on and pulls on the sweater, a jersey, over the one he's wearing. It's stiff and thick. One of Paul's, he thinks. Despite the sweat on his forehead, he pulls the thick jacket on too and stuffs what he thinks are socks into the pockets.

'Here we are.' Michael sounds tight, his voice deep and husky. He feels the truck dip and bump down the slipway. 'There's Yves.' The truck levels and pulls left before stopping. The back door opens and he sees the pale blur of Yves' face. 'Hello Stan. Grab your stuff. The boat's waiting. Tide's on the turn.'

He picks up the rucksack and shuffles on his bottom towards the door. His legs prick with pins and needles as he swings them down and Yves has to grasp his arm as he stumbles. 'Steady on, old chap.'

The words won't come.

'Come on.' Yves pulls him towards the glimmer of the sea and the light of the moon shines on a frothy white edge. A fishing boat is rocking in the shallows. He can just make out its shape; there are no lights on.

He turns back. Over his shoulder he can see three pale faces as Yves pulls him by the arm down the damp sand. 'Hang on. Let's keep your feet dry.' He feels a solid shoulder in his abdomen and the breath is pushed from his lungs. He holds tight to the rucksack which dangles over Yves' shoulder as the cold rises and he feels the whisper of moving water.

'Grab the rail…' It's salty beneath his hands as he hauls himself over, falling onto the deck. He sees a man, cap pulled low over his face, moving quietly, tying off ropes. Another man, younger, with a rucksack at his feet is sitting on a large wooden box watching him. Leaning over the rail, he looks down at Yves' face, eyes wide and mouth in a thin line, holding onto the side of the boat, up to his thighs in water. 'Good luck!' And he's gone. Stan can see his fair head diminishing. The sea swishes as he wades away.

Darkness descends again. The moon has moved behind a cloud. The boat's engine splutters. He lurches and clings to the sticky handrail, searching for a glimpse of the beach. All he can see is a dim, pale stretch and the dark land rising behind it. He feels the chill of the spring night rush away from him, taking his breath, as the boat speeds up and he sits down, back against damp metal and looks up. No stars.

*

Michael stood, his pulse slowing, the truck ticking against his back as he watched Yves guide Stan down the damp sand towards the dark water. The edge of the tide glittered; little waves shuddered and disappeared into the sand. There was very little wind. Spring was in the cool night air, a smell of green and growth, a promise of things to come. Ahead, the swaying white curve of a boat just visible, and a mast in the dimness. And Yves, hoisting Stan onto his shoulder, keeping his feet dry, wading out towards the boat.

Stan was gone. No words. What was there to say? He felt giddy and confused. He slumped back against the bonnet of the truck and took a deep breath. Meg's shoulder touched his arm and he glanced at her face, a white shape turned towards the sea, straining for a glimpse of the departing boat. Lily got back into the truck and closed the door with a soft click. The quiet was velvet black.

A heaviness and a silence had gripped the house since Meg had told them. They had not discussed any of it. His father worked all hours of the day, ate supper and went to bed. His mother appeared to sleep-walk through her chores and spent time with Amy, who shut herself in her room most of the day. Yves was busy with work; Michael didn't see him for weeks. He had turned to Meg and, together with Lily, they'd planned to get Stan out of Jersey. It wasn't safe for him to stay and Meg's friend George had offered a place on a fishing boat which was aiming to get to France. They'd had to wait for a spring tide and quiet seas.

Now he was gone. There was an emptiness, a gap created by his going, and above it all, a cloud of mirky knowledge, that things would never be the same again. He'd had no chance to ask Stan about that night. He'd only seen him once when they moved him from Trinity to the insurance office cellar. Stan wouldn't meet his eyes, kept his head down.

If Jacques had got to the coast of France… if his boat had survived the crossing, and he returned to Jersey… how would that feel? Michael couldn't imagine the conversation with his brother about the circumstances of his going or a family meal around the kitchen table. Jacques' chair had not been sat in since he had disappeared. It was pushed tight up to the table, half-hidden, its smooth curved oak back, shiny and dark with use, leant against the scrubbed tabletop, waiting.

But Michael wanted change, couldn't hold back time as his parents seemed to want to. Things must begin again; he needed his life to start. It was only a matter of time before the Germans surrendered, or the British came. Five years ago, he decided to be a vet. He wanted that opportunity now. He was ready to go to college, study for his Higher School Certificate, apply to veterinary college in England. He'd return to Jersey, work with farmers, buy a house on the coast, maybe at Le Hocq or Green Island. Would Laura return when the island was liberated? He closed his eyes and summoned her face; it was indistinct, blurred.

'Mike! Mike! Come on. We must go.' Meg was pulling at his arm and Yves was loading his bike into the back of the truck.

On the smooth dark of the sea, a half-moon slipped out from behind a smoky cloud and cast a path of white light towards the beach. There was no sign of the fishing boat.

APRIL 1945

On a warm, still April afternoon, Michael left his bicycle under the sea wall between Pontac and Le Hocq and headed out towards Icho Tower carrying a tin bucket and half a carton of salt. Jenny followed, splashing in the shallow pools and sniffing at the mounds of ribbon vraic. Le Hocq beach was still guarded; just one armed soldier today at the tower. On the eastern side, low-water fishing was permitted. He followed the sandy route to the left of King's Rock to where the end of a wall had been built into the rocks. A few rough blocks of blackened granite held together with crumbling pale cement and the khaki green of bladderwrack. On the coastal side of the wall were the remains of the nourrice; on the sea side a bank of sand, piled boulders and pebbles. This was where Stan and Jacques had buried Kurt's body. Six months ago.

He'd been there in late January and there had been no evidence of disturbance, just piled pebbles, boulders and sand. The winter tides and storms had shifted rock and spring had brought new growth of seaweed. He took a deep breath and moved on, paddling in his plimsolls down the meandering channel of water, trying to push the image of

Kurt's body trapped under rocks and sand, from his mind. What would be left now?

He was aiming for the sandy stretches below Icho Tower to the best razor fishing at the lowest of tides. At one point the channel met an inlet, the water ruffling cold into the shallows. He had to wade, up to his knees, and climb the rocky terrain on the other side before a larger sandy area appeared. He found a flat rock to sit on and called to Jenny who had avoided the water by taking the long way around.

'Here, girl. Let's just sit here before the last stretch. I don't think the tide's turned yet.'

Jenny came to be patted, pushed her wet nose into Michael's hand, and sat at his feet in the warmth of the spring sun. Both looked out to sea. Ahead, the tower squatted like a giant cork on the blackened rocky outcrop, the top half painted white as a warning to shipping. Gulls wheeled and cried overhead and the sourness of guano drifted on the breeze. To his left nothing but rocks and stones, reminding him of a picture of the moon's landscape in the set of children's encyclopaedias bought for them by Granny Nell; to his right a narrow strip of sand leading towards the edge of the deep inlet, glinting in the sunshine.

'I think I might have a dip. First swim of the year. You can stay here and guard my clothes.' He stripped off to his undershorts, kicked off his heavy plimsolls and made his way over the pebbly sand. He climbed down between sharp rocks and dropped into the water gasping at the cold grip on his warm chest. Kicking hard and splashing in a fast crawl, he completed a circuit and climbed out, wishing he'd kept his plimsolls on as he cut his foot on a limpet-covered boulder. As he bent down to examine the damage, a piece of driftwood caught his eye. It poked out from under a pile of vraic. He pushed the seaweed away and revealed a long, curved strip, with a green patch of paint on it and, at the end, a rusted rowlock. Bile rose to his throat and he froze, his heart thudding. No. It couldn't be. Could it? He limped back to his clothes, dragging them over his shivering body and pulling on his plimsolls. Nauseous and shaking, shadows filling his head, he turned over boulders and pulled at seaweed until his back ached and his hands were sore.

By the time the tide started turning, lapping around his feet, he had found three more pieces of rotting wood from the body of the boat and the remains of one of the seats. It was their boat. He was sure of it. Jacques didn't make it. The current must have pushed him into rocks. He stood and looked out towards the horizon, a grey line beyond Icho tower. He must have been dead all the time they were waiting for news. Jacques was dead. Dead. The shadows pressed inside his skull, his vision narrowing.

But… yet… why was the wreckage here, if Jacques had rowed out beyond Stone Beach? Surely the wreckage would have gone into the big channel, maybe coming in at the other end, the western side, near Brig-y-Don. And so close to the shore? And why had his body not been washed in?

He put all the bits of wood into his bucket and turned his face towards the coast, needing to get home, to escape the shadows, talk with someone. Jenny whined and barked at the water, rising now in the inlet. She put her head down and ran off into the rocks. Michael let her go, knowing it was no use trying to get her to swim. She'd find her own way back.

The warmth had gone when he got back to his bike. Clouds bulged grey and white overhead and his damp clothes clung to his sticky body. He hung the bucket on the handlebars and called for Jenny. There was no sign of her. Panic rising in his chest, his breath coming in gasps, he ran down the beach to where fishing boats leaned in the mud, anchor chains sagging. 'Jenny! Jenny'. No answering bark. He scanned the beach. The only movement he could see was a pair of German soldiers, digging in the soft mud near the boats, perhaps looking for crabs. The German army had not benefitted from Red Cross parcels and things were getting ever more desperate. 'Jenny! Jenny!' The Germans raised their heads and looked up at him before returning to their digging.

Michael turned and ran towards the tower; he'd get a better view from there. He scrambled over the boulders underneath the granite wall, onto Le Hocq beach and up the slipway towards the common. The guard at the tower stepped forward as he moved towards him. He held up his hands and called out: 'My dog… I'm looking for my dog. Have you seen a big black dog?'

The guard held out a hand to stop him. '*Was? Was wollen Sie?*'

'Dog. *Hund? Schwarze Hund?*'

'Oh, *jah. Hund.*' The soldier pointed towards the western end of the sandy stretch, towards witches' rock and headland guarding Green Island.

'Thank you. Thank you very much.' He turned and ran back down the slipway and over the pebbles and deep soft sand jogging towards the little bay under Brig-y-Don.

As he approached, panting with effort and climbing over the rocks and into the flat sand of the hidden beach, he could see Jenny near the big boulders under the cliff face, digging in the sand. Above, accessed by a steep path between the leaning fir trees, perched the square building of the children's home, Brig-y-Don.

Jenny did not raise her head when Michael called to him; she seemed intent on the hole she had created between two large boulders. His pulse slowing, relief flooding through him, Michael pulled off his itchy plimsolls and curled his toes into the damp sand, the cut under his big toe stinging as he walked towards the dog. The finding of Jenny lifted his spirits and, momentarily, the sun came out again, transforming the wet beach into a shining carpet, sprinkled with shells and tiny granite chips. Here and there, blue and green sea-glass glowed in the light. When he reached Jenny, all he could see of the dog was her hind quarters and black tail, wagging. Sand flew in an arc behind her.

'What have you found, Jenny? Don't eat it!' She was greedy; she'd gulp down anything smelly on the beach, often bringing it up later. It was probably a dead fish.

Jenny backed up and barked at Michael. At the bottom of the hole was a lump of something dark in colour, poking out of the disturbed sand. Fabric. Clothing. He knelt at the crumbling edge of the hole and reached in, pulling at the material. Rolling onto his stomach, he dug with both hands, scraped the damp grit away. A final tug and it shot out, wet sand stinging his eyes and peppering his head. It was a jacket, or most of one; a sleeve was missing and the dark red lining hung in shreds. A donkey jacket.

The breath was sucked from his chest and a mist crowded in his head. Shadows followed the mist, pressing on him, like a dark wave, suffocating him. Pulling himself back on to his knees, he clutched the jacket, eyes closed, and gulped air until the pain in his chest eased and he felt Jenny's rough tongue on his face. Feeling too shaky to stand, he pushed himself back against a boulder and smoothed the jacket over his legs feeling, in the coarse, sandy nap of the fabric, no trace of his brother. His palm felt a lump in one of the pockets. He fumbled with clumsy fingers on the swollen, leather-covered fastening holding down the flap and pulled out Jacques' cap. Under it, the cold metal of the button touched his fingertips. He rubbed the surface with his thumb finding the indentations: Hold Fast. Here was Jacques.

A surge of adrenalin and he was on his feet. What if? Would Jacques' body be washed up here? Laying the jacket on top of a boulder he searched among the rocks, scraping his arms and knees, feeling the warmth of dripping blood down his calf. Jenny watched him before setting off at pace sniffing towards the beginning of the rough path between the shrubs and trees winding up towards Brig-y-Don. Michael followed on shaky legs. Behind a black rock, yellowed in the crevices with furry lichen, Jenny was licking the toe of a boot. Michael, heart banging in his chest, reached down, dragged it out, heavy, full of sand and grit. A working boot. A farmer's boot, the tongue flopping forward, no lace, the leather scarred and scratched. Nothing else.

He sat in the damp sand, his head propped on the rock behind him, until his legs became numb with cold and he heard the sound of high-pitched voices. A group of children, some as young as five or six, others young teenagers, were descending down the path from Brig-y-Don, towels over their shoulders or under their arms, following two women who carried a picnic hamper. He couldn't talk to them. Couldn't talk to anyone. Getting to his feet, he stumbled across the sand following the dark imprints of his own footsteps, clutching the jacket with the Hold Fast button tight in one hand, the boot in the other. A cold sweat sprang on his forehead.

Feeling hollow and shaky, he slowed down, as the excited children's voices faded, and walked up to the sea wall, sitting in a patch of dry sand, hugging his knees, scanning the bay. Directly in front of him, surrounded now by the incoming tide, was Stone Beach. To his left, the rising cliffs of King's and Queen's Rocks blocked his view of where he'd been earlier, effectively creating a barrier between the Pontac side and the Le Hocq beach. So why was the jacket on this side and the boat wreckage on the other?

They needed to organise a search of the whole beach. He needed to talk to someone. Meg? Lily? He didn't think he could face his parents yet. Though they said little about Jacques, Michael believed that they still hoped that he'd made it to France. That he'd return. That somehow, the family would be whole again. It never would be. He knew that now for sure.

8TH MAY 1945

In front of Michael, his mother stood, her waist encircled by his father's tweedy arm, his hip tight against hers, hemmed in by the noise and laughter. He shouldn't have come. He was out of place here amongst the excited crowds. His mother had persuaded him. She felt as he did, that there was nothing to celebrate. And yet, she said, they should be there. Bodies pressed behind him and he shrugged away, cringing from the touch of a woman's shoulder who was bending over a child whining that she couldn't see anything.

The Royal Square was packed with people, shouting, singing, waving Union Jacks and Jersey flags. From the windows of offices, banks and shops overlooking the square, smiling faces leant out. Scraps of coloured paper, thrown by a woman from a high attic window, drifted through the branches of a bunting-decorated chestnut tree. Children bounced on their father's shoulders. Everyone faced towards the balcony of the courthouse, where loudspeakers had been hung, awaiting Churchill's broadcast. Bright summer dresses, shades of red and blue, despite the chilly breeze, glowed and danced. A sweet, flat smell of stale perfume hung in the air.

His mother turned to him, raised her eyebrows, gave a quick, forced smile, and pulled him closer, hooked her arm through his. He knew what she was thinking; he knew that she was trying to summon a moment of happiness, catch the mood in the crowd. A rush of something fizzed in his head.

He was looking forward to so much: being their own bosses again; more food, coal and gas supplies; no curfew; possibilities for his and Amy's futures. But a weight lingered over him. Much of the time he felt as if he was travelling inside a tunnel, the brick walls closed over his head, no semicircle of light to walk towards, just airless space.

Jacques was dead. They buried his body two weeks ago. Michael has tried not to imagine his death, the pain of being thrown against rocks, the panic of drowning, but he wakes sweaty and breathless in the night. His father would not allow him to see what was left of Jacques, found by him and Yves with a search party, in the rocks under the witches' headland, but he sees in his dreams a limp doll, limbs askew, eyes open, covered in vraic and sand.

The loudspeakers crackled and three bongs of Big Ben's bells echoed across the square. The crowd fell silent as the announcer spoke: 'This is London. The Prime Minister, the Right Honourable Winston Churchill.'

The deep, gravelly tones and measured rhythms of the familiar, confident voice rang out above the lifted faces of the men, women and children announcing the 'unconditional surrender' of the enemy. Cheering erupted, was shushed, and quiet descended again. Until: 'And our dear Channel Islands are also to be freed today.' There was a gasp from the crowd and Michael felt the blood rush to his face. Tears pricked and flooded his eyes. His mother's arm tightened around his. The world screamed and clapped and a flutter of something like joy rose to his throat. The rest of the speech was lost in the babble of laugher and voices. He caught phrases about the 'foul aggressor', the 'overwhelming power and resources', the 'evil doer… prostrate before us'. As the speech drew to a close, his mother, a real smile on her face, reached up and clutched him to her.

Churchill's voice rose: 'Advance Britannia. Long live the cause of freedom. God save the King.'

Michael wished he'd pushed harder for Amy to come. She should be witnessing this historic moment. Yves was somewhere close; he had waved to them before the speech started, a glass of beer in his hand and his arm resting on Bob's shoulder. Amy was alone in the house; she'd hardly left her room for months.

The bailiff stepped forward on the balcony of the court rooms and the Union Jack and red and white Jersey flag were hoisted together as he stood, a grin splitting his face, his hat in hand waving at the crowd. He offered a prayer for deliverance and announced the imminent arrival of the 'British Tommies'. There was another eruption of cheering and clapping.

'I want you all to feel that I am amongst you', Mr. Coutanche shouted. Throwing down the microphone, he disappeared from view before opening the front door of the courthouse to renewed cheers and yells of approval. The crowd surged towards him and Michael and his parents were driven forward by the bodies around them. 'God save the King!' Mr. Coutanche bellowed and hundreds of voices yelled back at him: 'God save the King!'

'And now, I will ask you to join me in singing the National Anthem,' he shouted and started the singing. Michael joined in, raising his voice as loud as he could in the mêlée around him. As the singing died down, the sound of church bells began, from the town church. Up and down the scale they rang, clean, clear notes. And then, as if to echo and spread the joy, on the wind from other churches across the town came more bells, mixing with the laughter and chatter of the crowd.

Michael's father, a smile on his lined face, turned to them: 'Let's go home.'

9TH MAY 1945

Low evening sunshine, creeping out from under a bulk of swirling grey cloud, skimmed the sharp pebbles and sandy gullies, smearing dark shadows behind boulders and mounds of stones. Michael stumbled as he waded down the main channel on Le Hocq beach, the water rushing before him towards the sea, dragging swathes of bright seagrass and ribbons of kelp around his ankles.

He was alone with the calls of seabirds. The 'kee-ar, kee-ar' shriek of terns and the insistent mewing of herring gulls filled the salty, still air. Then the nervous, shaky cry of an invisible curlew. These things didn't change. Yet everything had changed.

'Liberation' was the word everyone was using. He didn't feel free. The wide horizon penned him in, weighed him down; it was inescapable. What he knew. What he doubted. What he feared… Those things imprisoned him. There was a hunger, an emptiness in his gut and a fluttering panic in his head. His thoughts, loud, indistinct, couldn't settle.

Earlier he had watched the activity at the harbour from the heights of Mount Bingham, Amy silent at his side. A grey British naval pinnace, the red, white and blue flag fluttering at its stern, had rounded the walls of the harbour entrance, bouncing on the waves of the high tide. It was greeted by crowds of people thick on the walls and quays, waving flags. Like the murmur of a rough sea, he could hear the roar increase as two men in navy uniform, their white caps shining, stepped ashore and into a shiny black car. He watched its slow progress down the Albert Pier towards the harbour master's office where it was surrounded, mobbed by people. After a few minutes, a large Union Jack was hung out of an upper window and the cheers increased.

But he wasn't there. He wasn't part of it. How could he be? He had turned to his sister and his tight smile was returned; her face was his. In the lines on her forehead and around her mouth, in the clouded blue eyes, he saw hesitant pain. Like him, she couldn't speak of it, but it hovered, like a ghost, over her and between them.

Her hand had touched his arm lightly. 'Let's go home,' she had said.

When they returned to the farmhouse kitchen, the sight of the mutilated jacket, washed and pressed by his mother, on the back of Jacques' chair, and the single boot, sagging by the range, whitened by salt, had loaded his head again with shadows and he had turned away, searching for peace.

He reached Stone Beach. The rock reared up, large boulders piled below. The rolled-up bottoms of his trousers clung to his cold legs. The sun disappeared behind a wad of thick grey cloud. He rubbed at the stiffness of his old jersey on the worn arms and wished he'd taken his mother's advice and put on his jacket as well.

The rocks, wet and sticky under his hands, were cold and solid as he climbed around the rising rock, making for the flat shelf. When he and Amy rowed out on a high tide, they'd pull the boat onto the ledge while they swam. Or they did, before the occupation. He sat on the shining surface and dangled his legs over the edge. Below him piles of large, rounded stones and drifts of shells and granite grit almost covered the sandy cove. He lifted his eyes. Ahead of him the little bulk of Green Island rose and fell into a sparkling sea. To his left the grey of the sea melted into the greying horizon. To his right the land curved from black witches' rock, under the firs and falling trees below Brig-y-Don, across patches of yellow sand and stretches of flat rock towards the common and the sentinel tower, stripped now of wooden barriers and barbed wire.

Jacques was here. Somewhere. He'd always be here. Always young and strong.

The tide was turning. A swirl of water lapped into a rock pool. A streak of pale sunshine glittered on the granite. Michael took a deep breath and something cleared in his head, his shoulders lifted and a wave of calm travelled down from his wide eyes, floating through his chest and into his tingling legs. His hand reached into his pocket and felt for the smoothness of the button nestling in the corner. He rubbed at the wording under his thumb. Hold Fast.

Strength returned to his legs as he got to his feet. He climbed down onto the scattering of pink and grey pebbles and picked up an egg-shaped stone which fitted snugly into his palm. He put it to his lips, the cool saltiness against his mouth, before dropping it in a pool of clear water; with a plop and splash, it settled and darkened.

1ST MAY 1995

He unclipped Teddy's lead and the black Labrador, nose down, zig-zagged over the pebbles and sand, stopping occasionally for a sniff and a root in the seaweed heaped in wet piles left by the retreating tide. Looping the lead around his own neck, Michael took off his walking boots and socks, exposing white, bony feet, and rolled up the bottom of his trousers to just below the knees. A warm breeze teased his greying hair. He stood for a moment, curling his toes into the dry sand, inhaling the salty freshness and relaxing his shoulders. Stone Beach's rocks rose in soft mounds above steel-blue water. At the offing, a smoky roll of white and grey obscured the horizon; above, a rich, Marian-blue sky was feathered with cirrus cloud.

The red cap of Jane Le Brocq, who swam across the bay most days, moved steadily through a patch of white, glinting sun. Now in his seventieth year, he regarded himself as past the age of spring swims, decided a few years ago now that summer bathing, on a warm day, from a sandy beach, was the way he'd enjoy the sea.

Leaving his boots on a flat boulder next to the slipway, he set off, walking close to the low sea wall, toiling in the soft sand above the tide line, stepping over the fir cones spilt by the conifers near The Croft. As the beach curved around towards the headland, the dryness gave way to the cold cling of recently-covered sand. In his right-hand pocket, his hand closed around the letter he'd received that morning, and then pushed further down for the Hold Fast button, cool under the tips of his fingers.

When he had read Konstantin's confession, in Anna's letter, sitting at his late parents' scrubbed oak table earlier this morning, he had felt as if a window shutter, locked and bolted, rusted closed, had been opened suddenly, flooding his head with light, sharpness and clarity, sweeping aside shadows of the past, making sense, at last. He needed to read it again, close to where Jacques had died, before he shared the news with Amy and Yves.

If only he could have told his parents, buried for over ten years in St Clement's Churchyard, close to Jacques' grave, at the top of the slope under a flowering hawthorn tree.

If only he could have shared the story with Meg, who'd put flowers on Jacques' grave every week. Who'd tried for years, with her characteristic determination, to find out what happened to Konstantin after he left Jersey, giving up only when she became ill with the cancer that killed her.

If only he could have been a better husband to Laura, who he drove away because of his black moods, his periods of depression when he couldn't talk to her, couldn't look at their children. Could things have been different?

Later, he would telephone Lily. She wouldn't be surprised; like him she had always believed in Jacques. They would arrange for one of their chats, drink red wine and nibble cheese together in her conservatory or have a crab sandwich in the beach café at Archirondel, if the weather was good. The spark in her faded eyes still moved him. He'd try not to look at the grey roots of her red hair, the sagging skin of her neck, or the raised blue veins and age spots on the back of her hands. She'd smile and nod. They'd sit in silence. So much shared history, Laura used to say, frowning.

By the time he reached the little beach under Brig-y-Don, the sea had gone down enough for him to cross to the rocks where Jenny, Teddy's ancestor, had found Jacques' jacket.

Nothing had changed in that quiet corner for fifty years: big, blackened slabs of granite, looking as if they had tumbled down from the headland, littered the edge of the wild beach; pebbles rolled in the cream of the sighing tide; shells and grit sparkled in the weak sunshine; gulls called and swooped. In the shallows, a lone, white egret picked up his long legs, moving with dignity.

He settled himself, leaning back into in the curve of a hip-high boulder, and drew out the letter.

Sadovaya Street 649
Kolomenskoye
Orel
Russia

April 24th 1995

Dear Mr Le Breton,

My name is Anna Konstantinovna Baklanov. My father was Konstantin Leonidovich Ivanov. I think you knew him as Stan. He passed away at home three weeks ago. He died peacefully at the end, after suffering a long illness. I found your name, and part of your address, in one of his notebooks, which I discovered when sorting out his possessions. Most of the memoirs in the notebooks are about the war and the years he spent as a prisoner, and in hiding, in Jersey in the 1940s. He wrote about the farms, your family's, and another one, where he worked. He mentioned the kindness of your parents, Hélène and Paul, and Jacques, Yves and Amy, your siblings, I believe. Your name came up most often. He admired your sensitivity, your courage, though he struggled to tell you.

When he was confined to bed, we spent hours together talking. I asked him about his experiences. Like so many men of his generation, he rarely spoke of his suffering as I was growing up, preferring to keep his family separate from his terrible memories. He told me a little more about the awful conditions in which he, and many other foreign workers, were kept and the hard, physical work he was forced to undertake. He spoke of his escape from the Germans and became very tearful after mentioning your family's name. He was not an emotional man. It was the first time I have ever seen him cry.

He spoke of a secret, known only to him. He'd committed an 'injustice', that's what he called it. He hadn't told the truth. He wanted to put it right. He was not in his right mind during the years in Jersey, he said; he did not know himself. The suffering had taken something from him. He had lost his sense of worth, his sense of what was right and good.

He repeated the name 'Jacques' many times, called him an honourable man before he would tell me what happened. He wanted you to know that it was his fault, his crime, not Jacques'. He had stolen a rifle from Jacques and shot the German soldier in revenge for what had happened to him. At the time, he said, he felt great relief. He told himself that it was to protect your family, but in reality, he did it for himself.

A few days before he died, my father became very agitated. He recalled a terrible night. He blamed himself, called himself a coward and said that he could have saved Jacques, should have saved him. They had buried the German's body, at a place called 'Stone Beach'. The tide came in fast. It was stormy and he was afraid. He ran. Jacques fell, was lost. That was his word. Lost. My father tried to leave the island in a small boat, but it had smashed on the rocks close to the beach. He mentioned Meg, called her a saviour, said he'd betrayed her. He cried as he told me that he'd lied to her. His final words were whispered names: Michael, Jacques, Amy, Lily, Hélène, Paul, Yves, Meg. He repeated them, like a prayer.

After his death, the notebooks have been the source of great interest and comfort to me, though they are incomplete. I discovered more about you and your family's help and I am writing in the hope that I can find out more about my father's story. I am considering writing a book about his experience during the German occupation of the Channel Islands.

I am planning a visit, having been invited, representing my father, to the 50th anniversary of the liberation in May. It would be a privilege if I could meet you and your family.

With very best wishes and gratitude for your friendship with my father,

Anna

ABOUT THE AUTHOR

After a long and fulfilling career teaching English, with a passion for a wide variety of literature, Sarah Le Marchand began her own writing journey by completing an MA in Creative Writing with the Open University. Her first novel, *Hold Fast,* is inspired by her Jersey family's history and her long-standing interest in the German occupation of the Channel Islands from 1940 to 1945.